"Tate? Why

She blinked twice, as
"I wanted to apologize fo
brought you these."

He accepted the basket and set it down on the coffee table. The rich scent of cinnamon and cloves wafted up.

"These smell great, but apologies weren't necessary."

Her eyes twinkled as she held out her hand. "Okay, I'll take them back home then."

"Oh, no, you don't!"

He picked the basket back up and carried it across to the kitchen counter. As he turned back toward Tate, the towel came undone and dropped almost to the floor before he caught it. He was about to apologize for flashing her, even if it was an accident, when he realized that this time, Tate had made no pretense of looking away.

"See something you want?"

His voice came out little better than a growl. With even the slightest encouragement, he was going to be all over her.

She actually nodded. Her eyes stared into his briefly, then started a long, slow trip downward, taking their time. . . .

TURN THE PAGE FOR RED-HOT REVIEWS OF ALEXIS MORGAN'S SEDUCTIVE NOVELS. . . .

"INTRIGUING AND UNIQUE . . . COMPELLING CHARACTERS."

—*Romantic Times* (Top Pick!)

"MAGICAL, MYSTICAL, AND JUST PLAIN MESMERIZING!"

—*Wild on Books*

MORE PRAISE FOR ALEXIS MORGAN'S STEAMY PALADIN SERIES

DARKNESS UNKNOWN

"A fabulous read. . . . Passionate, hot, and very sexy."

—*Fallen Angels Reviews*

"Fresh and exciting with the same depth of character and emotional punch we've come to expect from Ms. Morgan."

—*Fresh Fiction*

REDEEMED IN DARKNESS

"Captivating, compelling, and totally hot!"

—Alyssa Day, *USA Today* bestselling author of *Atlantis Unmasked*

IN DARKNESS REBORN

"Utterly compelling. . . . Great sexual tension and action. Really terrific and totally unique."

—Katherine Stone, *New York Times* bestselling author of *Caroline's Journal*

DARK PROTECTOR

"An innovative story line, passionate protective champions, and lots of surprising twists."

—*Romance Reviews Today*

"A complex paranormal fantasy that pulls readers in from the first page and doesn't let them go."

—*Paranormal Romance Writers*

DARK DEFENDER

"Tons of suspense and drama. Morgan proves that she's . . . here to stay."

—*Romantic Times*

"An intense plot with twists and turns and wonderful surprises."

—*Paranormal Romance Writers*

. . . AND FOR HER TANTALIZING FIRST TALION NOVEL

DARK WARRIOR UNLEASHED

"This is great stuff!"

—*Romantic Times*

"A hero that is beyond a doubt an Alpha Hero. . . . A book that must go to the top of your must-read-as-soon-as-you-get-it list."

—*Simply Romance Reviews*

These titles are also available as eBooks.

Also by Alexis Morgan

The Paladin Series

DARKNESS UNKNOWN
REDEEMED IN DARKNESS
IN DARKNESS REBORN
DARK DEFENDER
DARK PROTECTOR

The Talion Series

DARK WARRIOR UNBROKEN
DARK WARRIOR UNLEASHED

ALEXIS MORGAN

Pocket Star Books
New York London Toronto Sydney

Pocket Star Books
A Division of Simon & Schuster, Inc.
1230 Avenue of the Americas
New York, NY 10020

First Pocket Star Books paperback edition March 2010

POCKET STAR BOOKS and colophon are registered trademarks of Simon & Schuster, Inc.

For information about special discounts for bulk purchases, please contact Simon & Schuster Special Sales at 1-866-506-1949 or business@simonandschuster.com.

The Simon & Schuster Speakers Bureau can bring authors to your live event. For more information or to book an event contact the Simon & Schuster Speakers Bureau at 1-866-248-3049 or visit our website at www.simonspeakers.com.

Design by Lisa Litwack. Illustration by Craig White.

Manufactured in the United States of America

10 9 8 7 6 5 4 3 2 1

ISBN 978-1-4165-6345-7
ISBN 978-1-4165-6397-6 (ebook)

This book is dedicated to my husband, Bob, my very own personal hero. Thanks for always being right there beside me as I reach for the stars.

Acknowledgments

A special thanks to the wonderful ladies at Village Yarn and Tea for taking the time to answer all my questions about the business of selling tea and for letting me sample your wares. Rest assured that your teas have spoiled me forever. Any mistakes are mine, of course, but my book is so much stronger because of your help.

Chapter 1

Jake blocked the way out. "Come on, Hunter, you don't have to do this."

But he did have to, if for no other reason than that the very thought had him shaking with fear.

"I won't be long." Hunter limped forward, hoping Jake would move before he had to force him to.

As Hunter stalked past his friend, Jake caught him by the arm. "Damn it, Hunter, if you won't let me go with you, at least let me get Jarvis."

Hunter jerked free of Jake's grip, hating being touched and hating the worry in his friend's eyes even more. "No, Jake. Wait here if you're that concerned, but this is something I have to do alone. The last thing I need is a babysitter. Don't follow me."

"Fine, but I don't like it." Jake stepped aside to lean against the cavern wall, his sword drawn and ready. "Holler if you need me, and I'll come running." Just like he hadn't when Hunter had last wandered down this particular tunnel.

Hunter walked away while he still could, the sour taste of bile burning his throat as he left the main cavern behind. It took him far too little time to reach the mouth of the correct tunnel. Time and pain had distorted his memory, making this specific place out to be the monster. But the limestone walls weren't his enemies. Their only sin was once offering his assailants sanctuary.

He kept moving forward one step at a time, ignoring the constant, bone-deep ache in his leg. The urge to break and run was riding him hard, but Hunter wasn't about to let the bastards win. Not this time.

The rough-hewn walls closed in on him, making it hard for him to breathe. His lungs constricted until he could no longer draw in enough air. He ignored the tight band of grief and fear blossoming inside his chest, concentrating instead on moving forward. Only another few yards to go, taking one painful step and then another. He'd make this journey or die trying.

Finally, when the tunnel widened out again, Hunter coasted to a stop. He reached out a hand to steady himself but jerked it back when he saw the rusty brown splotches that covered the walls. And the floor. And the ceiling. As far as he could see.

Dried blood. And all of it his.

He felt a wetness on his cheek. He touched it with his finger, too afraid to look. His logical mind said it wasn't blood; his fear screamed that it had to be. But it was just a single tear trickling down his face as he stood grieving for the man who'd died there. Thanks to the

Paladins' special DNA, Hunter's body had made the painful journey back from death. Even now his heart continued to beat and his lungs to draw breath. But although Doc Crosby had done his best to patch Hunter back together, modern medicine and good genes could only do so much to heal a shattered soul.

Hunter stood shivering in the chill of the underground chamber until temper, not fear, ruled his decision to leave. If he didn't go soon, Jake would come charging in to rescue him, not from their enemies but from himself. Hunter drew his sword and stared at its broken blade. He ran his hand down the jagged length of steel, drawing comfort from the cool touch of the metal. It was time to let go. He knelt down and gently laid the sword to rest right where he himself had died.

Then he turned his back on the past and walked away.

"Thanks for the ride." Hunter couldn't wait to get out of the car, but at the same time he was reluctant to leave Jarvis behind.

"You're welcome."

Jarvis stared out the windshield, the tension in his jaw a clear warning that he had something to say and was unsure of how Hunter would react. But his reaction was always the same these days: anger and rage. For the sake of their long friendship, though, he'd try to do better.

Hunter eased back in the seat and took his hand off the door handle. "What, Jarvis?"

His friend angled around to face him. "Hunter, you know I'm not much one for the mushy stuff, but I want to tell you what an honor it has been to serve with you all these years. I *hate* that you need to leave. We all do, but we also know that it's the best thing for now. You need to put some serious distance between you and this stretch of the barrier."

"Yeah." Even now he could feel it calling him, the need to stay close and defend it riding him hard. Leaving was for the best, even if he hated it. He didn't say that last part out loud because it would only make it harder on Jarvis and the others.

Jarvis made a move as if to reach out to Hunter, but he stopped, knowing Hunter's reluctance to be touched. "Buddy, believe me, if I could change things, I would. Having said that, I'm sending you out to Seattle because I trust Devlin Bane and Blake Trahern to make sure you get a square deal."

This time the bitterness spewed out before Hunter could catch it. "I'm sure they're both *thrilled* to be getting another crippled Paladin to babysit. Who knows? Maybe Penn Sebastian and I can form one of those touchy-feely support groups."

Jarvis hit the steering wheel with his fist. "Damn it all, Hunter, don't talk that way. Even with that leg of yours, you're still a better fighter than most Paladins and all of the guards."

"I'm glad someone thinks so." Because he definitely didn't. And it wasn't because of his leg.

"Give yourself time, Hunter. It's only been a couple of months." He reached into the backseat. "I've got something for you."

He handed Hunter a long, narrow box wrapped in

brightly colored clown paper and tied up with a big red bow. "You can thank Jake for the paper. Gwen did the bow."

Hunter stared at the gaudy package, his stomach doing somersaults over the possibilities. Everyone knew his sword had been broken. That didn't mean he was ready for another one that he might actually have to use.

"Go ahead and open it. It won't bite."

Hunter didn't need to look at Jarvis to know there was sympathy in his eyes; it was there in his voice. God, he hated that his fear was so obvious to his friends. To avoid further conversation, he tugged on the ribbon, and then ripped into the paper.

As he wadded it up and threw it into the back of Jarvis's Chevelle, he said, "Tell Jake Seattle isn't all that far away. I can and will get back at him for the clowns."

Jarvis's grin was wicked. "I'm sure he's counting on it."

Finally, when Hunter couldn't put it off any longer, he lifted the lid off the box. His throat closed up as he looked at what lay nestled in the tissue paper. If Jarvis thought Hunter was on the mend, why had he given him a cane? It was a beauty, all right, made out of black wood, maybe even ebony. The handle was a wolf's head carved out of ivory. Beautiful, yes, but a symbol of Hunter's weakness.

"Now, before you get the wrong idea, let me explain." Jarvis lifted the cane out of the box. "This belonged to my grandfather. Just like now, the authorities back in the day frowned on folks carrying a sword in public."

He pushed a small button at the top, then pulled on the handle, drawing out a razor-sharp sword. "My father said his dad had this custom-made. I figure you're not always going to need a cane, but this will allow you to carry a weapon with no one being the wiser."

Okay, so maybe the gift was acceptable after all. Hunter took the cane back from Jarvis. The wood was silky smooth, and the wolf's head fit his hand perfectly. "I'll take good care of it."

"More importantly, it will take good care of you. Now get going or you'll miss your flight."

Hunter reached for the door handle. At the last second, he reached out his hand to Jarvis. "Thanks for everything."

Jarvis didn't immediately let go. Instead, he tugged Hunter closer for a quick man-hug, the kind that said what neither of them had words for. For once, the brief intimacy didn't make Hunter want to dive for cover.

"I'll email you when I have an address and a new cell number."

"You'd better. If I don't hear regularly, I'll send Jake out there to kick your ass."

Hunter laughed as he got out of the car, mostly because it was expected. Then he retrieved his duffel and tucked his new cane inside to avoid any awkward questions from security. Waving over his shoulder, he disappeared into the crowd and left his world behind.

Devlin Bane sat at his desk with the phone to his ear. The wall behind him was covered with an interesting array of weapons. Hunter should probably be impressed, but he wasn't. Paladins collected swords and guns like other people did stamps. What did impress Hunter, though, was how much Devlin reminded him of Jarvis Donahue.

They were both big men, but then so was he. No, it was in the steady gaze that said they could see right through to the heart of a man. No doubt Devlin possessed the same highly developed bullshit meter that kept Jarvis one step ahead of both the Regents and the Paladins that served under him.

Okay, so maybe he could deal with Bane.

Devlin hung up the phone. "Sorry about that. I've been waiting all morning for that call."

"No problem." Hunter had nowhere he needed to be, nothing he was expected to do.

"I'd ask how your trip was, but I won't. For one thing, I'm not much into small talk. For another, I'd rather get to the point." Devlin's green eyes narrowed as his gaze met Hunter's head-on.

"Which is?" Hunter settled back into his chair, forcing his muscles to relax.

"What the hell are you doing here?"

So, okay, maybe Jarvis hadn't smoothed the way as much as Hunter had thought. Fine. If he wasn't wanted, he'd leave. But before Hunter could move a muscle, Devlin started talking again. He ran his fingers through his shoulder-length hair, frustration clearly driving him.

"Sorry, that came out sounding worse than I meant for it to. I know you needed to put some distance between you and the barrier in Missouri. Jarvis filled me in on what happened." He pegged Hunter with a hard stare. "By the way, nobody else around here knows the details. That's your story to tell."

The last thing Hunter wanted to feel was gratitude. He knew rumors were probably flying through the Seattle ranks, because Paladins gossiped like a bunch of old hens. It didn't mean he wanted them to know what really happened.

"My real question is are you here to lick your wounds or to work?"

Son of a bitch, this guy went right for the jugular. If he liked blunt, he'd get blunt. "A little of both."

Devlin lapsed into silence, clearly considering his options. Finally, he nodded. "Okay, here's what I can offer you. I'm not going to trust you or anybody else at the barrier until I know he can face what comes across it. None of us have any reason to love those crazy bastards when they attack, and you definitely have more reason than most to hate them. But here's the bottom line: if you're unsure of how you'll handle it, I won't risk my men's lives by asking them to fight next to you."

If Bane hadn't wanted to take on Hunter, why had he let Jarvis send him in the first place? "So you're saying maybe I should book my return flight to St. Louis?"

"That's up to you. There is an alternative."

Hunter had already come this far. He might as well hear the man out.

He settled back in his chair. "I'm listening."

"I'm sure you've heard about our interactions with the Kalith."

Hunter sneered. "Yeah, we heard you'd adopted a few strays. Didn't realize you were actually naming your pets."

Bane's big fist slammed down on the desk hard enough to topple a stack of files onto the floor. He ignored the mess as he leaned forward and snarled, "That attitude will get you nowhere, Fitzsimon. Like I said, I know what you've been through."

"Like hell you do!"

Some of the steam went out of Devlin's fury. He leaned back in his chair and stared at Hunter for a few seconds. "Maybe you're right, but you need to understand that things are different for us. I hate those crazy fuckers that attack every time the barrier goes down as much as the next guy. But around here, we consider the Kalith warriors like Barak, Lusahn, and Larem our friends and allies. All of them have risked their own necks to save lives—Paladin lives."

"So what? It's not like that evens the score."

Devlin shoved his chair back and stalked around to Hunter's side of the desk. "Lose the fucking attitude, Hunter, or I will personally stuff your worthless carcass on the next plane back to St. Louis!"

Hunter clenched his fists, but he held himself back. "Look, I'll try. Just don't shove them in my face."

"Shouldn't be a problem. I'm shipping your ass north of here."

Devlin reached across his desk, pulled a folded map out of the top drawer, and spread it out. He pointed to a spot on the enlarged map of the city.

"We're here in our headquarters located in the Seattle Underground. The barrier stretches through under the city here and here. The closer you get to the volcanoes, the more unstable it becomes. And just to make things more interesting, we've got tectonic plates crashing into each other right offshore."

Where was all of this headed? "Thanks for the geology lesson."

"Smart-ass," Devlin said with no real heat. "We do our best to guard the area, but you know there are never enough of us to go around. That means some spots are vulnerable."

He flipped the map over to show the entire state of Washington. "We've found out that there has been movement going in both directions across the barrier. Greedy bastards on both sides are making money at the cost of lives of our people *and* theirs."

Hunter didn't much care how many crazy Others died—or Kalith warriors, for that matter. He kept that little bit of information to himself, figuring it wouldn't pay to antagonize Bane any more than he already had. "Where do I fit in?"

Devlin pointed at a second spot some distance north of Seattle. "You may not have heard that one of my men spent some time on the other side of the barrier. While he was there, he discovered a small stretch of barrier we didn't know about. Evidently it's barely wide enough for two men to pass through shoulder-to-shoulder. To make matters worse, we have no idea how unstable the barrier is along there. What we do know is there's clear evidence that humans have been crossing there on a regular basis. But again, no idea how many or who. I haven't had anyone to post up there to keep an eye on things." Devlin looked up from the map with grim satisfaction. "But now I have you."

His phone rang again. While Devlin took the call, Hunter mulled over everything he'd been saying. They'd all seen Devlin's pet Other when Devlin had brought Barak q'Young with him, back when Trahern had been in Missouri. If Jarvis had known anything about Paladins crossing to the other side of the barrier, he hadn't said anything. What kind of crazy SOB would've done something like that?

When Devlin hung up the phone, Hunter asked, "So you want me to drive up there and take a look around?"

"No, we've done that. I want you to live up there for a while and assess the situation. You'll report directly to me. If you can't or won't handle the assignment, maybe I can find something else for you to do at headquarters. Take tonight to think about it and get back to me in the morning."

Hunter already knew what his answer would be, but there was no sense in rushing things. Might as well let Devlin sweat a bit. Earlier he had taken Hunter on a brief tour of the underground complex, as well as the admin building where the Handlers and the guards were stationed. Hunter's nerves were stretched to the breaking point from all those faces staring at him and pretending they hadn't noticed his limp.

The farther he got away from his own kind the better. Doc Crosby had warned him, though, that Paladins never fared well far from the barrier. This small bit of territory that Devlin was willing to cede to Hunter's care might just help him hold it together long enough to figure out what to do with the rest of his worthless life.

He gripped the wolf head on his cane and prepared to leave. "I'll check in with you in the morning."

"Not so fast. I promised Laurel that I'd invite you over for dinner tonight. Trahern and Brenna will be the only other two there, if that makes a difference." Devlin's face flushed a bit. "I should warn you, Laurel can't cook for shit, but don't let that stop you."

"This Laurel, is she the same Handler who helped save Trahern from the needle?"

"Yeah, she's the one."

Laurel's progressive attitudes had filtered their way through to other Handlers, including Doc Crosby. "Then I'll come. For her, I'd choke down dog food with a smile on my face."

Devlin nodded, muttering something under his breath that sounded a lot like "you might have to," then scribbled down directions and his address. "We'll eat around six. Call if you need a ride."

"Thanks. I'll see you at dinner."

It was only early afternoon, leaving Hunter with hours to kill. He'd spent most of his time on the airplane studying a guide book of Seattle that Jarvis had bought for him. If memory served, he was only a few blocks away from the waterfront. The walk would do him good and get him away from the prying eyes of the Paladins and everyone else who worked for the Regents.

Eventually he might have to get to know them, but not right now.

Trahern popped the cap off his beer and took a long drink. "Think Fitzsimon will show?"

"I don't know. He did seem more interested when he realized Laurel was the Handler who helped save your worthless ass. He might stand you and me up, but I suspect he'll show up for her."

"Last time I talked to Jarvis, he was pretty close-mouthed about Fitzsimon's problems." Trahern looked at Devlin, obviously waiting for him to fill in the blanks.

"All I can say is that this guy's problems make Penn Sebastian's seem like a walk in the park." Devlin adjusted the controls on the grill. "I know more. I won't say more."

The sliding screen door opened. Hunter glared at Devlin and then Trahern as he stepped out onto the deck. "It's nice to know you're a man of your word. My business is exactly that—my business."

"Fine by me." Trahern leaned over to snag another beer out of the cooler, then held it out. "Here."

Hunter accepted the drink and sat down. "Nice view."

"Thanks. I'm going to hate putting this place on the market." Devlin busied himself with straightening his barbeque tools.

"Why do it then?" Hunter picked up a handful of chips.

"Eventually the neighbors are going to notice that I haven't aged in all the years I've owned it. It's bound to draw unwanted attention."

Trahern looked around, a thoughtful expression on his face. "I'll probably have to do that myself one of these days."

Time to change the subject. "How do you like your steak, Hunter?" Devlin asked.

"Bloody and still mooing."

"That makes three of us. Brenna and Laurel like theirs a little less raw."

The screen door opened a second time, and two women joined them outside. "Talking about us again?"

Hunter studied them. Both were attractive but in different ways. As soon as Laurel got close to Devlin, the Paladin leader slipped his arm around her waist and pulled her in close. Lucky bastard, he was the first Paladin to ever dare date a Handler. When Hunter had first heard the rumors, he'd been surprised that the Regents had allowed the relationship to continue. Now that he'd seen the two together, he realized the Regents must have figured they'd stood to lose both Devlin and Laurel if they'd pushed it. The two were very obviously in love.

The same with Brenna and Trahern, but Hunter had already seen them together back in Missouri. She'd fought tooth and nail to drag her man back from insanity. Hunter liked that about her. He wondered if she know that Jake had a bit of a crush on her. Hunter figured it had started when from the two of them had been shot at the same time.

Laurel smiled at Hunter. "As soon as the steaks are done, we'll be ready to eat."

"Sounds good." He wasn't much for etiquette these days, but for Laurel and Brenna he'd make the effort. "Thank you for inviting me over."

"You're welcome." Brenna gave him a warm smile. "How are all the John Does doing these days?"

It took him a minute to remember that was the name Jarvis had told her to call all of the Paladins in Missouri when Trahern had breached security and brought her inside the compound without any authorization. Even if her late father had been one of the Regents, outsiders weren't allowed in the underground facility.

"They're all fine; Jake sends his regards. He said to tell

you that his computer game is about to be released. He'll be sending you one of the first copies."

He eyed Trahern briefly before adding, "The dragon Jake named after you is a real beauty. It even has your coloring."

Her face lit up. "He shouldn't have done that."

She was clearly pleased, even if Trahern wasn't. He grabbed Brenna's hand and tugged her onto his lap. "That's right. He shouldn't have."

Devlin laughed and pointed his tongs at Hunter. "You might want to warn your friend that Trahern doesn't share."

Laurel rolled her eyes. "For Pete's sake, it's just a dragon. I think it's sweet."

Devlin planted a quick kiss on her cheek, then started piling an obscene amount of barely cooked beef on a platter. "These are done. Let's eat."

Hunter followed them inside and took the place at the end of the table, uncomfortably aware that he was the odd man out. He'd been feeling that way a lot lately.

Tate Justice pulled back her lace curtain and looked outside to check the weather. It was misty and cool. Perfect. Maybe it was selfish of her to wish for light rain every day, but her business thrived when the weather drove people inside. When it was hot and sunny, she sat inside her tea shop all day by herself. On the other hand, that gave her more time to work on her book.

She poured herself a second cup of coffee, her secret sin. She might run a small tea shop, but she liked a good French roast with her morning granola. Sometimes she thought it was a bit sad that her worst vice was coffee. However, living as she did in the small community of Justice Point, there weren't all that many opportunities for sin.

Her daily to-do list was filled with the mundane activities of a small business owner and wanna-be writer. She read over today's list: check stock and call in an order for more tea, sweep the hardwood floors in the shop, do some laundry, and write her daily allotment of pages. Oh, yes, and pay the bills.

That last one had been carried over from the day before and the day before that. She'd run out of both excuses and time. She knew she had enough to cover all the bills, but after the past few weeks of particularly nice weather, it was a tight squeeze.

If only a tenant would magically appear for the furnished apartment over the garage. She'd posted it for rent a month ago, but so far there had been no takers. Most of the locals were too elderly to handle the stairs, and the village was too far from the bus route to the nearest college town to make it convenient for a student.

Someone would come along eventually. She didn't absolutely need the money, but it would give her budget a bit more breathing room. Sighing, she reached for the stack of bills and her checkbook. As painful as it would be, at least she'd be able to start her day with a clear conscience.

When Tate unlocked the front door of her tea shop on the first floor of her Victorian home, three of her favorite customers were already waiting for her. Collectively known as the Auntie Ms, Madge, Margaret, and Mabel were three elderly sisters who lived down the road. No one in Justice Point knew exactly how old they were, and Tate wasn't about to ask. Two of them were twins, though all three women looked enough alike that sometimes it was hard to tell them apart.

"Good morning, dear. Here are some of those cookies you like so much." Mabel shoved a plate into Tate's hands before heading for the sisters' favorite table in the shop.

"You shouldn't have."

She meant it. The sisters had to pool their limited resources just to get by. But no amount of arguing would stop them from making cookies for everyone in town. Tate made it up to them by sending them home with soup and other staples as often as they would let her. She understood pride and tried her best not to offend them.

The twins filed in behind Mabel, moving a bit slower with their matching walkers. When the trio was settled, Tate brought them a pot of their favorite tea and the morning paper. As usual, the Auntie Ms squabbled over who got first crack at the front page.

Tate swept the large front porch and fluffed the cushions of the wicker furniture scattered along its length. The checkers box was looking a bit ragged, and she made a mental note to bring out one of her empty tins to replace it. Nothing flowery or she'd get complaints from the two gentlemen who spent their afternoons trying to best each other at their favorite game.

Satisfied that everything was in order, she went back inside and started checking her inventory and making out her supply order. When that was done, she pulled out her laptop to edit the pages she'd written the day before. The hero was about to ride in and rescue the heroine from the villain. As a reader, she hated wishy-washy women and made sure the heroine was on the verge of saving herself already.

"Tate, dear, I think you have a customer."

Normally, Tate would've finished the sentence she was working on, but the excitement in Mabel's voice jarred her completely out of the story, derailing her train of thought.

Whatever had caught the attention of the Auntie Ms had them all sitting up straight and staring out the window. Tate couldn't quite hear what they were saying, but they reminded her of a flock of house finches twittering over the approach of a cat.

Tate came around the counter to get a better look but didn't see anything out of the ordinary. Before she could ask what was going on, the back doorbell rang. That was odd. The locals all knew to come around to the shop entrance.

"I'll be back, ladies," Tate told the sisters.

"Take your time, dear," Margaret said.

"Yes, all the time you need," Mabel added with a definite twinkle in her faded blue eyes.

"*We* certainly would."

That last remark came from Madge, which set all three of them off in a fit of giggles. What on earth had gotten into them?

The bell rang twice more before she made it to the door. Somebody was in a hurry. She turned the old-fashioned key to unlock the door and opened it to find nobody there. She stepped out on the back porch to look around, wondering if some tourist's kids were playing around.

Then she saw him. That was definitely no child. A man, easily several inches over six feet tall, was walking around toward the front of the house. She noticed he favored his right leg, but it didn't detract one iota from the impression of overwhelming masculinity.

She tried to speak, meaning to call him back, but all she managed was a squeak. Evidently that was enough, because he immediately spun around and headed straight for her, radiating aggression as he stalked back to where she stood. She instinctively backed up a step, but then stopped and held her ground.

He smirked at her reaction.

She'd see what the jerk wanted and then send him on his way with good riddance. "Can I help you?" she said.

He stopped a few feet from the porch. "That depends. Are you the owner?"

His voice was painfully hoarse, sounding like rough sandpaper, sending shivers through her. "Yes, I'm Tate Justice."

"Then you can help me. I saw your ad for the apartment. I want to rent it."

Oh, no. The first serious looker she'd had, and it had to be this guy. "You haven't seen it yet."

He quirked an eyebrow. "Are there any other places for rent in town?"

"Well, no."

"Then it doesn't matter what it looks like, does it?" He reached for his wallet and pulled out a wad of cash. "I believe the ad said first and last months' rent."

Visions of a balanced budget with a bit of cushion danced through her head before common sense took over. This guy was hardly what she'd had in mind when she'd run the advertisement. Even so, what grounds did she have to refuse him?

"Do you have any references?"

"No."

She studied his ragged jeans and the faded flannel shirt he wore unbuttoned over a white T-shirt. "Do you have a job? Locally, I mean."

"I can pay my bills."

That didn't exactly answer her question. Then she noticed he was carrying a cane. "I'll show you the apartment, but I fear it may not be suitable for you."

"And why is that?"

Now *this* was awkward. "The stairs are steep."

His eyes flashed with anger. "I can handle a few steps. Now show me the place if you insist, so I can get moved in."

It all boiled down to the fact that she needed the income and he needed the apartment. Her decision made, she met his gaze head-on and nodded.

"I'll get the key."

Chapter 2

It was obvious that her new tenant hated being stared at, but there was no way to avoid it. Considering the small size of Justice Point, Hunter Fitzsimon couldn't have been shocked that his moving a handful of boxes up a staircase would draw a crowd.

However, her neighbors had spent more than enough time ogling the newest resident. Tate waited until Hunter was inside the apartment, then she shooed everyone back around to their own yards. When Hunter came back out, he found himself alone, but if he was surprised, it didn't show. With the same look of grim determination, he returned to his truck for another load of boxes.

His limp was getting more pronounced, clear evidence that he'd made one trip too many up the stairs. She'd seen him carry in a duffel bag and a motley assortment of cardboard boxes but nothing that looked like food.

It would only be neighborly to take him some lunch. Making some extra sandwiches wouldn't be that much more bother than making just one for herself. Add a couple of soft drinks, or better yet a cold beer, one of her fresh blueberry muffins, and maybe an apple. No, make that two apples. He might get hungry later.

She tucked the food into a basket and set the sign in the shop window to say she'd be back in fifteen minutes. Timing her approach was tricky. She waited until he'd carried up another load. Picking up two of his smaller boxes, she followed him up the steps.

He exited the apartment just as she reached the top step. He immediately snagged the top box off her stack and stood glaring down at her. Tangled in the net of his angry gaze, his eyes green and smoky and framed by ridiculously long eyelashes, it took considerable effort for Tate to look away. He clearly wasn't thrilled to see her. Fine. He was her tenant, not her best buddy. But he still had to eat.

"I didn't ask for help." He shoved the box inside his apartment and reached for the second.

She hesitated before releasing it. "I know you didn't, Mr. Fitzsimon. I realize you are perfectly capable of hauling all this stuff up here by yourself."

He didn't respond. If anything, Hunter looked even angrier. When he held out his hands again for the box, she surrendered it.

"Thanks," he grumbled, and started back inside.

Before he could close the door, she stepped up on the small landing and blocked the door with her hand.

He prevented her from opening it any farther. "What now, Ms. Justice?"

"It's Tate, and this is yours." She all but shoved the basket at him. "It's lunch. I thought you might be hungry." She turned away. "No rush in returning the basket."

"Ms. Justice, I don't need—"

Ignoring him, she skipped back down the steps. When she reached the bottom, she looked back and smiled. "Look, I know you've got a lot to do, and I've got to get back to the shop. Let me know if you need anything."

The sound of the door slamming closed was his response.

Hunter watched his pesky landlady through the window until she disappeared into her behemoth of a house. His first instinct was to go after her and shove the basket right back into her interfering hands, but that was his temper talking.

She'd meant well. Earlier, she'd even run off all the nosy neighbors to afford him some privacy when she'd thought he hadn't been looking. Maybe she *did* understand that he wanted to be left alone. And the truth was, he was in no shape to drive anywhere just to eat. If he didn't rest his leg soon, he'd be in for a world of hurt.

After a final trip up the stairs, he limped over to collapse on the small couch and gingerly lifted his leg up to rest on the coffee table. Shards of pain ripped through his much-abused limb with lightning speed. Gritting his teeth, he kicked his head back and waited for the worst of it to pass.

On a scale of one to ten, the pain was an eight. Anything less than a nine didn't warrant a pain pill. His rule, not his Handler's. Doc Crosby had argued that Hunter would heal better if he stayed ahead of the pain rather than wait for the medicine to catch up with it.

But popping pills that made him queasy and dulled his brain would be just one more damn concession to his injury. He'd already lost too damn much; better that he grit his teeth and ride out the pain. Eventually it would fade to a manageable level. It always did. Meanwhile, he'd check out what Tate Justice had packed him for lunch.

He snagged the cold beer and popped the top. He didn't want to encourage her Good Samaritan act, but he definitely owed her one. The beer was a brand he wasn't familiar with, probably from a local microbrewery, but it tasted damn fine.

Figuring he shouldn't be downing alcohol on an empty stomach, he fished out one of the sandwiches and took a healthy bite. He wasn't much for bean sprouts, but the sliced ham was definitely a cut above the bologna he'd planned on buying for himself. By the time he'd finished the sandwich, an apple, and half the blueberry muffin, he felt a helluva lot better.

For the first time, he took a close look at his new home. It wasn't much space-wise, but he couldn't complain. Whoever had designed the apartment had done a decent job. He'd certainly made do with less in his life. The pillowtop queen-sized bed was a pleasant surprise, as was the oversized tub with spray jets. He planned on trying that out as soon as he unpacked and made a quick trip to the grocery store.

Right now, he was just glad to not be moving. He closed his eyes and let his mind drift. Since his leg had quit throbbing for now, he could use a little shut-eye. He'd drive to town later and maybe treat himself to a decent meal before coming back. Tomorrow would be soon enough to start learning the lay of the land surrounding Justice Point.

Tate opened the kitchen windows to dispel the smell of burned muffins. She had to admit she was more than a bit distracted. She set the charred remains aside to toss into the woods later. Her usual customers wouldn't appreciate charcoal-flavored pastries, but her four-legged friends weren't nearly as picky.

Once she stuck the replacement batch in the oven and set the timer, she'd sit down at the table and see if she could concentrate long enough to polish her latest chapter. That she could also keep an eye on the apartment over the garage was beside the point. Tate had no business spying on her new tenant, but she'd never been able to resist a puzzle, and Hunter Fitzsimon was definitely puzzling.

What was he doing here in Justice Point? As much as she loved the place, it didn't have much to offer a man like Hunter. He was obviously recuperating from a major injury, but he didn't seem the type to be drawn to quiet village life. The man was too intense to be satisfied with the slow pace of her boring life.

No! She didn't mean that. Her life was quiet, true, but calm didn't mean boring. Life with her mother had been unpredictable and chaotic. The only respite Tate had ever found had been her summer visits to her uncle's house, which now belonged to her. Bless Uncle Jacob's heart, he'd left her his ramshackle Victorian and enough money to live on for several years as long as she was careful. He'd made it possible for her to pursue her dream of becoming a published author.

Her mother had promptly demanded she sell the place, probably hoping Tate would then share the profits with her. But in case Tate's resolve wavered, Uncle Jacob had staged a preemptive strike against Sandra Justice's greed by stipulating that Tate couldn't sell the house for at least five years or the proceeds would go to charity. When her mother had heard the terms of the will, she'd stormed out of the attorney's office cursing her brother-in-law's idiocy and leaving Tate to find her own way back home.

It had taken Tate less than a week to break her lease, quit her job, and move into the house. Her mother had only spoken to her once since then, and that had been to ask for money. When Tate had explained she didn't have any, good old mom had hung up in a snit. No doubt Sandra would get over it eventually and reach out to Tate again, probably about the time her creditors started calling.

Meanwhile, Tate wondered what her mother would think of the newest resident of Justice Point. Sandra had always had an eye for a good-looking guy, but she preferred her men old, rich, and malleable. Glancing out the window toward the garage, Tate had to admit that she was strangely relieved her tenant didn't fit those demographics.

The timer on the stove chimed, reminding her that she was there to keep an eye on her baking, not Hunter. As she was setting the muffins out on the rack to cool, a noise outside caught her attention. She moved closer to the window and groaned as soon as she realized what was going on. One of the Auntie Ms was standing at the bottom of the garage steps and hollering. If they kept this up, Tate might very well lose her new tenant. However, short of posting No Trespassing signs, she didn't know how to keep people from bothering Hunter.

Besides, it wasn't her job anyway. She'd be better off keeping a wary eye on things and seeing how he handled the situation himself.

Hunter jerked awake, his well-earned nap ending abruptly, leaving him groggy and confused. It took him a second or two to recognize his surroundings. Someone was raising a ruckus right outside. He carefully lowered his leg to the ground and used the arm of the couch to push himself up to his feet. After grabbing his cane, he started for the door, ready to order Tate Justice to leave him the hell alone.

Only it wasn't Tate. Outside on the landing, he found himself looking down at a tiny old woman banging her own cane on his steps with a surprising amount of determination. There were a lot of things he'd done that he wasn't proud of, but abusing little old ladies wasn't one of them. He choked back his temper and aimed for somewhere close to polite when he spoke.

"Can I help you, ma'am?"

She stopped banging away at the step and peered up at him. "Young man! Come down here right now."

It would take an even harder heart than his to ignore her summons. He started down the steps slowly to avoid setting off his leg again. His visitor stood at the bottom and watched him through her thick glasses for several seconds before abruptly turning away.

At first he thought she was embarrassed for him as he awkwardly limped down the steps, which seriously pissed him off. Then he realized that someone else was headed in their direction. He didn't have to look to know that once again Tate Justice was intruding on his privacy. She was still a few yards away when he reached the bottom. The old lady immediately turned back toward him and thrust a plate of cookies at him.

"My sisters and I wanted to welcome you to Justice Point. We thought Tate would've had the good manners to introduce you around." She shook her head, looking sorely disappointed. "I'm Mabel. My sisters are Madge and Margaret. They would've come along to meet you themselves, but we didn't want to overwhelm you on your first day in town."

It was impossible not to like her feisty spirit. "That was nice of you, Miss Mabel. I'm Hunter Fitzsimon, and I have to admit to having a sweet tooth. These cookies will be greatly appreciated, so please thank your sisters for me."

She patted him on the arm. "I'll do that. You have nice manners, young man. Now I'd better get back home."

As she made slow but steady progress back up the driveway, he debated whether to wait for Tate to get up the courage to make her final approach or to go on back upstairs. He decided to wait, figuring she would make a better target for his aggravation.

"Well, have you taken root there, or did you want to say something?"

"I was going to try to head Mabel off at the pass but didn't get here fast enough. She and her sisters like to bake cookies for everybody in town."

"So what's the problem? Did you think I got my kicks being rude to old ladies?"

She shifted from foot to foot. "Not exactly, but I could tell you don't like being bothered."

He couldn't resist tweaking her temper a bit. "Maybe it's only nosy landladies I don't like bothering me."

Her chin came up and her dark eyes narrowed. "I wasn't being nosy. I was being neighborly."

"Obviously my mistake, but it's hard to tell the difference. At least now you can sleep nights, knowing that I don't eat old ladies for dinner."

Tucking his cane under his arm, he held the plate of cookies in his right hand and kept his left on the railing as he climbed the steps. When he'd gotten halfway, he looked back to see Tate still standing right where he'd left her.

"The show's over, sweetheart. You can go back to whatever it is you do besides stare out your kitchen window."

Ignoring her gasp of outrage, he continued on up, waiting until he was inside before risking another look. She'd almost reached her back porch, righteous indignation clear in every step she took. He set his cane aside and ate a cookie as he watched. Chocolate chip, his favorite. The sound of a door slamming carried across the lawn, making it clear that Tate Justice definitely had a temper.

For the first time all day, he smiled.

Hunter aimed the remote at his new television and started flipping channels while he reported to Devlin. "I've moved in, but I haven't had a chance to look around yet."

"How's the apartment?"

"I've lived in worse." Much worse. At least it had real walls and windows. He'd spent much of his life living deep in the caves that served as headquarters for the Missouri branch of Paladins. The light green paint and floral upholstered furniture sure as hell beat limestone walls and army surplus furniture.

"What's your landlord like? Did he ask many questions about what you're doing there?"

"It's a landlady, and if she's got questions, she hasn't worked up the nerve to ask them yet." But she would, and sooner rather than later.

Devlin was silent for several seconds. "We never talked about a cover story, did we?"

No, they'd been too busy shuffling Hunter out the door and on the road to his new duty station. "I've got one."

"Well, what is it?" Devlin asked, sounding irritated.

Hunter smiled, enjoying the game. "I thought if anyone asked, I'd just say I was looking to relocate to the Northwest and was trying to get a feel for the place."

"And if she asks why that particular spot?"

"I'll tell her I'm thinking about applying for a teaching job at one of the local colleges." He took pity on the Paladin leader and added, "I've even got the credentials."

He'd always thought teaching history would be fun, but Paladins couldn't hold outside jobs. There would be too many unexplained absences when the barrier went down, especially if one happened to die and needed time to recuperate.

"Good. One less thing for me to worry about."

"Like I'd stay up nights fretting about that." Hunter settled on a baseball game, more than ready for this conversation to end.

"You're a real charmer, Hunter. No wonder Jarvis kicked your ass out of Missouri." Devlin didn't sound all that mad. "Keep in touch or I'll send out a crew to check on you. Got that?"

"I don't need a keeper, Bane. You can send anybody you want to, but that doesn't mean I'll talk to them. You'll hear from me when I have something to report."

The silence coming from the other end of the line was heavy. Finally, Devlin sighed. "Like I said, keep me posted. You don't want me to be the one that comes up there."

When the line went dead, Hunter tossed the phone behind him, not really caring if it landed on the table or not. It wasn't like there was anyone he really wanted to talk to anyway. He missed Jake and Jarvis, but it was too soon to contact them. He wasn't ready to hear the concern in their voices. No matter how many times he told them he was fine, they knew he was lying. They'd done as much as they could to help him, but not everything broken could be fixed.

His interest in the ball game ended as the walls of the apartment abruptly closed in on him. In the space of only a few seconds, his pulse revved out of control and his lungs struggled with the increasingly thin air. Recognizing the onset of a full-blown panic attack, he grabbed his cane and concentrated on the cool feel of the ivory and textures of the carved handle. Without looking at it, he traced each line and curve, his intense focus giving him something to think about until he reestablished some semblance of control.

When he could finally move again, he pushed himself up off the couch and headed straight for the door, grabbing a jacket on the way out. Outside, he breathed slowly, deeply, and held his face up toward the night sky. The air was rich and heavy with the threat of rain, the damp scent of fir and cedar clearing his head. So far, so good. Closing his eyes, he reached out with his senses, trying to locate the small stretch of barrier that Devlin said was close by Justice Point.

There. He turned toward the woods that clung to the top of a rugged bluff above Puget Sound. It was there all right, a soft, soothing crackle and buzz in the back of his mind. More of a comfort than a compulsion, although that could change the longer he remained in its proximity. With his leg still unpredictable at best, he'd be better off to wait until daylight to find a safe path to the barrier so that he could see it for himself.

For now, he'd walk along the narrow road that led to Justice Point. There was a definite chill to the night, but he didn't care. The need to move, to walk off the darkness that crashed in on him whenever he was closed in too long, was more important than physical comfort.

Nights were the worst. In the daylight, the view out the windows helped hold the demons at bay. But as soon as the sun set, the ghostly memories of his tormentors crept closer, tearing at his hard-won control until it shattered. His fear made no sense, but then phobias weren't logical. It was no one's fault that he'd been in the wrong place at the wrong time and had paid dearly for that mistake. That didn't mean he didn't hate his friends for not having been there to save him and himself even more for thinking that way.

Time to get moving. He eased his way down the steps, favoring his good leg to make sure he didn't set off another bout of painful spasms. Upon reaching the ground, he started up the driveway, which circled around to the front of Tate's house.

Details were welcome distractions, like how good the cool air felt on his face and how the wind playfully teased his hair, reminding him he was long overdue for a haircut. As he passed by Tate's house, he noted that the first floor was dark, but light poured out of the windows on the upper floors. Did she live alone in that big monstrosity of a house? Her personal life was none of his concern, but he was in Justice Point to find out who'd been abetting the enemy. That meant he had to know who all the local players were. So far, he'd only met Tate and Mabel. Somehow he couldn't imagine either woman to be part of a grand conspiracy, but only time would tell.

For now, he'd keep walking.

Tate had no idea what drew her to the window at that exact moment. Wisps of clouds scuttled across the night sky, the wind driving them inland with their burden of rain. Hopefully they would be gone by morning. The tea shop was closed on Mondays, and she could use a nice day to get some work done in the yard.

She was about to turn away when she saw him. Hunter Fitzsimon was out walking. Somehow that didn't surprise her. He seemed to be an intensely private man, and walking after dark made it unlikely that he'd run into many people. At least he had the good sense to stick to the road. There were a few trails that led down the bluff to the rocky beach below, but they were treacherous even during the daytime when visibility was good.

If he'd turned in that direction, she would've felt obligated to follow him. And wouldn't he love that? He already thought she was a busybody. Although she'd occasionally rented one of her extra bedrooms to relatives and friends of her neighbors when they'd asked her to, he was the first real tenant she'd ever had.

Hunter was a far cry from the uncomplicated college student she'd envisioned her future renter to be. He definitely had more baggage than the few boxes he'd carried up to the apartment. She assumed it probably stemmed from whatever life-altering event had left him limping and hurting inside and out.

As rude as he'd been to her, she would've written him off as a lost cause, but then he'd been so sweetly polite to Mabel when she'd presented him with that plate of cookies. If he was going to snarl at someone, better that it was Tate than one of her elderly neighbors. But that didn't mean she had to like it.

She'd spent far too much time thinking about Hunter for one day, and it was past time to call it a night. At least she didn't have to be up at the crack of dawn tomorrow to get her chores done before opening the shop. She could sleep in, run a few errands, and then spend the afternoon working out in the yard if the weather cooperated. If it didn't, she'd sit out on the porch with a good book. Her to-be-read stack was getting out of control again.

She picked up the top book and wandered back over to curl up in the window seat in the corner bay window. She *hadn't* chosen the spot for the clear view of her driveway. It was none of her concern if Hunter Fitzsimon managed to find his way back to his apartment or not.

He was a big boy and could take care of himself. Even so, she kept a wary eye on the road outside as she read. The time stretched out as she turned page after page, the story failing to capture her attention. Finally, she tossed the book toward the pile and settled back against the cushions to watch the stars fade in and out as the clouds rolled in from the Sound.

As she relaxed, she floated somewhere just this side of sleep before slowly drifting into dreams about a mysterious stranger with moss green eyes.

• • •

The rain held off until Hunter had outdistanced the demons dancing inside his head. He'd exhausted his body some time ago, but it had taken far longer to wear down the sharp edges of his mind. Now it was time to turn around. He needed to get back before he lacked the energy to make it up the stairs. Sleeping on the ground even in the rain wouldn't kill him, but it would only draw more unwanted attention from the other residents of Justice Point.

He'd only been in town for roughly eighteen hours and he already had one of its citizens a little too interested in him. Hopefully Tate Justice would get over her need to keep an eye on him. If not, he'd have to figure out how to fix that. Her curiosity wasn't the only problem with having Tate Justice so close by.

It had been only a few months since his life had been ripped apart right along with his body. It had been even longer since he'd taken a woman to bed, and she'd been little more than a willing warm body. Hell, he couldn't even remember what the woman looked like, much less her name. After a brief, frantic coupling, he hadn't bothered to ask for her phone number, and she hadn't offered.

Which brought his thoughts right back to his pixy of a landlady. He normally went for leggy blondes, but what Tate lacked in height she made up for in compact curves, the kind that would cushion her lover's thrusts nicely no matter how he took her.

Of course, that was the last thing he should be thinking about. He wasn't there to indulge in lustful fantasies. He had a job to do for the Paladins, and even if Devlin had sent him up here as a favor to Jarvis, it was clear that the need was real. If someone from this world or Kalithia was stirring up trouble, Hunter would find out and put a stop to it.

Tightening his grip on the head of his cane, he imagined the sweet slide of its hidden blade twisting into the gut of an Other or the heart of a human traitor. He didn't care which as long as he could watch them die.

The lights were still on at Tate's. He stood in the shadows of the tall firs across the driveway and stared up at her figure in the upstairs bay window. Crazy woman. Why wasn't she tucked into bed like all the other residents of Justice Point? He was tempted to throw a rock at her window to startle her awake, but it would be too easy for her to guess who'd done it.

The last thing he needed was for her to get the idea that he was watching her as much as she was him. He had enough problems. Leaving the shadows behind, he cut across the grass to the garage. He took his time climbing the steps. All in all, the walk had done him good. After a long soak in the tub with the jets on high, he'd crawl into that big, soft bed.

The only thing wrong with that picture was that he'd be doing it all alone.

The rev of a powerful engine outside interrupted Tate's pleasant dream. She didn't remember the details, but there was definitely something about slow dancing wrapped up in the arms of a tall stranger. She could still hear the music, but her partner was a bit vague. Well, except for the reddish brown hair that brushed his collar and eyes that were a distinctive mix of gray and green.

She stood up and stretched. The brake lights of a big pickup truck glowed dimly in the darkness below. She couldn't tell what color it was, but even so it didn't look familiar. No one in Justice Point drove anything that massive. Obviously some stranger had picked the wrong turnoff and was following the loop back out onto the highway.

Odd, though, that he didn't have his headlights on. Maybe the driver was trying to be considerate by not shining them into the houses this late at night. She hoped he remembered to turn them on before he got much further.

That reminded her—had Hunter made it back to his apartment all right? It would seem so, since the only lights on in the apartment were in the bathroom and bedroom. She was pretty sure the living room light had been on when he'd left for his walk.

The grandfather clock down the hall chimed just once. It was definitely well past time for her to crawl into bed herself. As she pulled the blankets up over her shoulders, she smiled. Maybe if she fell asleep humming that same waltz, the mysterious partner from her dream would be willing to dance again.

His driver cursed and swerved back toward the center line, the road almost too narrow for two vehicles to pass each other without riding on the shoulder. "Have I mentioned how much I hate driving this road at night?" Joe asked.

"Yes, you have, Mr. Black. Repeatedly. It's been duly noted and given all the consideration it deserves."

Which obviously meant none. He didn't give a rip about how Joe felt. He paid him for his muscles and his willingness to do anything for money. Feelings didn't even make a blip on his radar, and they both knew it. Flipping on the headlights, Joe pulled out onto the highway and drove in aggravated silence.

"Slow down."

"Who's driving?" Joe sneered.

He hated it when Joe took the curves a little too fast, which was precisely why he did it.

Time to yank his leash again; it was growing more and more tiresome. "Need I remind you which one of us controls the money in our arrangement?"

Joe immediately slowed down. They only had about fifteen miles before they reached the interstate, and then it would be a straight shot back to civilization. Thank God. He couldn't imagine living in a hellhole like Justice Point. Why did they even bother giving the place a name at all?

They rode in silence. He only enjoyed classical music, while Joe leaned more toward twang and thumping bass. Since he couldn't stand the stuff himself, they'd long ago agreed to keep the radio off. Unfortunately, however, Joe couldn't keep his mouth shut for more than a few minutes at a time.

When Joe couldn't stand the oppressive quiet anymore, he asked, "Was there a message this time?"

"Is that really of your concern?"

"Not particularly. But if there wasn't, it usually means another trip up here sooner rather than later. I just want to make sure I'm available."

Would he never get their roles in this game straight? "I pay you to be available, Mr. Black. I hope this isn't a bid for more money. That would not please me at all."

Joe shot him a worried look. "No, sir, I wasn't asking for a raise."

"Good answer."

He also knew Joe hated being called Mr. Black, but one of the conditions of the job was that they never use their real names. When they'd struck the deal, Joe hadn't looked past the money being offered. He'd needed to get some creditors off his back, the kind who took late charges out of your hide with a knife. It had only occurred to Joe later to wonder why secrecy was so important when his duties only consisted of driving his employer up the coast once or twice a month.

All they ever did after parking the truck in a clump of trees was follow a trail down the bluff overlooking Justice Bay to a small cave. Sometimes there was an envelope waiting, sometimes not. Then Joe would drive them both back to Seattle and drop off his employer at a different location every time.

The money was good, the job simple, but Joe was starting to realize the money was a little *too* good and the job a little *too* simple. It would be some time yet before he would earn enough to pay off his bookie though. So for now, he'd do his best to keep his employer happy.

If that were to change, well, tragic accidents happened all the time.

Chapter 3

Tate sat cross-legged on the ground and stared at the flower bed. Something had been grazing on her flowers again. Short of installing an electric fence, there wasn't much she could do besides making the surviving plants look their best. It was a losing battle, but she wasn't going down without a fight.

A shadow fell over her. Based on its size and the heavy silence, it could only be Hunter Fitzsimon. They had managed to avoid each other for a couple of days. She wondered what desperate situation made him seek her out. She stood up before turning toward him.

"Did you need something, Mr. Fitzsimon?" She was rather proud of how calm she sounded, especially since her traitorous body took immediate notice of how very fine he looked in those worn jeans and a faded Tom Petty T-shirt. Even behind his sunglasses, she could feel the intensity of his gaze.

"Where's the nearest coin-op laundry?"

She eyed the stuffed pillowcase that he had slung over his shoulder. "I suppose there's one in Bellingham somewhere, but there's no need for you to drive that far. You can use my washer and dryer whenever you want. It's included in the rent."

Not that the idea had even occurred to her until now. She dusted off her knees and headed up the steps. "Come inside, and I'll show you where everything is."

Hunter followed in silence through the tea shop and into the kitchen.

"The laundry room is back here. I keep detergent and softener on the shelf above the washer."

"Next time, I'll use my own. I was going to buy some in town."

Big surprise. "That's fine. There's plenty of room on the shelf, so you don't have to carry it back and forth."

He nodded.

"Once you've started a load, come out to the shop if you'd like to wait for it to finish. I'm afraid I don't serve coffee, but—"

"I don't drink the stuff," he interrupted.

Hunter shoved his sunglasses to the top of his head and started stuffing his clothes into the washer. So he was a boxers guy, Tate noticed, and brightly colored ones at that. Of course, he had to catch her staring. His mouth was a straight slash of pure disgust.

Definitely time to move on. "I have pastries and tea, and today's paper is on one of the tables, too. I don't think anyone's gotten to the crossword puzzle yet." She was almost out the door when he spoke again.

"I'd appreciate some tea. Whatever you've got."

He was a tea drinker? He didn't seem the type, but okay. She'd make him some Pu'erh, a man's tea if there ever was one. Besides, it was rumored to have strong medicinal qualities. "I'll have some brewing for you. Want a muffin or scones to go with it?"

"Anything would be fine."

Anything? Like maybe a quickie behind the counter? Tate felt her cheeks flush. Oh, now that was a wicked thought. Just because Hunter was halfway approachable today didn't mean he was interested in being friends, much less anything more. She really needed to get out more, especially if Hunter Fitzsimon was going to be hanging around her shop regularly.

Luckily, a carload of tourists pulled up to the shop. They'd provide the perfect barrier between her and the enigmatic man who had just started her washer.

Hunter leaned against the counter and stared at the washer, willing it to work faster. Voices drifted in from that nightmare of a tea shop. He shuddered at the image. The cluster of small tables coupled with more lace and floral prints than he could stomach made him feel oversized, awkward, and pissed off. Normally he would've ignored such feminine trappings, but he'd focused on the decor rather than the seductive sway of Tate's hips and how well she filled out those jeans. Or worse yet, how much he wanted to peel them off of her.

Hell, he had to quit fantasizing about Tate Justice even if she did look at him with feminine interest in her eyes. Even before the attack he never messed with nice girls; they wanted a future he couldn't provide. Tate was definitely an innocent, not at all the type to be up for a meaningless romp in the sheets. The last thing he needed was to complicate his life even more by messing with a woman like that.

Maybe he should haul his wet clothes right back out of the washer and drive into town, except that would only raise more questions. With a curse, he left the utility room and headed into the tea shop, intending to let Tate know he'd be back when his clothes were done. Tate was chatting with a family seated near the window. She looked in his direction and gave a quick nod toward the far corner of the shop.

He followed her gaze and spotted the table she'd set for him. Next to a plate piled high with small pastries was a teapot and a mug sized for a man's hand. His temper stirred again, but even he wasn't enough of a jerk to blow her off, not when she'd gone to such effort to make him comfortable in her shop.

He maneuvered through the tables, sitting with his back to the wall, and slowly counted the seconds until his leg settled down. After adding two lumps of sugar to his mug, he poured the tea and took a sip. He didn't recognize the deep, rich flavor, but he liked it a helluva lot better than the cheap tea bags he bought at the grocery store.

He unfolded the paper and read the national news. He only skimmed over the local stuff because he wouldn't be in the Seattle area long enough to care about it. He folded the page, ready to start the crossword puzzle, before he realized he didn't have a pen. He was about to toss the paper on the next table when he saw Tate had left a pencil sitting by his plate.

Even that irritated him. He preferred ink when doing a crossword puzzle. No guts, no glory. She had no way of knowing that, but lately "reasonable" wasn't exactly in his vocabulary. He concentrated on the clues and filled in the small boxes, letting the rest of the world fade into the background. The peace wouldn't last long, but he'd settle for what he could get.

The door to the shop opened and closed, leaving the room blessedly quiet. He could remember when he actually enjoyed a crowd, especially when he and Jake went on a pub crawl looking for a good time. But not anymore. Now he needed silence and solitude.

A shadow fell over his table. He carefully filled in the last two letters on the puzzle before looking up. Tate gave him a tentative smile.

"The washer stopped. I can switch loads for you if you'd like."

The last thing he needed was for her to be handling his boxers—under any circumstances. "I'll get it."

He got up from the table and walked away, only belatedly realizing he should've thanked her.

Tate's day had been a long one. Business in the shop had come in fits and starts; one minute no one, and then several carloads at once. The menu was limited to a few sandwiches and pastries, so at least the prep work had been minimal.

Even so, one person could only do so much. In the back of her head, she'd been hoping that if a college student rented the garage apartment, she might have been willing to exchange working a few hours a week for reduced rent.

Somehow she didn't think Hunter would be interested. The image made her smile at the effect he'd have on her customers. He didn't exactly exude warmth and welcome, but that didn't mean he wasn't sexier than sin. Oh, yeah, any woman with a pulse would sit up and take notice when he spoke in that gravelly voice and took her order.

She'd spent far too much time thinking about him lately. She leaned back in her window seat and let his image fill her mind. His wavy hair needed a good trimming, and his clothes were chosen for comfort rather than style. She wondered why there was so much anger in his straight slash of a mouth and storm colored eyes. As much as she'd like to get to know him better, he'd made it abundantly clear that he wanted to be left alone.

But why? Perhaps he'd always been a loner, but somehow she didn't think so. She suspected the accident that had damaged his leg had left him wounded on the inside, too.

She opened her book again, determined to lose herself in its pages. The author was one of her favorites, and the story was the kind she was trying to write herself. But after only a few pages, her eyes kept wandering off to see if Hunter had left on one of his nightly prowls. He'd only been there a few days, but she'd already noticed his habit of walking after most folks had gone to bed. He'd even gone out the night before despite the heavy rain.

She'd been tempted to have a hot cup of tea waiting for him. Oh, yeah, that would've gone over well. Even if he'd accepted the mug from her, he'd have given her yet another angry lecture about leaving him alone.

Speak of the devil. Hunter stepped out of his apartment and started down the steps. But instead of heading toward the road as he had the past few nights, he turned toward the woods. She closed her book and leaned into the corner, hoping that he'd change direction.

But no, he was definitely heading for the trail that led down to the rocky beach below the bluff. He had no idea how treacherous the path could be at night, especially with his injury.

Without even realizing she'd made the decision to go after him, Tate was already tying her shoes. She ran downstairs and out the back door, flashlight in hand. There was a definite chill in the night air. Maybe she should've pulled jeans on over her flannel boxers and T-shirt, but there hadn't been time. Not if she was going to reach Hunter before he reached the steepest part of the trail.

Running in the dark could lead to disaster, especially if she sprained something vital. Impatiently holding her pace to a fast walk, she focused her eyes on the ground. Hunter wasn't as familiar with the terrain as she was, so with luck she'd catch up with him before long. She doubted he'd even taken a flashlight. He seemed to prefer the cloak of darkness, although with his injury it struck her as foolish.

Despite her caution, she tripped over a root just inside the tree line and stumbled forward, barely catching herself from taking a tumble down the sloping trail. She stopped long enough to shine her light into the trees ahead. Hunter was nowhere to be seen.

Had he turned back toward the road? There was no way to know for sure, so she'd continue on until she reached the sharp switchback. If she hadn't spotted him by then, she would turn back. The towering Douglas firs and cedars closed in around her, blocking out the moonlight. She paused to listen to the soft rustlings in the woods and the pounding of the surf on the rocks. It was as if she were alone in the world with no sight or sound of another human being.

The chill that swept over her had little to do with the ambient temperature. She'd never felt scared living in Justice Point, but then again she'd never ventured out in this part of the woods at night. Was she overreacting out of concern for Hunter? She fought against the urge to break and run for the safety of her bedroom.

The trail straightened out ahead, so she broke into a slow trot, swinging her flashlight in a wide arc as she ran. She tripped again and dropped it. The light died immediately, leaving her lost in total darkness. She stayed sprawled on the ground, waiting for her hands and knees to stop stinging. When she pushed herself back up to her feet, she was pretty sure she felt a trickle of blood running down her leg. Great. Just great.

It was time to surrender to common sense and turn back. She should head back to where the trees thinned. There she could see well enough to get back home without further mishap. She only hoped that she'd make it that far without running into Hunter. Some rescuer she turned out to be.

Then she heard voices. Turning her head to the side, she determined that they were coming from below her on the trail. She backed up a couple of steps. Who would be out in the woods this late at night? Well, besides her and Hunter? Tourists would be the most likely answer, but there was no campground down near the beach. It was also odd that she couldn't see any flashlights. Why would they be hiking in total darkness?

Maybe they'd spent the day picnicking and were only now heading back to their car. Trouble was she hadn't noticed any strange vehicles parked in town during the day. Then she remembered the other night, when that strange truck had driven past her house without any headlights. At the time she'd thought the driver was being considerate, but now she wondered if they'd been trying to avoid being noticed.

She had to get back to the house. Before she walked even a handful of steps, a strong arm wrapped around her waist and a hand clamped over her mouth. She tried to scream and fought to break free.

The arm tightened, cutting off her breath as a harsh voice whispered near her ear. "Damn it, Tate, hold still! Keep fighting me and we'll both get hurt."

Hunter! Her terror turned to relief. When she let herself go slack, he eased off on his stranglehold. Her lungs still weren't working at full capacity, but that had more to do with the unfamiliar sensation of being pressed up against a hard male body.

He whispered again. "I need you to do exactly what I tell you to. No arguments. Nod if you understand."

She nodded, his rough voice sending shivers through her.

"We need to get off the trail before they see us. Got that?"

She nodded again.

"Okay. Now keep quiet and follow me."

When he released her, her knees buckled. Cursing under his breath, Hunter caught her. This time he held onto her as he dragged her deeper into the shadows. Tate couldn't see more than a few inches in front of her, but Hunter seemed to know exactly where he was headed. Her best guess was that they'd gone about ten feet when he shoved her up against the far side of a thick tree trunk.

"You *would* be wearing white," he said, disgusted.

Since when was wearing a white shirt a crime? Before she could ask, he opened his leather coat and leaned in close to wrap it around her. She realized that between the tree at her back and the black leather, it would be almost impossible to see her. He was protecting her.

For a moment all she could focus on was the quiet rasp of Hunter's breathing, the warmth of his body surrounding her, and the scent of his skin filling her senses. Maybe she should be at least a little frightened, if not of the approaching voices, then certainly of the man who'd dragged her farther into the darkness with no explanation.

But what she was feeling for Hunter was definitely not fear. Instead, desire stirred in the back of her mind, wishing he'd press closer, harder. Was his hair as soft as it looked? Her fingers itched to find out. What would it feel like to be taken by a man with such strength, such anger? Her body melted and softened with need.

Her hands were trapped between his chest and her own, leaving her no room to move. Tension thrummed through his body as he cocked his head to one side, listening as the men passed by. She heard two distinct voices, but with her heart pounding in her head, she couldn't make out what they were saying.

Did Hunter know them? If not, why would he assume they were a threat? She fully intended to ask those—and a whole bunch of other questions—as soon as she had the chance. And if she didn't like Hunter's answers, she'd be looking for a new tenant come morning.

The bastards were gone, leaving Hunter stuck in the woods trying to figure out what to do about Tate Justice. He had a job to do, and it didn't include protecting a woman with too much curiosity for her own good. It didn't help his own control to know that she was attracted to him. But hot damn, it felt good to be this close to her tight little body. It would be so easy to yank those ridiculous boxers down and take her right there against the tree.

"Wait here," he said, shaking off the thought. "I'll make sure they're gone."

"But who were they?"

Her voice was anything but quiet. If she kept that up, she'd find out firsthand who, or what, they were dealing with.

"Hunter, answer me! Who—"

He silenced her the only way he could, crushing his mouth down over hers. Big mistake. Her lips parted, trying to protest his rough treatment, but they offered him the opportunity to deepen the kiss. It would've taken a far stronger man than Hunter to resist sampling the sweet taste of Tate Justice's mouth. He tightened his arms around her, pulling her flush up against his body as his tongue swept in and out of her mouth, stoking the fire between them.

It didn't take long for her to engage him in a fierce battle for domination, one he fully intended to win. He pushed his knee between her thighs, lifting her up onto her toes to ride his leg. She gasped, but he couldn't tell if it was outrage or pleasure. He didn't care. No doubt she'd clean his clock for him later, but he was willing to risk a few bruises for the chance to get his hands on that luscious ass.

When Tate fisted her fingers in his hair, he half expected her to use the hold to break off the kiss. Instead, she slid her tongue against his and rocked her hips. Holy God, he wasn't the only one racing straight toward catastrophe here. No matter how much his body screamed to get closer, to lose their clothes, to bury his cock deep in the damp heat pressed against his thigh, he knew in that direction lay total disaster. Tate Justice was not the kind of woman a man fucked up against a tree, even if she seemed up for it. Right now she was riding high on an adrenaline rush that he knew she'd regret as soon as she crashed.

He eased her back to the ground and stepped back away from her, reluctantly putting some distance between them. He had to get away and quickly. But before he left, he adjusted his coat on her.

"Put that on properly before you freeze your ass off."

Thanks to his Paladin high-octane eyesight, he could see her far more clearly than she could see him. Her eyes were huge, the expression on her pixie face caught somewhere between fear and fury. There was no question the woman had passion. At least the darkness hid the painful evidence that he'd enjoyed their momentary embrace way more than he should have.

He picked up his cane and stalked off to assess the situation. As soon as he reached the clearing, he heard a powerful engine start up. Even if his leg was up to the chase, they'd be gone before he got close enough to figure out who they were.

Cursing a blue streak, he started back down the trail to collect Tate and drag her interfering butt back to the house. Devlin Bane would have his head for screwing up like this, especially because of a woman. Or maybe not, considering he'd let Barak q'Young live because Bane's lover had asked him to.

It was too much to hope that Tate had stayed put. She'd managed to find her own way back to the trail. It'd serve her right if he left her to fumble her way home alone, but he couldn't do it. Telling himself that he was only protecting his favorite leather coat from inevitable disaster, he followed her.

"Give me your hand."

Tate started at the sound of his voice.

"You were gone too long."

He heard a hint of fear in her words and bit back a snarl. "At least I came back."

She latched onto his hand and held on tightly as he hauled her annoyingly cute ass back up the trail.

They reached the edge of the trees without further mishap. But as soon as there was enough light, she jerked her hand free and walked beside him. He was surprised she didn't stomp off in a huff and leave him behind.

Son of a bitch, she was showing her steps to accommodate his limp! Would the woman never learn? The last thing he wanted was her pity. Even though he'd pay for it later, he sped ahead until she was almost running to keep up.

Stepping up on the porch, she turned to look down at him. Maybe she thought the high ground would give her some advantage, but she should be smart enough to know he couldn't be intimidated.

Hunter joined her on the porch, standing close and glaring down at her. "What in the hell did you think you were doing out there half-naked in the dark?"

Her chin immediately came up in a stubborn tilt, but her eyes slid to the side, avoiding his gaze.

"That's my business."

So he was right; she'd been on a rescue mission.

"I will say this once, and I want you to listen: Leave me alone. Period. I've been taking care of myself for longer than you can imagine."

Instead of agreeing, Tate changed the subject. "Who were those men?"

He decided to give her the honest answer. "I don't know."

He *did* know that they might not have even been human. But the last thing the Paladins wanted was it to get out that wack-job Kalithians had been visiting this world for centuries.

"If you didn't know, why did we have to hide? They were probably just tourists." She sounded like she was trying to convince herself it was true.

"They may not have been. I'd rather err on the safe side."

Hunter knew it was time to make tracks for his apartment. The walk back from the woods had cooled down his body's response to holding Tate in his arms. But the longer he lingered, the harder it was to remember why he hadn't tried to finish what they'd started. And as much as it infuriated him that this little slip of a woman had jettisoned all common sense to come charging after him, it also touched him.

"Leave me alone, Tate. Got that?" he said, getting in her face one last time.

She executed a perfect salute, the brat. "Yes, sir, roger that."

Before he could walk away, she grabbed his arm. "But *you* get this, Hunter Fitzsimon. If you go tumbling off that bluff because you're too bullheaded to listen to reason, don't blame me."

Okay, that was cute. He looked down to keep her from seeing him smile. What the heck was that on her legs? He sniffed the air—fresh blood.

"What did you do to your leg?"

She shrugged. "I tripped over a root."

He took her arm again. "Come with me before you bleed to death."

The cut wasn't serious, but knowing she'd been injured because of him made him see red—again—as he dragged her into the house.

He yanked a chair out from the table. "Sit down," he snapped. "Where's your first-aid kit?"

"I can—"

"Tate, where's the kit?"

She rolled her eyes and flopped down on the chair. "Behind the counter out in the shop."

His leg was killing him, but he ignored the pain and tried not to limp. If Tate got the idea that she'd been right about the trail being too much for him, she'd be back up in his face about it or baking him cookies or some other crap. He rummaged around behind the counter until he found the small box with a red cross on it. On the way back to the kitchen, he grabbed a couple of clean washcloths and a bar of soap from the hall bathroom.

She was sitting right where he'd left her. He filled a bowl with warm water, soaked one of the cloths at the sink, and worked up a lather. The soap would probably sting her scrape, but she deserved a little pain for being such a big one.

The woman didn't have a lick of sense. The two men out on the trail might have been dangerous, but then again, so was Hunter. Before he was injured, he would never have lifted a hand against a human woman. But being tortured to death had left his temper unpredictable. He didn't want to hurt Tate, but there were times when he might not be able to control himself.

Or even remember later what he'd done.

Hunter pulled a chair closer to Tate and motioned for her to rest her legs in his lap. It took several tries to wash away all the caked-on blood and dirt. He smeared some antibiotic cream on her scrapes and covered the one deep cut with gauze and surgical tape.

"Anything else hurt?"

She held up the palms of her hands. "They're not bad though. A little soap and water, and they'll be as good as new."

Eyeing her bruises, he shook his head. "Yeah, right. We'll see if you're still singing that tune in the morning." Not that he planned to be anywhere near her tomorrow.

As he cleaned up the mess he'd made, he realized he was using it as an excuse to hang around Tate's old-fashioned kitchen. It was definitely time to get out of there, especially since she hadn't yet brought up what had happened between them. Maybe she got shoved up against a tree for a brain-rattling kiss so often that it wasn't worth mentioning, but he doubted it.

"I'm out of here."

She immediately stood up, wincing as she did so. "Thanks for the first aid."

"If you minded your own business, it wouldn't have been necessary," he reminded her. "I've got better things to do than play nursemaid to you."

She hobbled over to block the door. "Yes, well, maybe I thought you were more important than the possibility of a little spilled blood."

He caught her jaw with his hand and angled her face up to look straight at him.

"No, I'm not, little girl, so next time leave me the hell alone."

"You better get your eyes checked, mister, because I'm not a little girl. In fact, I'd bet we're about the same age."

"Like hell we are." He probably had ten years on her. "I'm not talking about years, sweetcakes, but experience. I'm out of your league."

Tate looked insulted and even a little hurt. "I don't remember hearing you complain back there in the woods."

She crowded closer, her blue eyes daring him to deny it. Then she moved in for the kill and kissed him. Her tongue swept in and out of his mouth, tempting him down the road toward utter ruin. He had to stop this, had to, but God, she tasted so damn good and felt even better. Another few seconds of this and he'd be shoving her back onto that kitchen table, taking her any way he could. He couldn't wait to find out if she tasted that sweet all over.

Tate moaned and dug her nails hard into his arms. The pressure was enough to cut through the madness that had possessed him. He wrenched his mouth away from Tate's. Holding her at arm's length, Hunter stared down at her swollen lips and defiant smile, praying for his brain to kick back into gear.

The words finally came, snapping out of his mouth with the power and speed of a cracking whip. "I'll say it one more time. Stay away from me."

Then he stepped around her and out into the darkness, where he belonged.

Chapter 4

"Tate, dear, what did you do to your leg?"

Mabel stopped just inside the door of the tea shop, her two sisters hovering beside her as they stared at Tate's bandaged knee.

"I tripped and fell out in the yard, but I'm fine. It looks worse than it is."

That was a lie. Everything ached, and a poor night's sleep didn't help. She'd dreamed about being chased by shadow people with spooky voices. Then there was the part where she'd had mind-blowing sex up against a tree with a mysterious lover and then again in her kitchen. But she wasn't about to share her smokin' hot dreams or her late-night adventures with three elderly ladies with heart conditions.

"I'll get your tea and scones."

Margaret and Madge made their way to the table, but Mabel stood her ground. "Where's that nice young man, Tate?"

Nice young man? "Do you mean Hunter Fitzsimon?"

"How many young men live in Justice Point, Tate? Of course I mean Hunter."

"I haven't seen him this morning." At least not since he left her kitchen well after midnight. "Why?"

Mabel headed for her favorite chair. "We want to thank him for mowing our lawn yesterday."

Tate blurted, "For what?"

Mabel turned an eagle-eyed look in Tate's reaction. "He found our old push mower out behind the house, sharpened the blades, and then mowed the yard. The place sure looks good."

Tate probably shouldn't have sounded so shocked, but the man spent all his time telling her to leave him alone, that he didn't want to be bothered by anyone. And yet he did a kind deed for three elderly women.

"That was nice of him, and I'll tell him so when I see him."

That is, if he'd let her get within speaking distance of him. She brought the ladies their tea before returning to her laptop. Staring at the screen, she realized that the hero in her story had undergone several radical changes. The book, set in the Old West, had all the usual components—a schoolteacher, a sheriff, and a gunslinger. When she'd first started outlining it, she'd planned on the lawman being the one to save the day. But for some reason, the sheriff came off as weak sauce compared to the gunslinger.

How had the story veered so far off the course she'd laid out? The heroine now ignored the straight-laced sheriff in favor of the strong, silent man with a gun—and a limp. Tate highlighted the last few pages, intending to delete them, when the shop door opened. She stood up, ready to greet her customer, her smile fading when she saw who it was.

Why was Hunter just standing there, taking up space, and staring straight at her? Before she could put together a coherent thought, the Auntie Ms spoke up.

"Mr. Fitzsimon! Come join us."

"Yes, please do!"

Hunter met Tate's gaze from across the room, as if daring her to comment. He slowly made his way through the shop to take the fourth seat at the ladies' table, angling it so that he could stretch out his legs. He leaned his cane against the windowsill behind him.

She knew better than to smile over the picture the foursome made—three tiny, gray-haired women and one oversized, glowering male. So instead of hunting down her digital camera, she made Hunter a pot of Pu'erh, snagged a couple of blueberry muffins, and carried them over to the table.

"Morning, Hunter. Nice to see you out and about so early."

She injected extra cheer into her voice and added, "These ladies were just telling me how *sweet* you were to mow their lawn."

"They baked me cookies again." His voice was rougher than usual and more defensive.

So that's what it was; he didn't like feeling in debt to anyone. She set down his muffins and tea. "Enjoy."

When he reached for his wallet, she waved him off. "It's on the house."

Tate went back to her computer, doing her best to ignore the conversation across the room. The three sisters were ardent baseball fans, and from the sound of things, they were trying to convince Hunter that the American League was vastly superior to the National League. Tate doubted that their staunch belief that the local team consisted of the "nicest young men" carried much weight with Hunter.

But she had to give him credit for listening to them, rebutting their arguments with some of his own. He had the three women eating out of his hand, twittering and giggling like schoolgirls.

Was he this nice to everybody but her?

She forced her attention back to her story. Maybe it was time for the gunslinger to get shot. Nothing lethal, but painful for sure. The heroine might patch him up, but she wouldn't be gentle or sympathetic about it. Yeah, that felt right. He might eventually earn the heroine's love, but he was definitely going to have to work for it.

She lost herself in the drama, letting it unfold before her. As she finished her fifth page, a shadow fell over her. Knowing who it was, she took her time saving the file before closing it.

"Yes, Mr. Fitzsimon, what can I do for you?"

"I came by to see if you were okay." The bite in his voice made it clear that he wasn't happy about being there.

"Thanks for asking, but it's really not your concern. After all, I thought we'd already agreed that I would stay out of your way and you would stay out of mine. That's hard to do if you insist on coming into my tea shop, Mr. Fitzsimon."

His eyebrows snapped down in an angry line. "Quit calling me that, Tate."

"Why should I?"

"Don't you think it's a bit formal, considering you had your tongue down my throat last night?"

She gasped. "You started it!"

Now, that sounded *real* mature. She bit back the urge to rail at him some more. "Was there something you wanted from me?"

So that wasn't the smartest way to phrase it. She tried again. "Why are you here?"

"Where's your lawn mower?"

"In the garage. Why?"

"I'm going to use it to trim my nails. Why the hell do you think I want it? I need the exercise and thought I might as well be useful."

"Don't expect *me* to bake you cookies."

"I don't expect—or want—*anything* from you." He crowded closer, his eyes a swirl of green and gray.

Refusing to be cowed, she slapped her hands down on the counter and glared right back. "Well, that's certainly a relief!"

"Tate Justice! That isn't like you!" Mabel and her sisters were clearly shocked by the heated interchange.

Ignoring Hunter, she forced herself to smile at them. "Sorry, ladies. I didn't sleep well last night, and I guess it affected me more than I realized."

Reaching behind her, she picked up a key ring and tossed it to Hunter. "The one with the blue tag will unlock the side door to the garage. There should be a full can of gas in the back corner."

Hunter made no effort to hide his smirk as he snatched the keys out of the air. "I'll return them when I'm done."

She dropped her voice to a sarcastic whisper. "Ooh, goody, something to look forward to." Then, for the ladies' benefit, she said a little louder, "Thank you, Hunter. I so appreciate everything you do for me."

But the victory went to Hunter when he smiled and whispered back, "You made that clear last night when I had you up against that tree."

Her hand itched to smack him, but they still had an audience. He walked away before she could come up with a remark scathing enough to draw blood. Instead, she cleared his dishes and set them aside to do later. Shoving the man firmly out of her mind, she sat back down at her computer. Maybe it was time to give the gunslinger a nasty infection.

He probably should apologize to Tate for provoking her in front of her customers, but that wasn't going to happen. The longer she stayed mad at him, the better, because she'd be more likely to keep her distance. One of them had to be smart about it. When he'd walked out of his apartment this morning, he'd planned on heading back down the bluff to see if those late-night visitors had left behind any clues. Bane would be wanting another progress report soon. But instead, Hunter had veered away from the trail and walked straight into the tea shop to check on Tate.

Turning the key to the garage door, he gave in and

grinned. The look on her face when he'd sat down with the Auntie Ms had been priceless. Those old ladies were a kick, but the real fun was watching Tate fume over behind the counter.

He stepped into the dim garage and flipped on the light. One look at the lawn mower and he knew why Tate's yard looked like it had been cut with dull scissors: the mower was covered with more rust than paint. In fact, the whole garage looked like it hadn't been touched in years.

After topping off the gas tank, Hunter wheeled the mower outside, hoping it ran better than it looked. It didn't. He had to give the cord half a dozen hard pulls before the engine sputtered to life. After pushing the machine through the ankle-high grass for less than ten feet, it died with a puff of blue smoke.

He ignored the searing pain as he kneeled down to check the spark plug. Judging by its condition, the mower hadn't been tuned since it was new. He shoved it back into the garage. Not about to settle for the rusty hodgepodge of tools scattered around the workbench, he hauled in his tool box from the back of his truck. By the time he had the engine in pieces, he found himself whistling along to his iPod.

What was up with that? Then it struck him that he was feeling *good*. It had been so long since he'd taken pleasure in doing anything that he'd almost forgotten what it felt like. Twice in the past twenty-four hours he'd experienced something other than pain and anger.

The first occasion had been last night when he'd shoved Tate Justice up against that tree and kissed her in a fit of temper and desire. Just thinking about it made a rush of heat pool just south of his belt buckle. In the blanket of darkness, with her scent filling his senses and his tongue tangling with hers, he'd felt whole.

He'd definitely had his share of women over the years, but he couldn't remember a time when a simple kiss had taken him from zero to sixty in less than a heartbeat. Maybe it had only been the adrenaline rush from knowing his enemies had been but a few feet away, or maybe because it had been so long since he'd touched a woman. But neither of those answers seemed right.

That was why he'd gone to check on Tate, to see if there was something about her that explained his irrational behavior. He still didn't have an answer, other than the fact that he liked the way she stood up to him, giving as good as she got.

He finished reassembling the mower and wheeled it back outside for a test run. He yanked the cord and the engine caught on the first try.

If his leg held up, he could still get the lawn mowed before lunch, leaving him the afternoon to go exploring.

She was watching him again. It wasn't really her fault though. If the man didn't want to be stared at, he should keep his shirt on. There wasn't a woman in a hundred miles who wouldn't admire watch all that sweat-slick skin gleaming in the sunshine. Then there were his muscles that flexed as he shoved that old lawn mower across her yard. The sun brought out the red in his hair, and he looked extra scruffy because he hadn't bothered to shave. Yep, she could probably sell tickets and make a fortune.

Even if a crowd had gathered, she was the only one who knew firsthand how it felt to be crushed between that scrumptious hard body and a tree trunk. She'd keep that little tidbit to herself.

He'd been out there for almost two hours without a break, and his limp had grown more pronounced. Before she could start second-guessing herself, Tate filled a large tumbler with crushed ice and fresh-brewed tea. She waited by the back porch until he rounded the corner and was heading toward her. When he spotted her, he frowned and slowed down. She held up the glass and the pitcher to show that she came bearing gifts. He jerked his head in acknowledgment and shut off the mower.

He took the glass, almost dropping it when his fingers accidentally brushed across hers. His eyes flared wide as she jerked away, a sign he'd felt the same shot of heat that she had. Rather than acknowledge the connection, he concentrated on the glass of tea, downing about half of it.

"Thanks," he said halfheartedly.

"You're welcome." She took a cautious step closer. "I appreciate your doing this, and I can't help noticing the mower sounds different."

He shifted from foot to foot and stared past her. "I tuned it."

Why was he being so nice all of a sudden? "It was on my to-do list but I hadn't gotten to it yet. This place keeps me hopping."

"Seems like an awfully big place for one person." His gaze swept over the house and then out toward the bluff.

She shaded her eyes with her hand. "It is, although I love every inch of the place. My uncle left it to me in his will, so I've only been living in it for a few months. I spent a lot of time here with him while I was growing up, though, so it's always felt like home."

If she thought sharing a bit of her own past would spur him into doing the same, she was sorely disappointed.

He shoved the glass at her. "I'd better finish up. Thanks again."

Then he walked away, leaving her staring after him, wishing he wouldn't go.

Hunter put the lawn mower back in the garage and puttered around the workbench, straightening up the tools and throwing out the trash. It wasn't his mess to clean up, but it gave him an excuse to rest his leg before tackling the stairs to his apartment.

He'd overdone it mowing the whole yard at once, but stubborn was part of the Paladin package. Maybe he would've quit if he hadn't noticed Tate watching him. It stung his pride knowing she'd hurt herself last night because she'd been worried about him.

Stupid woman. He wanted to shake some sense into her. What if he hadn't been the one who'd reached out of the darkness to grab her? He suspected that at least one of the men who'd passed by had been human, but he didn't know for sure. He shuddered to think what a pair of light-hungry Kalith would've done to her.

He picked up his cane, pushed the release button, and slid out the sword. He set down the ebony cover and took a few practice swings with the blade. It lacked the weight of his old weapon, but it had its own lethal grace.

He brought the blade up in salute to an imaginary opponent and went through his old training routine, concentrating on control rather than speed. The stretches gradually eased the tightness in his back and legs. With his eyes closed, he could almost imagine that he was back in Missouri banging blades with Jake and the others. Damn, he missed his friends. But until he could face them as equals again, they were all better off without him.

He'd already pushed himself enough for one day, so he stopped after only one set. Still, it was another step back toward normal. After putting the cane back together, he walked out into the bright sunshine and around to the staircase. As soon as he turned the corner, he came to an abrupt halt. A familiar basket was sitting on the bottom step.

He glared over at the house, but for once Tate had the good sense to stay out of sight. When he picked up the basket, intent on taking it back, a note fluttered to the ground. He grunted in pain as he reached down to pick it up.

He unfolded the paper, which simply read Thanks. He wadded it up and carried the basket up to his apartment. Some battles weren't worth fighting, but he'd have to draw the line somewhere and soon. Tate was already too interested in his activities. He was here on a mission, not to get involved with the locals. But as he unwrapped the sandwich, he had to admit that maybe it was already too late for that. There were all too many ways he could imagine getting involved with Tate, most of which started with getting naked with her and going from there.

For once, luck was on Hunter's side. He'd decided to wait until early evening to head for the woods to check out the cave. He needed to find a place to hide while he watched the entrance to see if the strangers returned. The only real tactical problem was crossing the backyard without being spotted. As he gathered supplies and loaded them into his backpack, he heard Tate start her car and drive off. There was no telling how long she'd be gone, but if he left immediately, he could make it into the woods without being seen.

He left his apartment lights on, hoping she'd think he was home when she returned. He needed to explore without worrying what trouble Tate might stumble across in another well-intentioned, but misguided, attempt to save him. From what she'd said, she'd been living in Justice Point only a few months. Had she seen something that made her think the woods were dangerous at night, or had it been his weak leg that had her worried?

As he crossed the lawn, he tried running a few steps to test out his leg. Other than a few twinges, it seemed to be holding up. He slowed back to a walk, not wanting to push it, but satisfied that his strength was returning. Doc Crosby would be pleased when Hunter called in his next progress report.

Once he stepped into the shade of the Douglas firs he studied the ground carefully, hoping to find footprints. As far as he knew, Kaliths all wore smooth-soled boots, so any prints they left should be easy to distinguish from human ones.

A short way down the trail he noticed a red flashlight lying in a jumble of roots. Tate had most likely dropped it when she'd fallen. He stuck it in his backpack.

A few feet farther down the trail, he spotted some prints, but they were clearly his and Tate's. Looking around, he spotted a good-sized cedar a short distance into the woods, which had him grinning. He might have been able to silence Tate in some other way, but a full body press had done the job just fine. Once she'd gotten over the shock, she'd definitely gone for the gusto when she'd started kissing him back.

He had no business hoping for a repeat performance, but hot damn she'd felt good in his arms, the soft crush of her breasts against his chest, her fingers tangled in his hair. If there ever was a next time, he wanted it to be somewhere a lot more comfortable than up against a tree, and with a lot fewer clothes. His bed or hers—it didn't matter as long as they were skin to skin.

Once again, he reminded himself that he had no business thinking about his landlady that way. It was definitely time to get back to work, but he couldn't help grinning. As uncomfortable as it was to hike with a hard-on, he bet Doc Crosby would be happy to hear that Hunter's leg wasn't the only body part that seemed to be returning to full strength.

Good thing the cave was right where Devlin had said it was because otherwise Hunter would've missed it. Standing on the rocky beach below, he could barely see the mouth of the cave peeking out from between a pair of boulders. From the trail above, the cave was all but invisible. No wonder it made such a perfect secret rendezvous point for the humans who were collaborating with those bastard Kalith.

The only way to reach the cave was to sidle along a rocky outcropping that ran the length of the bluff from just beyond the cave and back toward the trail. He studied the surrounding terrain carefully, looking for a place that offered a clear view of the cave entrance but would allow him to remain out of sight.

It wasn't going to be easy. Finally, he settled for a spot farther down where the hillside curved out toward the water. The cluster of trees and undergrowth offered the only substantial cover with a good view of the cave.

After setting up his equipment, he decided to take a quick trip inside the cave. Sidestepping his way along the outcropping, he hoped like hell he'd never need to defend the cave in a hurry. Between the loose gravel and occasional roots sticking out of the hillside, it would be all too easy to take a header and dash his brains out on the beach below. On the positive side, the difficult approach would be equally hard for his targets. No one would be making a quick getaway unless they managed to sprout wings.

At the edge of the entrance, he squeezed behind the closest boulder and listened carefully. All he heard was the faint buzz from the barrier. At the moment, it sounded healthy and strong. No time like the present to get acquainted with his own little slice of high-energy hell.

Hunter had to duck to enter the cavern, but inside, the ceiling was high enough for him to stand. The light from outside only extended a short distance into the cave, so he set a lantern on an outcropping. Devlin hadn't provided Hunter with any diagrams of the interior, so he'd make his own.

Using a tape measure to check the width and depth of the main room, he sketched the general layout. The whole room was only about twenty feet wide and twice that deep. He ignored the barrier, preferring to focus his attention on one thing at a time. When he finished measuring, he snapped several pictures with his camera, taking several shots of the camping gear stashed along the side. Obviously someone had spent some serious time there, but there was no way to know if the camper was human or Kalith.

Finally, Hunter gave in to the pull of the barrier and walked toward it. It was the smallest expanse of barrier that he'd ever seen. The portion that ran through Missouri was broken up into several stretches, but none this small. Holding his arms straight out, he could reach from one side to the other. Two, maybe three, adults could cross through it at a time. Depending on how unstable the barrier was, it would severely limit the number of people who could pass from one world to the other.

Although why the hell a human would want to risk entering an alien world was beyond him. He still had a hard time believing even *one* of Devlin's men had done so. There was no way those blue stones were worth risking lives over, but obviously someone disagreed.

Time to get outside and into position before darkness fell. It was doubtful that whoever was using the cave would do so in the daylight. Justice Point was too small for such odd behavior to go unnoticed, and Others had the added problem of sensitivity to too much light. He might have a lot of long nights ahead of him until he could figure out if they had a regular pattern for their meetings with the Kalith.

As he settled into his makeshift blind, he vowed that he'd bring a blanket and a huge thermos of coffee next time. Drawing his sword and setting his revolver within easy reach, he leaned back and opened his book. The light wouldn't last much longer, but he planned on taking advantage of it as long as possible.

Tate hated mornings like this. She hadn't slept well, mainly because she'd dozed off on the window seat while waiting to see if Hunter went out for his walk. Stupid, she knew, but she couldn't help it.

She had to get over this obsession. Maybe she should take Mabel up on her offer to set her up with her late husband's nephew Matthew, the IRS agent. After all, at least Matthew had a job, which was more than she could say for Hunter. Other than the fact that he walked around looking like sex personified, she had no idea what he did all day.

The shop door opened. Speak of the devil. That's what she got for thinking about him so much.

"The usual and a couple of muffins." His voice sounded rougher than usual, maybe because it was early. He took the corner table again after snagging the newspaper off the counter.

"What kind of muffins? I have blueberry, oatmeal raisin, and raspberry," she asked, adding tea leaves to the pot.

"Surprise me." He was already bent over the crossword puzzle, clearly done with any attempt at conversation.

She carried his order to his table, setting the teapot and plate down with more force than necessary.

He looked up from his paper. "Is something wrong?"

"No, everything is fine and dandy."

Except that he looked worse than she felt. Guilt made her ask, "How about you? Are you okay?"

His eyes flashed stormy. "Yes."

How could he put so much temper in a single word? He looked as if he was about to say more when the sound of a loud pickup pulling up out front distracted them both. Tate didn't recognize the man climbing out of the cab of the truck, but Hunter clearly did.

"Son of a bitch."

He was up and stomping out the door before Tate had a chance to say a word.

She couldn't hear what the two men were saying, but their body language spoke volumes. Clearly Hunter wasn't greeting a long-lost buddy, nor was he bringing the man into the shop to share his pot of tea. Instead, the two of them stalked off toward Hunter's apartment.

She would've followed their progress from window to window, but a pair of her regular customers had just pulled into the parking lot.

By the time her customers left, Tate had given up on Hunter's coming back. She dumped his cold tea and wrapped up his muffins in case he wanted them later. His *friend*'s truck was still parked out front, so they must have settled their differences.

She wished she'd gotten a better look at the other man. The quick glimpse had left her with the impression that he was as tall as Hunter but slightly broader. They'd even moved with the same powerful grace, despite Hunter's slight limp; maybe they had served together.

That idea brought her up short. He'd never said a word about how he made his living, much less that he'd been in the military. There was just something about him that convinced her she might be on the right track. As she made the rounds, wiping down the tables and straightening up the shop, she paused by the window and looked toward his apartment.

The man definitely had secrets, but that only made her more curious about him. He'd hate knowing that, but she didn't really care. After all, a woman had a right to know something about a man who'd brought her to her knees with a simple kiss.

On second thought, she took that back—there'd been nothing simple about that kiss at all.

Chapter 5

Once Hunter got over the initial anger at D.J.'s unannounced arrival, he grudgingly admitted that maybe it wasn't a bad idea to share what he'd learned so far with one of Devlin Bane's most trusted lieutenants. Which, in truth, wasn't much.

"Want a beer?"

"Always," D.J. said with a grin. "Because in the words of the great philosopher Jimmy Buffett, it's five o'clock somewhere."

Of course, it wasn't yet noon in Justice Point, but Hunter wasn't one to quibble over details. He pulled two cold ones out of the refrigerator and popped the tops. D.J. looked at the label before taking a drink.

"I thought I'd tried most of the local microbrews, but this one is new to me."

Hunter dropped down next to D.J. "They're all new to me, but I'm working my way through them. So far, this one is my favorite."

D.J. took a long swig and nodded. "I can see why."

Hunter was a patient man, but judging by the way D.J. tapped his foot, he was not. Hunter decided to wait the man out. Let him be the one to lay his cards on the table. It didn't take long for the Seattle Paladin to break.

"So, Dev sent me up here to see how things are going, but don't take offense." D.J. gave Hunter a sheepish grin. "Really he just wanted to get me out of town for a few hours."

"And why is that?"

D.J. snickered. "It seems that someone uploaded a very creative computer virus to Colonel Kincade's computer. He's the Regents' favorite lapdog in the area, by the way, a coldhearted bastard who hates us almost as much as we hate him."

"So what did this creative virus do?"

"I don't know exactly." The wicked gleam in D.J.'s eyes belied his statement. "Something about dancing pigs and fireworks popping up no matter what file he tried to open. I'm sure it will fix itself in about"—he glanced at his watch—"another hour or so."

Hunter choked back a laugh. "The miracle of modern technology."

"Yeah, ain't it great?" D.J. laughed. He took another long drink. "So what do you have for me to take back to Devlin?"

Hunter pulled out his rough sketches and spread them out on the coffee table. "I figured most of the activity would be at night, so I went down the trail while it was still light to explore the cave. I took measurements and pictures while I was there."

He handed his digital camera to D.J. "Night before last I checked out the trail for the first time and heard two men coming back up from the beach."

That got D.J.'s attention. "Human or Other?"

"I didn't get close enough to tell. I ran into a complication that prevented me from being able to follow them."

It was too much to hope that the Paladin would let it drop. "What kind of complication?"

"My landlady saw me heading out into the woods and wanted to warn me that the trail wasn't safe at night. I had to stop her from blundering right into them." The memory still made him furious. That woman didn't have the sense God gave a goat.

"Did she wonder why you thought they might present a danger to the two of you?"

"If she did, she didn't say so. I'm playing it pretty low key, hoping she'll forget about it."

Fat chance of that happening, but he didn't want D.J. reporting that Tate might be a problem. If she continued to interfere with Hunter's business, he'd be the one to deal with it.

D.J. frowned. "Our preliminary information on this place said an older guy owned that house. When did that change?"

"A few months ago. The previous owner died and left the place to a relative." Maybe D.J. would assume that Tate was older, too.

"Name?"

Damn, Hunter wished he could keep her out of this, but refusing the information would only make things worse. "Tate Justice."

The Seattle Paladin typed the updated information into his laptop, then uploaded the pictures from Hunter's camera.

"Anything else I should know?"

"No, just tell Devlin that the next time he wants an update, call. I don't want to draw attention to myself by having a parade of Paladins marching through here on a regular basis." He gave D.J. a pointed look. "We're not exactly inconspicuous."

Then he opened the door, a less than subtle hint that it was time for D.J. to be hitting the road.

"Will do. Won't promise he'll listen. The man's a law unto himself."

D.J. filed past Hunter and headed down the steps. There was no need for Hunter to walk him back to his truck, but he didn't want to chance D.J.'s running into Tate alone. For once, he thought his luck was going to hold long enough to see the Paladin safely on his way. But no, the door of the tea shop opened right before D.J. reached his pickup.

Tate stepped out into the bright sunshine with a paper bag in her hand. "Hunter, you left these behind this morning. I thought you might want them."

"Thanks." Maybe if he kept conversation to a minimum, she'd leave. Fat chance.

The cool smile she'd offered him warmed up considerably when she turned it in D.J.'s direction. "Hi, I'm Tate Justice."

The Paladin flashed a wicked grin at Hunter over her head. "Nice to meet you, Tate. I'd say Hunter told me all about you, but I don't believe he mentioned how lovely his landlady was. Imagine him trying to keep something like that secret."

"Shut up, D.J." Hunter knew he should just walk away because anything he said was only going to encourage the jerk.

D.J. leaned against the front fender of his pickup as if prepared to settle in for a spell. "Now, is that friendly, Hunter? And after I drove all the way up here just to make sure you're all right. Tate, you'd think the man didn't want me here for some reason."

Great. No sleep, his leg hurt, and now he had this asshole yanking his chain. Hunter took one step forward, his cane in his left hand, his right in a fist, enough of a show of strength to ensure the man knew he wasn't joking.

"I've already said good-bye once, D.J. Don't make me say it again."

D.J. laughed. "Well, obviously I've worn out my welcome. Tate, I hope to see you again soon." He dutifully got in his pickup and started the engine. As he backed out, he grinned and saluted her with a quick flick of his hand, then drove off.

Hunter wanted to punch the guy and then kick himself for feeling that way. Rather than say anything to Tate, he did an abrupt about-face and walked away. And, of course, she followed right behind him.

He spun around to face her. "Now what, Tate?"

She blinked and took a step back. "Here!" she snapped, throwing a paper bag at him. "Take your stupid muffins."

Since he'd missed breakfast thanks to D.J.'s untimely arrival, he supposed he should be grateful to Tate for her kindness. But as long as she was mad at him, maybe she'd quit crowding him. So instead of apologizing, he decided he was overdue for a little time away from Justice Point. He had plenty of time to drive to Bellingham, grab a quick lunch, do some grocery shopping, and still get back in time to get down to his blind before dark.

Maybe when he returned, he would be more in control. He didn't handle surprises well these days. Short of posting a sign outside his apartment that said Stay the hell away from me! he didn't know what else he could do to make it clear that he needed to be left alone. Some days were better than others, but too many people making too many demands made his skin hurt and shot his control all to hell.

He gunned the engine and peeled out, sending up a spray of gravel. Childish, yes, but too bad. It was a whole lot better than punching somebody.

"Mr. Black, I have need of your services. I assume you'll be available at the usual place and time."

Joe cringed. He hated that name, but his mysterious jerk of an employer had been adamant that neither of them use their real names. He was paid in cash, all calls were made on prepaid cell phones, and he wasn't allowed to ask any questions other than when and where.

He reminded himself that he needed to earn more money before he could afford to quit, and these extra runs helped a lot. For now, he'd jump through all the hoops necessary to keep that cold, hard cash rolling in.

"Yes, sir, I'll be there."

"Rent a car this time. We may have a guest on the return trip."

"I assume you'll want a full-size sedan."

The phone went dead before he had finished the sentence. He hated it when the man did that. But on the other hand, his employer was hardly the kind of man he'd want to hang out with at the local watering hole. A little civility wouldn't hurt, though.

Thoroughly disgusted with the whole situation, Joe signaled the bartender to bring his check, although he wanted another beer for the road. But the one time he'd picked up his employer with alcohol on his breath, his pay had been docked by a couple of hundred dollars. The next time, he'd been told, he'd be working for nothing.

What did the old coot do down there on the beach anyway? Joe had been tempted to ask more questions just to see what was really going on, but there was a predatory gleam in the older man's gaze that kept him from giving in to curiosity. If he learned too much, the price for that knowledge might be more than just a few measly dollars.

It was time to take one last look around the shop to make sure everything was cleaned up and put away. Tate was about to turn off the lights when she spotted a familiar face peering in through the door. She hurried over to see what had Mabel looking so worried.

"Hi, Mabel. I was just locking up. Did you need something?"

The older woman looked disappointed. "Oh, dear.

I didn't realize what time it was. I guess it's too late to have a cup of tea."

Tate held the door open and stood back out of the way. "Never for you, Mabel. Come on in and have a seat. I'll be right back with your tea."

"Won't you join me, Tate? It's been awhile since we've had a chance to visit."

Mabel sat down in her favorite seat. Tate carried two pots of tea over to the table and set them down.

"Would you like a little something to eat? I have a few scones left."

"That would be lovely."

"Where are your sisters?" It was unusual to see one of the aunties out and about alone.

"Napping. Sometimes I think that's all they do." Mabel broke off a piece of a scone to nibble on. "Most days I join them, but I'm feeling a bit restless today."

"Is something wrong?"

The older woman sighed heavily and stared out the window. "Today would've been my sixtieth wedding anniversary."

Tate was torn. Did she offer congratulations or condolences? She settled for, "What was his name?"

"Tommy." Mabel smiled at the memory, her sadness gone for the moment. "He was a handsome one, Tate. You might not believe it looking at me now, but I was considered a beauty back in the day. I could've had my pick of a dozen men, but one look at those smiling black Irish eyes of his and I was a goner."

She fumbled for the wallet in her purse, then laid

a well-worn photo on the table for Tate to see. It was hard to see the woman sitting next to her in the pretty young face smiling in the picture, but there was something about the eyes and the way she held her head that looked familiar. Mabel was right. Her Tommy had been a handsome man, and his military uniform only emphasized his athletic build.

"I bet he turned his fair share of heads, Mabel. I like his smile."

"I did, too." Mabel traced his face with her fingertip. "He had a laugh that made everyone around him want to join in. But he was deadly serious when it came to serving our country. I suppose it's old-fashioned to describe a man as a warrior, but that's what my Tommy was."

Tate was getting a bad feeling, but she had to ask. "How long has he been gone?"

"Close to fifty years."

Tate's heart broke. "What happened?"

There was such pride in the old woman's voice when she answered. "He was career military. They never told me the details, just that he was gone. I have all of his medals back at the house. I should show them to you sometime." Mabel blinked rapidly several times.

Tate patted Mabel on the shoulder.

"Thank you for sharing about Tommy with me."

A commotion outside interrupted, drawing the ladies' attention outside. Hunter's truck was pulling up in front of the garage. Tate ignored the surge of relief that washed through her. He'd left in such anger that she'd had to wonder if he'd even be back. Not that she cared—much. After all, the man had been an absolute jerk earlier when his friend had been leaving. She'd done nothing to deserve his bad temper.

Mabel stared out the window for a few seconds. "Looks like your young man is headed this way. Wonder what's in the box."

"He's not my young man, Mabel. He's my tenant."

"Well, I'd better be getting back." Mabel picked up her cane and stood up. She took a couple of steps, then stopped. "Tate, you know I'm not one to go around giving advice where it's not wanted."

She paused, waiting for Tate to say something. "I know that, Mabel," Tate finally responded.

But it was obvious Mabel thought Tate needed some advice now. "Young lady, there isn't a day that goes by that I don't miss my Tommy, and I would've given up my own life to spend even another day with him."

Her chin came up and she met Tate's gaze head on, her pale blue eyes burning brightly. "It's not easy loving a warrior, but that just means they need it all that much more."

Then she walked away, leaving Tate sitting there in stunned silence. Who said anything about love?

The timing couldn't have been more perfect. Hunter quickened his pace to catch up with the woman stepping out of the tea shop.

"Miss Mabel, I was hoping you and your sisters could use some fresh blueberries. I bought more than one man can eat."

"We would love some. That was sweet of you to think of us," she said with a pleased look.

His laugh sounded rough even to his own ears. "I don't think anyone has ever described me as sweet before."

"Well, there's sweet and then there's *sweet.* You're the kind where the taste is subtle but lingers for hours." She smiled, the gleam in her faded eyes more than a touch wicked.

Hunter set the tray of berries down on Tate's front step and took out two pints for the three sisters to share. "Why, Miss Mabel, are you flirting with me?"

Her giggle sounded like a young girl's. "If you have to ask, then I'm not doing a very good job of it, am I?"

"I'm flattered." He offered her his arm, shifting his cane and the berries to his other hand. "May I walk you home?"

"That would be nice, especially since my sisters are watching from the window. They'll be jealous, you know. It's been a long time since a handsome man came calling on one of us."

He leaned down and kissed her papery cheek. "Then the men here in Washington must all be fools."

"You sure can be charming when you want to, Hunter," she said as they started up the sidewalk to her front door. "You might do better to use it on Tate Justice instead of wasting it on me."

What could he say to that? The last thing he needed was Tate to think he was flirting with her, especially after the other night.

"She'll have to settle for me trying harder to be polite."

"You can offer her more than that, young man. She hasn't had an easy time of it, you know. Not with that vulture of a mother always hounding her for money." Mabel grimaced. "I shouldn't spread gossip, even if it's true."

"Don't worry, it's already forgotten." He supported Mabel as she climbed the three steps to her door, then he handed her the berries.

"Thank you again. Think about what I said."

"Yes, ma'am," he promised, wishing his fingers were crossed. He wasn't about to tell Mabel that the only thing he wanted to offer Tate was a few hot and sweaty nights between the sheets.

But now it was time to wave the white flag and present his peace offering to Tate. As soon as his temper had cooled, he'd regretted his actions. D.J. was a different matter. Paladins were used to each other's tempers and tended not to hold grudges about it.

After picking up the cardboard carton he'd left at Tate's door, he popped a couple of blueberries into his mouth, savoring their sweetness. It reminded him of what Mabel had said. Jarvis and Jake would howl over someone thinking a Paladin was sweet. It really showed how insulated ordinary people were from the nightmare Paladins faced every day. Men like him were anything but sweet, but that was how it should be. People like Tate and the Auntie Ms deserved to keep their innocence.

The door opened—he'd lingered too long. Tate stood staring at him, her expression unreadable.

"I thought you might like blueberries." He held out the box, hoping she'd take it and disappear.

Instead, she crossed her arms over her chest. "Why would you care what I like?"

Sometimes it was easier to just bend over and take the licks. "Because I was a jerk. Happy now?"

"Not completely, but I'm getting there." She stepped outside. "I wasn't trying to crowd you this morning. I know better. You've made sure of that."

Hadn't he just admitted to being a jerk? What else did she want from him? There was only so much groveling he was willing to do.

"Look, do you want the berries or not? I said I was sorry."

"No, you said you were a jerk." She held out her hands. "But thank you. Apology accepted."

"Okay, then." But instead of handing her the box, he picked out a ripe berry and held it up to her mouth. He felt the soft brush of her lips against his fingertips from his head to his toes.

"Delicious." He wasn't talking about the blueberry, and they both knew it.

"Hunter?"

She was staring at his mouth, leaning slightly forward as if waiting for him to kiss her. He needed to get away from her—or a whole lot closer. When she looked at him with those clear blue eyes, what did she see? The man he used to be would've been flirting, seeing how far she would let him go. But he wasn't sure who he was anymore, much less how to approach a woman like Tate.

"Do you want to have dinner with me?" he asked.

He wasn't sure which of them was more surprised by the question. His first thought was to retract the offer, but he couldn't find the words. Maybe he'd get lucky and she'd refuse.

No such luck.

She took a step back before answering. "Sure, why not? Where do you want to go?"

Now that was a good question. Most of the restaurants he'd tried in town had drive-thrus. "I'll let you pick. I like Greek, Italian, and any place that serves rare steaks."

She looked shocked. "Oh, I'm sorry, but I'm a strict vegetarian. I only eat at organic restaurants. You know, yogurt, tofu, and fresh veggies. I know the perfect place!"

Tofu! He winced. How did he get out of this now? A drive-thru sounded better by the second. Still, he'd offered.

He tried to look enthusiastic. "Okay. Tofu it is. Can't wait. I'll meet you out here in an hour."

That's when he noticed Tate struggling to keep a straight face. When she couldn't contain it any longer, her laughter rang out bright and clear.

"Oh, God, Hunter, if you could've seen your face!" She used her free hand to wipe the tears from her eyes. "I'm sorry, that was mean, but I just couldn't resist."

He gave in and gave her a reluctant smile. "I probably had that coming."

"Yes, you did. But I'd love a steak dinner. I know a good surf-and-turf place that's not too far or too expensive."

That stung. "I'm not worried about the prices, Tate. I can afford it."

She grimaced. "I didn't mean it that way. I meant the food is great, but the decor isn't fancy and people can come casual. You couldn't get me into panty hose this time of year."

He'd be a lot more interested in getting her out of them, but he doubted she'd want to hear that. "Sounds good. Meet you here in an hour."

"Okay, then." She started back inside. Then she called after him, "And thank you for the berries. They're my favorite."

"What to wear, what to wear?"

Sometimes she wished she had a cat. At least then she'd have someone to talk to besides herself. Tate stared at the three outfits she'd picked out.

She put the jeans back in the drawer. "Too hot, too casual."

The shorts and matching top went next. "They'd be cool enough, but they're white. With my luck I'd drip something down the front."

That left the sundress. She held it up in front of her and stared at the mirror. The color played up her tan and made her eyes look bluer. Slip on the white sandals and she'd be set. Besides, she was running out of time if she wanted to shower.

Twenty minutes later, she stood at the window watching Hunter start down the steps from his apartment. Butterflies had taken up residence in her stomach, mostly because she wasn't sure exactly what this was supposed to be. Two friends going Dutch treat? That would be okay with her, but she suspected he was planning on paying for both of them. A steak dinner was a tad extreme for an apology for his short temper. Besides, that's what the blueberries had been for.

Which left a date. Did that even make sense, when he'd been working so hard to keep her at arm's length? But here she was, all dolled up. Hunter had on khaki pants and a sports shirt with the sleeves rolled up, showing off his powerful forearms. Her heart did a double flip. Even with his cane, there was no mistaking the masculine strength in the way he moved—or the way her body reacted to him.

Time to go. She stepped outside and locked the door behind her. Rather than wait, she met him halfway. He tried to be subtle about checking her out, but his smile had too much heat in it for her not to notice.

"You look great."

"Thank you." She warmed, basking in his approval. "So do you."

His expression said he doubted that, but he didn't comment. "Are we ready?"

"I am if you are." *For dinner. Just dinner.*

They walked over to the passenger side of Hunter's massive pickup truck. Oh, dear. She hadn't been thinking about the logistics of climbing up into the cab when she'd decided to wear a dress. She reached for the grip and pulled herself up, all too aware of how high her skirt rode up as she did so.

When she was settled, she expected Hunter to shut the door, but he seemed mesmerized by her legs. She tugged her skirt down a bit farther and then reached to close the door herself. When she moved, Hunter blinked and shook his head. Then he slammed the door.

O-kay, then. They'd been together less than ten minutes and already he was mad. That should make the rest of the evening interesting.

Hunter followed Tate's directions to the restaurant, doing his damnedest to keep his eyes firmly on the road. One glimpse of those tanned legs as she'd climbed into the truck and he already had a world-class woody. Hopefully she'd assumed the trouble he had walking around to his side of the truck had been due to his usual limp. A bit of black humor had him smiling: At last he had a reason to be thankful to the Others for the damage they'd caused.

He doubted anyone else would find that funny, including his companion.

"The restaurant is at the end of the block on the right."

"I see it."

They rode in silence while he found a parking spot. He got out of the truck and considered his options. If he let her climb down, he'd be right back where he started the trip—hard and hurting. To forestall that event, he handed her his cane and picked her up by the waist, lifting her down to the ground.

His unexpected move startled a gasp out of Tate. "Next time warn me!"

He liked crowding her a bit, so he held his ground, trapping her between himself and the truck. "What is it they say? It's easier to ask for forgiveness than for permission."

"And if I don't want to forgive you?"

Her hand came up to rest on his chest as if to push him away, but he caught it in his and held it there.

"Well, then I'd have to find some way to earn it. You know, buy you some more blueberries, or"—he lifted her hand to his mouth—"I could do this." He pressed a soft kiss to her palm, letting his breath tease her skin.

"Or maybe this." Moving slowly, letting her make the final decision, he leaned in close to brush his lips across hers. "What do you say, Tate? Forgive me?"

When she didn't immediately answer, he kissed her again, this time a little slower, a little longer, wrapping his hand around the curve of her neck. He kept the kiss short and gentle in comparison to their earlier ones. But the effects still burned through him like fine scotch.

He rested his forehead against hers. "I probably should say I'm sorry for that, too, but I hate to lie."

Her mouth quirked up in a half smile. "In that case, I'll settle for the truth."

Stepping back, he took her hand. "Come on, then. Let's go find you that steak."

Chapter 6

Hunter could've eaten cardboard for dinner and not complained as long as he could stare across the table at Tate Justice. The soft overhead light brought out the highlights in her short blond hair and the sparkle in her pretty blue eyes. Her mouth was driving him crazy, making him wish they were somewhere far more private than a restaurant.

They kept the conversation light, managing to avoid potential mine fields like his past, her family, and politics. But it didn't take long for them to get into a good-tempered argument over books, sports, and whether men had to watch chick flicks in equal proportion to the number of beat 'em up, blow 'em up movies they dragged their dates to.

He lost that one. She even warned him that she'd be keeping score if they ever went to the movies together.

Tate laughed at the expression on his face when she described her movie collection to him. Finally, she relented and admitted that she also had a shelf of films with explosions and great sword fights.

"How about dessert?"

"You bet." She grinned across the table at him. "Normally I'd pretend not to want any and then eat half of yours, but their strawberry shortcake is to die for. I'll have to put in about eight hours on the treadmill at the gym tomorrow to make up for it."

"Let's make it two," he told the waitress. Turning back to Tate, he picked up where they'd left off. "I didn't know you belonged to a gym."

"I don't. I sort of own one. I still haven't given you the full tour of my house, have I? My uncle wanted the place to be sort of a community center for Justice Point, so there's a mini fitness center behind the tea shop. It doesn't get much use because so many of the residents are elderly, but the equipment is top of the line. There's a treadmill, weights, an elliptical machine, and some other stuff. Feel free to use it anytime."

"Thanks, I might just take you up on that."

Silence settled easily between them. He couldn't remember the last time he'd enjoyed an evening out so much. It was a shame it had to end.

Hunter glanced around to check on the waitress's progress on their dessert, and spotted her over by the window.

It was dark outside.

His stomach clenched, and he grabbed onto the edge of the table for support. Shit! Where had the time gone? This time of year it stayed light in the Northwest until close to ten o'clock, so they'd been sitting in the restaurant for over three hours.

The waitress walked toward them, blocking his view of the window. She set down two enormous helpings of strawberry shortcake. The sight made him sick. Too sweet, too perfect, too much everything.

He had to get out, get home, get away before he lost control. Where the hell was the door?

"Hunter, is something wrong?"

"No!" His voice, ruined right along with everything else, grated on his own ears. "I've . . . no, we've got to leave. Now."

He held onto coherency long enough to throw a pile of money on the table. Too much, probably, but the price of freedom was always high. Right now he'd sell his soul to get outside, where the stars overhead would give him enough room to breathe without screaming.

His leg was stiff from sitting so long, but he managed to lurch his way to the front door, only dimly aware of the waves of worry following him as Tate struggled to keep up.

Outside, he leaned against the building. He'd reached the sanctuary of the darkness. The glare of neon and streetlights diluted the comfort, but anything was better than being shut inside four walls. Tate moved up beside him as he coasted to a stop, unable to go another step farther. Besides, where could he go to outrun himself?

"The truck is this way." Tate motioned toward the far side of the parking lot.

Her voice was calm, soothing, but he noticed that she kept her distance. Who could blame her? Not when he'd gone from fine to fractured with no warning. He squinted, trying to focus. What was he looking for? Oh, yeah. The truck. His truck. One step and another and another after that. Success, he was definitely making progress.

"Give me the keys, Hunter. I'll drive."

He didn't argue. He wouldn't want to ride with him at the wheel either. When they reached the truck, she opened the passenger door for him. Turnabout was fair, he supposed. But there was one problem. He couldn't stand the thought of being shut up inside the cab. Not even with Tate. Maybe especially with Tate when his control was shot all to hell.

"I'll ride in back." He pushed past her, heading for the tailgate to climb in.

"But it's starting to rain," she protested, holding her hand out to catch a few drops to show him.

He shook his head, refusing to listen. "I can't, Tate."

"Okay," she conceded, but clearly not happy about it. At least she wasn't trying to drag him off to the ER.

He stretched out in the bed of the truck, staring straight up at the night sky. The engine rumbled on, the vibration feeling good to him as the brush of the air rushing past cooled his skin. All he needed was to focus, to touch the smooth ivory . . . his cane! Where was it?

Pure panic had him flailing around in the truck bed, hoping to find it and knowing he wouldn't. The last time he remembered seeing it was at the restaurant, when he'd set it down on the extra chair at the table. Son of a bitch! Darkness that had nothing to do with the night blotted out his vision. The weakness made him ashamed, but if he didn't get the cane back, he'd fly apart and never find all the pieces again.

He raised up and pounded on the back window of the cab with his fist. The truck swerved back and forth. Damn it, he'd scared her, but they had to go back. Now, before it was too late.

She eased the truck over to the shoulder and rolled down her window.

"What do you need, Hunter?"

He caught a glimpse of his reflection in the rearview mirror as he leaned down to talk to her. Poor Tate, no wonder she looked a bit rattled. He looked like a madman, with his hair windblown and his eyes glazed over with fear.

"My cane. I left it at the restaurant."

"They're probably closed now. We can get it back in the morning."

He slammed his fist down on the roof of the cab hard enough to leave a dent. "No! I need it now."

Tate jumped at his outburst, but then gave a slow nod. "Okay, then. Sit back down before I swing the truck around. Wouldn't want you bouncing out on the pavement."

Her calm acceptance helped him gather up the tattered edges of his control and pull himself back together, enough so he could breathe and count the seconds as they sped back into town. Bless Tate's heart, she slid through stop signs and only flirted with the speed limit to get back to the restaurant. She didn't mess with the parking lot, stopping right in front of the entrance.

Hunter looked over the side of the truck. Crap, she'd been right. The front lights were off. Tate knocked on the door, and when that didn't work, she tried again using both fists. Finally, someone inside pulled back the curtain to look out through the window next to the door.

Evidently they tried to tell her the place was closed for the night, like she wasn't smart enough to figure that out for herself. Tate started pounding again. Finally she stopped and stepped back.

"I'm sorry. I know you're closed, but my friend left his cane at our table. I would've waited until tomorrow, but it's a family heirloom and he has to leave first thing in the morning."

Her words struck hard blows to Hunter's chest. Common sense said she was only saying that as an excuse to make them hunt for the cane. Even so, under the circumstances he wouldn't blame her for wanting him out of her apartment. If she asked him to leave come morning, he'd be packing up and looking for a new place to hide from the world. Devlin Bane wouldn't be happy, but Hunter was more concerned about Tate. If he'd scared her enough to want him to leave, he would go.

The jerk in the restaurant left Tate standing there in the rain while he ostensibly went hunting for the cane. Couldn't he have let her come inside for a couple of minutes? It made Hunter want to punch something, or better yet, someone. Before he could climb down out of truck to do just that, the guy was back. He opened the door only far enough to shove the cane out to Tate, then yanked it shut again.

Retribution would have to wait.

"Here you go, Hunter."

As soon as his hand latched onto the cane, he focused all his attention on it. Closing his eyes, he traced the cool, hard carving of the handle. As he stroked the ivory with his fingertips, his pulse gradually slowed, at least enough that he no longer feared his heart would burst.

The familiar touch, combined with the soft rumble of the truck's engine as they tore through the damp night, helped bring back his awareness of their surroundings. They were almost at the turnoff to Tate's place. Ordinarily he would've been relieved to be back in familiar territory, but not this time. He was in no shape for long discussions, even if he could bring himself to tell Tate the truth about himself.

But somehow he doubted she was going to simply hand him his keys and disappear into her house. Maybe by morning he would've found some way to explain what had happened, but right now he could barely string two coherent thoughts together. As the truck slowed for the final turn, he braced himself for a bumpy ride that had nothing to do with the ruts in Tate's driveway.

Tate turned off the engine, then rested her head against the steering wheel. Boy, oh, boy, she really did not want to leave the quiet sanity of the truck cab. The seat was wide enough for her to stretch out. Maybe she should just lock the doors and sleep there, safe and sound.

Not that she was in any danger from Hunter Fitzsimon, at least not physically. She squeezed her eyes closed, trying to block out how he'd gone from friendly to frantic in a heartbeat with no explanation. One second he'd been anxious for dessert and the next, he was charging toward the exit.

Then there was the whole cane thing. He'd made it all the way to the truck without it, so he didn't need it to walk. Yet clearly he couldn't make it home without it.

There was a light knock on the driver's side window. Time to face the music.

She pulled the keys out of the ignition and grabbed her purse. Taking a deep breath, she opened the door and slid down out of the seat. Hunter made a move as if to catch her but then jerked his hand back.

For a moment neither of them spoke, caught up in that awful in-between of needing to say *something* and knowing there was nothing to be said. Nothing that would matter anyway.

"Are you all right?" His voice was softer now.

"I'm fine." She stepped far enough away from the truck to shut the door. With her back to him, she asked, "Are you?"

"I'll see you to the door," was all he said, which was no answer at all.

"I don't need—"

He cut her off midsentence. "Tate, I will walk with you to the door or I'll follow you to the door. Your choice."

She *so* didn't want to do this. "Fine. Suit yourself."

But when she tried to walk around him, he blocked her path. "We'll never get to the porch this way, Hunter. I don't know about you, but I'm tired." He moved closer, his face outlined in stark clarity by the security light above the garage. She wanted to offer him the comfort of her touch but wasn't sure she could bear being rejected. Instead she waited patiently for him to spit out the words he was all but choking on.

Finally, he looked up at the sky, as if he could find the answers up there, written in the clouds as they passed.

"Look, Tate, all I can say is I'm sorry if I scared you, and I'll understand if you want me out of here. Just give me tomorrow to pack up and I'll be gone."

Having delivered his speech, he stalked away, heading off into the darkness. His words cut through her exhaustion, leaving pain and denial in their wake.

She chased after him. "Hunter? What are you talking about? I may be tired, but I'd remember if I'd issued an eviction order!"

He didn't even slow down.

"If you're talking about what I said to that guy at the restaurant, it was only because he kept insisting I come back when they were open."

That didn't even slow Hunter down. She kicked off her sandals, ready to run after him if necessary. "Damn it, Hunter, I *don't* want you to go."

Hunter stopped at the edge of the trees, once again becoming part of the shadows, reminding her how well the darkness suited him. "All the more reason I should."

And then he was gone.

It took her a few more seconds to find the strength to turn back toward the house. She made it to the porch alone, despite his promise to walk her there. Before stepping into the kitchen, she studied the woods for a few seconds. Although she couldn't see him clearly, she knew Hunter hovered only a short distance inside the tree line, waiting and watching until she reached the safety of her home.

She lifted a hand to let him know she was okay. Sure enough, there he was, a dark blur blending into all of the other shadows. Had he waved back? She'd like to think so, but she doubted it.

But then again, he ran so hot and cold on her, maybe that had been a branch she'd seen moving in the wind.

Tate walked through the darkness to her bedroom upstairs. She was too tired and strung out to maintain her usual vigil in the window seat. Tomorrow would be soon enough for her to check on Hunter.

She got ready for bed, hoping for a good night's sleep. She was going to need all her strength if Hunter had indeed made up his mind to leave. If so, it was doubtful that she'd be able to convince him to change his mind, but she planned to try. She smiled as she pulled the covers up to her chin—she might even play dirty and sic the Auntie Ms on him. He might be willing to walk away from her, but she bet he'd have a hard time saying good-bye to those three ladies.

He stood in the trees watching the house long after Tate's lights went out. When he finally moved, everything hurt, and his leg screamed in pain. Doc Crosby had warned him that stress and tension always attack the weakest part. Hunter tightened his grip on the cane until it hurt, the distraction helping him find his way through a darkness that had nothing to do with nighttime.

Exhaustion made it difficult to breathe, much less move, but he needed to do something before he sought out his own bed. Paladins didn't let injuries get in the way of the job, not if they still had the strength to hold a sword. Hunter might be only a shadow of the man he once was, but duty still mattered. He followed the tree line around to the back of Tate's yard, where the trail led down toward the beach.

Poised at the edge of the woods, he looked back at the house one last time, wishing like hell he knew what to do about Tate. He'd scared her badly tonight, but she'd shoved her fear aside and gotten them both home safely.

Home. Shit, he had no business and no right to think of that apartment as home, any more than the nondescript room deep in the cave in Missouri had been. Both were little more than places to sleep when he wasn't needed for his strong sword arm, like the Paladin who'd lived there before him and the one who would move into it now that Hunter was gone.

He was okay with that. So often the names of individual soldiers, the ones who bled and died, were lost in the dim memory of history. It was only their accomplishments that were remembered. Paladins lived and died to protect the world. Their names didn't matter, only that they did the job they were born to do.

It was time to get to work. He'd check the cave and stand watch for a while. And not just because he wasn't ready to face being indoors yet. He looked back toward the house one last time, meaning to start the long hike down the bluff. But as his gaze swept across the lawn, his eyes caught on something in the grass.

A pattern. Someone had passed by Tate's house, and fairly recently. The grass was heavy with moisture, so whoever had walked through it had left a trail. He circled wide, tracking the footprints back to their start near the road. Two men had walked side by side, straight past the house and right to the trail where Hunter had been standing. What's more, there was a return trail only a few feet away.

Son of a bitch! Two men might have gone into the woods, but three had come out. Devlin Bane was going to have his head when he found out that Hunter had been in town on a date when their enemy had crossed the barrier. Most likely the man would send Trahern and company up to kick Hunter's ass off the cliff for a screwup of this magnitude, and Hunter wouldn't blame him a bit. He hit Devlin's number on speed dial and left a terse message.

It was probably too late to accomplish anything tonight, but he'd go down to the beach anyway. Maybe the bastards would come waltzing back before dawn. And when they did, they would die. Not because they were screwing both of their peoples for filthy lucre but because they'd brought their greed to Justice Point.

Innocent people lived here. Good people, asleep in their beds with no knowledge of the nightmare that existed on the other side of that barrier. And if he had to bleed out the last drop of his life's blood to preserve that innocence, then so be it. With sword drawn, he began the long march down to the beach.

Tate woke to the sound of birds singing and someone pounding on her front door. She wasn't sure which one annoyed her more.

She made a quick stop in the bathroom and stumbled downstairs as she pulled a sweatshirt on over her tank top. At the bottom of the steps she paused, waiting to see if the pounding started up again, hoping her visitor had left.

"I'm coming, I'm coming," she muttered.

Tate unlocked the door and yanked it open, ready to rip into someone. After all, the shop's hours were clearly posted. One look outside, though, and the words died on her lips.

"You're back." Hunter was going to be pissed.

D.J. nodded, not looking any happier about the situation. "Where's Hunter?"

She blinked at him, trying to decide if the tone in D.J.'s voice was worry or anger. "He's not here, if that's what you're asking. His apartment is over there."

D.J. shifted his weight from foot to foot and back again. "I know that. But if he was *there*, I wouldn't be *here*, would I? His truck's parked by the garage, his apartment is empty, and his bed doesn't look slept in."

His words burned away the cobwebs in her head, leaving only fear. "Let me get my shoes on. I'll help you look for him."

D.J. nodded, although her near panic had clearly startled him. "I'll wait here."

She ran to the back door, where she always kept a pair of old sneakers for gardening. They had holes in the toes and broken laces, but right now high fashion wasn't her concern.

True to his word, D.J. was standing right where she'd left him. If she wasn't so worried about Hunter, especially after how they'd parted company last night, she would've found D.J. amusing. Had she ever seen a grown man vibrate with so much penned-up energy?

When she stepped outside, she was relieved to see that Hunter's truck was indeed still there. She hated knowing that she'd halfway expected both it and him to be gone this morning. So if he was gone, he hadn't driven.

"Did you check the bed of his truck? He likes to be out at night. Maybe he dozed off there." But she couldn't imagine him sleeping through D.J.'s arrival.

If her question surprised Hunter's friend, it didn't show. "No, but I'll go take a look."

He jogged over to the driveway but shook his head after looking in, and even under, the truck. Well, she hadn't really expected it to be that easy. Darn it, she should've insisted that Hunter stay with her last night, even if they had to spend the night on the back porch.

Could he be over at the Auntie Ms mowing the lawn? She didn't want to worry the sisters, so she forced herself to walk toward their house. If Hunter was there, she should be able to see him from the street.

Sure enough, there he was, shirt off, the sun glinting off the red undertones in his hair, looking as if he didn't have a care in the world other than pushing that old mower through the grass.

She wanted to hit him. She'd gone to bed worried about him and woke up to the same rush of concern. He spotted her coming toward him but didn't stop. Instead, he flipped the handle over on the push mower and started back across the yard.

Did the jerk he really think ignoring her would

work? He should know better by now. She caught up with him before he'd made it halfway across. Another couple of steps and she planted herself firmly in his way. Without hesitation, he went around her, leaving her standing in a patch of long grass feeling stupid.

This time she put her hand over his on the handle of the mower.

"I'm busy here."

His voice was cool, disinterested even. She might have even bought it if she hadn't felt the tension in his hand before he jerked it out from under hers. Rather than give him hell for scaring her, she gave him the message she'd come to deliver.

"Your friend D.J. is looking for you."

"He's not my friend."

She rolled her eyes. "I don't care if he's secretly your mother, Hunter. He dragged me out of bed to look for you. Now go talk to him so I can get back to my own business."

Her mission complete, she walked away. She could hear Hunter coming up behind her. Rather than let him catch up, she cut across her yard and walked straight inside without looking back. Inside, she leaned against the counter and waited for her pulse to slow down.

Darn the man, anyway! She'd been so worried about him last night, but he seemed fine this morning. She'd have thought she'd overreacted, but D.J. had been concerned about him, too. Well, maybe now they could both relax—or maybe not. The memory of how he'd acted last night was too fresh for her to forget that easily. He might have pulled himself back together but for how long?

The clock upstairs chimed softly, warning her the morning was slipping away. She had very little time to get things ready before opening the shop. On her way up to her bedroom, she walked past a mirror and came to a screeching halt. Oh, God, she looked like something straight out of a horror film. Her hair was mashed flat on one side, and she still had faint blanket marks on her face. Coupled with the ratty shoes, oversized sweatshirt, and flannel boxers, she made quite a fashion statement.

It was a wonder Hunter hadn't run screaming in the other direction. Served the man right if she did scare him a bit, though. Feeling cheerier, she headed into the bathroom to get cleaned up. While she wouldn't mind giving Hunter a few nightmares, she couldn't afford to do the same to paying customers.

Tate was mad at him. Good. Although it was hardly his fault that she'd gone into panic mode just because D.J. had shown up unannounced and hadn't been able to find Hunter. He'd had to fight to keep a big grin off his face when she'd come charging up to him over at the Aunties' house. Seeing how she looked fresh out of bed had had a predictable effect on him, but luckily she'd been too intent on getting right up in his face to notice what had been going on further south.

He'd much rather go after her than deal with D.J., but duty called. No doubt Devlin had sent D.J. scurrying up here in response to Hunter's message last night. Next time he'd make it clear that he didn't need or want reinforcements unless he asked for them. Maybe eventually they'd even believe him.

Speaking of whom, where was the idiot anyway? He caught a movement out of the corner of his eye and spotted D.J. heading for the woods with a duffel bag in his hand. Hunter put two fingers in his mouth and let loose with a shrill whistle. When the other Paladin immediately whipped around, Hunter started toward him. Maybe they'd have more privacy in the woods.

"I take it Tate found you."

"She did." Hunter let a little of his temper show. "The question is why you dragged her out of bed to hunt for me?"

"You left Devlin a message saying there'd been some action last night. When you weren't in your apartment, I thought she might know where you were."

"She's my landlady, not my keeper."

"Glad to hear it. Think I'll stop in her shop for something hot before I head back." Then the bastard had the balls to leer back toward Tate's house.

Hunter crowded in close, getting right up in D.J.'s face. "Leave her alone."

D.J.'s eyebrows snapped down over his eyes. "Like you said, she's not yours. That makes it none of your business if I want to check out her . . . pastries."

That did it. Hunter's fist connected with D.J.'s stomach, sending the other man staggering backward. His retreat didn't last long. D.J. flung his duffel to the ground and came charging straight back. Hunter sidestepped, deflecting the brunt of D.J.'s attack. Even so, the other

Paladin had a good thirty pounds on Hunter, all of it muscle, and he used it to his advantage to get in a few good licks of his own. But what D.J. didn't have was the powerful need to protect Tate.

Hunter knocked D.J. to the ground and stood ready to beat some sense into the hapless fool when D.J. held his hands up in surrender.

"So I was wrong. She *is* yours."

Hunter wanted to deny it, but it was hard to under the circumstances. He tried anyway. "No, she's not. What she is, though, is innocent. I don't want her dragged into our world."

"Okay, I hear you." The Paladin drew a ragged breath as he sat up.

"Good. Now, how about we get back to business?" Hunter held out his hand to pull D.J. back up to his feet. "Sorry I lost my temper like that."

The other man dismissed the apology. "Don't sweat it. I have that effect on most people."

Hunter couldn't help it. He laughed, but winced at the pain in his jaw and flexed his hand. "It's been awhile since I punched somebody. But, damn, that felt good."

"For you maybe." D.J. picked up his duffel. "But I'm glad to be of service. Now show me what you found last night."

"It's not much, but somebody came through. I know that much for certain."

He led the way into the woods, feeling as if he'd just turned a major corner. It *had* felt good. In fact, damned good. So what if it took a bloody nose and a few bruises to feel alive again?

Chapter 7

Hunter's leg was killing him. He hadn't slept more than a couple of hours after he'd come back up from the beach last night, and the scuffle with D.J. hadn't helped. Pride kept him from asking D.J. to slow down, if that was even possible for the Seattle Paladin. From what Hunter could see, D.J. only had three speeds—fast, faster, and fastest.

It didn't help that the day was miserably warm. Considering all the years he'd lived in Missouri with its hotter-than-hell summers, he should've been accustomed to a little heat, but then he'd spent most of his time underground in the constant chill of the limestone caves. At least it would be cooler once they were down by the beach.

"D.J., hold up when you get down to that next bend in the trail. That's where we turn off for the cave."

When Hunter caught up with the other Paladin, he pulled the sword out of his cane and carefully set the wooden cover to the side of the trail where he could retrieve it on the way back. D.J. unzipped his duffel and pulled out a double-bladed ax and a sword.

"Nice blade you've got there, Hunter." He held up his own weapons. "Any suggestions?"

Hunter gave a low whistle. "The sword. There's not room inside the cave to swing an ax, and that's a damn shame. I'd like to see you in action with that beauty."

"Maybe one of these days you'll get a chance." D.J. returned the ax to his bag, handling the heavy weapon as if it were no heavier than a baseball bat. "Thanks to the volcanoes, we get to dance pretty often in this region."

Hunter understood the dark memories in D.J.'s voice all too well. "I saw St. Helens, Mt. Adams, and Rainier when I flew in. It was quite a sight, not to mention I see Mt. Baker every time I go into town. Having volcanoes hovering in the distance takes some getting used to."

D.J. nodded. "They're beautiful to look at, but personally, I hate every last one of them. I figure they stay covered in snow year round because they're such cold-hearted bitches."

Hunter couldn't fault him for thinking so. "We don't have volcanoes in Missouri, but we've got a major fault line where the river deposits have never fully solidified. We get the occasional big shaker, but we also get the kind of quake that comes in swarms, all low-level intensity, but enough to screw up the barrier for weeks."

D.J.'s smile was sympathetic. "Oh, well, keeps us employed."

"Yeah, nothing like job security."

Not that he had that anymore. If Devlin decided

Hunter was no longer needed, what then? But now wasn't the time for a pity party.

He pointed at the narrow ledge with his sword. "We have to sidestep our way across that to reach the cave."

D.J. stood back. "Lead the way."

The two men made their way across without mishap. Although judging by the way D.J. practically dove into the cave, he wasn't overly fond of the experience.

As soon as they stepped into the dim interior of the cave, Hunter cursed. Paladins had better-than-average night vision, but a little light wouldn't have hurt. "Sorry, I didn't think to grab a flashlight before we came down here."

"Not a problem. I've got one in my bag." Then D.J. sighed. "Which is on the other side of the ledge."

"Just a minute. Let me check something."

Hunter carefully made his way over to where the unknown camper had left his gear. Sure enough, there was a pair of flashlights tucked into the bag of supplies.

"Here."

He tossed one to D.J. and turned the other one on, focusing it on the cave floor. There wasn't enough loose dirt and sand to hold footprints very well, which was probably a good thing. There would've been no way to know how old any prints were anyway, but it also meant that he and D.J. wouldn't be leaving any signs of their own visit for their targets to notice.

D.J. did a slow three-sixty, studying his surroundings. "I'd guess it's not much of a cave by Missouri standards, is it?"

"It's big enough to have a stretch of barrier. That's all

that counts." Hunter pointed at the camping gear with his light. "And it's big enough for someone to be using as a back door into our world."

Hunter slowly approached the barrier. "Speaking of which, how come Devlin hasn't had you guys blow this place all to hell before now? Back home Jarvis just had a team of Paladins cave in a tunnel the Others were using to escape from."

D.J. knelt down to study the camping gear. "Yeah, we heard the bastards caught some poor SOB and carved him up like a Thanksgiving—"

Then he stopped midsentence, a look of horror on his face. "Oh, shit, Hunter, I'm sorry. I wasn't thinking. If you want to deck me, I won't fight back."

For once Hunter's first reaction wasn't anger. He actually laughed, although he wasn't sure if that surprised him or D.J. more.

"Thanks for the offer, but don't sweat it. It could've been worse." Not really. Being tortured to death was about as bad as it could get.

D.J.'s expression pretty much said the same thing, but at least he let it drop.

"But to answer your question, Hunter, we haven't blown it up for a couple of reasons. One is that it would be hard to make it look like natural causes brought down the hillside. But mainly because the bad guys don't know that we've found this place, which gives us our first real shot at catching them. If we close this spot down, then they'll move their operation someplace else we don't know about yet."

Hunter nodded. "Makes sense. Hopefully we can

nail the bastards sooner rather than later. I haven't been here long enough to see if there's a pattern to their behavior yet, but I keep watch every night." He backed away from the barrier. "If you've seen everything you want to see here, I'll show you where I've set up my blind."

D.J. handed Hunter the other flashlight. Once he had them stowed back where they belonged, Hunter led the way along the ledge back to the trail. He put his blade back into its cover while D.J. picked up his bag.

"See if you can figure out where my camp is."

D.J. studied the beach below, the trail above, and the woods where the bluff jutted out into the bay. "If I were going to pick a spot, I'd look for someplace up there so I could see them coming," he said, pointing to the trail above them.

"Good. That's what I wanted to hear. There are actually a couple of different approaches down to the beach, so our uninvited friends might not be coming from the trail by Tate's house."

He pointed across toward the far slope. "I set up about halfway down that rise over there because it's the only place where you can see both directions of the trail as well as the cave entrance."

"Not bad, Hunter. Devlin will be impressed. I know he'll appreciate the additional intelligence on the setup."

"Well, if you've seen enough, let's get out of here. I'm pretty sure they only come and go at night, but I'd rather not be seen hanging around down here just in case they do have someone keeping an eye on the place."

They walked along in silence until they reached the top of the bluff.

"Want to grab some lunch?"

D.J. looked surprised by the offer. "Sure. I assume we're not going to Tate's?"

"No, I thought we could drive into Bellingham. Tate only offers tea and a few pastries."

That much was true, but it was also true that he'd prefer to keep anything to do with his real purpose for being in Justice Point separate from Tate and the other residents. On a personal level, the last thing he wanted was D.J. sniffing around Tate.

"Okay, sounds like a plan. Although I suspect that Tate might offer more than tea. You just don't want her offering it to me."

"Remember that free punch you promised me? Keep jerking my chain, and I might just take you up on it."

D.J. clapped him on the shoulder. "Okay, okay. Tate Justice is *definitely* off limits."

Then he added, "But if that changes, let me know."

Tate took advantage of a quiet spell to top off the tins of tea. She drew in a deep breath, letting the familiar scents soothe her. Some of the teas were spicy, some pungent, and some even smelled of dried grass. To her, they all smelled like home. Her uncle had been the one constant in her world, and this old house a refuge against the chaos of her mother's lifestyle.

Maybe a cup of her favorite Darjeeling would perk her

up. She filled a pot with hot water and set it to steep while she made herself a sandwich. She carried it all over to the table where Hunter usually sat, not that she picked it for that reason. It was the one spot where she had a clear view of the road that ran by the front of her house as well as her driveway.

Hunter had left with D.J. over two hours ago. The two men had looked awfully chummy considering how adamant Hunter was that they weren't friends. Of course, he was equally insistent that she needed to steer clear of him, yet he'd invited her to dinner. The man needed to learn how to make up his mind.

Though that didn't keep her from hurting for him. Last night had been nothing short of disaster. It didn't take a genius to recognize that whatever had happened to him was still causing some pretty severe aftershocks. He'd been fine right up until dessert, but somehow she doubted that strawberry shortcake had caused his near meltdown.

It was a puzzle all right, one that he wouldn't let her close enough to solve. Ignoring the stab of pain the thought caused her, she pulled out her laptop. Maybe getting lost in her story would help. She'd left the gunslinger at the heroine's mercy as he fought off the infection from his wound. Maybe it was time to have the sheriff come knocking at the door, a quick reminder to the heroine who the real good guy was.

The sheriff was handsome, kind, and . . . boring, Tate realized. He might think to bring the heroine flowers or even some pretty ribbon for her hair, but none of that seemed to matter. The gunslinger, on the other hand, was surly and carried enough baggage with him to stock a luggage store. Yet he was the one who made the heroine's pulse race and curled her toes when he'd finally given in and kissed her in a fit of anger.

Tate suspected the direction her novel was heading meant that both she and the heroine were in deep, deep trouble. Even so, she was on a roll. The heroine had just reluctantly agreed to go for a buggy ride and picnic with the sheriff. She hated leaving the gunslinger alone while he was so sick, but she couldn't risk the two men seeing each other. The lawman would feel obligated to save her from her outlaw, and that was the last thing she wanted.

Before Tate could describe their outing, a car pulled up in front of the house. She quickly saved her file and started to clear the table, ready to wait on a potential customer. Then she recognized the car and groaned. What was *she* doing here? Tate considered turning the Closed sign around and pretending to be gone, but that never worked.

If her mother was desperate enough to show up on Tate's doorstep, it meant she had nowhere else to go. Delaying the inevitable would only make things worse.

Tate opened the door. "Mother."

The other woman sailed into the shop in a cloud of cloying perfume. "Now, Tate, you know I prefer to be called Sandra."

That was true, and it was petty of Tate to refuse to do it. She forced a smile, pretending that she was glad to see her only parent. "I know, but that doesn't change the fact that you are my mother or that you're forty-six."

Sandra looked insulted. "I'm not a day over forty, and you know it."

Some things never changed, especially Sandra's problems with addition. Tate was twenty-six, and according to her birth certificate, Sandra had been twenty when she'd given birth. Somehow, those two figures added up to a smaller number every year. At this rate, Tate would eventually be older than Sandra, but logic had never been a strong suit for her mother either.

"Would you like a cup of tea, Mother?"

Sandra perched on the edge of the chair Tate had just vacated. "I'd rather have coffee."

"This is a tea shop. I don't serve coffee."

She didn't have to look in Sandra's direction to see the combination of disappointment and petulance on her face. Those were the only two expressions her mother ever wore when they were alone together, just as Tate always gritted her teeth and prayed for patience.

"Fine. I'll have a cup of that same stuff you gave me last time."

It was just another indication that they both lived in her mother's self-centered universe. Tate offered over fifty varieties of tea, yet she was supposed to remember which flavor her mother had tried months ago. But of course, she did. Sandra's visits were always memorable, if not pleasant. She reached for the Lady Grey and a pot.

She set a plate of cookies down with the tea in front of her mother and then picked up her laptop. Sandra didn't know about Tate's dream of being published, and Tate wanted to keep it that way.

"You know I don't eat sweets, Tate. That's how I've managed to keep my figure all these years. I'm still a perfect size six."

And Tate wasn't. Her mother also towered over her by almost five inches, giving Sandra the willowy model look she was so proud of. Except for her blond hair and blue eyes, Tate had taken after her father's side of the family.

"Would you like a sandwich instead?"

"If it's not too much trouble. One piece of bread, lean turkey, no mayo. If you don't have turkey, then lean ham will do."

Tate took her time assembling the sandwich, relieved to get a brief respite from Sandra's company. Although she loved her mother, their relationship was complicated. Somewhere along the way their roles had reversed, making Tate the responsible one.

Most of the time that was all right with her, but once in a while she wished she could be the flighty one most men adored. Accepting her uncle's gift of this house and the chance to write was the closest Tate had ever ventured to doing something wild. Well, up until she'd met Hunter Fitzsimon.

As she cut up a carrot and some celery to add to her mother's plate, the bell over the shop door rang again. She needed to hurry out and greet her customers before her mother could say anything to them.

Too late. Worse yet, she recognized the rough voice immediately. Caught up in her mother's unexpected arrival, she'd missed seeing that Hunter had returned. This was disaster in the making.

Her mother had never met a man she didn't like, even if her preference was for older, richer ones. Her concentrated efforts to hold off the changes time wrought had paid off for her. Despite Tate's teasing Sandra a bit about her real age, the woman did look more like Tate's older sister than her mother.

Bracing herself to see yet another man enamored of her mother, Tate walked back into the shop. To her surprise, Hunter was sitting by himself, staring out the window with his back toward Tate's mother. Sandra looked confused and not a little insulted by his obvious lack of interest.

"Here's your sandwich, Sandra."

Her mother's eyes flared at Tate's use of her given name, but she didn't say anything. Instead she gave the back of Hunter's head a pointed look. Rather than answer the unspoken question, Tate went behind the counter to fix Hunter a pot of tea.

"Here you go, Mr. Fitzsimon." She handed him the morning paper with his order.

He looked up at her with a knowing gleam in his eye. "Thank you, Ms. Justice. I'd like a couple of those muffins when you have time."

"Coming right up."

She brought him the muffins and threw in a scone for good measure, telling herself it wasn't a reward for him not being instantly enamored by her beautiful mother.

Tate was at a loss as to what to do next. She really wasn't in the mood to hear what had brought Sandra to Justice Point. As much as she still wanted to corner Hunter and find out what had really happened last night, she wouldn't air his personal business in front of anyone, least of all her mother.

She kept herself busy behind the counter dusting the

shelf that she'd cleaned only the day before and rearranging the display of teacups and matching saucers in the glass counter. What next? Alphabetizing the teas? Finally, she settled in with her laptop and tried to concentrate on her story.

Melinda, the heroine, was antsy, wanting to get back home to her patient. The handsome but boring sheriff wasn't stupid; he knew something was up. He was convinced he'd make Melinda a damned good husband, but it was becoming obvious that she didn't think so. To prove his point, he kisses her.

Tate stopped to think. How would that kiss feel? Before Melinda had met Chance, she would've jumped at the chance to have the sheriff court her. Was she foolish enough to give up the security the lawman would offer her for the dark appeal of Chance? Tate realized she was staring across the room at Hunter and nodding.

Oh, yeah, that's exactly what Melinda would do.

As if sensing her interest, Hunter slowly turned in her direction. Hating that he'd caught her staring, she blushed, trying her best to ignore the tingle of awareness, which had nothing to do with the embarrassment that flooded through her. It was as if his gaze had weight, caressing her skin with a palpable heat.

The scrape of a chair across the wooden floor reminded them both that there was a third person in the room. Hunter turned his attention back to his crossword puzzle as Tate immediately closed her file and prepared to deal with her mother.

"Tate, I need the key to the apartment over the garage."

Oh, God, this wasn't going to be pretty on so many levels. Her mother wanting to move into the apartment was the subject of several of Tate's nightmares. Her mother's fortunes must have had a serious downturn for her to want to stay in Justice Point. She was not going to be happy to find out that Tate had rented the place out.

"I'm sorry, but the apartment isn't an option. You can have your usual room upstairs for a few days." Hopefully that's as long as Sandra was planning to stay.

Obviously her mother had other plans. "I'd prefer some privacy, so I want the apartment. It shouldn't take you much time to make it livable for me. You owe me that much, considering you didn't see fit to share the proceeds of your uncle's estate with me. I still think that lawyer misunderstood Jacob's intentions. After all, I'm his brother's widow."

She ignored the fact that Tate was Jacob's only niece, and Sandra had never been anything but hateful to him anyway. Tate didn't bother to state the obvious, since Sandra never saw past her own selfish needs.

"The apartment is already livable, Sandra, and someone is living in it. I rented it out."

"Tell them to move out." Sandra pursed her mouth so hard that there was a white line around her lips.

Hunter carried his dishes over to the counter. "She can't. I have an ironclad lease for the next six months, with an option for six more if I want them."

The look on Sandra's face would've been funny if it hadn't portended a major hissy fit.

"And you would be?" she said with a great deal of snark in her voice.

"I would be your daughter's tenant," Hunter said, his voice rough and low.

He smiled at Tate, deliberately ignoring her mother. "I'll be up at the Auntie Ms finishing the lawn if you need me for anything."

And didn't that just fry her brain with possibilities?

Both women stared after him until he'd sauntered out the door, leaving Tate alone to face her mother's anger. Rather than wait for the explosion, Tate gathered up the dirty dishes and carried them into the kitchen. Sandra wasn't far behind.

"Why did you rent that man my apartment?"

So they were back to that. "Mother, I'm sorry that you drove all the way up here only to be disappointed. That is hardly my fault, much less Mr. Fitzsimon's. I advertised for a renter. He answered the ad. It's that simple."

Most people would've called ahead, but Sandra wasn't other people. The world revolved around her. Tate had learned that early on, but that didn't make it any easier to deal with.

"Well, since you caused the problem, young lady, you can fix it. Make him leave."

That did it. "Mom, for the last time, I'm not going to ask him to move. He rented *my* apartment in good faith. He could sue me if I tried to break the lease now."

Sandra launched her next salvo with a strong undercurrent of triumph. "But where am I going to put all my furniture when it arrives?"

Suddenly the sandwich Tate had eaten felt like a brick in her stomach. This wouldn't be the first time that

Sandra had imposed on Tate's hospitality without asking, but she'd never dragged along all her worldly goods.

"Well, either you'll have to pay to store your furniture somewhere or else find an apartment in town. I'm sure you can find something nicer than living over my garage." She added soap to the dishwasher and punched the button.

"I can't afford the prices in town."

"You can store your stuff in the garage for a *short* time," Tate suggested, emphasizing the word *short*, "and stay with me until you find a job and get a few paychecks. Once you've got enough saved up to move out, I'll help you find a place."

There. She'd set down the limits—not that she expected Sandra to abide by them. She never had before.

"That garage is filthy!"

"There are cleaning supplies in the utility room. Use what you need." Tate busied herself washing the counter, not wanting to watch her mother play the martyr. Unfortunately she could still hear her. Sandra sighed and sniffed a little, as if fighting the urge to cry.

"You sound like your Uncle Jacob."

Tate rolled her eyes toward the ceiling, praying for deliverance or at least patience. "Thank you for saying so. He was a good man."

"It wasn't a compliment, my dear. He was a stubborn, unkind man. No wonder you're not married. Men like their women sweet and to take a little more care with their appearance."

If that was the case, how could Sandra explain her success with men? While she did maintain her appearance, Sandra was anything but sweet, especially when she was thwarted. She'd only get worse if Tate pushed back.

"I'm sure you're right, Mother."

Sandra changed tactics. "What do you know about this Fitzsimon? Did you check his references before letting him move in?"

"Mother, drop it. He's here to stay." Tate wiped her hands on a towel. "Now, if you want to spend the night, there are sheets in the linen closet. You've got plenty of time to get your bed made up, bring in your luggage, and get settled in before dinner. You can even squeeze in one of your naps if you hurry."

Sandra vibrated with anger. "Do you treat all your guests this way? If so, I'm surprised that you've stayed in business this long."

Tate reached for a mixing bowl. Baking always soothed her after one of these conversations.

"No, I don't ask actual customers to make their own beds. I assumed you weren't planning on paying me, but let me know if I'm wrong about that."

"I don't know how I raised such an ungrateful daughter." This time the crack in Sandra's voice sounded real.

Tate set the flour back down. "Okay, Mother, what's really going on? We both know you hate this place, so something must have happened to drive you to such desperate straits."

"Not that you care, but Edwin and I broke up."

Edwin? The last time she'd heard Sandra mention a man it was Louis something.

"I'm sorry. Had you been seeing him long?"

"Long enough that we were living together. But we had a fight, and I had to leave. He said some perfectly horrid things to me."

Sandra allowed a single tear to trickle down her cheek before taking a deep breath and putting on a brave expression. Probably to avoid ruining her mascara.

"I'm sorry to hear that." Tate pulled out her recipe box and looked for the card for pumpkin muffins. "I'd help you get settled, but I've got to get things ready for tomorrow."

"Fine. Let me know when you have dinner ready."

Tate listened to Sandra's footsteps retreat. She did her best to ignore the sound of her mother's multiple trips out to her car and up the steps to the room she always used. After dealing with Hunter last night and her mother today, it was no wonder Tate's head was about to explode.

It might take several batches of baked goods to restore her equilibrium. With Hunter's sweet tooth, the extras wouldn't go to waste. Besides, she owed him for making it clear to Sandra that he wasn't going to give up his new home.

Suddenly her head didn't hurt so much.

Hunter reached for his beer and took a long drink. God, it felt good to relax. Between spending most of the night perched on a pile of rocks waiting for the bad guys to show, hiking his ass back down to the beach with D.J., and mowing the Auntie Ms yard, he was ready to stretch out and not move for a week. Or maybe ever again.

He cranked up the hot water another notch, hoping the near-scalding water would help ease the stiffness in his leg. The jets of water surrounded his body with a gentle massage that felt like heaven. He sank down lower, until only his head was above the waterline.

He'd allow himself a solid half hour in the tub before seeking out his bed. Paladins knew how to grab sleep whenever they could, so catching a few z's in the middle of the afternoon wouldn't be a problem. He'd set his alarm, though, to make sure he had time to grab a bite before heading back down to the beach before nightfall.

Maybe Tate's clearly unexpected company would keep her distracted long enough for him to get past her eagle eyes for once. The woman took far too much interest in his business, although that was his fault, too.

Odd that she hadn't asked him any questions about last night. Either she was too freaked out and wanted to forget it even happened, or she was being sensitive and not wanting to upset him by bringing the subject up. He wasn't sure which irritated him more.

Speaking of Tate's guest, that woman was a piece of work. He might not have immediately realized the woman was Tate's mother when he'd entered the shop, but he'd known she was trouble at first glance. He'd never had much use for pit vipers. And it didn't take a genius to figure out what Mabel had been talking about the other day when she'd slipped up and mentioned her.

He smiled. Mrs. Justice hadn't much liked it when he'd refused to pay homage to her beauty when he'd walked into the tea shop. She'd liked it even less when she'd found out that he was occupying the apartment she'd staked out for her own. If Tate had asked him, he would've considered moving out, because family came first. But he'd heard the panic in her voice when her mother had announced that she was moving in.

He didn't know why he'd decided to lie about having a lease, but he didn't feel the least bit bad about it. Not with that harpy sharpening her claws on her daughter.

Time was up. He needed to get to bed. Bracing his hands on the side of the tub, he stood up and gingerly put weight on his right leg. The pain was far less than he expected. As long as he was careful, he should be able to get to sleep without taking a pain pill.

After he toweled off, a jaw-cracking yawn had him hurrying to get horizontal. He slung the towel over his shoulder and strolled out into the living room buck naked. He'd thrown all of his clothes in the hamper and hadn't brought any clean ones into the bathroom, planning to sleep in the nude and get dressed later.

Unfortunately, there was one small thing he hadn't planned on: Tate standing at the door looking in his window.

Chapter 8

Son of a bitch! Short of hitting the floor facedown and risk bruising something precious, there wasn't much he could do to rectify the situation. Damn the woman! How many times had he told her to stay away?

He had to give her credit, though, for toughing it out. He would've expected her to go stumbling ass over end down the steps in full retreat. Instead Tate stood her ground, her eyes pinned on his ceiling as if it had suddenly become the Sistine Chapel. Judging by the bright pink flush on her face, she'd already seen about all there was to see. His perverse sense of humor had him considering doing a three-sixty in case she'd missed anything important.

Instead, he snatched the towel off his shoulder and wrapped it around his waist before jerking the door open.

"You can look now." Although the towel didn't cover much.

She peeked at him with one eye, as if to make sure. He half expected her to rip into him, but instead she used the tip of her tongue to moisten her lips. It was probably due to nerves rather than lust, but his cock didn't care.

When she still didn't speak, he tried again, giving the basket in her hand a pointed look. "Tate? Why are you here?"

She blinked twice, as if trying to clear her head. "I wanted to apologize for my mother's behavior, so I brought you these."

He accepted the basket and set it down on the coffee table so he could check the contents. He couldn't unwrap it one-handed, and he was holding the towel together to prevent any mishaps. The rich scent of cinnamon and cloves wafted up.

"These smell great, but apologies weren't necessary."

Her eyes twinkled as she held out her hand. "Okay, I'll take them back home then."

"Oh, no, you don't! I didn't mean to sound ungrateful." He picked the basket back up and carried it across to the kitchen counter. As he turned back toward Tate, the towel came undone and dropped almost to the floor before he caught it. He was about to apologize for flashing her, even if it was an accident, when he realized that this time, Tate had made no pretense of looking away.

"See something you want?"

His voice, always rough these days, came out little better than a growl. With even the slightest encouragement, he was going to be all over her.

She actually nodded.

He started toward her, ready to throw in the towel, so to speak, on his resolve to keep her at arm's length. Her eyes stared into his briefly, then started a long, slow trip downward, taking their time. He let her look her fill, liking it when her breath shuddered when she got as far as his cock, fully erect and jutting straight out at her. After lingering there briefly, they continued downward. That's when everything went to hell.

"Oh, God, Hunter! Your leg!"

His ego wasn't the only thing deflated by the dismay in her voice and what he suspected was pity in her gaze. Fury, dark and hot, burned through him, aimed directly at himself. For a few minutes he'd actually forgotten that he was no longer the guy who liked to flirt and enjoyed the company of a pretty woman.

No, he was the guy who'd died and should've had the good sense to stay that way.

He jerked the towel up to hide the jagged scar that cut across his thigh at an angle from his groin almost to his knee. Eventually it would fade to a faint silver streak under his skin, courtesy of his Paladin DNA, but right now it was still vivid and raw.

When she started toward him, he backed away, shaking his head. "Go home, Tate. Now."

"But why? I'm sorry if I offended you, Hunter. I knew you had a problem with your leg, but I didn't realize it would be that bad," she faltered, obviously trying to dig herself out of the hole she found herself in. "Please, give me another chance."

"To what, Tate? To pity me? I don't need that, not from you, not from anyone." He threw the towel aside in disgust. He hated the way his leg looked, but damned if he was going to run and hide either.

Once again Tate surprised him. Women—and most men—had the good sense to back away from a man like Hunter when he was riled up. But she came straight for him, looking determined and spoiling for a fight.

"I don't remember saying anything about pity. You're sensitive about how your leg looks. Fine, I get that, but don't go putting words in my mouth."

By now, she stood close enough for him to feel the warmth of her body and breathe in the faint scent of cloves and cinnamon on her skin.

"Next time, just warn a person, you big jerk." She inched closer. "But when you asked if I saw something I wanted, I said yes. *That* hasn't changed."

Her hand settled on his chest. With a slow smile, she trailed her fingers across his skin, tracing down until she skirted his burgeoning erection and brushed lightly across his scar.

"I'm sorry this happened, and I'm sorry you hurt. But if you're thinking a little thing like a scar or a limp makes me think less of you, you don't know me at all."

She leaned in close to plant a soft kiss on his chest.

That's all he needed.

He took her hand and led her straight to his bedroom.

Tate's lungs had forgotten how to work. From the second she'd knocked on Hunter's door only to see him walk out of the bathroom wearing nothing but a frown, she'd been having trouble drawing in enough oxygen.

And now she was being towed along in Hunter's wake, headed straight for his bed. She wasn't sure how they'd got to this point, but she planned to make the most of it.

God, that man had an ass to die for, and the rest of him was built like a god. She hadn't been lying about his scar, either. Whatever accident he'd been in had been horrific, but it didn't detract in the least from Hunter's powerful masculinity.

Stopping just short of the bed, Hunter turned to face her, his eyes stormy and intense. "Are you sure about this?"

She liked his slight hint of insecurity. Actions always spoke more eloquently than words. She inched closer, giggling a bit when his erection kept her at an impressive distance. Feeling a boldness she'd never felt before, she wrapped her fingers around the velvet and steel of his cock and tucked it up between them so she could settle her body against his strength.

"I'm sure, Hunter. Are you?"

He frowned as he brushed the back of his fingers along the side of her face and down the curve of her neck. "I've been wanting this from day one, Tate."

His lips followed the path of his fingers, his warm, moist breath tickling her skin and sending shivers up her spine. She grabbed his shoulders for support, loving the flex and play of his powerful muscles.

"You have me at a disadvantage," he murmured in her ear as he tugged her T-shirt up to slide his hand along the small of her back.

"Why don't you do something to level the playing field?"

"You really want me to put on some clothes?" He nibbled on her earlobe.

She loved his teasing. "They'd only get in the way of what I have in mind."

His eyes darkened. "Fine, so that leaves you taking yours off."

"You don't want to help?" She reached for the hem of her shirt when he shook his head.

"Nope, since I took my own off, it would only be fair if you did the same."

He backed away and crossed his arms over his chest. "Besides, this way I get to watch."

His smile was pure temptation, and she found this playful side of Hunter irresistible. For the moment the shadows were missing from his eyes, replaced with a burning heat. She peeled off her shirt and tossed it aside. After easing her bra straps down off her shoulders, she flicked the front fastener open, but hesitated briefly before letting it slide away completely.

He groaned, his approval obvious. Feeling more confident, she turned away as she hooked her fingers in the waistband of her shorts and panties. She took what seemed like an eternity to slide them down her legs, bending over to push them as far as her ankles before stepping out of them.

"Tate, honey, you're killing me."

Hunter's voice was a low whisper, rasping over her nerves like a caress. She hadn't heard him move, but his hands settled on her hips, pulling her backside flush up against his erection. God, all that warm male strength made her purr, especially when his hands moved up to cup her breasts.

She straightened, soaking up the heat from all that luscious skin-on-skin contact. Hunter murmured his approval, nuzzling her neck as he kneaded her breasts and tugged gently on her nipples.

She never wanted him to stop—but she wanted so much more.

He loosened his hold on her. "Tate, baby, we need to move this act to the bed or I'm going to take you standing right here."

Oh, yeah, she liked that idea. Instead of heading for the bed, she walked straight past him to plant her hands on the dresser, cocked her hips out, then widened her stance in invitation. Then she looked back over her shoulder and gave him a come-and-get-it smile.

Obviously a man of action, Hunter was right there with her, staring into her eyes in the mirror. The predatory hunger in his eyes would've been unnerving if his touch hadn't been so gentle. His hand settled heavily on the center of her back and then slowly glided down over the curve of her bottom to gently probe between her legs.

Her body softened, dampening, preparing for him. She closed her eyes as he slowly parted her, testing her readiness with one finger, then two. As they continued a gentle rhythm of thrusts, he arched over her, letting her feel his weight as he trailed kisses down her spine and then her bottom.

His mouth, hot and demanding, sought out the center of her desire, his tongue lashing out with quick licks that had her biting her lip to keep from screaming with the sweet beauty of it.

"Hunter!"

His name became a prayer as she begged for more, for him to end the torment, to release the storm that was building deep inside of her. Then he stopped and rose up.

He was leaning over her again. She arched back and up, helping him to find her center, bracing herself as he thrust deep into her core. Her breath left her in a rush and then came in short pants as he worked his cock in and out, driving them both closer and closer to the edge. He gripped her hips, and the slap of his belly against her bottom almost drowned out the pounding of her heart.

Her head was resting on her arms, but then she raised up enough to watch her lover in the mirror. Hunter's expression was fierce, his eyes half-closed as his thrusts became relentless. She'd never experienced anything so wonderful or intense.

As the first ripple of her orgasm started deep inside, milking the silken hard length of him, he increased the pace, driving both of them harder and harder, until there was nothing left of her world except the sound and the feel and the scent of Hunter Fitzsimon.

He shouted. She screamed. Then the universe dissolved as Hunter shuddered deep within the heart of her. Afterward, everything shifted and settled into a whole new reality.

He was pretty sure he almost just died again. That's how good it was with Tate. But if he didn't get horizontal soon, there was a good chance he would spend the rest of the afternoon curled up on the floor. As long as Tate was there beside him, that would be fine, but the bed would be a lot more comfortable.

He carefully moved away from the warm sanctuary of her body and offered her a helping hand to straighten up. When she wobbled a bit, he swept her up in his arms and carried her to the bed, ignoring the screaming pain in his leg, determined to make it that far without dropping her.

Success! He settled her in the center. "I'll be right back."

After a quick trip to the bathroom to get a handful of condoms, he joined her under the covers.

He turned on his side and propped himself up to look down at her. "I've been remiss, I think."

She frowned a bit as she touched her fingers to his cheek. "I don't remember complaining about anything."

"But I never kissed you."

She pretended to pout. "Well, that does make you a bit of a cad. However, it's never too late to make up for past mistakes."

He closed the distance between them, hoping his kiss would tell her the things he couldn't say. Like how alive she made him feel and that her touch healed him in some amazing way.

This time the passion built more slowly, but it burned even hotter. And for the first time since he'd died, he knew peace.

• • •

"Stop!"

Tate froze, unsure what was wrong. She'd been getting dressed; she needed to get back to the house before Sandra returned. Shortly before Tate had brought the basket over to Hunter's apartment, her mother had taken off, saying she'd needed to check on a few things in town.

The last thing Tate wanted right now was for Sandra to figure out that she had spent the afternoon in Hunter's bed. *With* Hunter. The wonder of the experience was too new, too amazing to let her mother spoil it. Sandra was already touchy about Hunter living in the apartment. If she found out that he actually preferred Tate to her, there would be hell to pay.

Back to the matter at hand. "What's wrong?"

"I left marks on your skin." He pointed at a faint set of fingerprints along her hip bone.

"I hadn't noticed."

Besides, considering how long it had been since she'd last let a man get that close to her, she fully expected to feel a few twinges in odd places. But sex with Hunter had been unlike any she'd ever experienced before.

"I'm sorry if I was too rough." He circled her, checking her over for more damage.

She stopped him. "You weren't. Besides, I'm pretty sure I left my mark on you, too."

But when he turned around to check himself in the mirror there wasn't a single scratch or bruise to be seen. How odd. She'd distinctly remembered urging him on with her nails and leaving a love bite on the side of his neck.

When he saw her puzzled look, he kissed her on the

forehead. "Don't think so hard. Maybe I'm just a fast healer."

"Right." Although something in his tone made her think he wasn't really teasing. He pulled a clean shirt out of the drawer and put it on.

She really hated to see all those sleek muscles disappear. As she finished getting dressed, she said, "I'd invite you over for dinner tonight, but Sandra's still a bit unsettled. We probably won't be the best company."

"That's okay. I've got to be someplace anyway. I'll be out late."

Right up until that remark, he'd been approachable, but it felt as if he'd just slammed a door shut between them. Maybe she was being too sensitive and a little unsure about this sudden change in their relationship. Yes, that had to be it. Well, maybe. Regardless, it was definitely time to put some distance between them.

"I'll be going then." She hurried toward the door. "Enjoy your treats."

"I do believe I already have." Then he gave her a wicked grin. "Oh, you meant the muffins."

She hadn't gotten far when he caught her arm, swinging her back around to face him.

"What?"

"Is something wrong?" He cupped the side of her face with his callused hand, rubbing the pad of his thumb across her cheek.

She studied his face, trying to read the thoughts behind his stormy eyes. "No, not really. I didn't know something like this would happen, and I'm not sure how to act or what to expect."

He didn't smile, but his expression gentled. "I have no expectations, Tate. We'll take things as they come."

His lips were soft against hers, his kiss reassuring. Then he rested his forehead against hers for a few seconds. "I wish . . ." He started to say more but stopped.

Somehow she knew what he meant. He wished that this could've been more than an afternoon of shared passion. It was his way of putting some distance between them, putting things in perspective. He was offering her no promises, not even the possibility of a repeat performance.

"I know, Hunter. Me, too."

This time he let her go, but she felt his gaze follow her all the way to her kitchen door. Maybe she shouldn't be upset, but all she felt was sad.

Her mother was waiting for her. Of course. It was too much to ask for a few minutes to herself before having to deal with Sandra's demands.

Her mother launched her attack before Tate could even think to close the door. "So that's why you wouldn't throw him out of my apartment."

Tate jerked as if she'd been slapped, but then held her ground. "Not now, Mother. I need to start dinner."

Sandra stepped between Tate and the counter, blocking her way. "I notice you're not denying that you spent the afternoon letting that man work off his rent. How much of a discount did you give him?"

Tate stared at her mother in disbelief. They'd had their problems in the past, but Sandra had never before launched such a vicious attack.

"I cannot believe you said something that crass! My relationship with Hunter is none of your business."

Sandra shrugged. "I'm your mother, as you so often point out. Somehow you've managed to hold on to your ridiculous naiveté for far too long, but it's time you faced the truth, Tate. A man like that would only settle for you because there's no one else in this hellhole of a town under fifty."

Okay, Tate had claws of her own and knew how to use them. "Well, that's not quite true. *You're* here, aren't you? But Hunter didn't choose you, did he, Mother? Is that what this is all about? That, heaven forbid, a man actually prefers me to you!"

Tate's only warning that they were no longer alone was when her mother's eyes glanced at something, or someone, behind Tate. The older woman immediately backed away. Could this get any worse? Tate glared at Sandra briefly before turning to face her furious tenant.

"Hunter, I'm sorry you had to hear that."

He stared over her head toward Sandra, his face stone hard. "Don't be, Tate. I knew what your mother was the moment I saw her. It's not your fault she's a pit viper."

Tate could feel Sandra's outrage pouring from her in waves.

"Well, Tate, are you going to let him stand there and insult me?"

"Considering what you just accused us of, I figure he can insult you all he wants."

This was getting them nowhere. Tate forced herself to concentrate on Hunter, unable to face Sandra at the moment. "Was there something you needed?"

Hunter held out her basket, his knuckles white with tension. "I thought you might need this. Would you like me to throw her out for you? It wouldn't take long, and it would give me great satisfaction."

Sandra gasped. "You wouldn't dare!"

His smile turned sinister. "There's a lot I'd dare if you push me far enough. Rip into Tate like that again, and you'll find out firsthand."

"Stop it, both of you! I do not need this from either of you."

"Tate, he's the one—"

"Mother! Leave this room right now. I will deal with you in a few minutes." She wasn't sure if Sandra would go. But when it was clear that Hunter wasn't going to leave unless she did first, Sandra flounced out, playing the martyr with consummate skill.

Tate ached with a familiar pain, but one thing at a time. She tugged the basket out of Hunter's hand. "Thank you for returning this. I know you have plans for the evening, and I don't want you to be late on my account." She paused. "I'll be fine." Eventually. Maybe in a hundred years or so.

He knew it, too. "I'd take you with me, but I can't."

"I didn't expect you to." She gave him a gentle shove toward the door.

But instead of leaving, Hunter grabbed the notepad she kept by the phone. After scribbling something on the top page, he ripped it off and shoved it into her hand. "Here's my cell number. Call if you need me."

"That's nice of you, Hunter, but I've been dealing with my mother for a long time. I don't know what made her act that way. She's never been this bad before." Well, not often.

"No one's ever accused me of being particularly nice, Tate. I won't be at all happy if I find out you should've called me and didn't." He crowded close, glaring down at her. "Got that?"

His anger was intense, but it only made her feel comforted. Not even Uncle Jacob had been strong enough to face down Sandra. The only time he'd been able to thwart her was when he'd left his entire estate to Tate.

"Yeah, I've got it." She raised up high enough to kiss that angry slash of a mouth. "Thank you."

His arms yanked her in close as he deepened the kiss. For the moment, she lost herself, letting the gift of his taste and touch hold her problems at bay, even for only a few seconds.

Both of them were breathing hard when Hunter finally broke off the kiss. "I've really got to go, or I won't be able to."

She loved the note of regret in his rough voice. "I know."

"You'll call." It wasn't a question.

"Yes, I'll call, but only if I really need to. Now go, before you're late."

"I'll be gone most of the night, so don't wait up for me." He softened his words with a smile.

She blushed. She'd so hoped he hadn't noticed that she'd been waiting up to make sure he made it back from his nightly ramblings.

"All right."

But they both knew that wouldn't keep her from

checking for signs he'd returned if she happened to be up during the night.

One last quick kiss and he was gone.

"Mr. Black, something has come up unexpectedly. I'll be needing your services this evening."

"Yes, sir." Joe kept his voice calm, counting the seconds until he could hang up and start cursing. He hated having to cancel his plans. A buddy had won a pair of tickets to a ball game and had offered the extra to Joe. Good seats, too.

"You will pick me and our guest up at six o'clock. Make sure you bring the gift I bought for you. Here's the address where we'll be."

Joe dutifully wrote down the directions and signed.

The gift. That was one thing to call it. What was up with that guy that he was too paranoid to call a spade a spade or a gun a gun? He'd even paid Joe extra to spend time at the local firing range to improve his accuracy. He didn't know exactly how many innocent targets he'd blown all to hell since signing on for this job, but it was a lot.

He hung up the phone and checked his watch. He'd have to leave soon to gas up the car if he was going to make the appointed time. If he kept busy, maybe he wouldn't have to think about the "guest" Mr. White had referred to. There was definitely something off kilter about that guy, in addition to the fact that he rarely spoke. Joe couldn't place his accent, but it was strong enough to be difficult to understand. Most of the time, Mr. White simply stared out the window and rode in silence.

Where did he go when Joe dropped him off in the woods above the beach? Joe wasn't picky about how he earned his living, but he still had pride in his country. He'd hate to find out that Mr. White's mysterious companion had links to some terrorist group. He sure looked creepy enough with his pale skin and oddly streaked gray hair. If there were such things as vampires, he would fit the profile, that's for sure.

Even though Joe was joking, the idea gave him a lasting chill. He was thinking too much; it didn't matter if he liked the guy or even Mr. White. Joe was in this for the easy money, not to make friends with the bastards.

"Mother, dinner is ready."

It was the second time Tate had yelled up the steps, and so far Sandra had refused to make an appearance. Fine. If she wanted to sulk, so be it. Besides, eating by herself would make for a much more peaceful meal. Once Tate had eaten, she'd check on Sandra and get a few things settled.

Tate had no choice but to have it out with her mother over her earlier behavior. Tate was willing to put up with it, but only up to a certain point. Tonight Sandra had definitely crossed the line. Either she straightened up, or Tate would order her to leave. She wouldn't let Sandra ruin the nice life Tate had made here in Justice Point.

That didn't mean Tate was in a big hurry to have another confrontation. She ladled up a big bowl of soup and sliced a baguette. Sandra could heat up something later if she got hungry.

Rather than sit at the table and stew, Tate booted up her laptop. Maybe she could squeeze in a few pages before it was time to face the endless paperwork that went with owning a small business.

Where had she left off? Oh, yeah, the sheriff had just kissed Melinda. It was obvious to both of them that this relationship was headed nowhere, not as long as Chance was still in the picture. On the long ride back to her house, Melinda mulled it all over.

A smart woman would know which of her two suitors would be a solid, upstanding partner for life, providing a stable home life and would be a good father for any children she might have. Despite her education, it appeared that Melinda wasn't all that bright. She didn't want stable, and she didn't want upstanding. She wanted Chance. What's more, she wanted her children to have his green eyes.

He was waiting and watching as the buggy pulled up in front of her house. Even though she couldn't see him, she felt his presence. She waited for her escort to come around to hand her down out of the buggy, although she'd rather have climbed down on her own. She very much feared he might try to kiss her again, and she couldn't bear to have Chance watch. There was no telling what he'd do.

But no, as always, the lawman acted the perfect gentleman, even thanking her for an enjoyable afternoon when it had been anything but that. She didn't call him on the lie, hoping their friendship hadn't been irreparably damaged. When he disappeared down the road, she braced herself and went inside to face her outlaw.

Tate leaned back in her chair, satisfied with how the scene had turned out. She even knew what was coming next. Chance was furious that he'd had to hide behind Melinda's lace curtains and watch her ride away with his enemy. He'd been on the verge of going after them when they finally returned. Melinda looked guilty. Had they done more than share a little fried chicken?

He'd promised himself that he'd keep his hands off of her, knowing he couldn't offer her any kind of life. But now all bets were off. As soon as she walked through that door, he was going to have her, even if it was only this one time. . . .

"What are you doing?"

Tate jumped guiltily. How long had Sandra been standing there? More importantly, had she been reading over Tate's shoulder? God, she hoped not. The last thing she needed was for her mother to sully Tate's secret dream with her usual sarcasm.

"Finishing up some paperwork. It never ends."

She saved the file, and then closed the laptop. "Soup's still hot on the stove. Help yourself."

Sandra filled her bowl and hesitated, as if not sure what to do. Tate really didn't want her company, but they had to make peace sometime.

"Sit down, if you want to. I was just going to have seconds." So that was a lie, but her mother was looking lost and a lot older than she had just hours before.

Tate stirred her soup, feigning interest. They sat in awkward silence.

Finally, both women set their spoons down and pushed their bowls away. Tate leaned back in her chair, ready to come out swinging, but willing to give Sandra one last chance.

"Okay, so I was way out of line earlier." Sandra kept her eyes firmly on the table as she picked at a loose thread on the tablecloth.

"You think? You insult my tenant—"

Her mother's eyes jerked up to meet hers. "He's more than that, and you know it."

Tate prayed for patience. "What he is, Mother, is none of your business. Let's get something straight. For the last time, Uncle Jacob left me this place, lock, stock, and the garage apartment. It is not now, nor will it ever be, yours. Got that?"

"Rub it in, why don't you? I don't know how you manipulated him into—"

That did it. Tate slammed her fist down on the table hard enough to rattle the bowls and slosh soup over the sides.

"I did *not* manipulate Uncle Jacob. I had no idea he'd named me as his heir until the lawyer called. Maybe if you'd been nicer to him, Uncle Jacob might have handled things differently. But you weren't. You were always your usual selfish, self-centered charming self around him."

Tate need to move. Shoving her chair back from the table, she carried the bowls over to the sink and grabbed the paper towels to clean up her mess. Besides, they'd come in handy to sop up the tears that were streaming down her face.

"You never did understand me," Sandra sniffed, her eyes also brimming with tears.

"No, I guess I didn't. I still don't. What I do understand, though, is that this is *my* home and *my* business. I cannot have you here making my friends and guests as miserable as you do me. I will write you a check. It won't be much, but it should be enough to give you a start."

She paused to stare at the woman who'd given birth to her; she had in so many ways remained a stranger. "And this will be the last dime I give you. You're a big girl, Mother. Act like it."

Sandra snarled right back, "So you're throwing me out? Just like that? Over some man you hardly know?"

"Just like that, Mother, but not because of Hunter. This has been a long time coming, and we both know it. You're welcome to stay until morning, but then I want you out. Next time call before you barge in for another 'visit.' I may or may not have room for you."

Tate crossed the kitchen to stand by the sink, her back to Sandra, unable to face the disaster their relationship had become. She was done crying over a lost cause. Or at least she would be by morning.

Chapter 9

Damn it. His leg was cramping from sitting in one position for too long. He had to stretch, or it would only get worse. So far, the night had been quiet. But if that changed and he needed to move quickly, he wouldn't be able to unless he did something about it and soon. He'd have to risk standing up, even if he risked being seen.

He'd deliberately situated himself between a couple of good-sized cedars, knowing he could use them for cover as well as support if he needed to pull himself up. Setting his cane in easy reach, he began the arduous process of getting vertical, moving as slowly and quietly as possible.

The pain was manageable right up until he put his full weight on his leg. He drew in a sharp breath as he waited for the throbbing to ease up. Finally, he paced a few steps. Gradually the muscles relaxed and the pain ebbed. As he enjoyed the brief moment of peace, a noise caught his attention.

Someone was coming.

Judging by the noise, Hunter guessed there were at least two, maybe three, people coming up from the beach. It was too late for him to duck down, so he blended farther back into the shadows. Moving slowly, he hit the release button on his cane and withdrew his blade. He didn't plan on charging into battle against superior numbers, but he had to be prepared in case they spotted him.

Of course, there was no guarantee that it was his enemy approaching, but it was awfully late for a bunch of tourists to be hiking up from a picnic. Besides, they'd likely be talking amongst themselves. Whoever was coming up the side of the bluff had yet to say a single word.

His years of Paladin training kicked in, slowing his pulse, enhancing his senses, increasing his awareness of each breath his enemies took as they hauled themselves up the steepest pitch of the trail. Oh, yeah, two were definitely human, but the third was not. Hunter's blood boiled with the need to skewer the alien bastard who'd crossed into this world, bringing his darkness with him. He stood his ground, ignoring the sour mix of fear and hate on his tongue.

The two humans definitely deserved to die screaming for mercy for their betrayal of their own kind. If it was up to Hunter, that's exactly what would happen. But he was in no position to take on three men at once. Now that he knew for sure that the cave was being used regularly, he'd contact Devlin about sending some help. First, though, he needed to discover if there was a pattern to their appearances, because Bane didn't have the manpower to station multiple guards up here night after night on the off chance the bastards would show.

The three men stopped at the ledge leading to the cave. Two of them started across, leaving the third to stand guard. Hunter could easily kill him, but that would only put the other two on alert. The whole idea was to capture those involved, not to force them to find another place to cross the barrier.

It didn't take long. Even from where Hunter stood, he saw the bright flash of the barrier going down. A few seconds later it flashed again as it was restored. There'd been rumors coming out of Seattle that some of the Kalith warriors had the ability to bring the barrier down at will. It looked like that much was true, since it was unlikely that these bozos conveniently arrived just as the barrier went down.

Shortly after, the second human left the cave to join his companion. Together they set back down the trail toward the beach. Hunter toyed with the idea of following them, but he didn't trust the strength of his leg enough to risk it. If they heard him coming, it could turn ugly. While he hadn't noticed if the one man who'd gone into the cave was armed, the one who'd stood guard definitely carried a gun in his right hand. As good as Hunter was with a sword, it wouldn't save him from getting shot.

Besides, he'd have a hard time explaining a bullet hole to Tate. Considering how up close and personal they'd gotten, she was intimately familiar with his scars. A new one would definitely draw her attention.

That is, if they got around to a repeat performance. He was definitely up for it, but he wasn't so sure about

Tate. Her mother had done everything she could to tarnish her daughter's memory of the afternoon.

How had someone so cold and calculating given birth to a lovely, warm woman like Tate? He'd never raised his hand against a woman, but he'd come darned close to decking Sandra for tearing into Tate. How dare she accuse Tate of taking sex as payment? Didn't she know her own daughter better than that?

Obviously not.

He'd check on Tate in the morning. And he'd give the bad guys a few more minutes to make a clean getaway before he started the climb back up the bluff. Maybe he'd take another long soak in the tub before turning in. He'd sleep better if he did. Besides, maybe when he got out, Tate would be standing at his door again.

That was probably too much to hope for. Still, he'd definitely take that bath. Just in case.

She thought *she* looked bad when she got up, but Hunter had just straggled into the shop looking as if he hadn't gotten more than an hour's sleep. She couldn't point fingers, though. She'd heard the clock in the hall toll the hour, every hour, all night long.

Sandra had yet to make an appearance. Tate would give her another hour and then check to see what the holdup was. Maybe that was the coward's way of dealing with the situation, but Tate needed another cup—or three—of caffeine before she could face another potential battle.

The bell over the door rang again. The Auntie Ms filed in a cloud of perfume. Normally Tate didn't mind that they all wore different kinds, but this morning the miasma of floral scents was overwhelming.

Hunter looked up from his tea with a small smile. "Good morning. How are my favorite ladies?"

Normally the three women would've fluttered a bit at his attention, but Madge and Margaret barely nodded. Mabel, always the most outgoing of the three, didn't even respond.

Tate quickly filled their teapot and carried it over to their table.

"Mabel, is everything all right?"

Her smile was shaky. "I'm just having one of those mornings, dear. When you get to be my age, sometimes things don't feel quite right."

Her color was off, too, so that the circles of peach blush on her cheeks stood out against the sallow tone of her skin. When she went to sit down, Mabel suddenly toppled to one side. If Tate hadn't been there to catch her, she would've hit the floor.

Thank God Hunter was there. He swept the woman up in his arms and set her in a chair. He knelt by her side.

"Mabel, are you having any chest pains?"

She shook her head. "No, but I'm a little light-headed. This happens once in a while. I'm sure it will pass."

Hunter caught her frail wrist between his thumb and forefinger and counted her pulse. After a few seconds, he looked up at Tate. "Call nine-one-one."

Mabel protested. "That's not necessary. I'll be fine. Like I said, I get this way. A nap will set me straight."

"How about I drive you to the hospital myself?" Tate asked. "It's not far, and we'd all feel better if a doctor gave you a quick checkup."

Mabel looked to her sisters for confirmation. They both nodded.

"But what about the shop, Tate? You can't afford to lose customers over me."

Tate put her hand on Mabel's shoulder. "Friends mean more than money. We won't be gone that long. Besides, business is always slow when it's this nice out."

"All the more reason for you to be here for the few that do come in."

Hunter butted into the argument. "I'll run the shop for her, Mabel. You know she won't be able to concentrate if she's worried about you."

His offer stunned Tate, and at the same time she was grateful. She really wasn't worried about the money, but now Mabel would agree to go. Sure enough, her friend slowly nodded.

"Perhaps I *should* go."

When she tried to stand up, Hunter stopped her. "Wait until Tate gets her keys and then I'll carry you out to the car."

Tate ran to grab her purse. When she returned, Hunter already had Mabel in his arms and was carrying her outside. Her sisters followed. Tate unlocked the car and stood back while he helped get all three of the Aunties situated and strapped in.

Then he leaned in and planted a soft kiss on Mabel's

cheek. "Don't give the doctors too hard of a time. Let them do their job, Mabel."

"I'm not a complete fool, young man. Now you go take care of things for Tate."

"I will."

If Tate hadn't been in such a hurry to get Mabel to the hospital, she would've given in to the urge to hug Hunter. She didn't care if he locked up the shop as soon as they were out of sight, but his promise to fill in would keep Mabel from fretting, especially if the ER was backed up and they had to wait.

She started the car and backed out onto the street. The road to town was too narrow and crooked for speed, but Mabel was in no obvious discomfort. Maybe they should've called the medics, but Tate could have her at the hospital in about the same time it would've taken an ambulance to get to the shop.

For once all three of the sisters were quiet, making the drive seem much longer than it actually was. But finally, Tate turned into the emergency entrance and pulled up under the overhang. After turning on her flashers, she ran inside the entrance to grab a wheelchair. A volunteer immediately came up to see if he could be of help.

"Yes, I have three elderly ladies out in the car. If you'd help the two in the backseat, I'll see to their sister in the front. She's the one who needs to see a doctor."

"I'd be happy to."

Tate mustered up what she hoped was a reassuring smile and headed out to help Mabel into the wheelchair.

• • •

Hunter poked around behind the counter to see where Tate kept everything. He suspected he shouldn't be serving food without some kind of official okay from the health department, but too bad. He could handle the demands of any customer. How hard could it be to fill pots with hot water and throw in some tea leaves?

Next he studied the tins of tea and compared them to the various blends listed on the menu. Who needed this many flavors? What was wrong with the basics like black and green? Well, and Pu'erh, his newest favorite, not that he'd admit that to Tate.

The floor overhead creaked. It had to be that damned Sandra. He stopped to listen, tracing her footsteps, hoping she'd stay up there until Tate got back. On the other hand, he'd be just as happy to have her on her way right back to wherever she'd come from. He didn't give a rip what the woman thought about him, but he hated to see Tate in pain. If Sandra tore into Tate again, he'd stuff the woman back in her car himself—or maybe under it.

He'd done everything he could think of to get ready for any customers. Maybe while it was quiet, he should report in. He listened again to make sure that Sandra was still upstairs, then he stepped outside to call Devlin. The Paladin leader answered on the second ring.

"It's Hunter. I had company last night."

"Gee, that's great. Were these the out-of-town relatives that you'd mentioned might be stopping by?"

Hunter stared at his phone in confusion before he realized that there must be someone with Devlin, someone not friendly to the cause.

"Yes, the one from out of town went home last night. The other two were local, but I figure they'll be back for another visit soon. I'll let you know if I hear from them again."

"That's great. I know some of the other guys would like to see them, too. Say, can you hold a minute? I've got someone here."

Hunter was on hold before he could respond, leaving him no choice but to wait. He considered hanging up, but it wouldn't do to piss off the man for no good reason.

Devlin clicked back in on the line. "Sorry about that. I don't think you've had the pleasure of meeting Colonel Kincade yet. He's the Regents' resident asshole, and he's really been on a tear this morning."

"No problem. You wanted to be kept in the loop when I had activity. There were two humans and one Other through here last night. They came up from the beach this time rather than crossing through Tate's property. One of the humans stood guard on the trail while the other two went into the cave. The Other didn't come back out."

"Could you follow the two humans when they left?"

"Not without being heard." Especially with his leg, but he figured that was none of Devlin's business.

"Okay. Let's do this. I'm going to send D.J. back up there with some friends. Show them around and see if any of you can pick up any information from their trail. They'll be up this afternoon."

How the hell was Hunter supposed to play tour guide for D.J. and company when he'd promised to work in the shop? He'd have to figure something out. "Okay, but there's no guarantee my guests will be back anytime soon."

"I know, but now that we know they're still using that passage through to Kalithia on a regular basis, you'll need some backup. That is unless you like parking your ass out on that hillside every night."

He didn't need help doing his job, but it only made sense to have someone ready to step in if something went wrong.

"Okay, send them."

"Will do." Devlin's voice warmed up a bit. "And Hunter, I do appreciate your doing this. I really want to stop these bastards, and your being there might just make that possible."

As a rule, Hunter didn't deal with gratitude well. "Tell D.J. if I'm not at my place to try the tea shop."

Devlin snorted. "Tea shop? Don't you know Seattle is the latté capital of the world?"

"Justice Point isn't Seattle."

"No, I guess not. Keep in touch."

As usual, Devlin hung up without a good-bye.

"What are you doing here?"

Hunter considered ignoring Sandra completely, but he figured that would only set her off. There were a couple of ladies sitting in the corner messing with yarn and drinking the tea he'd made. The last thing he wanted was to get into a shouting match with Tate's mother in front of customers.

"I'm keeping an eye on things so Tate could take a friend to the emergency room."

He sipped his own tea and tried to figure out what

four-across was on the crossword puzzle. The clue was a five-letter word for an ancient weapon. He considered writing in "old ax," but he doubted that was what they were looking for. Obviously, he'd gone wrong somewhere.

"Why didn't she ask me to cover for her?"

Was that hurt he heard in her voice? Surely not. But when he finally looked up, she did look a bit bewildered. Rather than point out that Tate had no reason to think Sandra would've volunteered, he gave a gentler answer.

"There wasn't time. When the Auntie Ms came in, it was obvious that Mabel was ill. The only way she'd let Tate take her to the hospital was if she knew Tate wouldn't have to close this place down. I was handy."

Sandra seemed unsure about what to do next.

"Would you like me to make you a cup of tea?"

He didn't know which one of them was more surprised by his offer.

"I'd love some, but I can fix it."

He had to admit that she looked pretty comfortable behind the counter, putting her tea on to steep and warming up a scone in the microwave. When she picked it up, he used his foot to push out the chair across from him in an unspoken invitation to join him.

"Thank you." She broke off the point of her scone and topped it with some lemon curd. "Any idea when Tate will be back?"

"No. I guess it will depend on what's wrong with Mabel. Tate has my cell number, so I figure she'll call if it's something serious."

He went back to his puzzle. Yeah, he'd had some letters reversed. He crossed them out and smiled when he realized the "ancient" weapon was a sword. Well, that all depended on what crowd you ran with. True, some of his buddies fought with swords that had been handed down through their families, but blades wore out eventually. The Paladins kept their armorer busy making replacement weapons. Ancient was all a matter of perspective.

"Did you read something funny in the puzzle?"

Sandra had been so quiet that he'd almost forgotten she was there.

She pointed toward the paper with her teaspoon. "You were smiling."

"No, I was just thinking about some friends of mine."

When he didn't go on, she went back to stirring her tea. "I'd planned on talking to Tate before I left. Do you think she'll be upset if I'm gone when she gets back?"

Relieved would be a better guess, but he kept that thought to himself.

"I can always give her a message for you." As long as it was civil and wouldn't upset Tate.

"Tell her that I'm going back to Edwin. I called him this morning, and we talked things out."

"Does she know this Edwin?"

For the first time, he realized that Sandra hadn't bothered with makeup and looked more like her real age. He had no idea if that was good or bad.

"No, she hasn't met him, but he's a good man. If he has his way, though, she'll meet him soon enough." She pushed her cup and plate to the side. "I've never had much luck with men sticking around, including Tate's father. I'm sure she told you that I drove him off."

"The subject never came up."

"Oh. Well, I've always suspected she blamed me for him not sticking around. He was on one of his extended trips, if you get my drift, when he was killed in a car accident. He wasn't alone at the time."

"I'm sorry. That must have been tough for both you and Tate."

"Yes, it was. She loved her father. So did I, but that never seemed to be enough for him." She stared at the table, lost in thought for a few seconds.

"Anyway, Edwin wanted to make our relationship more permanent, and I panicked. He says he's willing to take things slower, but he still wants to marry me."

"How do you feel about that?" God, he couldn't believe he'd asked that. It was none of his business.

"Scared. It seems like I've spent my whole life feeling that way. Who knows, maybe it's time to change that. He's a good man." Then she smiled. "I guess I already said that, didn't I?"

"That's okay. Maybe you needed to hear yourself say it."

She drew a shuddering breath. "Tell Tate I'm sorry about yesterday. What I said was unforgivable, and I'll understand if she doesn't want to see me for a while."

The faint sound of a cuckoo clock could be heard from upstairs.

"Oh, dear, I hadn't realized it had gotten so late. I have to get packing. Edwin's expecting me for dinner." Sandra started to get up but then stayed where she was. "Before I leave, though, I want to know what your intentions are toward my daughter. She's not the kind to sleep with just any man who comes along. I hope you realize how special she is, even if I occasionally seem to forget that myself."

Intentions? Other than to get Tate back into his bed as soon as possible, he didn't have any. Couldn't have any. Paladins made for bad boyfriend material, much less anything more long term than that.

"That's between me and Tate."

He nodded in the direction of the two ladies still knitting away in the corner, hoping Sandra would think his reticence on the subject was discretion on his part. Nope, she wasn't buying that idea at all.

He held up his hand to forestall whatever she was going to say. "Like I said, Sandra, it's between me and Tate. I won't betray her confidence, especially with you. If she wants to talk to you sometime, fine." Not really, but it sounded good.

He went on. "Judging from last night, I don't see her pouring her heart out to you right now. I'm not about to do it for her."

Sandra drew herself up to her full height, a fierce look on her face. "Fine, but you heard me. She's inexperienced when it comes to dealing with men like you."

Now that pissed him off. "You don't know anything about me, lady."

He stood up. All too aware of the two women listening from the corner, he dropped his voice. "This conversation is over. Do Tate a favor and be gone before she gets back. Let me know if you need help with your bags."

Then he walked away.

• • •

It was a relief to be on the way home. According to Mabel, the doctors had checked her from head to toe and back again without finding anything too alarming. The dizziness was from a combination of a middle ear and sinus infection.

Her elderly friend shifted restlessly in the seat beside her. "Thank you for taking me, Tate. It's nice to know that it wasn't my heart, but there's no cure for getting old."

There was no denying that, so Tate didn't try. "Well, he did say that you'll feel better once that antibiotic kicks in and takes care of the infection." She pulled up in front of Mabel's house. "We're home, ladies."

She helped each of the sisters out of the car and then followed them slowly up to the house. When she had Mabel all settled in bed for a well-deserved nap, Tate made sure the other two were tucked up comfortably in their usual chairs in front of the television. Finally, she ran back out to the car to get the carry-out food they'd picked up on the way home. She'd gotten enough for the three women for lunch and dinner, knowing they'd be too tired to cook.

Satisfied she'd done as much as she could, she left them alone, promising to check in again later. Now back to the shop to see what disasters Hunter had run into serving tea. She'd thought about him off and on for hours, wishing she could've been there to see him pouring tea and bussing tables.

Hunter Fitzsimon was definitely a puzzle. There was

no missing the wary edginess he wore like a second skin, but he was kind to old ladies and the first to jump in with an offer to help. He mowed lawns unasked and had made her feel like the center of his universe when he'd held her in his arms.

Those were the positives. On the other side, he had no discernible job, pushed her away as often as he pulled her close, and obviously had some major problems arising from whatever had caused that horrific scar on his leg.

When she pulled into her driveway, she noticed her mother's car was gone. Would it be too horrible of her to hope that she'd really gone and not just made a run into town to pick up a few things? Maybe, but she tried not to lie to herself. Sandra was never easy to be around, and she'd been extra horrible this time.

That was when she noticed a large black SUV pulling in to park in front of the shop. How many customers had Hunter had while she'd been gone? She hoped he hadn't been inundated by too many or bored out of his mind by too few. Either way, she owed him big time for his help. Maybe she could slip in the back door and get in position to wait on these new customers and give him a break.

Hunter looked up from his book when she walked into the shop from the kitchen.

"Welcome home. How's Mabel? Is she okay?"

Her heart warmed at the concern in his voice. "The doctor said she'll feel better in a few days. She has a sinus infection and a middle ear infection."

"I'm glad it wasn't anything more serious."

Hunter closed his book and stood up just as the door opened and four men filed in with D.J. leading the way.

"Hey, there, Tate!" D.J. nodded at Hunter before stepping aside to let his friends walk past.

Before she could respond, Hunter screamed in outrage and lunged past her, almost knocking her to the ground. By the time she caught her balance, Hunter had shoved one of the other men up against the door frame and had his hands around the man's neck.

His victim frantically fought to pull Hunter's hands away from his throat, as did the other two strangers. D.J. had his arms around Hunter's waist, trying to yank him off the other man while Tate looked on in horror. As they rolled in her direction, she scuttled back behind the counter, wanting to hide but unable to tear her eyes away from the terrifying spectacle unfolding before her.

Hunter's face was contorted with such intense hatred that she barely recognized him. He was as out of control as he'd been the other night when he'd rushed out of the restaurant, but multiplied by a factor of ten or even a thousand. Inhuman growls came out of his mouth as he cursed and did his damnedest to choke the life out of his opponent.

D.J. and one of his companions finally succeeded in yanking Hunter off their friend. The two of them tossed him to the floor and then sat on him to keep him down. The fourth member of the group helped the injured man to a chair on the far side of the room.

"Damn it, Hunter, stop it before you hurt yourself!" D.J. threw his full weight across Hunter's chest. "For God's sake, you're scaring Tate!"

That last part must have gotten through to Hunter, because he suddenly collapsed back against the floor, his arms and legs limp. Slowly D.J. lifted up, allowing Hunter more room to breathe, but remaining in position in case he attacked again.

Hunter glared up at D.J. with wild eyes. "Let me at the bastards, D.J. Now."

Tate shivered at the venom dripping from each word he uttered. It was as if she was looking at a total stranger, not at all the man who'd carried Mabel to the car with such gentleness and care.

"Damn it, Hunter, I can't do that, and you know it."

"Get the hell off me, D.J., or I'll kill you, too!"

D.J. immediately flattened himself back down, knocking the breath out of Hunter in a loud *whoosh.* He glanced back over his shoulder.

"Tate, you might want to leave for a few minutes. This might get ugly." Then D.J. glanced at the man that Hunter had attacked. "Stand back. Lonzo and I will drag this crazy bastard outside and pound some sense into him."

Horrified by the threat, Tate gasped, "D.J.! You wouldn't!"

"Sorry, this is no time for delicate sensibilities, Tate. Please leave and take my friends with you. When this idiot comes to his senses, he won't like knowing you were here to watch."

Chapter 10

Hunter's world narrowed, until all he could feel was a craving to kill, even if it meant taking D.J. out to get to those pale-eyed freaks. Those bastards weren't going to get their hands on him, not this time, playing their vicious games, slicing and dicing him until the floors and walls ran red.

"Damn it, Hunter, quit!"

Hunter shifted his focus back to his enemies and feinted to the right and then back left, sneaking past D.J. to grab the closest Other by the neck. The fucker's skin was warm, his pulse throbbing under Hunter's hands as he squeezed, slowly choking off his victim's air supply. Oh, yeah, this was sweet; he reveled in the chance for some payback.

The other Paladin joined D.J.'s efforts to pry Hunter loose. He kicked out to the side, trying to hold them off. He wouldn't let them win, not this time, especially with his own kind siding with his enemies. Where the hell was his sword?

Desperate to do the most damage he could before they overwhelmed him, Hunter tightened his grip. But his prize was ripped from his grasp, sending Hunter falling backward to the floor with two Paladins doing their best to keep him from bucking them off of him.

He screamed out his frustration. He had to kill. How would he ever heal if he didn't? That was his job—to kill Others, to make them pay for raping his world, raping his mind, and ripping apart his soul. He'd tear out the bastards' hearts with his bare hands and regain his honor.

Hunter whipped his head back and forth as he spewed out his hatred and his fury. Then he spotted her. Tate. Oh, God, Tate. Save her. The monsters had her; they were leading her away! His stamina was fading, but the sight of the woman—his woman—with his enemy recharged him. With a sudden burst of energy, he dislodged D.J.

But before he could kick his legs free of the second Paladin and charge to Tate's rescue, D.J. snarled, "Damn it, Hunter, I didn't want to do this."

Then D.J. clocked Hunter in the side of his head. Once. Twice. Finally, in a burst of bone-jarring pain, all Hunter's anger disappeared under a cold blanket of darkness.

Tate's stomach roiled from watching Hunter's explosion of violence. What had set him off? It clearly wasn't D.J.

or the one called Lonzo who had him foaming at the mouth with the need to fight or kill.

That left the two men D.J. had told her to get out of the way. But considering Hunter's reaction to them, would she be safe alone with them? Before she could decide the answer to that, they were standing beside her. The fact that both of them towered over her made her even more skittish.

"I'm sorry, Ms. Justice. You have no reason to trust either of us, but I do think it is best that we leave the room. Your friend Hunter will calm down when he can no longer sense our presence."

She couldn't place the man's accent even though it sounded vaguely familiar, but his quiet dignity and sympathetic tone helped convince her that leaving was best. How odd that both men had dark hair shot with gray when their faces placed them in their early thirties. Were they related? But now wasn't the time for idle questions.

She started out of the room. "Come this way."

Once they were in the kitchen, she motioned the two of them toward seats at the table. The second man had yet to say a word, not a surprise considering the bruising on his throat. She pulled a large bag of peas out of the freezer.

"Here, maybe this will help."

"Thank you for your kindness." He tried to smile but winced in pain. The rough gravel in his voice sounded worse than Hunter's usually did.

The silence from the shop seemed ominous. She needed something to do to keep busy. Tea. Without even asking if they'd like some, she filled her favorite teapot with hot water and added loose tea leaves, choosing a combination designed to soothe the throat. Her hands were shaking, and the cups rattled in their saucers as she carried them to the table.

The bells over the shop door rang out, their sound jangling her already rattled nerves. Where were they taking Hunter? She started to charge out after them, but before she'd gone two steps, her way was blocked.

"Please, Ms. Justice. You can trust D.J. and Lonzo to help Hunter regain control. They have a great deal of experience in such matters."

"But he's hurting." Her eyes stung with tears.

"That he is, and with good reason. But as D.J. said, when Hunter can think clearly, he will not appreciate an audience, especially you."

Although he made no move to touch her, Tate suspected he would if that's what it took to prevent her from leaving the kitchen.

"Fine. I'll wait. But if they hurt him, I will call the police and press charges, even if he won't. Is that clear?" She had to tilt her head back at a painful angle to look him in the eye.

He surprised her when he smiled. "I have great admiration for a woman fierce enough to defend her man. I am blessed to have such a lady in my own life."

Hunter wasn't her man. Not really. But she couldn't deny that her first instinct was to lash out at these four men for hurting him.

"What's her name?" she asked on her way back to the

counter to pour the tea, not that his answer mattered. It just gave her something to concentrate on.

"Lacey Sebastian. I am Barak q'Young, by the way, and my silent friend here is called Larem q'Jones."

Such odd names. Barak sat back down at the table, staying between her and the shop. He apparently took his guard duty seriously.

"This tea is blended to soothe sore throats. I don't know if it will help you or not, but I like the flavor even when I'm not sick," she said as she handed Larem a cup.

"Thank you." Larem winced when he spoke, but he sighed with relief when he sipped the tea. "This feels quite good."

Barak agreed. "If circumstances allow for it, I would love to explore your selection of teas. I do drink coffee, but I have found I prefer tea. Have you owned this business long?"

She allowed herself to be distracted. "My uncle opened the shop almost thirty years ago. I spent a lot of time with him as I was growing up. I always liked to experiment with different blends of herbs and spices."

She noticed that Larem had set the peas back down on the table. "Do you need another bag? I can get you some more if that one's already thawed."

"No, I am fine." His voice was much clearer.

Odd. She had thought his neck was badly bruised, but the faint streaks of purple had already faded to red. Before she could comment, Lonzo appeared in the doorway. He looked at the two men first.

"Larem, are you all right?"

"Yes, I'm fine."

Lonzo turned his attention toward Tate. "How about you? I'm figuring we scared you a bit."

No use in denying that. "All I want to know is if Hunter is okay."

Lonzo nodded and smiled at her. "More or less." Then he gave Barak a pointed look. "He's got himself back under control for the moment. D.J. said for you two to come back into the shop so he can introduce you."

Larem knocked back the rest of his tea and nodded his thanks to Tate. Barak did the same, bowing slightly before following his friend back to the shop.

Lonzo hung back. "Give us a minute or two to settle a few things, and I'll come back for you. We don't want to overwhelm him again."

That did it. She was willing to cooperate up to a point, but this was her home, her shop. And Hunter was her friend; she wasn't sure these guys could make the same claim.

"I wasn't the one who set him off this time."

"This time?" Lonzo frowned. "He's done this before?"

She shouldn't have let that slip. If Hunter wanted them to know he was having problems, it certainly wasn't her place to be telling them. Rather than elaborate, she asked a few questions of her own.

"Who are you, anyway? What are you to Hunter? And why did Larem and Barak upset him like that?"

"All good questions, Ms. Justice, but Hunter will have to be the one to explain." He quickly backed out of the room, leaving her no chance to demand answers.

She'd wait, but not for long. Opening her utensil drawer, she pulled out her favorite rolling pin. If they didn't let her close to Hunter soon, she was going out there and knock a few heads together. Even if she needed a stepladder to do it.

Shit, this was bad. Hunter would be lucky if Devlin didn't haul his worthless ass back to Seattle and have someone shove a needle full of toxins in his arm. He'd been out of his head with the need to hurt somebody, and that's all it took to condemn a Paladin to death. But, damn it, they should've known better than to let their pet Others drop in on him unannounced.

Neither Barak nor Larem had made a single aggressive move in his direction, but it rubbed his control raw to have them within reach and off limits. They knew it, too. It was no accident that D.J. and Lonzo sat flanking him; there was no question whose side they were on, and it wasn't his.

"Hunter?"

Oh, God, Tate. She sounded tentative as she poked her head into the shop. As soon as she spotted him, she headed straight for him, but the anger in her eyes was directed at his companions. When he saw the rolling pin in her hand, the big knot in his chest eased.

He gripped the edge of his chair to keep from charging across the room to her. It was the second time he'd gone into meltdown in front of her. This had to stop. He'd lost too much of himself in that Missouri cave to ever come back from the edge. Even if she wasn't terrified of him, he was terrified *for* her. What if he attacked her the next time his brain checked out and the rage took over?

"Are you all right?" She stood just out of reach, clearly unsure of her welcome.

"For now."

He kept his eyes focused on the table in front of him, but he saw her flinch in response to his abrupt answer. When he didn't elaborate, she backed away.

She cleared her throat and spoke again, this time in her best hostess voice. "Okay, gentlemen, since things are under control here, I'll leave you alone. Before I go, would anyone like tea?"

Hunter didn't trust himself to speak, so he nodded. Barak and Larem did as well. Lonzo finally answered for all of them as the silence dragged out.

"Don't go to any trouble for us, Ms. Justice."

"It's no trouble. It's my job."

She retreated to the counter and busied herself filling pots and setting out cups and saucers. When she had everything ready, D.J. went to help her. He winked as he picked up the tray. She did not look amused.

Hunter realized that if he hadn't been in such a foul mood, he would've laughed at the sight of two Others—make that Kalith warriors—and two Paladins drinking out of Tate's fussy china cups. She'd set his usual mug down in front of him, which the other men eyed with no little jealousy. Without a single word, Tate had shown them who belonged in her shop and who didn't. It didn't change anything, but he appreciated the gesture.

Once they finished their tea and the plate of warm

scones she'd brought, they could get down to Paladin business. But not here.

Gradually his four companions started talking amongst themselves. It was odd to hear Larem and Barak discussing the local baseball team's season with Lonzo and D.J. If he closed his eyes, it was impossible to tell who was human and who wasn't. Maybe that was a good thing, but right now it only made it harder for him to maintain control.

He interrupted their conversation. "Gentlemen, I don't know about you, but I could use a long walk."

"Sounds good." Barak nodded and then approached Tate, pulling out his wallet. "How much do we owe you?"

D.J. shifted slightly toward Hunter, ready to intercede if necessary. But there was no need. Even if Hunter hated having an Other pay for him, Tate was already shaking her head no.

"My treat today. Next time I'll let you buy." She kept her eyes focused on her computer screen. She offered him a small brown paper bag. "I thought you might like to try this tea. It's one of my custom blends."

"I thank you for your hospitality." Barak dropped some bills in the tip jar anyway. "Perhaps next time, I'll bring Lacey with me. I suspect the two of you have much in common."

Hunter walked out the door without looking back. It was the right thing to do, to start putting some distance between himself and Tate Justice, even it felt as if he'd ripped all of his old wounds open, leaving him bleeding and raw. As he stumbled down the steps, he drew what comfort he could from the cool feel of his cane's ivory handle.

D.J. hustled to catch up with him when they were out of direct sight of Tate's house. "Why aren't we headed back down the way you showed me the other day?"

"I don't want anyone seeing us showing too much interest in the trail."

"Meaning Tate."

Hunter smacked D.J. on the arm. "You think? Devlin tells me to play this low key and then you lead a fucking parade right into town. If you'd called ahead, I would've met you somewhere else." He spun around to face D.J. head-on. "And you could've warned me who you were bringing with you."

Hunter shifted the grip on his cane so that he could wield it like a club. D.J. eyed it uneasily, which showed he was smarter than Hunter thought. "I don't know what the hell you and Devlin were thinking, D.J. Maybe we could've avoided that whole fucking mess if you had called ahead."

Lonzo moved up beside Hunter. "And maybe we wouldn't have. We're all sorry Tate got sucked in like that, but we had to find out how you'd react if the five of us are going to be working together. Now we know."

Hunter stared back at the two Kalith males. Neither of them made a move in his direction, but he recognized warriors when he saw them. They hadn't attacked him even though he'd given them enough provocation. Hunter knew that what had happened to him hadn't been their fault, but it felt damned weird thinking that way.

He relaxed his hand to let the cane slide back down to its normal position. Ignoring the two Paladins, he stuck his hand out to the one he'd choked. It was hard to tell who was more surprised by the gesture.

"Let's start over. I'm Hunter Fitzsimon, and I'm sorry I attacked you."

Larem's smile started in his eyes. "I am Larem q'Jones. If it's any comfort, I'm still trying to figure out how I ended up with a Paladin for a roommate."

He nodded in Lonzo's direction. "However, fighting a common enemy has made the transition easier."

Barak laughed softly and offered his hand to Hunter as well. "My mate-to-be is the sister of a Paladin, and my own sister now lives with another of the Seattle Paladins. It makes for interesting family dinners."

Hunter studied Barak for a second or two. "I knew of you from your visit to Missouri when Trahern was there, but that was all. I regret my lapse in control." Oddly enough, he meant it.

"From the strength of your reaction, I suspect you had ample provocation." Larem rubbed his neck. "I hope that we're past that now."

Unfortunately, Hunter's control was too hit-or-miss to promise that. "Let's just say I'll try my best to maintain when I'm around you and leave it at that."

"That is all we can ask," Barak said in his quiet way. "Now, Devlin said you had a stretch of barrier in a cave for us to look at."

Feeling better than he had a few minutes ago, Hunter led them down to the beach from the far end, taking the same approach that his late-night visitors used.

"They came this way, but the last time they cut through Tate's backyard to the woods. I assume they use different routes to prevent anyone from picking up on any patterns. Last night they weren't talking, but they weren't particularly quiet in their approach. Previously, when they came up the trail and past Tate's place, they talked the whole way."

"Ballsy of them." Lonzo knelt down to study the trail. "It's impossible to know for sure, but I think this print was made by a Kalith, since the sole is smooth. These others pretty much have to be human."

Hunter nodded in agreement. "Come on. We need to haul ass if we're going to get around that point up there before high tide. We can check out the cave and then go uphill from there back to where you parked."

The five men walked single file around the narrow strip of rocks still above the tide mark. Once on the other side, the beach widened back out. Hunter stopped and looked back.

"Maybe they choose their route based on the tide tables. It's probably safer for them to come this way if they want to avoid being seen. But if the tide's in, they have to come down the hill or go wading."

D.J. nodded. "That makes sense. Good thinking."

"We can post someone up there to watch this direction." Hunter pointed up the bluff a short distance. "Getting up there won't be easy, but it's less likely we'd be spotted."

They continued on, winding their way up the hillside toward the narrow ledge that led to the cave. Hunter pointed out where he'd been hiding when the enemies had made their appearance. Then he led them, sidestepping, across to the cave.

Hunter stood back, watching to see how Barak and Larem responded to the barrier. Both men stood within arm's reach of its shimmering surface while the three Paladins waited in silence.

Finally, Barak spoke. "This strip would be relatively easy for someone with my talents to bring down on command."

"Your talents?" Hunter asked, although he suspected he already knew the answer.

"There are those rare ones among our kind who are gifted with the ability to work with stone and the barrier. My sister and I both have the gift. It is safe to assume that the Kalith who passed through here last night does as well."

Larem looked disgusted. "That narrows the field down to no more than a handful of possible culprits."

"The Guildmaster being at the top of the list." There was no mistaking the bitterness in Barak's voice. "I would give a great deal to catch him on this side of the barrier."

Hunter had no idea who the Guildmaster was, but it was obvious that both Lonzo and D.J. had at least a working knowledge of him.

"He seems more the type to send someone else to do his dirty work." Lonzo shifted his weight, his hand on his hip, as if reaching for the sword he wasn't carrying. "Wouldn't Berk be keeping a close eye on him?"

Hunter was starting to feel as if he were watching a foreign film with no subtitles. "Okay, I'm lost here. Who's the Guildmaster and who's Berk?"

Barak was the one to answer. "In our world, we have

warriors who serve to protect our people. They work in groups of four, in what I believe you would call a squad. The leader of such a group is a Sworn Guardian, the other three serve as his or her Blade. The Guildmaster is the man who is in charge of all of the Blades in a given region. Unfortunately, the current Guildmaster is a man of no honor."

Larem took up where Barak left off. "He has betrayed our people in many ways. Berk is one of the Sworn Guardians working to catch those who have been dealing with someone from your world, trading our blue stones to the humans. We don't know what the Guildmaster gets in return."

"Well, I guess the next time he passes through, we'll have to ask him." Hunter's smile had nothing at all to do with being friendly.

Larem surprised him by clapping him on the shoulder. "I will enjoy being part of that particular discussion."

Hunter winced at the contact, still not comfortable with being touched. Well, except by Tate, but that was over. At least he managed to control his reactions enough to not take another swing at Larem.

As the men watched, the intense colors of the barrier flared brighter. As they fluctuated, streaks of sickly green and yellow flowed through the stream of energy.

"Son of a bitch! It's going down." Hunter hit the button on his cane and yanked the blade out, ready to protect his companions. "Back out of here. If they come across, you don't want to be trapped in here unarmed."

Both D.J. and Lonzo had drawn small revolvers, but

the narrow confines of the cave made it no place to start shooting. Possible ricochets weren't the only problem. The barrier could be ripped apart by bullets. "Come on, Barak, Larem, get moving."

Larem did as they asked, but Barak stood his ground. He held his hands out in front of him, palms forward. Sweat poured off his face, as if he struggled to push against an invisible foe.

Hunter froze, staring at the barrier. Slowly at first, and then more rapidly, the putrid colors faded away, leaving behind only the vibrant colors of the barrier when at full strength. When the last bit of sallow green was gone, Barak slumped forward and let his hands drop to his sides.

D.J. stepped forward to offer support. He wrapped Barak's arm around his shoulders, then muscled him toward the mouth of the cave.

"He'll be all right in a few minutes, but let's get out of here in case his fix doesn't hold. It's doubtful that a bunch of Others are waiting to come party at this particular site, but you never know. I'd rather be outside the cave, where we can use our guns if necessary."

Hunter waited until the other four were safely outside before he joined them, as he was the only one with a usable weapon. Outside, Barak was leaning against one of the boulders. He looked marginally better than he had only a few seconds before.

"Are you okay, or do you need a few more minutes?" Hunter asked as he stood with his eyes sweeping the trail both above and below the ledge.

Barak remained where he was. "As long as we go

slowly, I'll be all right. Working with the energy is never easy, and I'm out of practice."

They all waited quietly until Barak pushed himself upright and started back toward the main trail. Hunter motioned for the rest to go ahead of him.

"Let D.J. take the lead, because he's been here before. I'll bat cleanup."

Hunter waited and watched the path down to the beach for several seconds to make sure they weren't being followed. Or at least that was the excuse he told himself. The truth was that he needed to put a little room between himself and his companions.

If they wondered why he was slow to follow, they didn't say anything. He was hanging in there, but the past twenty-four hours had been a bitch. Even now, it was all he could do to face the two Kalith with any degree of control. That they were dressed in human clothes helped, but only a little. Years of fighting their insane kin had left him with a hair-trigger temper that screamed at him to attack before they could. Being tortured had only served to hone that particular instinct.

About halfway up the hillside, Larem dropped back to walk beside Hunter. If Hunter thought the Other was doing so to accommodate his weaker leg, he'd kick the bastard down the bluff to show him just how well said leg still worked.

But when Larem seemed sure the rest of the group couldn't hear their conversation, he spoke. "I don't know why I feel compelled to tell you this, but I want you to know that I did not choose to live in your world."

As focused as Hunter was on his own situation, he

recognized some of the same resentment and anger in the Kalith warrior's voice and eyes.

"Then why are you here?" Not that he really wanted to know. Or did he?

"Barak came here expecting to die. Instead, he saved Devlin's woman from a human who would've killed her. Rather than being a martyr for our people, he became a hero to yours a second time when he saved the woman he loves. Her brother is a Paladin. You may have heard of him—Penn Sebastian."

Hunter nodded. Penn was the other Paladin who could no longer fight at the barrier. Even if the two of them had that in common, or maybe because they did, Hunter had no interest in meeting Penn. Was he a bastard for feeling that way? Probably, but hanging out with Penn would make this change in his life seem too real, too permanent.

"So what did they do, drag you here kicking and screaming?" Hunter asked.

And if so, why didn't he just go home?

Larem stared up the trail, but his eyes were focused on something only he could see. "Lusahn q'Arc, Barak's sister, served our people as a Sworn Guardian. As Barak explained, Guardians are much like your police, only more than that. I was privileged to be part of her Blade, one of the three warriors who fought at her side. Barak was trying to meet with her, to work out a way for the Paladins and our Guardians to fight these common enemies who have betrayed both our peoples."

"So what happened?"

"Barak's woman was kidnapped by humans. So instead

of Barak meeting with Lusahn, your Cullen Finley crossed into my world. While he was there, we were all betrayed by Lusahn's former mentor. Both of my Blademates were murdered by traitors who left a trail that laid the guilt on Lusahn and myself. Had I stayed, I would've been executed. In fact, Lusahn and I both would have died at the hands of the Guildmaster. Instead, with the help of Barak and three of the Seattle Paladins, we are here."

"And you hate it." Where was Larem headed with all of this?

"Not so much anymore. I have made a few friends. I like baseball." His smile was fleeting. "But I lacked purpose until Devlin asked me to assist you in this hunt. I will understand if my continued presence causes you to wish me gone, but I would offer you the use of my sword."

Obviously he didn't mean that Hunter could borrow his weapon. Despite his unusual way of speaking, it was clear that Larem was a warrior in need of a battle, just as Hunter was. Although Hunter might not be fighting alongside his friends, at least he was still in his own world. How much worse would it be to have lost all that, especially through no fault of his own?

And how weird to realize that he had more in common right now with his enemy than he did with Jarvis and Jake, not to mention the rest of the Paladins he'd spent his life serving with. Maybe he owed Larem a few explanations of his own. If Devlin had been true to his word, no one from this region knew the complete truth about what had happened to Hunter.

"In Missouri, we defend a stretch of barrier that runs

off and on through a system of limestone caves and tunnels. I got stupid and went wandering alone and ran into a bunch of . . ." He hesitated, not sure what to call them.

"A bunch of Others, as you call them," Larem suggested with only a slight hint of bitterness in his voice. "They are no longer Kalith when they seek the light in your world."

There was no pretty way to describe what had happened, so he didn't try. "They took their time and a great deal of pleasure in torturing me. They cut me to shreds." He slapped his thigh with the palm of his hand. "I almost lost my leg. The only reason I didn't is that I died, and that took all of the fun out of it for the bastards."

Next, his hand went to his throat of its own volition. When he spoke, it felt as if he had a mouth full of gravel. "My vocal cords were ruined from screaming."

Larem came to an abrupt halt. He picked up a rock and threw it as hard as he could against the nearest tree, knocking a hole in the bark. "Those *bastards!* Killing an enemy in battle is one thing. There was no honor in what they did. And there's no shame in needing time to recover from what they did to you. Wounds of the soul take the longest to heal."

Hunter stared at the Kalith warrior, whose fury on his behalf was both a surprise and a gift.

"I could use your sword, Larem." Once again he offered his hand to his companion, but this time with a great deal more enthusiasm. "Would you like to stay at my place tonight? We can get some dinner and then stand watch. I doubt that our quarry will make another appearance so soon, but you never know."

"I will tell Barak and the others that I won't be returning with them tonight." This time his smile seemed more genuine. "I brought a pack with me, just in case."

Up ahead, D.J. was pacing restlessly just inside the tree line. Barak and Lonzo ignored him, no doubt familiar with the Paladin's high energy.

"Took you two long enough."

Hunter decided to yank D.J.'s chain a bit. "What's the matter, D.J.? Don't tell me you're jealous."

Larem let out a bark of laughter. "I didn't know you cared so much, D.J. Maybe I should be flattered, but I'm truly not."

All three men were now staring at Larem and Hunter as if they'd sprouted polka dots and horns. Hunter couldn't blame them. He was a little surprised by how things were playing out himself.

"Larem has offered to stay and stand guard with me tonight. Maybe two of you can relieve us tomorrow night."

Lonzo studied Hunter and Larem for several seconds. Whatever he saw had him nodding. "Fair enough. One of us will return with Barak late tomorrow. But if the barrier decides it's time for us to dance, it may be Penn who comes. Hope that's okay."

It would have to be. "Sure." Especially since the wounded Paladin would be standing guard with Barak, not Hunter.

"Okay, then, the rest of us will head back to Seattle. We'll let Devlin know what's up."

Back at the SUV, Larem pulled out his pack as the others piled in. Waving good-bye, the three men drove away.

When they were completely out of sight, Hunter looked at his guest. “Let’s drop your stuff off in the apartment, then head into town for dinner. What sounds good?”

“Did I mention that I’m a vegetarian?”

Hunter pretended a disgust he really didn’t feel as he unlocked his door. “Well, that leaves out the steak house. How about Japanese then?”

“I’ll trust your judgment.” Larem tossed his bag on the floor.

“Considering my luck, that might be a mistake.” Hunter glanced outside. “One more side effect I’ve yet to get past is that I need to be outside at night, or you’ll see more of what you saw earlier.”

“No big deal.” Larem shrugged with a smile. “One of my favorite things about your world is takeout.”

Chapter 11

Tate paced back and forth, working herself up into a fine temper. She made the turn again and came to an abrupt halt. Who was she mad at here?

Definitely D.J. and company for upsetting Hunter. It was clear that he'd had another flashback of when he'd been hurt, but it was unclear what about Barak and Larem had set him off. If they really were his enemies, then why did D.J. bring them to visit? Besides, he'd obviously made peace with them once he'd gotten himself under control.

So, how upset was she with Hunter and why? Finally, she decided she was pretty darned mad, but not because he'd attacked Larem. It was obvious that he had no control over his flashbacks.

No, now that she thought about it, her anger stemmed from his treatment of her afterward, when he'd gone back to being all buddy-buddy with his posse. She hadn't expected him to introduce her as if they were a couple; their relationship was too new for that. She wouldn't have been any more comfortable with it than he would have, although Barak *had* made that reference to her defending her man. All Tate knew was that she'd neither said nor done anything to give Hunter the impression that she had any expectations.

But was civility too much to ask for? No, it wasn't. Did Hunter think she was going to curl up on his lap and toy with his hair while his friends were there? Pout when he didn't spend every second catering to her every whim?

Was she overreacting? Yes. Well, maybe. No, not completely. There'd been a definite chill in the air when she'd come into the shop to reassure herself that he'd been all right. Granted, some men didn't want to appear weak in front of their buddies. Was that his problem? God, she hoped not. She had little sympathy for that attitude, especially since she'd never given him any reason to think she'd embarrass him.

She walked down the steps and looked around. The SUV was right where they'd left it, so the four men were still in the area. Deciding it was none of her business where they'd gone or what they were up to, she started walking to the Auntie Ms house. One of the twins would've called her if Mabel had taken a turn for the worse, but she'd promised to check in on them. Besides, she badly needed something to do.

Madge saw her coming and met her at the door. "Come in, dear."

"Thanks, Madge. I wanted to see how Mabel was feeling."

"She's still in bed and fussing about it. That usually means she's on the mend."

Madge's eyes twinkled with good humor. It was good to see that the worry was gone from the twin's expression.

"I won't stay long if it will tire her out."

"Actually, the company will do her good. She gets pretty dizzy if she sits up too long, and she can't read either. You know my sister. She's not happy if she's not busy."

A querulous voice called out from the next room. "Tate, is that you?"

Madge and Tate exchanged a conspiratorial smile. "I'm coming, Mabel."

The light was dim in the older woman's bedroom, and she looked frail lying there in bed. When Mabel struggled to sit up, Tate hurried to help her. She tucked two extra pillows behind Mabel for support.

"Thank you, dear. I don't mean to be a bother."

Tate patted her on the arm. "You're never a bother. Besides, what are friends for?"

Mabel kept her eyes closed while she moved, probably hoping to hold off the waves of dizziness from her infection. But at Tate's admittedly rhetorical question, they popped wide open and looked at her with hope.

"Would you have time to read to me for a few minutes? I tried to get Margaret to, but she doesn't care for my taste in books."

No surprise there. The twins preferred thrillers and mysteries, while Mabel was a huge fan of romances of all kinds. Lately, she'd been reading paranormals and Westerns.

"Sure, I'd be glad to. I closed the shop early. Everybody must be out enjoying the sunshine." Usually she would've used the time to write, but she couldn't concentrate while she wondered and worried about Hunter and company.

There was an untidy stack of books sitting on the bedside table. Tate picked up the top one and pulled a chair over to sit beside the bed. Opening to the bookmark, she started to read aloud. Mabel settled back against her pillows with her eyes closed and a smile on her face.

For the first few pages, everything went smoothly. It didn't matter to Tate that she had no idea what was going on in the story. The writer was one of her favorites, and it was easy to lose herself in the flow of words and imagery. The Western had all her favorite elements: a sheriff trying to come to peace with his past, a feisty heroine, and a real bad guy, not at all like the handsome gunslinger in her own story.

Maybe she should ask Mabel to read her manuscript. She trusted her friend to be fair and honest. What would she think about the gunslinger? Tate suspected that Mabel would root for the unpredictable, compelling gunslinger over the boring lawman. Tate smiled, wishing she could've known her elderly friend when she'd been young and in love with her warrior husband.

"Tate? Are you all right?"

"What? I'm fine." Then she realized that as she thought about her own book, she'd stopped reading.

"I'm sorry, Mabel. I got distracted."

But her friend's eyes narrowed and then came into sharp focus. "Okay, what's that young man done now?"

"What young man?" Tate asked, but they both knew she was just buying time.

"Hunter Fitzsimon, unless you have more than one handsome man staying with you."

"He's not staying with me!" Tate protested, although she could feel her face heating up.

It wasn't a lie, after all. He was renting her apartment, not living with her. The one time they'd crossed the line between tenant and landlord, they'd been in his place, not hers.

"You know what I meant. Now what has you upset?"

The temptation to confess it all to Mabel was riding her hard. Even if Sandra had stuck around, she was the last person Tate would trust to help her with matters of the heart. Mabel, on the other hand, was the perfect mix of pragmatic and romantic to understand what was going on in Tate's head.

But not now. Perhaps tomorrow, if Mabel was feeling more like her old self.

"Hunter's fine. He's out with some friends." Tate made a show of checking to see where she'd left off reading.

"You're upset with him."

It wasn't a question, but Tate answered anyway. "He confuses me."

"And that's a bad thing? It takes longer than a few days to get to know anybody very well. Throw in a bunch of hormones, and things get even more complicated."

"It's not like that, Mabel." At least not anymore from the way he was acting.

"Now, young lady, which one of us are you trying to convince with that bunch of malarkey? You've been acting different since the moment you laid eyes on him. Not only that, but he's been looking back."

He'd done a lot more than just look at her, but Tate wasn't about to admit that to a bedridden elderly woman.

It wouldn't hurt to share a bit, though. "I've never met anyone like Hunter before. He's never said what he does for a living or how long he plans to stay. That same man who came by before is back, with three more just like him."

"Do you think they are brothers or cousins?"

Tate stared at the book in her lap, as if the answers to all of her questions would magically appear on the printed page.

"No, they're not related, at least not all of them," she added, thinking of Barak and Larem. "There's just a sameness about them, like they've all had the same training or played the same sport or something."

Mabel nodded, as if Tate had confirmed her suspicions about Hunter. "I haven't seen these other gentlemen, but I would guess what you're sensing is that they've served together."

"You mean in the military?"

She thought about that horrible injury to Hunter's leg. Had he been hurt in the war? Her heart hurt over the prospect. It would also would explain the two episodes of sudden violence. Post-traumatic stress disorder had been in the headlines recently. Hadn't outbursts of anger been one of the common symptoms?

Mabel was speaking again. "The military is definitely a possibility, but it could've been some kind of police work or homeland security or even a fire department," Mabel said. "All of those careers tend to have similar effects on those involved." Her smile was wistful. "My Tommy and his friends were like that, too. Even though

exhausted themselves with some incredibly acrobatic maneuvers, Tate was ready for a long nap herself. She closed the book and stood up.

"I need to get home so I can finish cleaning the shop and get things set up for tomorrow. If you need anything, though, don't be a martyr. Call me and I'll come running." She leaned down and kissed Mabel on the cheek before removing the extra pillows so she could lay back down and sleep.

"Thank you for visiting, Tate." Mabel's smile was a bit wicked. "And I appreciate your reading to us. It brought back some fond memories."

"T.M.I., Mabel! Way too much information!" Tate laughed, though, as she left the room. Her friend was definitely on the mend.

Out in the living room, the twins had turned the television back up to its usual level now that the dramatic reading was over.

"Bye, ladies. I'll see you tomorrow."

When Tate returned home, she noticed D.J.'s car was gone, as was Hunter's truck. Not her business, she reminded herself. At least she'd have some peace and quiet while she gave the shop a quick touch-up. When the floor was swept and the sugar bowls filled, she'd throw a couple of batches of cookies in the oven and measure out the ingredients for the scones she'd make in the morning. She'd keep an eye out for Hunter, of course, not that she was worried about him.

With everything that had happened, it seemed like

her mother had been gone for days rather than a matter of hours. She didn't want to risk calling Sandra until she knew what had happened to result in her leaving. It never paid to deal with Sandra without having all the facts first. Her mother had a real talent for twisting everything to fit her own selfish take on things. That was the only reason Tate wanted to talk to Hunter.

Yeah, right. She picked up the broom and went after the crumbs under the tables with a great deal of enthusiasm. Just because she and Hunter had had sex—granted, it had been red hot, brain-melting sex—that didn't mean that she had any claim on him or wanted one. She knew that.

Once she finished sweeping, Tate decided the window on the garage side of the shop needed cleaning. There were definitely fingerprints on the glass that had to come off. She'd get around to the other windows tomorrow or the next day. Granted, a side benefit of washing that particular stretch of glass was that it afforded her a perfect view of the garage and therefore Hunter's apartment.

God, she had it bad.

Hunter liked the salty tang in the air. On the way into town they'd spotted a small park overlooking the Sound and had decided to eat dinner there. Both men were new to the Pacific Northwest and still felt a bit like tourists when it came to soaking in the beauty of the Cascades to the east and the islands and Puget Sound to the west. Besides, staring at the landscape gave Hunter an excuse not to talk for a while.

Most people felt it necessary to fill a lull in conversation with meaningless chatter, but Hunter's dinner companion seemed at ease in silence. Maybe it was just Larem's demeanor, or maybe he knew Hunter wasn't comfortable sharing tempura with a Kalith warrior yet.

"I hate to admit it, but Devlin was right about you," Hunter said, breaking the silence.

Larem had been about to take a bite of rice, but Hunter's comment made him drop it on the table. Both men ignored the mess.

Larem set his chopsticks aside and took a long drink of his iced tea before responding. "Most of the time Devlin does his best to ignore me. I suspect I'm a problem he doesn't know how to solve. I can't imagine that he had much good to say."

Hunter frowned. "Actually, when I first landed in his office, I made a comment, which I won't repeat here, that set him off big time. He specifically mentioned you, and Barak and his sister. Something about you being considered friends and allies and that you were different from those we cross swords with on a regular basis."

That clearly surprised Larem. "I knew he tolerated us, but I've always assumed it was because circumstances gave him no choice."

"That might be true," Hunter said with a smile. "But he said he'd throw my worthless carcass on the first plane back to Missouri if I couldn't adjust to the way things are out here."

Pale gray eyes studied Hunter for several seconds. "So, can you adjust?"

"I guess we'll see, won't we?" He picked up his chopsticks and began eating again.

"I guess we will." Larem laughed softly before adding, "But do me a favor?"

"What's that?"

"If you decide you can't adjust, give me a chance to draw my sword before you attack. I find it undignified to defend myself with words when my enemy has a blade." Not that Larem seemed all that worried about the possibility.

"Fair enough," Hunter told him. "Although if my Cardinals ever face your Mariners in the post-season, all bets are off."

Larem nodded gravely. "I stand forewarned."

"We'd better finish up here and get into position. I want to be ready if company comes calling tonight."

He'd been dreading another night on the hillside, but with Larem close by, he wouldn't feel quite so isolated. And if that wasn't an odd turn of events, he didn't know what was.

"Mr. Black, I'm afraid our usual trip north has to be postponed for another few days. I regret the short notice and any inconvenience it may cause you."

Joe doubted that Mr. White gave a rip how he felt about anything. As far as Joe could tell, there were only two things his employer cared about: money and himself.

"That's all right, sir," Joe lied. "I can use the time." To get rip-roaring drunk, but he knew better than to share that part.

Mr. White sounded disgusted. "As you well know, Mr. Black, circumstances can change in an instant. I would hate to call upon your services only to find out that you were—*incapacitated.*"

Joe stared at his phone. The man on the other end was too damned spooky. It was like he had a direct line to Joe's most secret thoughts. "Not a problem, sir. I might have a beer or two with friends over a friendly game of pool, but I quit drinking myself stupid years ago."

"You may lie to yourself all you like, but don't presume to lie to me, Mr. Black. I'll be in touch."

As usual, the line went dead before Joe could respond. God, he really hated that man. On the other hand, he had the next few nights off. He'd head for the local watering hole and nurse a beer while checking out the singles scene. Who knows, maybe he'd get lucky. A warm and willing woman beat a six-pack of beer hands down. And better yet, no hangover.

Feeling much better about life in general, Joe headed home to clean up. Would putting fresh sheets on his bed jinx him? Either way, it was a risk he was willing to take.

Hunter plunked down at his usual table in the tea shop. It had been several days since he'd stopped in. He and Larem had spent three of the last four nights on that godforsaken bluff with nothing to show for it but sore asses from sitting on the rocky ground. D.J. and Barak had finally showed up last evening with Penn Sebastian in tow, apologizing for the delay but not bothering to offer excuses. Shit happened—they already knew that.

But at least Penn and Barak had covered lookout duty last night. They planned on getting a hotel room to sleep during the daylight hours before returning to the bluff for two more nights. Hunter's own Kalith houseguest had ridden back to Seattle with D.J. As Larem had climbed into D.J.'s car, he'd promised to return when Penn and Barak were scheduled to leave, provided he could get a ride. The barrier had finally stabilized, but there was no predicting how long it would last. If the Paladins were busy staving off an invasion, Larem would be without wheels.

Funny, Hunter had grown so accustomed to Larem's dry sense of humor and soothing nature that he'd all but forgotten Larem wasn't human. It was only when he mentioned something like not being able to drive that Hunter remembered his new friend was from another world.

But right now, despite Hunter's first full night's sleep in days, he couldn't relax, and it sure as hell wasn't because Larem had waved good-bye. The cause of his unrest was a petite blonde with bright blue eyes. He'd caught the occasional glimpse of her over the past few days, but he'd kept his distance.

What pissed him off was that Tate had made a point of ignoring him, too. He'd caught himself preparing to wave if she'd looked in his direction, only she never had. He no longer sensed her watching him when he mowed her lawn. Nor had Tate's name come up when he'd stopped by to make sure that Mabel was feeling better and to see if the Auntie Ms needed anything from town.

Despite his vow to put some distance between himself and Tate, he hadn't realized how much it would bother him to sever the connection completely.. Was she all right? Had she heard from Sandra again? When he'd woken up that morning, it had occurred to him that he hadn't finished telling her what had transpired between him and her mother.

So that was his excuse for coming into the tea shop. Unfortunately, despite the nice weather, it looked like everyone within ten miles had all come at once. Tate was efficient, but she was looking a bit overwhelmed. Should he offer her a helping hand?

A low rumble caught his attention. A tour bus pulled up outside and women were already streaming off it, heading straight for the shop. He got up to warn Tate, who had just carried a tray full of dirty cups and saucers into the kitchen.

She looked up from loading the dishwasher, clearly not happy he'd invaded her domain.

"I was going to get to you."

Maybe when hell froze over, but they'd have that discussion later.

"I thought you'd want to know that you have a busload of customers on their way into the shop." The bells above started chiming like crazy, as if to confirm his tale.

Tate looked a bit shell-shocked. "A whole *busload*? Where am I going to put them all?"

"That's your problem. I'm here to do dishes and fill pots of hot water." He made shooing motions with his hands. "Go. I'll take care of this."

She wiped her hands on a towel. "Okay, if you're sure."

"I'm sure. I'd ferry the clean stuff out, but I don't have a health certificate."

"God, you're right. Okay, I'll go take orders. If you'll fill the pots, I'll add the tea. And when you get a second, there are more pastries in the freezer. If you'll set them on the counter, I'll defrost them when I come back with the first set of orders."

"Will do."

It didn't take long for the two of them to fall into a rhythm. He kept the dishwasher running and a line of pots ready to fill as she needed them. When things finally slowed down, he was surprised to see that two hours had flown by. The noise coming from the shop had lessened considerably, a good sign that the rush was over.

He leaned against the counter as he counted down the seconds until the dishwasher shut off again. Once he emptied it, he'd head home before his leg gave out. In case Tate didn't return before he left, he scribbled her a note. They'd reestablished some of their previous rapport, and he didn't want to blow it by letting her think he was avoiding her. Any information he had to give her about her mother had waited this long. Surely it could wait until he was able to stand without pain.

A few minutes later he made his way across the yard toward the garage. He was leaning heavily on his cane and having serious doubts that he'd make it up the steps. God, he hated this! How was he ever going to get his life back if he couldn't manage a few steps without crawling?

"Hey, Hunter!" a familiar voice called out.

He froze midstep, wishing like hell he could just ignore Penn Sebastian's greeting and continue on alone. That wasn't going to happen, though. Carefully schooling his expression, he turned to face them.

"Penn. Barak."

Barak nodded in what Hunter was coming to realize was his typical quiet, reserved way. Penn was only slightly more outgoing.

"We thought we'd stop by and see if you wanted to have dinner." Penn shot his future brother-in-law a dark look. "And since it's my turn to pick, we're going somewhere that serves big, bloody steaks."

He looked to Hunter for sympathy. "Last night we ate vegetarian lasagna and salad. The closest thing they had to *real* food were the anchovies in the salad. And tough guy here even picked those out."

Barak took the teasing with his usual equanimity. "How about the night before? You ate fish and chips, and I had to live on slaw."

When it became obvious that the squabble would continue indefinitely, Hunter jumped in. "Why don't we call out for pizza? I've got plenty of beer."

"Perfect," Penn agreed. "You and I can get a couple of extra larges with the works, and the alien here can have a veggie."

"Alien? What planet are you from?"

All three men spun in unison to face Tate. How the heck had she managed to sneak up on three highly trained warriors without any of them noticing?

Barak smiled warmly. "Tate, I don't believe you've met my fiancée's idiot brother. Penn Sebastian, this is Hunter's landlady, Tate Justice."

The Paladin shot Barak an offended look before

holding his hand out to Tate. "Nice to meet you, Tate. I'm sorry that you have to put up with the likes of D.J. and Barak. Hunter and Larem are okay, but they too lack my charm."

Tate arched an eyebrow. "Don't forget your humility."

Hunter had to laugh. She always gave as good as she got, and he liked that about her. Despite his belief that it was best they limit the time they spent together, maybe it was okay as long as they had a buffer to keep things from getting out of hand. Besides, she had to be exhausted.

"Look, we've decided to get pizza for dinner. Would you like to add one to the order?"

"Actually, that's why I followed you. I was going to drive into town to pick up something to eat, because I couldn't face the thought of cooking tonight."

"What's your pleasure?" Penn asked.

Something in his voice made it clear that he was talking about more than her favorite toppings. Hunter's temper instantly flared. Now was not the time to lose control, not with Tate standing there. Not again.

"I know what she likes," he announced, pinning Penn with a dark look. "I'll call in the order."

When Barak saw Tate roll her eyes, he offered her a smile. "Shall we go upstairs and leave these two to finish pounding on their chests?"

She giggled. "Let's. I know the pizza number by heart. The food should get here by the time they're done beating each other bloody."

She swept past Penn and Hunter, patting each of them on the cheek as she passed. Barak smirked as he followed her up the stairs. When Hunter realized Penn's eyes were focused on the tight fit of Tate's jeans, he elbowed the Paladin.

"Knock it off," he growled.

"Oops, sorry." Penn's grin was unapologetic. "I take it you've got dibs on her."

"What I have on her is none of your business." God, could he have worded that any worse?

Penn laughed and started up the stairs, allowing Hunter to follow at his own speed. The brief delay in hashing out their plans for dinner had given him time to rest his leg. He still wasn't going to win any races, but at least he'd been spared the embarrassment of asking for help.

He could hear Tate's soft voice mixed in with the deeper male ones. What did she think of Barak? Did his unusual coloring mean anything to her? Not that he was worried about any uncomfortable questions she might ask the Kalith warrior or Penn. Like all Paladins, Penn was a practiced liar when it came to what he did for a living or where he disappeared to when duty called. Barak had secrets of his own to protect, and Hunter was sure the man had a plausible cover story.

She hadn't asked Hunter himself much about his own past, maybe because she knew he was recovering from an injury. He dreaded the day she did start asking questions, though; he'd really hate lying to her.

But the bottom line was that he'd do it anyway.

Chapter 12

Tate noticed that Hunter had become a night owl, their paths rarely having crossed over the past week. His friends came and went, sometimes stopping in her shop to say hello, sometimes not. Barak, especially, seemed intent on trying every tea she offered, but Hunter rarely came with him.

It was tempting to pump Hunter's friends for information, but she refrained. She suspected they were as closemouthed in their own way as he was. At least when he was with them, he was friendlier than he had been when he'd first arrived.

Good for him, but she couldn't help but wish that she was the one he'd turned to for companionship—of all kinds. Depending on her mood, she ran the full gamut of emotions about their one bout of hot sex. On a good day, she accepted it for what it was—a fun romp between two consenting adults. On a downswing, she had to wonder if she'd misread his response to the whole episode.

Then there was today, when she wanted to track him down and demand answers to all of her questions. Where had he come from? How had he gotten hurt? What did he do for a living? How long was he going to stay? And, finally, how dare he ignore her after everything they'd been through, in bed and out?

It didn't help that her mother had finally called. Evidently Sandra had gone crawling back to Edwin. If she was telling the truth, they were working hard to fix what was broken in their relationship. According to Sandra, Edwin was a nice man who wanted a wife. She, on the other hand, wasn't sure she was cut out to stay with one man for the long haul. However, she'd promised Edwin she'd try. What mattered was that they were still together. It was a start.

If Tate wasn't mistaken, her mother had actually sounded happy and hopeful. The big shocker was that Sandra was applying for jobs and hadn't even hinted once that she needed Tate to send money. Even if miracles could happen and Sandra was finally growing up, the call had left Tate unsettled.

If her mother could face her demons, Tate should face hers, even if her particular demon didn't want to talk. Maybe he was afraid she'd read more into that one afternoon than he was ready for, but how was she supposed to know what he was thinking if he wouldn't even talk to her?

For once, none of his buddies were around. Earlier, she'd braced herself for a confrontation and marched over to his apartment to have a talk, only to find him gone. So now she was waiting and watching for him to return.

The hours dragged by as she watched late-night television, trying to stay awake. Every fifteen minutes she looked out the window to see if the lights had come on in his apartment. So far, they remained depressingly dark.

Thirty more minutes and then she'd turn in. But she'd set her alarm for earlier than normal to give herself time to go pound on his door at the crack of dawn. If he was going to cost her sleep like this, then she would return the favor.

She checked all three of her vantage points. The first one gave her a view of the road. After checking both directions and seeing no sign of Hunter, she moved to look out toward the garage. No lights and no Hunter climbing the steps.

That left the woods out back, not that she could see much past the first few trees. No Hunter. No suspicious shadows. No luck. She plopped back down in her chair and tried to concentrate on the movie. In fifteen more minutes, she'd make the rounds again.

Why was it so important for her to see him tonight? The honest answer was she didn't know. There was just something driving her to make sure he was all right. Sure, she'd like to know if he'd been avoiding her, but it was more than that.

She checked the clock. Only twelve more minutes to go. She hoped he was okay.

Nights perched on the rocky hillside were taking a toll on Hunter's ass, not to mention his leg. He wasn't even supposed to be on duty, but D.J. had called to say they were running late, and he'd asked Hunter to fill in. An hour later, he'd called again to say they'd been further delayed. Basically, Hunter should expect them when he saw them.

Because Hunter hadn't planned to be there so long, he hadn't brought all of his usual gear with him. Lately, he'd actually considered bringing down a folding lawn chair but had decided against it. He couldn't guard the place 24/7 and didn't want to risk anyone stumbling across his chosen spot. He supposed he could always take the chair back and forth each night, but that was a pain, too. Besides, it would only increase the risk of Tate getting too curious about what he was up to every night.

She'd gone back to watching him. Even from a distance he could feel the weight of her gaze and all the questions swirling around in that busy brain of hers. Barak had reported back to him that she'd been friendly when he'd stopped in to try another one of her teas, but she hadn't pressed him for information of any kind, much less about Hunter.

They all thought it was a bit weird that she wasn't more suspicious of three Paladins and two Kalith warriors, even if she didn't know them by those descriptions. He still wondered if he'd been mistaken about the odd look she'd given Barak and Larem that first day. He'd been too fractured at the time to trust his own perceptions of the events, but he was certain there had been something surprising about her reaction.

But both Larem and Barak had been around off and on since that day, and she'd treated them both with the same friendly courtesy she did everyone else. Maybe

Hunter should drop in for tea tomorrow and see if he could work the conversation around to them.

He rolled his shoulders and slowly stretched his leg before starting back up the bluff. He checked his watch. When D.J. and company finally did show up, they could finish out the night, but he'd had enough. Besides, based on their enemies' previous arrivals, if they were going to come calling, they'd have done so by now. If Penn or one of the Kalith warriors had been there with him, they could've taken turns dozing. He could only do so much alone.

Leaning on his cane, he stood up. On the whole, his leg had continued to improve, but these cool, damp nights near the water didn't help it much. It always took him a few steps before he could trust it would support his weight.

He gathered up his empty cans and sandwich wrappers and stuck them in his pack. He slung it over his shoulder and started up the trail, taking his time to enjoy the night sounds and the distant whisper of the waves washing up on the beach below. His night vision enabled him to walk through the darkness without tripping over rocks and the occasional root jutting up in the path ahead.

It wasn't until after he'd covered half the distance up the hillside that he realized he wasn't alone. Two men were headed directly for him, probably both humans, since they carried flashlights. Their voices drifted toward him, but the distance was too great for him to understand much. One made mention of a flat tire, his voice hot with anger. The other made placating noises but mumbled too much for Hunter to decipher his reply.

If Hunter hid in the trees along the trail, maybe he could learn something that would help Devlin and company track the bastards back to their lair. Moving slowly so as not to draw their attention, he started toward the deeper shadows in a thick cluster of trees.

But as he took a step to his left, a familiar sound coming from right behind him made his blood freeze. The rasp of cold steel sliding out of its sheath had him spinning around to face the closer threat. A Kalith warrior headed straight toward him, his blade up and the promise of death in his pale eyes.

Hunter needed to buy enough time to draw his own sword out of the cane, so he swung his pack at the charging Other. The straps tangled on the Other's blade, jerking the canvas bag from Hunter's grasp and at the same time deflecting the blow meant to separate his head from his neck.

He retreated back into the trees to make it harder for the bastard to get off a clean swing. He could still do Hunter considerable harm, but the limited space would reduce how much power the Kalith could put into his attack.

Hunter pushed the button on his cane and yanked the blade clear of its ebony sheath. He considered using the wooden casing as a club but figured it would shatter the first time it blocked an attack. Besides, he didn't want to be the one to tell Jarvis he'd fucked up his family heirloom beyond repair.

He must be nuts to be worrying about such a stupid thing right then! He had bigger problems, like figuring out where the two humans had gone. They might not have swords, but they probably did have guns. One way or the other, he was outnumbered. At best, he could hope to take as many of the three down with him as he could.

Now that he was properly armed, he smiled at the circling Kalith. "Okay, you bastard, bring it on."

There was no way for Hunter to keep track of the humans, not while he was facing one of the best swordsmen he'd ever come across. The Others he usually faced were out of their minds in battle lust, making them desperate and careless. This guy was coldly calculating in his attacks, doing his best to back Hunter into a thicket, which would leave him no room to maneuver. Hunter charged forward, ducking to miss another well-placed swing of his enemy's sword.

Or at least he tried to duck. He'd had enough sword cuts over his career to know that this one would be painful and bloody but not fatal. Too bad the fight didn't end there. Instead, the coppery scent of Hunter's blood scented the night air, driving his opponent to try even harder to finish him off.

But that wasn't going to happen, even if Hunter had to turn tail and run. He'd already died too many times at the hands of this Kalith's buddies. Ignoring the pain in his arm and the cramping in his weak leg, he watched for an opening, figuring he'd only get one good shot at taking this guy out before his human friends showed up to join the party.

He feinted forward, then dropped back just as quickly, which made the Kalith lunge right at him. Perfect. Hunter swung his narrow blade out and then up, right into the Kalith's side. The point sliced through clothing and flesh with equal ease, sending the Kalith stumbling backward to the ground.

Hunter yanked his blade free of his enemy's gut. As he prepared to finish the job, a gunshot rang out through the night. The impact knocked Hunter sideways over the edge of the trail, sending him bouncing down the hillside.

He wanted to scream, and God knows, he *needed* to scream. But between the bullet hole in his side and the wind being knocked out of him, all he could do was whimper. The quiet of the woods slowly settled around him as he prayed for the darkness to ease his pain and hide him from his enemies.

Hushed voices came closer, and then faded away. What were they saying? The calmer one was adamant about getting the Kalith back to the cave and shoving him back to the other side, where his own people could stitch him up. That made sense: they wouldn't risk a human doctor discovering the anomalies in the Other's blood, which would mark him as anything but human.

The crazed one wanted to charge down the hillside, looking for Hunter. They probably wouldn't give him a vote in their final decision, but Hunter really preferred that they take care of their friend. He even started to raise his hand to get them to call on him before he realized what a stupid move that would be.

God, what was wrong with him? He couldn't remember if blood loss always made him this giddy, but he definitely wasn't firing on all cylinders at the moment. He was cold, he hurt, and he wasn't sure he could hold off sliding into oblivion for much longer. Maybe he'd stave off the darkness if he thought about something other than his pain and his enemies. Tate. Yeah, he could think about her.

Those blue eyes and how they'd looked as he'd made love to her, driving them both hard toward the finish line. How her soft body cushioned his much bigger, harder one. How sweet she'd tasted wherever he'd kissed her. Oh, yeah, that was better. Lots of details came to mind. How her breasts had fit his hands perfectly and her body had fisted his cock like a warm glove. God, he wished he'd told her how good it had been for him.

The darkness nipped at the edges of his mind again, and this time there was no stopping it. If he was going to die again, at least his mind was in a better place. His last thought was that he'd really like to live long enough to make love to Tate Justice again.

The thirty-minute deadline had come and gone over an hour ago, and Tate still couldn't relax enough to go to sleep. What was wrong with her? If Hunter wanted to stay gone all night long, it was none of her business. He was a grown man and could take care of himself.

But something kept drawing her back to the window, to check one last time to see if he'd made it home safely. His truck was parked right where it belonged, but it had been there the whole time. Where had he gone on foot?

He was down on the trail again. He had to be. The idiot, hadn't she warned him how dangerous it was once the sun set? But big macho man that he was, he thought he was immune to a simple trip and fall that could knock him senseless or break his neck. What he chose to do, stupid or not, wasn't her problem, she reminded herself for the millionth time.

Which, of course, was why she'd put her jeans and shirt back on before heading out the back door, a flashlight in her hand and her cell phone in her pocket. She'd march down to the beach to find out one way or the other if her renter had lost what few marbles God gave men to play with. Once she had Hunter in her sights, she planned on ripping into him but good. He was long overdue for a lecture on common sense and courtesy.

That is, if he was all right when she found him. If he wasn't, she'd deal with his injuries and *then* lecture him on common sense. Either way, she was going to get it through his thick skull that he shouldn't take unnecessary risks. She understood that it was hard for him to be inside once the sun went down. But he could find a safer place to outpace his demons than a rough trail that wound through the woods and down a steep bluff.

She stopped when she got to the porch. Maybe she should check his apartment first in case he'd slipped past her vigil. It wasn't as if she'd been watching for him every minute. She sprinted across the grass and up the steps. As she raised her hand to rap on the door, she was reminded of the last time she'd appeared at his door unexpectedly.

And look where that had gotten her—on her back in his bed. Well, that wasn't going to happen tonight. She was here on a rescue mission, and that was all. But the images of that afternoon left her breasts feeling heavy and a heated ache between her legs.

Ignoring her body's hunger for his, she pounded on the door again. When there was no sign of life inside the apartment, she tried the knob and found it unlocked. Feeling guilty for invading Hunter's privacy, she ventured inside.

"Hunter? Are you here?"

She flipped the switch next to the door and blinked at the glaring brightness. From where she stood, she could see that both the bathroom and the living room were empty. That left one more place to check. The memories of the last time she'd crossed the threshold of his bedroom had her hesitating to push the door open, but finally she did.

The bed was rumpled, as if he'd made a halfhearted effort to make it, but it was definitely unoccupied. Feeling an odd mixture of disappointment and relief, she backed out into the living room. Okay, she'd eliminated one possibility. That left the beach.

She turned off the light on her way outside and pulled the door closed. Rather than immediately heading down the steps, she waited for her eyes to readjust to the darkness. From where she stood, she could see most of her backyard, as well as the road that ran along the front of her property. She thought she heard the low rumble of a powerful engine in the distance.

She leaned forward, as if those couple of inches would help her hear better. Yes, there was definitely some kind of vehicle at the far end of the road, but it was too distant for her to make out any details. Was that same truck back? There was no way to know for sure, but the mere possibility ramped up the sense of urgency she'd been battling all night.

Hunter was in trouble, though how she knew that she had no idea. She just did. Within seconds she pounded down the steps and took off for the woods. She had to find him. Inside the tree line she slowed down, knowing she wouldn't be any good to him if she didn't keep her head.

She kept her light focused on the ground just ahead of her feet, determined not to make the same mistakes she made last time. Even if Hunter was lurking in those same shadows, that would be all right. At least she'd know he was okay, and they could finish what they'd started up against that big tree. But no, she soon passed the spot where Hunter had grabbed her that first time, and there was still no sign of him.

As she went farther along the path, she began sweeping the flashlight in a broad arc, looking for a sign that someone had recently passed through. So far, nothing, but rather than finding it reassuring, her pulse was doing a salsa.

As her light made a return sweep, it caught the edge of something that looked out of place. She slowed down and repeated the same arc, this time slower. There, on the left. Keeping the flashlight focused on the scrap of red poking out from under a bush, she hurried forward.

It was a backpack, but there was nothing that identified it as Hunter's. One of the straps had been sliced in half, and there was a long gash along one side, the kind made by a sharp blade. Her stomach cramped tight with fear. Now was the time for panic. Focusing on the ground, she looked around for any other evidence. She muttered a heartfelt curse when she spotted a familiar-looking black tube and bent down to pick it up.

Although it was missing its ivory handle, she knew she was looking at Hunter's cane. How had the wolf's head broken off without damaging the wood? More questions and damn few answers.

She studied the ground, spotting a few tracks that looked fresh, but they told her nothing. Having gleaned what little she could from the ground, she studied the bushes and undergrowth around the area. Several limbs were bent and a few were broken off entirely, as if there'd been a fight.

Should she start calling Hunter's name? No, only as a last resort. Whoever had attacked him—if that's even what had happened—could still be lurking in the area. She was taking enough of a risk just using her flashlight.

As if to underscore the need for caution, she heard what sounded like a moan. She froze. Closing her eyes, she concentrated on trying to distinguish that same soft noise from the normal murmurings of the night.

There it was again. Cautiously, she approached the edge of the trail where it dropped off sharply. One of the low bushes was torn out by the roots, and another one showed definite signs of having been squashed flat. If Hunter had veered off the path there, it hadn't been of his own volition, that was certain.

She had to find out for sure. If he was down there, he could be badly hurt—or worse. The going quickly got dicey, leaving her no option but to tuck her flashlight in the waistband of her jeans to free up both hands. Grabbing onto saplings and low branches, she made her way down the first ten feet before stopping again. Leaning against the stout trunk of a cedar tree, she pulled out the flashlight to take another look around.

Oh, dear God! Even with the dim light and dark shadows, she knew that was no downed tree she was looking at. It took all the willpower she could muster not to go tearing down the hillside to reach Hunter. If she was going to be of any help to him, she had to approach cautiously.

He stirred slightly and moaned. He was obviously hurt, but definitely alive.

"Take it easy, Hunter. I'm coming," she called out softly, pitching her voice so that it would reach him but not echo through the woods.

Instead of calming him, her words had him thrashing around and muttering about swords and killers and guns. Was he experiencing another flashback, or trying to warn her? It didn't matter; she wouldn't abandon him. Once she knew how badly hurt he was, she would call for help.

She sat down and scooted down the hill on the seat of her pants, exchanging a bit of dignity for safety. When she reached Hunter's side, she shifted her position to kneel beside him. He'd lapsed back into a silence more worrisome than his earlier agitation.

"Hunter, I'm here. Are you okay?"

He clearly wasn't. Time to call in the cavalry. But when she flipped open her phone, she groaned. No reception. She'd have to administer rudimentary first aid, and then climb back up to where she might be able to call out.

Holding the flashlight in one hand, she started at his head and worked her way down his powerful body, checking for injuries. She ignored the scrapes he'd collected on his slide down the hill, knowing they'd be painful but not life threatening. The deep gash on his arm was a different matter.

She pulled off her flannel shirt to use as a bandage. The fabric proved to be too strong to rip into strips with just her hands. Hunter seemed the type to carry a pocketknife, but before she could search his pockets, she saw what he had clasped in his other hand. Was that a blade of some kind? She reached across his chest to yank it from his hand.

She recognized the wolf's head immediately and was surprised at how long the actual blade was when she finally worked it out from under Hunter. What was he doing with a sword? Even as she started cutting into the flannel, she put two and two together. The black tube was the sheath for the sword, allowing Hunter to carry a lethal weapon in plain sight. The question was why he felt the need, but she'd have to wait until later to demand an answer.

"I'm sorry if this hurts, but I've got to stop the bleeding," she explained as she wrapped his arm, although he gave no sign of hearing her. The cloth was already soaked through by the time she tied the knot, so she wrapped one of the shirtsleeves around his arm, hoping to slow the bleeding until the medics could get to him.

"I'm going to check the rest of you for injuries,

Hunter. You look pretty banged up, but I think most of it is from falling down this hillside."

She kept up a one-sided conversation as she searched for other injuries. His other arm seemed sound, and his legs were both straight, with no obvious breaks or open wounds. Then she pulled up his dark T-shirt, realizing for the first time that all the blood wasn't from the cut on his arm. She'd never seen a bullet hole up close before, but she was looking at one now.

"This is going to hurt, but I'll be as gentle as I can."

She braced herself for the worst and rolled Hunter toward her to check for an exit wound. Was it a good thing that she found one? How the heck was she supposed to know something like that? They sure didn't cover that topic in the first-aid course she'd taken. But a bleeding wound was a bleeding wound, regardless of the cause. She hacked up some more of her shirt to make a couple of thick pads. Now, to hold them in place. The question was how. His belt might work. She unbuckled it and yanked with all her strength to pull it free from the loops in his jeans.

That was the easy part. It was much harder to work it under him and cinch it down over the makeshift bandage. There wasn't any more to be done until she got some help, although she hated to leave him alone even that long. Would his cell phone work when hers hadn't? It was worth a shot.

"I'm going to try your phone, because my cheap service doesn't do well down here."

She patted down his pockets, hoping he hadn't lost the phone or broken it in the fall. Luck was with them.

The reception wasn't great, but she should be able to get a call through to 911.

"Hang in there, Hunter. I know it feels like we're out in the middle of nowhere, but the fire department and the aid car will be here in no time."

And the police as well, but she didn't say so. She hoped Hunter had a good explanation about how he'd come to get shot and stabbed, not to mention why his own sword was covered in blood. At least the inquisition couldn't start until he was stabilized and conscious.

"Okay, I'm dialing. Help's on the way."

"Don't call." Hunter's voice was rough and weak; there was no mistaking the steel behind his demand.

Good, he was awake, but he still needed help. "Sorry, but I can't get you back up the hill by myself. I have to call for help."

Before she could enter the second number, Hunter's hand clamped down on her wrist hard enough to bruise. The sudden motion startled her into dropping the phone. As she scrambled to pick it up, she tried to tug her arm free of his grasp.

"Hunter, let go of me." Her voice cracked with fear. "Even if I could get you up on your feet, you're bleeding too badly to make it back to the house."

"I'll be fine. No calls. No police." His eyes burned with intensity, giving his words the strength his voice lacked.

She shivered. "You're scaring me, Hunter."

"Sorry."

He closed his eyes and waited for the world to quit spinning. She was right; they needed help, just not the local authorities. The question was, who? His list of possibilities was short. Then there was the problem of getting Tate to go along with his choice. Hoping it would help convince her that he wasn't crazy, he released her arm. Good. She stayed next to him rather than bolting for cover.

"D.J. is seven on my speed dial. Call him." He drew a ragged breath, the pain from his arm and his side making it hard to concentrate.

"What good's he going to do? Especially if he's any distance away?" Despite the doubt in her voice, she was already flipping the phone open.

"Tell him what happened. He'll know what to do."

She nodded as she waited for D.J. to pick up on the other end. Bright woman that she was, she put the call on the speaker phone so Hunter could hear and be heard.

"Yo, Hunter. What's up?" The Paladin sounded like his usual carefree self.

Hunter felt Tate brace herself. "D.J., this is Tate. Hunter's been shot and stabbed. He needs help but won't let me call nine-one-one. I'm going to anyway."

When D.J. spoke again, he was all business. "No, don't. He's right, Tate. That would only put him in more danger. Where are you now?"

"We're about halfway down the trail to the beach that starts at the back of my yard, right below that sharp switchback. He fell down the hillside, so we're off the trail completely."

"Are the bastards that did it still around?"

Tate's head whipped around, as if that thought hadn't occurred to her. "No, at least I don't think so. I heard a truck leave right before I came looking for him."

D.J.'s voice sounded more relaxed. "Okay, that's good. Keep an eye out, though. Can Hunter walk?"

"I don't think so. He's bleeding from a bad cut on his arm and a bullet wound on his side." Her voice grew calmer the longer she talked.

"What have you done for him?"

"I cut up my shirt with his sword and used it for bandages."

That last remark set off a string of curses that had Hunter wincing. This was a clusterfuck of monumental proportions, and experience told him it was going to get worse as the cold chill of death crawled up his extremities.

D.J. gave them their marching orders. "Okay, Tate, here's what you do. Stay with him. I'm just pulling up your driveway, so I'll be there with reinforcements in a matter of minutes. Stay put and we'll come get him. Got that?"

She shook her head, as though D.J. could see through the phone. "He's hurt too badly to wait much longer. The authorities can transport him to the hospital for treatment." Her voice dropped to a low whisper. "Oh, God, D.J., he's lost so much blood."

D.J.'s voice softened. "Look, Tate, I know it looks bad, and maybe it is. But if he's awake and talking, he'll be fine. The last thing Hunter wants or needs is to end up in a civilian hospital."

"Civilian? Are you telling me that you two are in the military?"

Skepticism dripped from every word as she stared at the bloodstained sword lying on the ground beside him. Hunter didn't blame her one bit, but all that mattered was that she did as D.J. asked.

"I'll give you ten minutes. Any longer than that, or if he gets worse, I'll do whatever it takes to get him the help he needs. Got *that*?"

D.J. laughed. "Yes, ma'am. Call me if anything changes."

"I will." She closed the phone.

"Thanks, Tate," Hunter whispered.

He tried to touch her hand, hoping to offer her a bit of comfort, but he couldn't move his arm. Poor Tate—while he knew his body would eventually start working its special healing mojo, she didn't. As far as she knew, he was an ordinary man, one who could die and stay that way.

Tate moved away and avoided looking at him, focusing all of her attention on the trail above, as if she could make D.J. appear faster through sheer willpower. She sat with her arms wrapped around her waist, looking so alone and scared. Hunter hated knowing that her fear was because of him. A situation like this was exactly why there could never be anything serious between them. He just hadn't expected that truth to hurt more than being both skewered and shot combined.

"Sorry you got involved in this."

He wasn't sure if he'd spoken aloud or if he'd only thought the words. Maybe it didn't matter, because if Hunter died in front of Tate, Devlin would be forced to replace him. One way or another, this could be his last night with her. He sucked in as much as air as he could and tried one more time.

"Sorry, Tate."

This time she looked directly at him, but her silence was nothing more than he deserved.

Chapter 13

Joe signaled and moved over into the fast lane, hoping to get this screwed-up night over with as fast as possible. Knowing the explosion was coming any second, he kept his eyes firmly on the road ahead and counted off the seconds until his employer finally blew his cork.

Mr. White slammed his fist down on the dashboard. "What a fucked-up mess!"

Now wasn't the time to speak up. Better to avoid drawing any attention to himself while the old bastard vented. Mr. White would get around to berating Joe eventually, but later was better than sooner. If there was a God in heaven, they'd be back in Seattle before his name reached the top of the list of things his employer was pissed off about. Unfortunately, Joe's luck ran out only seconds later.

"And what were you thinking, shooting your gun like that? We're lucky no one called the cops before we got away." By now, Mr. White's voice lost all its heat and became ice cold.

"That guy was about to kill your business partner. I was thinking that would be a bad thing." If it wasn't, that made it pretty clear how far professional loyalty would get him with his boss. At the first sign of trouble, Joe would be jettisoned just like that pale-eyed bastard had been.

"I don't pay you to think."

He was getting damned tired of the insults. "No, you pay me to drive, and you're the one who wanted me to carry a weapon. If you meant it to be just for show, you should've said so."

Silence. The adrenaline from actually pulling the trigger had left him riled up and ready to fight. Maybe he shouldn't have shot his mouth off, but at that moment he didn't much care. If he got fired, Joe would miss the money. But sometimes cold, hard cash wasn't worth the bullshit you had to put up with to earn it. Maybe he'd calm down long to apologize before the trip back to town was over, but he doubted it.

To his surprise, Mr. White blinked first. "You're right, of course, Joe."

That was the first time the man had called Joe by his real name. Somehow it didn't leave him feeling all warm and fuzzy. More like chilled to the bone and wishing he had installed an ejector in the passenger seat. He'd be using it right now and celebrating when Mr. White bounced off the highway and into a ditch. If that didn't kill him, then at least Joe would've had a head start on getting out of town.

"Do you think your friend will be all right? Or the one I shot?" It was hard to tell how badly hurt the one man had been since his weird coloring was so pale to begin with. The other one had tumbled down the hillside before Joe had had a chance to see how much damage the bullet had done. He guessed he'd know for sure when he read the morning headlines.

Mr. White shrugged, clearly not concerned. "The one you shot was most likely dead before he hit the bottom of the hill. If not, who's going to believe anything he says anyway? Especially about being stabbed with a sword."

He laughed and turned his cold eyes in Joe's direction. "As far as my associate, if he received care soon enough, we should hear from him tomorrow or the next day. If so, we'll be returning to the cave again. However, if he doesn't contact me, it may be awhile before I need you again. I'll have to wait for his replacement to make contact."

Okay, so maybe Joe wouldn't die for shooting the crazy jerk who'd pulled a sword out of nowhere when Mr. White's business associate had gone on the attack. This whole situation just kept getting weirder and weirder. Who goes around carrying a sword in the first place? Well, besides the guy they were up there to meet, that is.

Joe had tried to convince himself from the beginning that the guy was some kind of reenactor, but despite his odd clothing and insistence on wearing his sword, that was clearly not the case. Even in the dead of night it had been easy to see that the two men had known how to swing those swords and had seriously meant to kill each other.

"You're thinking too hard about things that are none of your concern, Mr. Black. Tonight's events have complicated the situation, but we'll deal with it. Wake me when we're at the drop-off."

They were only about twenty minutes out, but Joe was just as happy to let him doze off. As long as the man was sleeping, Joe could pretend he was alone and everything was under control.

Even if it wasn't.

Tate wished Hunter would say something, anything, especially if he could tell her this was all a bad dream. Not that she'd believe him. It was hard to ignore a bullet wound, not to mention a vicious cut from a sword. Then there was the pungent smell of drying blood in the air.

A bubble of confused laughter threatened to break loose. Here she was, an aspiring romance writer who loved swashbuckling heroes and had a thing for a certain badass gunslinger, yet there was nothing at all romantic about this situation. Unlike the spunky heroine in her book, Tate was scared. Terrified, in fact. It wouldn't take much to shatter her control—a loud sound, a footstep, a leaf falling from overhead.

Gunshot and sword wounds were ugly, bloody messes, even though Hunter wasn't complaining. Actually, other than that last sigh, he'd been totally silent. Oh, God, was he even breathing? She scooted closer and rested her fingertips against his throat, hoping against hope to feel a steady pulse. His skin was cold and clammy. One beat . . . two, then his chest moved slightly, enough to reassure her that he was still breathing, though it seemed awfully shallow and irregular.

Where the heck was D.J.? She checked the time. Another two minutes and she'd start dialing whether Hunter and D.J. liked it or not. Then she heard the welcome sound of rapid footsteps on the trail above. At least she hoped they were welcome. She stared up the hillside, grateful for the shadows concealing their location but also wishing she could see more clearly.

Hunter shifted next to her. He rolled slightly to his left and tried to push himself upright before she could stop him.

"Stay still or you'll start bleeding again."

Ignoring her advice, he continued to struggle to sit up, leaving her no choice but to help him. That didn't mean she had to like it.

"If you bleed to death, don't blame me."

Hunter winced in pain as he used her support to get to his feet. "Tate, unless you're the jerk who shot me or the one who stabbed me, none of this is your fault."

She moved to stand beside him so he could lean against her. "Do you know who did this to you?"

"Not by name."

Okay, she knew he was hurting, but cryptic answers weren't going to cut it. Not when she had his blood on her clothes and hands. Had the attack been directed specifically at him, or had he stumbled into the wrong place at the wrong time? She kept her voice low even though she really wanted to rip into him.

"But you did expect something like this could happen, or why else would you be carrying a sword." She felt him stiffen, warning her that he was going to choose his words very carefully.

Finally, he sagged back against a tree for support. "Tate, you have to believe that I never meant for you to get drawn into this."

Which was sort of an answer, she supposed. "Why the sword?"

His words came in stutters and starts. "A friend knew I was having . . . problems . . . from my injuries . . . like the other night in the restaurant . . . holding the wolf's head helps me focus. The cane . . . a family heirloom made in the late 1800s."

That didn't explain how Hunter had come to be stabbed or how he'd managed to draw blood with his own weapon. But right now, she was too tired to care. Once help arrived, they could take over Hunter's care. Personally, she planned on going home, jumping into bed, pulling the blankets up over her head, and doing her best to pretend none of this had happened.

Later, when she was rested and could think more clearly, she'd corner Hunter and demand better answers to her questions. If he refused to respond, or if she didn't like what he had to say, she'd be looking for a new renter.

Yep, that was her plan.

Before she could convince herself that it was a good idea, she asked, "Who exactly is *them,* Hunter?"

"Shhhh!" he hissed, his eyes wild, his mouth grim. "Not now. They're coming."

Then Hunter grasped his sword with both hands and stood ready to defend their lives.

She studied the top of the ridge, finally spotting the dark figure standing outlined against the horizon. "Tate! Hunter! Where the hell are you?"

Thank God, it was D.J. and company, and Tate could breathe again.

"Here we are!" she called out as she waved the flashlight to catch their attention.

Another figure appeared, pointing in her direction. "Down there."

She wasn't sure, but she thought it sounded like Larem. "Take it easy coming down. It's slippery and steep."

Like they couldn't see that for themselves, but she seriously didn't need to deal with any more major injuries right now. It didn't take long before she could make out three men slip-sliding their way down the hillside. D.J. was the first to arrive. As he dusted off his backside, he studied Hunter.

"How bad is it?" He turned his flashlight full on Hunter's face. The stark light emphasized Hunter's pallor.

When he didn't answer D.J., Tate spoke up. "He's lost a lot of blood, but he's still standing—barely."

"Glad to hear it, because we brought a first-aid kit but forgot the shovel." That remark came from Penn Sebastian. "Besides, digging a grave on this hillside would be a bitch."

She did not appreciate the humor. "Listen, you jerk, that's so not funny."

Penn winced as he set the kit down beside her. "Sorry, Tate."

She started to rip into him some more, glad to finally have a target for her anger and her fear, when Hunter's sword dropped from his hands. It hit the ground only a heartbeat before he landed right beside it, facedown in the dirt.

He didn't move, not even a twitch, nor did he make a sound. Before Tate could respond, D.J. dropped to his knees beside Hunter's still form and rolled him over to do a cursory examination. In the darkness, D.J.'s face revealed nothing of what he was thinking, but something in the set of his shoulders gave his thoughts away.

"D.J.? Is he . . ."

She couldn't give voice to the possibility, but the look D.J. exchanged with Penn spoke volumes.

"No, no, no . . . he can't be. I shouldn't have listened to him. This time no one's stopping me from calling the police."

She pulled out the cell phone, but before she had a chance to punch a single number, D.J. grabbed it from her hand. Fury and fear had her lunging at him, intent on doing serious harm unless he relinquished the phone. Before she could do any damage, Penn wrapped his arms around her from behind, successfully trapping her in between the two men.

As they continued to scuffle for control of the phone, Larem shoved past them.

"Fools, stop it! Maybe I can help him!" he shouted and flung himself to the ground at Hunter's side.

Tate froze in horror as the normally sedate Larem yanked a long, narrow knife out of his boot and raised it over Hunter's chest. She screamed as the blade slashed downward. D.J. pushed her toward Penn before diving down to catch Larem's arm. He succeeded in stopping him, but both men shuddered as they each struggled for control.

D.J. glared at the other man. "Larem! What the fuck are you doing? For God's sake, I thought you two were friends."

"We are! Now let me go before it's too late. Maybe he doesn't need to die again, not like this."

"What can you do?"

D.J. sounded calmer, but he didn't release Larem. Were they both crazy? Nothing they said made sense. Die *again*? What did that mean? All she knew was they still weren't calling for help.

"At least try CPR!" she pleaded.

Something. Anything. Neither man paid her the least bit of attention. Tears burned acid hot down her face as she waited for this nightmare to end, but it just went on and on.

Larem's words came out in ragged gasps as he fought to regain control of his weapon. "You know Barak's ability to control stone? It's not the only gift to fade away among our people. The gift of healing is another."

"And you have it? This gift?" Somehow D.J. sounded both hopeful and skeptical at the same time.

Larem nodded. "In the darkness of my world, I could sometimes ease pain or slow bleeding. But stories have been passed down from past generations that back in the days of light, our healers could perform true miracles."

"And you've been in the light for some time now." Slowly, D.J. nodded, then released Larem's arm. "See what you can do."

This time when Larem raised the blade, he began chanting in a strange cadence. As the rhythm of his words sped up, he used the razor-sharp edge to cut away Hunter's shirt, peeling the blood-soaked cloth away from his skin with a sickening wet sound.

Next, Larem held his knife up, as if making an offering to an unknown god. At that point, he shouted to the heavens and plunged the blade hilt deep, straight into Hunter's chest.

Horrified to the point of being numb, Tate sobbed as she collapsed onto the ground. He'd killed Hunter, right there, right then. How could anyone live through such a vicious attack?

"Son of a bitch!"

Clearly horrified, D.J. continued to curse while Penn stared down at Hunter's ravaged body with a look of utter despair on his face. Larem went back to chanting as he swayed back and forth over Hunter, his voice growing more ragged and ever more desperate.

Finally, he grasped the hilt of his knife and yanked it back out. As the blade slipped free, Hunter's eyes flew open and he let loose an agonized scream that ricocheted off the rocky hillside and echoed up into the night sky.

When he drew a second breath, the tension in his body abruptly drained away.

"What the hell just happened?"

Hunter's voice was weak, but the words sounded like the "Hallelujah Chorus" to Tate's ears. As soon as Larem and Penn sat up, she pushed them aside to get closer to Hunter, who lay blinking up at her, sharing her confusion.

He tried to lift his head to look around, but he was unable to hold it up for long. "How did I end up on the ground? Did I pass out?"

How do you tell someone he'd just been dragged back from the edge of death by being stabbed in the chest? She didn't believe it herself, and she'd had a front-row seat to the spectacle. She struggled for words.

But Penn had no problem at all. "You died, and your good buddy Larem here jump-started your worthless ass using his knife and some kind of Kalith mumbo jumbo."

D.J.'s sudden grin turned wicked, his teeth gleaming in the darkness. "Gotta say being stabbed in the heart looked like it hurt like a bitch. But since you're breathing regular again, I don't figure you've got much to complain about."

Hunter's eyes sought out Larem, asking the questions he didn't seem to be able to ask aloud. The other man shrugged.

"Seemed like a good idea at the time. You were already dead, so I figured you wouldn't be any worse off if it didn't work."

Then they all laughed—even Hunter managed a wheezy chuckle. Were they *insane*? Yes, they had to be. She moved away, ready to bolt for home and the sanctuary of her bed. Come morning, she'd do whatever it took to put her world back on track, but right now she needed to put some distance between herself and these crazies.

As the men hovered over their fallen friend, she gathered up the tattered remains of her control and took a step up the slope. Then the fear she'd been fighting since leaving the safety of her bedroom took control, and violent shakes wracked her body. Her legs gave way, sending her plummeting toward the ground.

"Oh, hell, she's going into shock."

She was dimly aware of strong arms managing to cushioning her fall and then of being hoisted in the air against someone's chest. Her head was buzzing, making it hard for her to distinguish voices as they carried on a discussion over her head.

"I'm going to get Tate the hell out of here."

Penn nodded. "Let's get them both up to the house. Devlin wants a full report ASAP, and then we can decide what to do about all of this, especially her."

The voices sounded as if they were coming from the bottom of a very deep well. Even so, she recognized Larem when he asked, "Is the best way up or down?"

D.J. was the one holding her, because she heard his answer rumble through his chest. "I'd say down. We can control our descent better than trying to drag Hunter's sorry ass up that hill."

Larem loomed over her. "Tate, are you all right?"

"Get real, you idiot. Hell, no, she's not okay, not after getting dragged into our world with no warning." D.J. sounded more disgusted than angry.

Their world? Just one more thing that made no sense, but right now her head was too foggy to make sense of much of anything. She struggled to get down.

"What about Hunter?"

"Hold still, Tate, before both of us go flying headfirst down this bluff! Hunter will be right behind us." D.J. started moving, traversing the remaining distance in fits and starts.

When they were safely on level ground, she insisted that he set her down, but her legs refused to hold her. He immediately swept her back up in his arms. "Okay, we'll do it the hard way."

Larem caught up with them. "Hey, Tate. Can you take this? Hunter will need it."

He held out Hunter's reassembled cane. Once again it looked handsome and harmless. But as she took it, she knew she'd never forget that inside that beautiful exterior lurked a deadly weapon.

And she suspected the same was true about the men who surrounded her. Once again the darkness swirled through her head and dragged her down into blessed oblivion.

The morning sun peeked through Tate's bedroom window as Hunter sat in the corner watching her sleep. After patching him up, Larem and the others had tried to order Hunter to bed, leaving one of them to patrol Tate's house while she slept. Fat chance. It was his job to stand guard over her while she was so vulnerable. Once she was awake, she'd probably kick his worthless hide out to the street. Until then, he was staying right where he was while D.J., Penn, and Larem sacked out in Hunter's apartment.

As the hours passed, he managed to doze off a couple of times, but then he'd dream about that Other charging after him with death in his eyes. Then he'd jerk back awake, his pulse racing. Sitting in the darkness, the cool feel of the ivory handle on his cane vanquished the last shadows of the nightmare.

Better yet, thanks to Larem's efforts, his arm was already healed. The bullet holes would take a few more hours, but even the stab wound inflicted by Larem had all but disappeared. By midday, Hunter would be back to where he was before the attack. Hell, even his leg felt better, but nothing seemed to ease the heavy ache in his chest.

How was he supposed to explain his resurrection to Tate when he was having trouble dealing with it himself? Even more, how they were going to deal with Larem's newly discovered ability? By all reports, Barak was understandably reluctant to use his gifts to aid the Paladins. Would Larem feel any different? But now wasn't the time to worry about that.

All things considered, Tate had done all right last night, holding herself together until help had arrived. Far better than most folks would've done when confronted with the truth of the world the Paladins lived and died in.

What had she been thinking by charging off to rescue him again? Bless her heart for wanting to, but he'd warned her to stay out of his affairs for good reason. That Other and his human buddies wouldn't let one headstrong human female get in the way of profit.

Tate could've been killed. His hand gripped and released the ivory wolf head over and over again as he remembered the sweet feel of fighting his enemy, sword against sword. Even better was how close he'd come to ridding both this world and Kalithia of one more crazy. Earlier, he'd wiped the bastard's blood off his blade just as he had so many times in the past, but this time it had been a validation of Hunter's worth as a warrior.

Since waking up in Doc's lab all those months ago to find himself stitched together, he'd wondered if he'd ever be able to face his enemy again. The answer was yes, and it felt damn good to know that.

"Shouldn't you be lying down somewhere?" Tate was awake, her huge blue eyes blinking at him. She looked sleepy and worried, and more than a little bit afraid. At least she wasn't screaming.

"I'm fine. I was more worried about you." He clenched both his cane and the arm of the chair, fighting to keep himself from crossing the room to her bed.

She sat up, the sheet pooling around her waist. He waited for her to notice that he'd changed her clothes for her. She'd probably hate knowing he'd done so, but her shirt and jeans had been soaked with his blood. He'd wanted her to wake up mad rather than have her face such an awful reminder of what had transpired in the woods.

It didn't take her long. She peeked under the sheets, then gave him a suspicious look. "I don't remember changing when I got back. Come to think of it, I don't remember how I got here at all."

"When you collapsed, D.J. carried you up here. I figured you'd sleep better in something clean."

He'd also given her a sponge bath to get the rest of the dried blood off her skin. The memory of sliding that soapy cloth over her smooth skin, pretty much from head to toe, was one he'd cherish for a long time. Even now, he was instantly aroused and aching as the images filled his mind.

"Don't." Tate pulled the sheet back up.

"Don't what?" Although he knew.

"Don't look at me like I'm on the menu at your favorite restaurant. Not after last night," she snapped.

"Damn it, Tate, I can't help that you have that effect on me. It doesn't mean I'm going to act on it."

"Darn straight you're not." She studied him from across the room, her expression puzzled. "You almost died last night, but you look fine, almost like it never happened."

Time for some plain talk. "You know perfectly well that isn't true. I didn't almost die."

She held the edge of the sheet in a white-knuckled grip. "Don't lie to me, Hunter. I was there."

"I know you were, but you didn't see me *almost* die. What you saw was me *really* die. It's not the first time that it's happened, and it won't be the last."

Tate blanched at his brutally honest statement of the facts. But after everything that had happened, she deserved the truth no matter how unpalatable, even if it was going to cause major problems for him and possibly the whole organization. She'd shined that flashlight right on the worst of his injuries and had had a front-row seat when Larem had stabbed him in the heart. There's no way she was going to believe that his wounds had only been minor scratches.

"That's not possible." Tate shook her head slowly, trying to find some way to deny what she'd seen with her own eyes. "Is it?"

"I told you once before—I heal fast." He held his arm for her to see. The cut was completely closed, leaving only a faint scar. Despite the severity of the wound, it would be only another in a long line of painful memories in a matter of days.

"Stand up and lift your shirt," she demanded.

He set the cane aside and did as she asked, turning slowly so she could see both sides.

"Come here." She crawled out of the covers to kneel on the edge of the bed.

Getting this close to her in that position was not a good idea, but right then he wasn't thinking with his brain. He crossed the few feet that separated them and held his breath as she traced his scars with a feathery light touch of her fingertips.

His cock hardened, wanting some of that gentle touch for itself. He shifted his stance, hoping she wouldn't notice the renewed strain on his zipper. No such luck. Tate's hand had come to rest right above the wound on his stomach. When she noticed what was going on a few inches south, she jerked back with a hiss.

"What's going on, Hunter? And don't try lying to me. Not anymore."

She stared up at him with enough fear in her eyes to really piss him off. Maybe she had good reason, but after what they'd shared, she should know better. Right then he would've promised her anything, but the truth was easy. He owed her that much. No matter if he'd be breaking his vow to the Regents by doing so, he was going to tell her everything she wanted to know.

"Okay, but put some clothes on and meet me downstairs." He forced himself to walk away, pausing at the door to look back. "Unless you want me to join you in that bed."

When she jerked the sheets up to her neck, he had his answer.

Chapter 14

While he waited for Tate to come down Hunter made breakfast. She was already seriously upset with him, messing up her kitchen could hardly make matters worse. Besides, he needed to keep busy.

The floor overhead creaked. She was up and moving. Good. The sooner they got this over with, the better. He cracked half a dozen eggs into a bowl and put six strips of bacon into the skillet to fry while he set the table. What else?

A knock on the back door answered that question. He unlocked it and stood back as D.J. and Larem filed in. Penn was right behind them. As soon as he set foot in the kitchen, he sniffed the air and smiled.

"Breakfast! Good, I'm starving."

Would it be cowardly to have the three men there as a temporary buffer between himself and Tate? Probably, but that didn't stop him from pulling another dozen eggs out of the fridge.

"If you want to eat, the plates are in that cabinet, and the knives and forks are in the drawer below it."

He turned the bacon, all the time listening for the telltale creak of the steps to warn him that Tate was on her way down. There. She hesitated briefly at the top. Perhaps she'd heard the commotion and realized that she'd be facing more than just Hunter. Or maybe she needed one last moment to gather up her courage.

Resisting the urge to go to her, he put the bacon on paper towels to drain and poured the eggs into the skillet. By the time Tate finally made her appearance, he'd served up three plates' worth of food and shoved his friends out the door with orders to stay at his place until he came for them.

When he turned back, Tate was standing in the doorway staring at the mess on the counter.

"Sorry. I'll clean up, but I wanted to get the guys fed and out of here in a hurry." He filled two mugs with hot tea and set them on the table. "Come on and have a seat. I may not be the best cook in the world, but even I can make edible bacon and eggs."

She sat down and wrapped her hands around her mug, absorbing the heat as he dished up the rest of their meal. She didn't seem inclined to talk, and he was in no hurry to spill his guts. Not when it meant that he'd be back over at the apartment and packing up all his possessions five minutes after he was done talking.

Despite his claim to the contrary, his breakfast tasted like sawdust. He carried the plate to the sink and kept himself busy washing the dishes, all the while feeling the burn of Tate's gaze boring straight to the heart of him.

He knew she had questions, and he would answer each and every one of them to the best of his ability.

Her chair scraped across the wooden floor. He accepted the offering of her plate, the last excuse he had to avoid talking. As he wiped the last dish dry and returned it to its proper spot, it felt as if the seconds were counting down until the warden was going to throw the switch.

He turned to face her. "Want to take a walk?"

"No. I want answers." To emphasize her plans to stay put, she sat back down at the table and refilled her mug.

Okay, a deep breath then. He flipped one of the kitchen chairs around and straddled it, resting his arms on the back as he faced her. "Ask away."

"What are you?"

Ouch. Not *who,* but *what.* The distinction hurt. Did she think he was some kind of cyborg out of an old science fiction movie? He resented the inference, especially when she knew all too well just how human he was, but he bit back the urge to lash out.

"Okay, here it is in a nutshell. Our world shares a barrier with another one. When there's an earthquake or volcanic eruption, the barrier goes down and that's where the trouble starts. The crazies from that world come pouring across, out of their heads with the need to kill. Men like me fight to stop them before they can escape."

She rolled her eyes. "Yeah, right. Sounds like a new series from the sci-fi channel on cable."

He slammed his fist down on the table, causing the tea in her mug to slosh out on her hand. So that wasn't his smartest move. He grabbed the dish towel and tossed it to her.

"Look, I know it sounds far-fetched, but that doesn't make it less true."

Clearly skeptical, she gave the scar on his forearm a pointed look. "So why do you heal like you do? And what's all this about you dying again? Are you talking about some kind of out-of-body experience?"

Oh yeah, this should be fun. "At some point in the past, some of those beings from the other world managed to wade into our gene pool. My ability to heal, as well as my ability to come back from death, are gifts from my long-lost alien ancestors."

Tate looked out toward the garage. "And your buddies out there—they've got that same gift?"

Okay, so now he was outing his friends, too. "Penn, D.J., and Lonzo all do. Larem is actually from Kalithia, the other world, only he didn't cross over all crazy like most of them do. That trick he pulled last night was news to all of us, so I can't say for sure what he can and can't do."

She nodded slowly, clearly still skeptical. "So that would mean Barak is an alien, too."

He answered even though she hadn't really phrased it as a question. "Yes, he is."

Her expression was bleak. "And you really did die last night."

He nodded.

"And before you came here, when your leg was hurt so badly, you died then, too."

He shuddered at the memory. No way he was sharing those details with her. "Yes, but that wasn't the first time, and it will happen again. That's how it is for my kind. Eventually, though, we use up all of our get-out-of-jail-free cards."

She flinched. "Is there a name for what you are?"

He straightened his shoulders, showing his pride in his answer. "To the few who know about us, we're known as Paladins. No one knows for sure, but we suspect that some of the knights who bore that name were our ancestors."

"I'm not saying that I'm buying all of this, but if it's true, then how come no one knows about this stuff?"

"Think about it, Tate." He took a drink of his tea before continuing. "Most people couldn't handle knowing that we all live under the constant threat of alien invasion. And if any government agency got their hands on us, God knows what they'd do. Some would want to breed us or clone us or some such shit. Imagine the power of having an army that is damn near impossible to kill. Just as many would want to exterminate us for not being completely human."

She shivered. "So are you or Larem going to do some kind of mind meld and erase my memory of all of this?"

He set his mug back down with a bang and glared across at her. "Hell, no. First of all because no one has that power. Secondly, if I didn't want you to know the truth—my truth—I would've just disappeared after putting you to bed last night."

She met him glare for glare. "Don't get all huffy with me, Hunter Fitzsimon. How do I know what's possible and what's not? You didn't see Larem save your life by sticking a bloody knife in your heart. And you didn't hear yourself scream when he pulled it out."

"No, and I'm sorrier than you'll ever know that you did see all of that. Of course, if you hadn't followed me out there, none of this would've happened."

She shoved her chair back from the table and closed her hands into fists. "And you would've bled to death out there without anyone to help."

"I bled to death anyway," he reminded her. "But I would've been all right." Eventually. Maybe. He didn't add that, or the part that if he'd come back out of his head crazy, he might have murdered everyone in Justice Point before D.J. or one of the others could track him down and kill him. "All you did was put yourself in danger for no good reason."

She slowly rose to her feet and pointed toward the door. "I think you need to leave. Now."

"Why?" he demanded, although he knew. "Because you don't like my answers? I warned you to stay away from me. I never asked you to sit up there in that window and wait up for me every night. It's not my fault you didn't listen."

"Maybe you're right." She stalked around to his side of the table and glared down at him, her mouth a straight slash. "But you let me think it was because of your problem dealing with your injury. If you'd told me the real truth from the start . . ."

This was getting them nowhere. He stood up, towering over her. He was petty enough to enjoy watching her back up a step to lessen the effect of his superior height. He followed right after her when she moved back again.

"If I'd told you the real truth, Tate, you would've never rented me the apartment in the first place."

"Could you blame me?"

When she moved back again, she came up against the counter. He closed in, trapping her with one hand on either side of her. He was enough of a predator to enjoy this little game of cat and mouse.

Tate ducked under Hunter's arm and looked around for a safe place to go. Definitely not upstairs. The porch was also out of the question. The last thing she wanted was to be a spectacle for the neighbors, not to mention Hunter's friends. She circled around to the other side of the table. Hunter let her get a few steps away, but then he started prowling after her again. She should've been angry, but her traitorous body was reacting in a whole different way. Her breasts felt heavy and a familiar ache settled low in her body, growing stronger with each step they took.

"I didn't advertise for some kind of freaky alien tenant, you know."

She regretted the words as soon as they slipped out. Unless she was mistaken, that was hurt she saw flash through Hunter's eyes before they turned stormy.

In a sudden move, he trapped her against the table. He leaned in close, forcing her to arch back to keep any distance between them.

"I'm not some kind of freaky alien, Tate." Temper made his voice sound huskier than normal. "You should know. You've seen, touched, and tasted damn near every inch of me." His breath danced over her skin.

Oh, yeah, she had. And right now some of her favorites of those inches were pressing against her belly, reminding her all too well of how good they had felt.

"And I don't remember you complaining about me being your tenant when I . . ."

His whispered reminder of exactly what he'd done to her—not once, but several times—had her skin flashing hot and then cold.

"Don't!"

"Don't what, Tate? Don't talk about it? Don't try it again? Maybe you should spell it out for me. We aliens don't always understand what you humans really want."

"That isn't funny, Hunter."

"I agree. In fact, I'm feeling pretty damned serious right about now—not to mention horny as hell."

He was going to kiss her. She knew it. He knew it. And they both knew that if she let him, all bets were off. She gave his chest a shove, seeing if he'd grant her that much breathing room. When he did, still allowing her the final decision despite his anger and his desire, she knew all was lost. There might be no future for the two of them, but there was now.

She reached up to tangle her fingers in his hair none too gently. "This won't change anything, you know."

He cupped the side of her face and stared down at her for the longest time. Finally, he answered as he brushed his thumb back and forth across her cheek. "I know. But that doesn't seem to keep me from wanting you."

Then all chance for further discussion was gone. His mouth crushed down on hers, demanding entry, demanding surrender, maybe demanding forgiveness. She didn't know if she could give him what he wanted but she did know that if she didn't at least try, she'd never forgive herself.

God in heaven, the man knew how to kiss. After his initial assault, his touch gentled. She'd never been seduced by just the gentle sweep of lips against hers or realized that the soft brush of fingertips across her breasts could make her ache straight through to the heart of her.

She did some touching of her own, smiling when she heard the hitch in Hunter's breathing.

"Like that, do you?" She trailed her hand downward, stopping just short of her intended target, waiting for his approval.

"Woman, you'll be the death of me." He rested his forehead against hers and sighed, then frowned when she laughed.

She sent her hand sliding downward to stroke him through the thickness of his jeans. He moaned and leaned into her, murmuring his approval and his pleasure.

"Want to go upstairs?" she whispered.

He shook his head. "Don't think I can wait that long."

Then he reached behind her and tested the strength of the table with his hand. Evidently satisfied with what he found, he grinned at her, his intent clear.

"Hunter?"

"Tate," he echoed.

Scandalized, she sputtered, "Anyone could walk up on that porch and see us."

He shook his head as he spanned her waist with his strong hands and lifted her up onto the table. "Your friends never use that door and mine know I'll kill them if they set foot out of my apartment without my express permission."

She should've objected, should've marshaled her defenses. But how could she concentrate on things like logic and common sense when he was busy peeling down her jeans and panties and unbuttoning her shirt? Maybe she could've come up with the right words, but then he was once again leveling the playing field. How was a girl supposed to think straight with him showing off that sculpted physique just for her?

Raising her arms in invitation, he stubbornly stayed just out of reach.

"Tell me you want this. That you want me, at least for right now. That's all I'm asking."

"You know I do."

"Then say it, Tate."

"I want you. I want this. And I want it now."

Then he stepped into the cradle of her arms, all signs of gentleness gone, making it clear that this was to be a claiming. He undid the front clasp of her bra and pushed it out of the way. His hands cupped the lower curve of her breasts and plumped them, rubbing his thumbs over her nipples until they pebbled up.

"Sweet," he murmured as he nuzzled them both before capturing one with his lips and suckling hard to a point just shy of pain.

"Hunter!"

She slowly lowered herself back to lay flat on the table, at the same time scooting closer to the edge of the table to wrap her legs around his hips. He held back, ignoring her unspoken hints. Instead, he knelt down on one knee as he spread her legs wide with a long, slow caress up the inside of her thighs. He focused his eyes right on the apex, leaving no doubt about his intentions.

Sensations came too quickly, overwhelming her—first his warmth, then his breath, then the merest touch of his tongue right at her core. When she whimpered, he pressed closer and smiled.

"Like that, do you?"

He kissed her again, this time more thoroughly, using his lips and teeth and tongue. It was too much and not enough. When she arched her back, he pressed her back down on the table, holding her in place with the weight of his arm. When he eased his fingers deep inside of her, the gentle invasion caught the first ripple of her climax.

"That's it, come for me, Tate."

Hunter took pleasure in watching Tate lose all control at his touch. Her mind might question how she felt about him, but on some level she trusted him. She wasn't the kind of woman to let just anyone make love to her on the kitchen table.

Before she could gather up her defenses again, he was going to take her again, this time without holding back anything. He rose to his feet, leaning in over her to lift her legs high against his shoulders. Cupping her bottom with both hands, he settled his cock against her nest of curls and rocked back and forth several times. Tate bit her lower lip as she waited for him to plunge deep inside the slick heat of her body.

Hunter hesitated only seconds to let her adjust to the abrupt invasion before slamming into high gear, pounding into her with all of his strength. The old table creaked and groaned as he established a hard, driving rhythm. The two of them fit together perfectly, the heat they generated burning through him like fire.

The small noises she made each time he withdrew only to return again drove him crazy. He needed to slow down if he wanted this wild ride to last, but he'd lost all control. Faster and faster, deeper and deeper, until he no longer knew where he left off and Tate began. For the moment, they were one.

This time, when an orgasm ripped through her, she took him screaming across the finish line with her. Both of them shuddered and shook. She moaned. He shouted. They both rode out the waves of pleasure until he collapsed against her from the sheer wonder of it all.

Despite the beauty of what they'd shared, when he kissed her, he could taste the sadness and feel the goodbye. It damn near killed him to withdraw from her, to help her up, to step away.

As he did so, it suddenly hit them that temper and frustration had blinded them both to the need to use protection.

"Uh, Tate, we forgot . . ."

Her eyes widened when she realized what he was talking about, but she cut him off before he could say more. "It's not a problem. I'll be fine."

"But—"

"I said I'll be fine."

She eased down off the edge of the table and picked up her clothes. With each moment, she gathered up more of her dignity and used it to distance herself from him. The separation hurt like a son of a bitch, especially after what they'd shared.

He yanked up his pants and tucked in his shirt. "I'd better get over to the apartment to see what D.J. and the others are up to."

He paused at the door, hoping she'd say something, anything. When she finally spoke, he wished that he hadn't waited.

"I think it's best if you find someplace else to live, Hunter." Her voice cracked. "I'm sorry, but . . ."

He didn't want to hear it. Not now. Maybe not ever. Stepping out onto the porch, he risked a final look back. "I'll move into a hotel until I find something more permanent."

He drew no comfort from the fact that she looked as shattered as he felt. She'd managed to put her jeans back on, but he noticed her shirt was buttoned crooked.

"You can leave your stuff in the apartment until you do."

"Thanks."

Then he walked away while he still could.

Could this day get any worse? Penn and D.J. seemed oblivious to Hunter's foul mood, but there was no mistaking the sympathy in Larem's pale eyes when Hunter walked into the apartment.

The argument about how to handle the cluster fuck that was Hunter's life didn't help.

"I don't give a rat's ass what Devlin thinks. He has no room to talk when it comes to relationships the Regents might deem inappropriate. Tate needed to be told the truth. End of story."

Then he gave Larem a long, hard look. "What did you guys tell Devlin about last night?"

D.J. frowned, while Penn avoided any eye contact. "Nothing yet."

"Good, let's keep it that way for now. God knows what the Regents would do to Larem after what he did."

There was no mistaking Larem's relief as he nodded to each man in turn. "I thank you."

Uncomfortable with the gratitude, Hunter said, "Now let's get moving." He shoved his way past D.J., determined to take the lead in both the trip back down to the cave and the conversation. That way he could control the pace. If he left it up to D.J., they'd be at a dead run most of the way down the slope.

The two of them walked in angry silence until the trail widened out enough for D.J. to fall back into step beside him. Hunter did not want to be having this conversation, but D.J. was determined to continue the discussion.

"You know the Regents are going to raise hell if they find out you broke silence."

"Like they did when Trahern brought Brenna into our installation without permission?" Hunter smacked his forehead, "Oh no, I forgot. They let it slide because her father was one of theirs, didn't they?"

He stopped to catch his breath and to renew his argument. "Tate's a smart woman. Even if I hadn't told her a damned thing, she already knew that my injuries had completely healed in less than twenty-four hours, and the reason the four of us are hiking our asses up and down the bluff this morning isn't because we need the exercise. Anything I told her was just filling in the blanks."

D.J. stood next to him, shifting his weight, his energy level running high even for him. "But having suspicions is different than handing her the facts, Hunter. Right now, if she went to the authorities and told them her boyfriend got shot and stabbed, they wouldn't believe her. How can they when those supposed fresh wounds have all but disappeared? And even if they managed to track the Kalith back to the cave, I doubt his two buddies left any evidence for the cops to find."

"I'm not her boyfriend." He had to deny it even though he wanted to be far more than that to her. "And besides, if she was going to call the cops, she'd have done it already. We can trust her."

He started walking again, relieved to reach the steepest section of the trail, forcing D.J. to fall back behind him again. He hated knowing that D.J. was right. The only reason the Paladins were able to do their job was that so few people knew about them. If their existence became public, the military and the government would step in and screw things up for everybody. They'd want all of the Paladins to serve in the armed forces. Who wouldn't want soldiers who were nearly impossible to kill? But then who would defend the barrier?

Then there was the whole impact once it became known that intelligent life existed on other worlds. Oh, yeah, and by the way, only an unstable energy barrier kept the crazies at bay. Wouldn't that make for interesting headlines on the evening news?

The more he thought about the entire situation, the worse his mood became. He needed a target for the anger that chewed at his gut and burned along his nerves. And hey, D.J. was handy. Hunter considered the best plan of attack. He couldn't pull his sword. It wouldn't be fair, since the other Paladin wasn't sporting any steel at the moment.

The cane might have other uses, though. He shifted his grip on it, considering its effectiveness as a club. Oh, yeah, the balance was perfect, and the ivory handle would make a nice impression on his companion's thick skull.

Before he could make his move, D.J.'s heavy hand came down on his shoulder from behind. "I wouldn't try it, good buddy. Not that I mind a good dustup now and then, but do you really want to explain a whole new set of bruises to your woman?"

Hunter shook free of D.J.'s grasp and turned to face him. "She's not my woman."

"You keep telling yourself that if it makes you feel better." D.J.'s eyes twinkled with good humor. "But my guess is that Tate checked over last night's crop of injuries pretty thoroughly this morning."

That did it. Hunter's fist connected with D.J.'s mouth with a loud crack. The force of the blow left Hunter's hand hurting like hell, but at least he'd wiped the smile off D.J.'s face. To his surprise, the Paladin didn't strike back.

"You just going to stand there?" he asked, bracing himself to take this to a whole new level.

D.J. spit some blood on the ground. "Pretty much. Figure I probably had that one coming. Besides, you were about to explode from frustration. Now maybe you'll be able to think more clearly while we explore the cave."

The man was clearly insane, but Hunter couldn't deny that he'd burned off a little of his temper. He picked up the cane before heading on down the trail to meet up with Penn and Larem. They were waiting by the ledge that led to the cave.

Penn looked at D.J. and then back to Hunter, a grin starting to spread across his face. "I was going to ask what took you so long, but I can guess. What did he do this time?"

"Nothing."

Penn snorted. "Then why the split lip?"

"He tripped on a tree root and ran into my fist when I tried to break his fall," Hunter said with a straight face. "I feel real bad about it, too."

D.J. started to laugh but winced when it stung his lip. "All right, assholes, that's enough. I can't help if I'm clumsy. Let's check this place out."

Hunter released his sword and started across the ledge with Larem close on his heels, followed by Penn. D.J. remained behind to stand guard.

They paused at the entrance of the cave, letting their eyes adjust to the dim light. All of them had good night vision, but the bright sun outside had a stronger effect on Larem. Inside, they spread out.

Penn knelt down to study something on the floor of the cave. "You definitely cut him good, Hunter. Someone made a half-assed attempt to hide the blood spatter, but they missed some."

"Good, although I'd just as soon have found his body than his blood." Maybe that was cold, but it was honest.

Larem stopped short of the barrier. "I'd guess you came pretty close to killing him; he definitely wasn't moving all that well on his own. Looks like they practically shoved him across once he brought the barrier down. I'm guessing it was the Guildmaster himself. I don't know anyone else strong enough to control the barrier while bleeding that badly."

Penn moved up beside him. Hunter thought it had to be the strangest sight he'd seen in a long while. Who would've ever thought to see a Paladin standing shoulder to shoulder with an Other as allies rather than enemies? Hunter might have a hard time thinking Larem or Barak would choose to save him over one of their own kind, but obviously Penn and D.J. didn't feel that way.

Hunter glanced at Penn's sword hand, the poor bastard. Even if Hunter's leg would never come back to one hundred percent, at least he could still wield the Paladin weapon of choice. What was Penn going to do if he never regained the use of his hand?

Penn happened to glance back at that moment. He frowned and balled his fist. "Knock it off."

Sensing an apology would only piss Penn off even more, Hunter focused his flashlight—and his attention—on the floor of the cave. "It's clear both humans were in here last night."

Larem stepped back from the barrier. "Has it occurred to either of you to wonder why they didn't return to finish Hunter off? Unless they assumed he was dead. But if they wanted to keep their little enterprise secret, they wouldn't risk leaving a witness."

Hunter *had* been wondering the same thing. Last night, most of his fear had been for Tate's safety. Even if the bastards had shot him a few more times to make sure they'd gotten the job done, he would've pulled through. Tate wouldn't have been so lucky.

So why hadn't they come gunning for him once they'd sent the injured Kalith back to his own world? The answer was obvious.

"Maybe one of them suspected killing me wouldn't work. That's the only thing that makes sense."

Penn was already nodding. "We've known all along that the Kalith were working with someone on our side. Whoever it is has to have ties to the Regents organization, but we haven't been able to figure out who it could be. Every time we manage to identify someone, he ends up dead. The guard who attacked Laurel died falling across the barrier, but Devlin would've killed him anyway."

Hunter paced the narrow width of the cave. "Yeah, and the Regent who was behind the attacks back home in Missouri was murdered while inside our headquarters. That had to be an inside job."

Larem joined in. "Then some died in the earthquake that almost killed Barak as well."

Penn's smile was brutal. "Can't exactly blame that on anyone except their own stupid selves for getting trapped in a cave with a pissed-off Kalith warrior in the middle of an earthquake. Served the bastards right. Besides, they got off easy because they died quickly. I can guarantee they wouldn't have if they'd still been breathing when we dug them out."

He looked back at the barrier. "My sister and I would've both been dead if it hadn't been for Barak's ability to hold off the mountain's fury long enough for me to get her to safety. We almost lost him."

No wonder the Seattle Paladins had adopted Barak and Larem as their own. It was time to get back to the apartment. Hunter needed to find a place to live, and they weren't finding much here anyway.

"I think we've seen everything. I doubt they'll be back tonight, since their Kalith contact was injured, but someone should keep watch just in case."

Larem shot him an odd look. "Is there some reason you won't be able to do it?"

Hunter thought about lying, saying he needed some rest because of his injuries, but he couldn't bring himself to do so. "I won't be here. Tate asked me to move out, and I promised to get a hotel room until I can find another apartment."

For several seconds, an uncomfortable silence settled over the hillside as they stepped out into the late-afternoon sunshine.

Penn finally spoke up. "Well, that sucks. You can crash with us. Devlin told us to hang out up here for a few days to keep an eye on things."

Normally Hunter would've resented the Paladin leader issuing orders without consulting him first, but in this case it was for the best. Besides, he tried to pick his battles when it came to bucking any decisions handed down by Jarvis, and he figured it was only smart to treat Devlin's edicts in the same way.

"Sounds good. She didn't mention you guys needed to leave, and my rent's paid up until the end of the month. If you think it's more comfortable, feel free to use the apartment."

D.J. rolled his eyes and grumbled. "Comfortable my

ass. Have you tried sleeping on that couch? It's a foot too short and feels like it was upholstered with rocks and rusty springs. Personally, I'm looking forward to sleeping in a real bed, even if Penn does snore."

"Me? It sounded like someone was grinding boulders on your side of the room."

Larem laughed and clapped the two Paladins on the shoulder. "We flipped a coin, and I won. These two had to share while I slept well in the silence of my own room."

"Yeah, well it sounds like you've got a roommate now, and I snore—a lot." Hunter moved up beside Larem. "In fact, they gave me my own insulated room back in Missouri because I kept setting off the earthquake alarms."

The Kalith warrior's attempt to hide his horror had Hunter grinning. "Aw, buddy, don't sweat it. I'm just jerking your chain."

Penn and D.J. both cracked up. Larem finally joined in the laughter as they continued up the hillside. "Hunter, it will be my honor to share my room, but you might want to remember one thing about Kalith warriors."

"What's that?"

"We understand the concept of revenge quite well." His smile showed a few too many teeth to be a happy expression.

"I'll remember that."

"See that you do."

Chapter 15

Son of a bitch! He slammed the phone down. Why wasn't Joe answering?

Did nothing ever go right? He paced the width of his office and back. No word from that idiot Guildmaster either, not even to say that he'd survived the night. Maybe he hadn't, but that was the fool's own fault. If he hadn't tried to take on that Paladin with his sword instead of letting Joe simply shoot the bastard, none of this would've happened.

Granted, if he was right about the intruder's being one of Bane's boys, he wouldn't have stayed dead after a simple gunshot. But once he'd been immobilized, the Guildmaster could've slipped back to finish the job when Joe hadn't been there to watch. No, it was better to let Joe think he'd killed the guy, even if he now had a bunch of pissed-off Paladins to deal with and perhaps a dead partner.

Where was the justice in that? He'd spent years cultivating this partnership with the Kalith leader, and both of them had profited nicely by the association. Not that he'd care at all if the Kalith was dead, as long as his replacement could pick up where his predecessor left off. But according to Devlin Bane's reports, there was a group within the Sworn Guardians determined to stop the leak of blue garnets out of their world.

The Guildmaster had barely managed to keep his job after the Paladins' unauthorized foray into the other world. When the news of their little adventure had spread through the Regents, he'd wanted to dismantle the entire Paladin organization in Seattle and scatter those fools all over the world. It had taken him days to rein in his temper enough to look at the situation with a clear head.

Breaking up the close-knit group would've served no purpose. In fact, it would've been counterproductive. Paladins took care of their own. Threaten one and you had them all breathing fire down your neck. So instead of banishing them all to obscurity, he'd gritted his teeth and continued to frustrate any way he could.

That, in fact, was his favorite pastime. Speaking of which, maybe it was time for another round of mandatory tests. That always set Trahern off, which was fun to watch. Not that he gave a flying fuck about the results, only that it kept the Paladins off balance and riled up.

He'd give the Guildmaster another day to recuperate. Kalith warriors didn't heal quite as fast as Paladins did, but it was close. Maybe he should make the next trip up to Justice Point by himself. Having Joe with him would only complicate matters. In the past, he'd stayed overnight at the bed-and-breakfast where Jacob Justice, the owner, had always been up for a good game of chess to pass the time. Should he risk it? Of course, if any of the Seattle contingent was hanging around, he'd be dead meat.

At least his recent visits had all been at night. The Paladins might not be watching so closely when the sun was up, especially knowing the Kaliths' sensitivity to light. No one there had seen him. He should be safe enough, especially if he kept his stay brief, just one night.

Walking to the minuscule window in the corner of his office, he stared out at the Seattle skyline. Sometimes it felt as if the entire world conspired against him. What was wrong with wanting to retire early and rich? That certainly wasn't going to happen on the pittance the Regents paid him, so he was building up a little nest egg for himself. If a few people died along the way, that just left more for him.

As far as he was concerned, it was capitalism at its best.

Tate frowned at the flowery teacup in her hand for a long time before finally setting it down, reaching instead for the one mug on the shelf. Hunter's mug, or at least it used to be before she'd kicked him out of the apartment and her life.

Somehow, sipping a strong brew of Darjeeling from the heavy piece of crockery offered her the only comfort she'd been able to find. Stupid, she knew, but the solid weight of the mug somehow eased the pain that had settled in her chest since Hunter had left her kitchen. Left her.

She poured the hot liquid from the plain teapot she'd also used for Hunter. Was she a glutton for punishment or a fool for clinging to the few reminders she had of the time he'd spent in her life? Probably a little bit of both.

Although, to be honest, even though he'd vacated the premises, he certainly hadn't vacated that huge place in her heart he'd managed to carve out for himself. When he'd tossed his duffel in the back of his truck and backed out of the driveway, heading for God knows where, she'd watched in silence. Not because she'd had nothing to say, but because the sight had made her skin hurt and her lungs quit working.

She'd wanted to scream that it was all his fault, but that wasn't true. He'd warned her off repeatedly, but she hadn't listened. Instead, she'd let herself pretend that he'd just been the average guy next door. Well, he'd been next door all right, but he and the crowd he ran with were anything but average.

His explanation of who and what he was had sounded insane. Trouble was, she had seen too much to deny the truth. Hunter wasn't completely human, and those parts that were alien in origin gave him special abilities. All of that freaked her out, but at the same time she was grateful to his long-lost ancestors for donating that magical DNA—it was all that had kept Hunter alive this long. A sly voice in the back of her mind reminded her that it hadn't been Hunter's alien genes that she'd been admiring when he'd finally cornered her against the kitchen table, though.

No, he'd been all man as he'd reduced her to a quivering mass of hormones with his touch. And it wasn't mere lust that had her aching now. No, she feared it was another *l* word, one she couldn't bear to let herself admit. Not now, not when it was too late.

Her tea had grown cold, but she didn't want it anyway. All of this wallowing was getting her nowhere. There had to be something she could do to occupy her mind. It was Monday, so the shop was closed, leaving her free to do whatever she liked. She didn't feel like shopping, but she needed to be active.

Her yard was in good shape and wouldn't need mowing for another few days. Maybe she should head over to the Auntie Ms and do theirs for them. With Hunter gone, they'd be back to using a lawn service, something they could ill afford on their budget. The three women did their best to be independent and take care of themselves. But if they'd accept help from Hunter, they surely wouldn't mind Tate lending a helping hand. They could bake her cookies if they felt the need to pay her back.

She put on her garden shoes and headed out to the garage to get her lawn mower, trying to ignore how much junk Hunter had cleaned out of the garage or how nicely the lawn mower ran since he'd tuned it up. Nope, she wasn't going to think about him.

That plan lasted as long as it took her to push her mower the short distance to the Auntie Ms house. Not only was the front yard neatly mowed but the bushes had recently been trimmed as well. Darn, she should've thought of this sooner. Judging by the amount of work that had been done, they'd obviously already spent a small fortune on getting the place spruced up.

She was about to go back home when a movement at the back of the house caught her attention. At first she thought she was imagining things, seeing what her heart wanted to see, similarities where there were none. Whoever she'd glimpsed out of the corner of her eye had gone back around the corner, where she could no longer see him.

For her own peace of mind, maybe she should go look at the Auntie Ms new gardener, even introduce herself to the man. That way he'd know that someone was looking out for the elderly ladies. Then she'd know for certain that her mind had been playing tricks on her.

With a strange mix of reluctance and determination, she cut across the lawn, heading for the backyard, all the while hoping that Mabel and her sisters were taking their afternoon naps or were too caught up in their soaps to notice her.

Mentally rehearsing her little impromptu speech, she rounded the corner of the house, only to come up against a newly laid brick wall. Except this "wall" wore a T-shirt and ragged jeans. It also had a familiar shade of reddish brown hair and stormy gray-green eyes.

Her heart stopped before her feet did, slamming her right up against Hunter's chest. Only his quick reflexes prevented them both from tumbling to the ground. There were words she should be saying, questions she should be asking, but all she could do was stand there and stare up into his angry eyes.

• • •

Hunter waited until he was sure Tate regained her balance and then made himself let go of her. Not that he wanted to, but it was for the best. Her initial response to seeing him might have been surprise, but temper was sure to follow. After all, she'd done her best to banish him from Justice Point. And even though he understood her reasons, it still irritated him.

Tate swallowed hard, trying to regain the ability to talk. She glanced at the open window behind her and dropped her voice to a harsh whisper, probably not wanting the Aunties to hear her rip into him.

"What are you doing here?"

He crossed his arms over his chest and widened his stance, making it clear that he was going to stand his ground. "I live here."

She shook her head slowly, as if struggling to make sense of what he was telling her. "No, you left with your friends and said you'd be back to pick up your stuff."

"That's right. I did."

He was toying with her, but he couldn't seem to help himself. Not when all he really wanted to do was yank her right back up against his chest again and kiss the living daylights out of her. She'd probably knock him upside the head for trying, but the pain might just be worth it. It certainly couldn't be any worse than what he'd been suffering since leaving her kitchen.

"So you can't plan on moving back into the garage apartment like nothing ever happened." Her voice started to increase in volume, but she immediately quieted down when he gave the window a pointed glance.

"I don't need to. I said I live *here*." Which was true,

but he was going to let her puzzle it out for herself.

"Hunter Fitzsimon, you're not making a bit of sense."

He shrugged. "Not my problem. Now, if you'll excuse me, I have chores to do."

Before he could take two steps, she did an end run, grabbing his arm and planting herself directly in his way. Her simple touch sent a jolt of high-powered need racing through him. The predictable effect on his anatomy was so intense it hurt.

He leaned in close, crowding her, and growled, "Touch me at your own risk, Tate. I'd let go damn quick if you don't want a repeat of what we did in the kitchen the other morning. I'm sure I can think of a few things we haven't tried yet."

Her eyes flared wide in fury. But before she could tear into him but good, the door behind them opened and Mabel stepped out onto the porch with a glass of lemonade in her hand.

"Why, hello, Tate. I didn't know you were out here or I would've brought you a glass, too. I figured Hunter might need a break about now from all the hard work he's been doing for us." She held on to the handrail and carefully walked down the steps. "Isn't it wonderful that he's going to be staying with my sisters and me for a while? That's a real shame about the plumbing problem in your garage apartment. I hope they can get it fixed soon."

Then the elderly woman smiled at him, showing off her dimples. "Well, not *too* soon. We like having such a handsome young man around. He works too hard, of course, no matter how many times we tell him that we don't expect him to earn his keep."

"How nice for all of you, Mabel."

Tate's smile for her elderly friend appeared genuine, nothing at all like the snarky one she shot in his direction. So be it. Two could play at that game.

"I was going to stop by and ask if you'd called the plumber yet, Tate. I'd like to know when it will be livable again so I can move back in." There—let her field that ball.

Her voice dripped sugar. "Why, yes, I have, Hunter. Unfortunately, he can't get a crew here for days, perhaps weeks. That's why I suggested you might want to look for alternative housing. You know, like in town."

Mabel wasn't a fool. She glanced from Hunter to Tate and then back again. "Okay, you two. What's going on?"

"Nothing, Mabel. Everything's fine."

Tate's attempt to placate her friend flopped big time. The other woman drew herself up to her full height and sighed heavily.

"Tate Justice, I never thought I'd see the day that you'd lie to me. This has all the earmarks of a lover's quarrel. Are you two fighting?"

"No, we're not fighting," Hunter hastened to assure her, but then realized that left her assumption about them being lovers unanswered. Before he could address that issue, Tate spoke up.

"Our relationship is nothing like that, Mabel. Not that we have a relationship at all." Then, as if realizing how ridiculous that sounded, she tried again. "What I mean is I'm his landlord, nothing more."

"I'll repeat what I just said, since you didn't seem to understand me. I don't like being lied to. Now maybe it's yourself you're lying to, but I can tell you this much. I've had my share of landlords over the years, but never once did we shoot sparks like you two do whenever you get within ten feet of each other."

Then she shook her finger at Hunter. "And you, young man. I suspect you've also misled me and my sisters about the circumstances which led you to our door. You can still stay with us because I issued the invitation and won't go back on my word. However, I suggest you do what you can to mend the fences between you and our Tate here. Do I make myself clear?"

What could he say to that? "I'm sorry about all of this, Mabel. Why don't you let me see you to the door so Tate and I can talk in private?"

"All right, but I expect a full report."

As he helped her up the steps, he kept a wary eye over his shoulder to see if Tate was going to bolt. But no, she stood there waiting right where he'd left her. Judging by her expression, their talk wasn't destined to be a pleasant one. That was okay. He was in the mood for a good dustup, as D.J. would call it.

As soon as Mabel was tucked safely back inside the house, he braced himself for combat and marched back to where Tate stood waiting. He stalked past her without waiting to see if she'd follow him. If she didn't, he'd toss her over his shoulder and haul her off into the woods so they could rip into each other in private. In fact, he almost wished she'd refuse. Right now a few caveman tactics held definite appeal.

He stopped a few feet away. "Well, are you coming?"

Tate slowly shook her head, more than a hint of suspicion in her expression. "Why can't we talk here?"

He jerked his head back toward the house. "Because those women might be a little hard of hearing, but they're not deaf and they're not stupid. If you want to discuss all the pertinent details of the past couple of weeks in front of them, fine with me. I just thought you'd appreciate a little discretion."

Before he could take more than a step in her direction, she was on the move.

"Where are we going?"

Anywhere he could get her to go, like back to that big cedar where he'd first kissed her. But somehow he doubted that's what she meant.

"For a walk." He shot her a heated glance. "Or we could talk in your kitchen. We'd have plenty of privacy there."

She immediately veered across the yard, heading directly for the woods where the path led down to the beach. "Stop it, Hunter. We both know that wouldn't be smart."

Maybe not, but when it came to Tate Justice, he wasn't feeling very intelligent. He fell into step beside her, content to let her take the lead. As they walked along in silence, he struggled to find something to say, something that would ease this awful strain between them. It wouldn't do to get too comfortable. Nothing had changed.

And the bottom line was he didn't want to hurt her any more than he already had.

A short time later, they reached a clearing that looked out over the islands dotting that stretch of Puget Sound. He wondered if he'd ever get used to the incredible beauty that the locals seemed to just accept as a matter of course. Or if he'd be there long enough to find out. His goal in coming to Seattle was to find out how much of his old life he could salvage. Despite his longtime friendships with Jarvis and others back in Missouri, he was finding life here in the Pacific Northwest unexpectedly appealing.

And not only because of the woman standing next to him.

"So why did you wangle an invitation from Mabel and her sisters to move into their house?"

"I needed someplace to stay. My reasons for coming to Justice Point haven't changed. The danger hasn't gone away." He shifted his stance slightly in order to keep her in his sights while still watching the waves crash on the rocky beach below.

She rubbed her hands up and down her arms, as if she found the shade of the trees too cool for comfort. "I see. And your buddies, where are they?"

"Why do you care?" Maybe he could've put that a little better, but being this close to Tate and not being able to touch her made it hard to control himself.

"I just want to make sure that you aren't *all* imposing on my friends."

That did it.

"If you're that worried about the Aunties, I can always move back into the apartment. As I recall, the rent's paid for another two weeks."

Just that quickly, her expression went from angry concern for her friends to guilty. "I was going to refund your money, but I didn't have a forwarding address. I'll go get my checkbook."

"Keep it."

For the first time she looked straight at him. "No, I'm the one who asked you to leave, so I owe you."

He fisted his hands to keep from reaching out to shake some sense into her. He doubted it would work anyway, and touching her would be mistake of monumental proportions.

"You don't owe me a damn thing, and I don't want you to pay me back, Tate. What's more, I'll be insulted if you try."

She was definitely his equal when it came to stubborn. "But it would only be fair—"

"Who gives a rip about fair? Nothing about this is fair." If life were fair, his landlord would've been an elderly man, not the feisty beauty standing beside him.

"Hunter, I want—"

"You gave up all rights to wanting anything from me, which only shows how smart you are." He ran his hands through his hair in frustration. "Look, I can't leave the area, not until the problem I was sent here to handle is resolved. The other night made it clear that it isn't a one-man job, so Larem and the other guys will be hanging around, too."

He glanced back toward the house behind them. "I wanted to stick close by, so I conned my way into staying with Mabel and her sisters. I'd just as soon have stayed in the apartment, but that didn't work out. So here's the deal: I'll continue to stay out of your way and you'll stay out of mine. When it's safe to leave, I will. I understand why you don't want me around."

Her eyes looked glazed, as if she was fighting tears, but it was hard to tell in the dark shadows of the trees. Damn it, the last thing he wanted was to make her cry, but he'd meant what he'd said. He'd do his best to stay out of her way until he could safely disappear from her life altogether.

"Do we have a deal?"

"I don't guess I have much of a choice, do I?"

He'd been right. There was a tear slipping down the curve of her cheek. She ignored it, so he did too.

Then she did something totally unexpected. She stepped close enough to whisper near his ear, "But you're wrong on one count, Hunter. I do want you, and *that* is the real problem." Then she kissed his cheek and walked away.

Tate resolutely turned her attention back to her book, doing her best to ignore a certain former tenant. Okay, the man was going to drive her crazy, if she wasn't already there. Hunter was holding to his promise to leave her alone, yet he still found ways to remind her that he was close by. Like yesterday morning, when she'd unlocked the door of the tea shop to find a container of fresh-picked blueberries sitting on the porch. Or when she'd made a trip in to town and returned to find her lawn mowed.

Right now, he was leaving on one of his nightly

prowls. It was a relief to know he wasn't headed for the woods at the back of her property. But that probably meant one or more of his friends were down on the beach. She worried about them almost as much. But the real problem was that watching him stroll by in the darkness was a surefire guarantee that she'd be dreaming about him. Again. And she suspected that he'd been watching her too. Before he'd realized that she'd spotted him standing in the shadows across the road. She hoped that he was as miserable as she was.

It certainly didn't help that the Auntie Ms still made their daily trip to her shop for tea and the paper. Somehow they always managed to turn the conversation around to the latest thing Hunter and those nice friends of his had done for various residents of Justice Point.

Windows had been washed, minor repairs made, cars tuned up, and enough wood split to keep the drafty old Victorian homes heated for much of the coming fall and winter. Tate kept telling herself that she wasn't jealous, that she was actually happy for her friends, many of whom were elderly. An uneasy mix of the two feelings was closer to the truth.

The handyman marathon probably served two purposes for Hunter and company. It gave them something to do when they weren't patrolling for aliens, but it also gave them an excuse to hang around without people wondering what they were up to. Had anyone bothered to wonder why they had so much free time on their hands? Probably not, even though they certainly didn't act like the usual tourists who visited the area.

Not that any of it was her concern. She had enough to

take care of without worrying about . . . Hunter. There. She'd admitted it. No matter how things had turned out for the two of them, she didn't want him hurt. As long as he was still hanging around Justice Point, he was in danger. Hadn't he been hurt enough? How much could that super-duper secret organization he served ask of one man, special genes or not? Who did they think they were?

She'd seen his scars and his pain. He deserved a better life than more of the same until he was all used up. They all did.

That did it. Slamming her book closed, she marched down the stairs, determined to confront Hunter. He had no business risking his life—or lives in his case—so carelessly. Righteous indignation carried her as far as the road. Determination took her a bit farther. Temper and plain old-fashioned stubbornness kept her going until she reached the turn in the road where the trees blocked out the last bit of light from the houses behind her.

The darkness settled her. She paused to breathe in the spicy scent of the fir trees and the faint dampness in the breeze rolling in from the Sound. The silence was comforting rather than frightening, because she wasn't really alone. Not with Hunter standing right behind her. Perhaps she was fooling herself, but she could swear that she could feel the warmth of his tall, hard body despite the distance between them.

"I don't suppose it would do any good to remind you that there are scary things that go bump in the night around here."

His husky voice rasped over her nerves with a powerful jolt.

She slowly turned to face him. "Scarier than you?"

The bit of moonlight through the trees wasn't enough to allow her to see him clearly, but that didn't matter. Her mind and heart were plenty able to fill in the blanks.

"I'm not all that scary." There was a hint of a smirk in his answer.

"No, but you can't deny that you're dangerous." Especially to her heart.

He moved closer. She let him.

His fingers skimmed down her arm as he whispered near her ear, "Why did you follow me, Tate?"

"Because I'm angry." Although she didn't sound that way, even to her own ears. No, she sounded needy.

"What have I done this time?"

As he spoke, he shrugged off his jacket and wrapped it around her shoulders. The leather held both his body heat and his scent. She should've refused it, but the comfort of its buttery soft warmth eased her spirit.

"I'm not mad at you." She sighed. "Well, yeah, I am, but that's not what I'm talking about now. I'm really, really furious at those people you work for. How dare they treat you and your friends with such disregard for your well-being? You aren't some kind of weapon meant to be used up and tossed away."

She got right up in his face. "I want to give them a piece of my mind as soon as you can arrange it. Now would even be better."

Hunter jerked back a step. How the hell was he supposed to respond to that? There was no way he could let her near the Regents, even if he'd been wanting to have the same discussion with them for years now. But Paladins fought until they could fight no more. That was their fate, no matter how they felt about it. He just wasn't used to someone other than his band of brothers giving a damn about the cost to their souls.

Tate wasn't going to be satisfied with platitudes or bullshit about the secrecy demanded by his employers. He wouldn't put it past her to go on a holy crusade if he didn't head her off at the pass.

"Some things are the way they have to be, Tate, regardless of how they seem to an outsider." Thanks to his night vision, he saw all too well how that last word hurt her.

He seemed to spend a lot of time trying to apologize to this woman. "Look, I didn't mean it that way. But there are reasons for the way we live. Maybe someday we'll figure out a better way to do things, but for now it's best to maintain the status quo."

Her silence puzzled him. She tended to shoot from the hip, so he had no idea what was going on in that head of hers. The wisest course of action was to walk her back home and then run like hell before he forgot his promise to leave her alone. Yeah, she'd followed him, but that didn't absolve him of all responsibility, not when he'd given his word.

She turned away from him. "I hate this, Hunter. I can't concentrate on anything, wondering where you are and what you're doing and if you're hurting again. Still. More."

He eased up behind her, circling her waist with his arms, trying to comfort her. When she slowly leaned back against him, he bent down to rest his head next to hers, soaking up the seconds before common sense reared its ugly head and he forced himself to walk away.

"I wish I could pull one of those mind melds you mentioned and take this all away from you, but I can't."

She reached back over her shoulder to rest the palm of her hand against his face. He closed his eyes to better savor the touch. "I wouldn't want that."

"Not even now? After all you've seen and heard?"

She turned in his arms. "Not even now, especially after all I've seen and heard. I might not be able to understand how you live your life, but I don't regret having *known* you, Hunter Fitzsimon."

Her eyes were huge in her face when she added, "Not in any sense of the word. Because you know what, no matter what happens from this point on, nothing is going to change the fact that I love you."

Then she raised up on her toes and kissed him as if her life, and maybe his, depended on it.

Chapter 16

Hunter leaned his forehead against hers and closed his eyes. "You have to know I never meant for that to happen."

She managed a small smile. "I know, and I'm not asking for anything in return. I just couldn't stand for you to eventually walk away without knowing how much I care about you."

He struggled to respond, his own emotions were a fucked-up mess. If words existed that could describe them, they weren't in his vocabulary.

"In a perfect world, I would tell you . . ." He stopped there, unable to go any further with that particular thought. "But this isn't a perfect world. It's my world, and I won't drag you into it."

"Too late, big guy. I'm already there. At least for right now."

He knew he should walk away—or, better yet, run.

But for this one moment, he had Tate in his arms, with her love for him in her eyes, and his heart in his throat.

The last thing he'd expected when he'd set off on his nightly walk was a chance to hold Tate again, much less hear those words from her. Sure, he'd hoped to catch a glimpse of her up there in that window seat, reading a book while she pretended to not be watching for him. They'd both been skating the edges of their promise to stay away, but now they'd blown the whole deal to hell and back.

And, frankly, he didn't give a damn, not with Tate so close. An hour from now, or maybe tomorrow morning, they'd have to rebuild those walls. But not now. Not yet.

His hands sought out the warm silk of her bare skin underneath her soft cotton T-shirt. Could she sense how right it felt to be skin to skin again, even if only that much? God, he hoped so. He didn't want to be the only one on the verge of a total meltdown under the starlit sky.

"Hunter, please . . ." she murmured as she kissed his jawline and did a little burrowing of her own.

He moaned as she gently raked her nails down the length of his back, pressing her body against his. He eased his hand down across her waist to trace the curve of her bottom, lifting her higher, holding her closer, wishing he could lay her down and love every inch of her the way she deserved.

His conscience might not let him strip off her clothes and take her right there in the woods, but he could at least pleasure her. It was amazing how easy it was to ignore the vow he'd made to protect Tate, even from himself, no matter the cost.

The elastic waistband of her pajamas proved no barrier at all as he sought out the center of her desire. She jerked with surprise, then murmured her approval as he touched and teased her with the same sweet, syncopated rhythm that marked the dance of their kiss.

He smiled against Tate's lips, sensing how close she was to coming apart at the seams. Oh, yeah, this was going to be incredible for her, and he would be happy with that. He'd have to be. But then headlights flickered through the woods as a car drove past out on the road. The sudden illumination startled Tate, and she immediately pushed herself free from his touch.

She stood there, just out of reach, breathing hard and looking adorably rumpled. Slowly she shook her head, as if to clear away the passion-induced cobwebs. Finally, she tugged at her flannels, pulling them back up firmly around her waist and holding his jacket closed over her chest.

"What are we doing here, Hunter?"

"I would think the answer to that would be obvious." He kept his voice calm and level, but inside he was screaming with the need to finish what they'd started.

She shot him a disgruntled look. "That's not what I meant, and you know it."

"Then tell me where we go from here, Tate, because tonight could be all we have."

"Yes, I know, but I've also never asked you for more than you could offer."

No, she hadn't. She'd given him so much, making him realize what a selfish bastard he'd become. He knew full well how he felt about her. The least he could do was tell her.

He reached out to her with his hand and his truth and threw the dice. "I've never said this to anyone else, and saying it now won't change anything, but I do love you, Tate. Let me show you how much."

Then he held his breath and waited for her answer.

She had to be out of her mind. When she headed to the sanctuary of her bedroom, she wasn't going alone. She took Hunter's hand in hers, her throat tight with the need for his touch. "Let's find someplace more private to continue this discussion."

His smile heated her through and through.

As they walked back toward the house, they took their time and enjoyed the journey. She'd never thought of the simple act of holding hands as foreplay, but the solid feel of his fingers entwined with hers was revving her engine like crazy. Small tingles of warmth glided up her arm and spread through her body.

In the shadows cast by the streetlights, Hunter stopped to pull Tate into his arms. His soft lips contrasted sharply with the slight roughness of his skin against hers as he kissed her and his tongue danced with hers. God, he tasted like male heat and temptation.

She liked that he wasn't rushing to finish what they'd started, instead taking his time to relish each moment. He made her feel cherished and loved, and that was enough. It was all they had, but she wasn't going to dwell on that. Not now.

He seemed content to simply hold her, but she wanted more. "Let's go upstairs."

They walked into the house through the back door and straight up the steps. The last time Hunter had been in her bedroom was when she'd woken up to the shock of him alive and well after being stabbed through the heart. She shoved those memories out of her head. Despite the differences in his DNA, she knew he was a good man. That's all that mattered.

That and the fact that he loved her.

She left his side long enough to turn down the bed and to fetch a box she'd picked up at the pharmacy on her last trip into town.

"We'll need these."

Hunter smiled his approval when she handed it to him. "Good thinking. I'd hate to have to make a run into the city right now."

He set the box on the bedside table and reached for the bottom of his T-shirt. Tate caught his hands in hers. "Let me."

Then she proceeded to strip him of all the trappings of civilization. His shirt, his pants, everything. Finally, using all of the tools at hand—tongue, touch, and taste—she stripped him of all control.

"Woman, you're killing me here," he groaned. "Enough of that."

Then he pulled her back up to her feet and turned the tables. Her clothes disappeared, carelessly tossed about while he murmured his approval of each patch of soft skin he uncovered. She knew herself to be ordinary, but Hunter made her beautiful with the worshipful way he touched her, his eyes burning bright and greedy.

Finally, he settled her on the bed, his weight pressing down on her as he took her deep and hard. She cried out, loving the give-and-take and the way their bodies fit together.

He paused, pushing himself up to arm's length from her, his stormy eyes looking a bit rueful. "I want to go slow, but I can't. Not this time."

Even as he spoke, he was moving over her, in her. She wasn't about to complain and told him so while digging her fingertips into the bunched muscles of his world-class backside.

"Give me all you've got, Hunter. I can take it. I want it." Then she locked her heels around his hips, angling her body up to better meet his thrusts.

He braced himself and then cut loose, relentlessly driving them both to the brink. The skin on his face was pulled taut as he strained for both control and completion. Having that effect on such a strong man was heady stuff, as Tate fought to push him over the edge.

It didn't take long, and he dragged her screaming over the precipice with him. The warm cocoon of her bed shattered into a billion little pieces, and she wasn't sure they would ever fit back together again. Hunter's powerful body shuddered and shook as he poured out his passion deep inside her. Tate held on for dear life and rode out the storm.

And then, for the first time in days, she knew peace.

Hunter was pretty sure he'd died—again. His heart had certainly stuttered to a stop and his lungs had surely burst as he and Tate had crossed the finish line. But even a dead man should have better manners than to crush his lover—at least until he was ready for round two.

He mustered up enough energy to roll to the side, taking Tate with him and tucking her in close beside him.

"That was amazing." She sighed and snuggled closer. "Think we woke the neighbors?"

Had he ever laughed with a lover? He didn't think so. "I'm surprised that D.J. and company haven't come charging in with their swords drawn to make sure we weren't under attack."

Her soft laughter warmed his soul as her hand wandered down his body. "I'll be glad to tell them this particular sword is more than capable of handling any situation that should arise in here."

Oh, yeah, when she touched him like that, he felt invincible.

He lifted her up onto his chest, shifting so that she straddled his hips. "In that case, let me show you some of my favorite moves."

Her eyes lit up. "Okay, let's see what you've got."

"Hold on, then, because it's going to be one heck of a ride." He grasped her hips and held her still until their bodies were once again joined.

Tate sighed, her fingers flexing on his chest like a contented cat's. With a siren's smile, she leaned down close for a long, deep kiss that only served to fan the flames higher as their passion burned. Once again, he wasn't sure he'd survive the experience, but at least he'd die a happy man.

• • •

Morning came way too soon. Normally Tate enjoyed waking up to a bright sunny day. But not this time, not knowing if this was not only the first time she'd wake up in Hunter's arms but the last as well.

"Don't think about it so hard," he said groggily. "We don't have to get up yet, do we?"

She reached up to touch his face, liking the roughness of his morning beard. "No, not yet."

"Good." Then he touched his lips to hers.

God, the man sure knew how to kiss. He nibbled at her lower lip before slipping his tongue inside her mouth, inviting her to join in and play. She wrapped her arms around his neck as the passion once again flared white hot between them. Hunter thrust his knee between her legs, the pressure easing her ache a little, but not nearly enough.

His hands explored every inch of her body, even places she'd never known were so erotic, all the while murmuring hushed descriptions of exactly what he planned to do to her. Some of his ideas shocked her, but she still couldn't wait for him to follow through.

Hunter's stormy eyes met hers, his smile wicked as he began a long journey down her body, following the trail his hands had blazed only moments before. He kissed his way down her throat, paying special attention to the pulse point at the base of her neck. Once again, he nuzzled her breasts, whispering his praise as he suckled one and then the other.

She giggled when his breath tickled her belly button

and the slight curve of her stomach. But then he settled between her legs, sliding his arms under her thighs, tilting her hips up at a higher angle. Was he going to . . . oh, yes, he was. He kissed her most private place, his breath warm and moist. Her head kicked back on the pillow as myriad sensations flashed through her.

Then his tongue, velvet smooth and soft, tasted her. He growled with pleasure, the slight vibration causing her inner muscles to contract as her body prepared for what was to come. He shifted slightly, freeing up one hand as he eased first one finger and then a second deep inside her.

"Hunter!"

"Like that, do you?" He worked his fingers in a slow rhythm.

"Faster," she whispered as she thrust up against his hand.

"I thought we'd take our time this morning." He maintained the same pace but used his tongue in counterpoint. "How's that?"

She couldn't lie. "Not enough," she rasped.

He immediately increased the pressure with his tongue and the speed of his wicked fingers. "Come for me, Tate!"

Pleasure exploded through her body, starting deep inside her core and spreading outward. Hunter left her shuddering with the aftershocks while he opened another condom. Then he was back, spreading her legs wide as he positioned himself at her body's entrance.

Digging her heels into the mattress, she waited for that first powerful thrust when he'd claim her. For all his promise to go slow, once her body adjusted to the abrupt invasion, he didn't hold back at all. She reached over her head to hold the bottom edge of the headboard as he drove into her.

She chanted his name as he withdrew and plunged and withdrew again, the sensation blocking out everything else. Her entire existence narrowed to just the two of them straining to become one, their bodies blending, fitting together with such perfection that it brought tears to her eyes.

Then he rolled to the side onto his back. She rose up over him and began rocking, loving the control he'd ceded to her. He used one hand to capture her breast, teasing her nipple into a sharp point. At the same time, he slipped one finger between where their bodies were joined, putting pressure on just the right spot.

She slowed down, loving the way he made sure that his pleasure was hers as well. As much as she wanted it to last forever, the pressure was building and building. Her body bucked against his, riding them both hard until Hunter suddenly arched up with a loud holler as he grabbed her hips with both hands and held her immobile. His shuddering release deep inside of her triggered her own, until they were both lost in a maelstrom of lightning and thunder.

She closed her eyes against the swirling chaos and collapsed against his sleekly muscled chest, holding on for dear life. His arms cradled her gently and stroked the length of her back. She wasn't sure, but she thought he kissed the top of her head.

"Are you all right?"

She smoothed her hand up his arm. "Far better than merely all right. I'm not sure there are words for how good I feel."

He chuckled. "Maybe we need to make some up. How about wonderistic?"

"Or splendorific?"

"Yeah, that works. I just wish—" He stopped midsentence, a frown erasing his good mood. Then his body stiffened, and not in a good way.

"Somebody is at the door." He lifted her off to his side. "Let me get cleaned up and dressed so I can distract them."

"I'd rather ignore them." Even though she knew that wouldn't work.

"So would I, but it's probably D.J. and the guys. We have business to attend to." Although neither of them had moved an inch, suddenly there was a yawning gap between them.

She reached up to brush his hair back from his face. "Business that doesn't include me."

His arms tightened around her. "Tate, we both know it has to be that way. I won't risk your getting hurt because of me and the world I live in."

The world that would someday destroy him, but now wasn't the time to throw that in his face. She'd promised not to ask for more than he could give, and she wouldn't betray his trust. But already the pain was settling back in her chest, knowing he was so close to disappearing from her life.

But with a smile and a hug, she'd send her warrior lover off to face his battles, just as women had been doing for millennia. That didn't mean she wouldn't weep for them both when she was alone. And she would be alone for a long time.

This time she heard the knock at the door downstairs, an impatient demand that she be up and moving. Knowing further delay would only prolong the inevitable, she threw back the covers and trudged into the bathroom.

Hunter remained motionless as Tate left the bed and walked away, taking his heart with her and leaving only darkness behind. Despite the bright sunshine streaming in through the window, the day promised to be the first in an endless parade of dark ones for him.

He hoped like hell that Tate wasn't hurting as much as he was, but he knew she was. Why else had she cranked up the radio in the shower so loud? Despite her efforts to hide her tears, his sharp Paladin hearing made it all too clear. His first instinct was to go to her, to offer what comfort he could. But it would change nothing. The sooner he got out of Tate's life, the sooner she'd get over him and vice versa.

Yeah, right, like that was going to happen anytime soon. Back when he'd regained consciousness to find himself strapped down to Doc's stainless steel table after being sliced and diced, he'd known it was going to be a long, hard crawl back to normal. One step at a time. One day at a time. But this particular pain was going to be a bitch to deal with, because he wasn't the only one hurting.

The banging downstairs was getting louder. Whoever was pounding on the door was going to make a handy target for Hunter's temper. He yanked on his jeans and yesterday's shirt and stomped down the stairs ready to start swinging. Halfway down, it occurred to him that it might be Mabel or one of her sisters looking for him. After all, he hadn't gone home last night.

Time to calm down. No matter who was at the door, they weren't responsible for Hunter's foul mood. If it was one of the Auntie Ms, he'd reassure them that both he and Tate were fine. If it was a stranger, he'd offer tea and scones to keep them occupied until Tate came downstairs. But if it was one of his friends, well, he'd cross that bridge when he came to it.

He turned on the overhead lights in the shop. One glance out the door made it clear that the impatient customer was a stranger to him. Hunter flipped the sign to Open and unlocked the door. A man, perhaps in his late fifties, turned his temper on Hunter.

"It's about time. The sign clearly says the tea shop opens at nine. It's almost ten."

For Tate's sake, Hunter bit back the urge to tell the jerk to fuck off, offering instead a cool, "Can I help you?"

"Where's Jacob Justice? And who are you?" the man snapped as he pushed past Hunter into the shop. "I've been coming here to play chess with him for years, and I've never seen you before."

"I'm new." Hunter walked back to the counter, needing to put something solid between himself and the irritating customer. Obviously this guy hadn't heard about the former owner's death. It didn't feel right that Hunter should be the one to break the news, especially if this guy was indeed an old friend of Tate's late uncle. He could at least make some effort to make the older man feel welcome.

"Would you like some tea?"

Judging from the man's reaction, Hunter suspected his smile hadn't come across as particularly friendly. Too bad. At least he'd tried.

"I'll have Earl Grey, and make sure you heat the teapot first."

"Don't worry. I know how to make tea." The man's autocratic demeanor was making it even harder for Hunter to remain civil.

"I should hope so, considering it's your job."

The man sat at the table in the far corner, out of sight of both the door and the windows. Something about the man's behavior was off, although Hunter couldn't quite pinpoint what it was.

He'd planned on being gone before Tate came down, but he hated to leave her alone with this jerk. Maybe he'd check in with D.J., and then come back to keep an eye on the situation until the man moved on. To hurry it along, he carried the tea over to the man's table.

"Will there be anything else?" He deliberately crowded close to the table, forcing the man to lean back to meet Hunter's gaze.

Even so, the man took his own sweet time pulling his attention away from his newspaper. "Any business I have left with Mr. Justice is for his ears only. And don't think I won't mention the surly nature of his hired help."

Tate was coming. Time to get moving.

• • •

The bell above the shop door jingled just as Tate's foot hit the bottom step. She didn't need a crystal ball to know that Hunter had just made his escape. Pasting a bright smile on her face took some effort, but she didn't want to scare away innocent customers by greeting them with tears streaming down her face.

"Good morning. . . ," she started to say before she recognized the solitary man tucked away in the darkest corner of the shop. "Oh, Mr. Kincade, how nice to see you again. It has been a long time."

Well, that was a lie. Not about the time that had lapsed since she'd seen this particular man, but that it was nice to see him again. Unlike her, Uncle Jacob had been blessed with the patience of a saint. All she could remember was how hard her uncle had worked to please Mr. Kincade. The tea was always too hot, too cold, too weak, too strong. The bed in his room was too hard or too soft. Everything was always *too* something.

But Kincade had been one of the few who'd been her uncle's equal at chess, so Jacob had tolerated his occasional stay. They'd spent hours huddled over the chessboard, each game hard-fought. She crossed her fingers that Kincade had stopped by for tea and nothing more.

"Ms. Justice, I see you're back for another visit with your uncle. I hope you don't mind if I steal away some of Jacob's time to play chess." His smile looked a bit forced as usual.

Oh, no, he hadn't heard. She'd had to break the news

to a number of old customers, and it never got any easier. As raw as her own emotions were right now, the last thing she wanted to do was think about the other important man in her life she'd lost.

"Mr. Kincade, I'm sorry to have to tell you that my uncle passed away a few months ago. He left me the house and tea shop, so I live here now."

Kincade set his cup down hard, his eyes wide with shock. "I am so sorry, Ms. Justice . . . Tate. Jacob was a good man, and I know he meant the world to you." The sincerity in his voice didn't quite warm up his eyes. "The world has lost a great chess player. I will miss him."

"We all do, Mr. Kincade. I know he always looked forward to playing you."

"That's sweet of you to say." He looked around the tea shop as if really looking at it for the first time. "I can see that you've made a few changes."

"Not many, except that I've made the tea shop my main focus."

"Does that mean you've closed the bed-and-breakfast? I was hoping that my usual room would be available just for tonight. I know that I should've called ahead, but your uncle always accommodated my erratic schedule."

The last thing she needed right now was an unexpected guest. On second thought, maybe it was. Anything to keep her hands busy and her mind occupied.

"I usually don't rent out rooms anymore, but I guess I can make an exception for an old customer."

"If you're sure it wouldn't be too much of an inconvenience, I would really appreciate it. My business associate is supposed to meet me here sometime late tomorrow, and I have no way of reaching him."

That was weird. "You can't call him?"

Kincade shook his head. "I'm afraid that would be difficult if not impossible. He'll be traveling a long distance to get here and is out of cell phone range, at least until he crosses the border. I suppose I could take a cab back to town and return in the morning to meet him here."

She forced a smile. "Since it's just one night, I'll be glad to have you stay. Let me refresh your tea. After I get things organized down here, I'll prepare your room."

"I appreciate this, Ms. Justice." He went back to his newspaper.

She poured him another pot of tea before disappearing behind the counter. It had been a few days since she'd last worked on her novel, although she'd been mulling over the plot in odd moments. So far, the end of the story remained shrouded in shadow.

Her heroine was definitely in love with the outlaw but had serious doubts about his suitability as a potential husband. The sheriff would be a good man to spend her life with—reliable and unlikely to end up behind bars or dancing at the end of a rope. On the other hand, she knew the longer the gunslinger hung around, the more likely he was to meet a bad end.

Decisions, decisions, decisions.

But in her heart, Tate knew that she and the heroine had both made their choice. Hunter wasn't an outlaw or a gunslinger, but he was a warrior fighting on a frontier that few people even knew existed. The gunslinger was just as much a product of his time as the sheriff, and the heroine knew in her gut that he would die to protect her. The real question was if he was willing to do whatever it took to live for her. Why was that so much harder for the hero to do than dying? Tate's heart ached for her fictional counterpart.

Hunter was the same. Despite how outlandish it sounded, she believed that he'd already given his life over and over again to keep humanity safe from the perils of another world. He'd definitely died down on the bluff to keep the evil from reaching Tate. Even now, he was with his friends making plans to continue their mission, regardless of the price they had to pay.

The cold, brutal truth was that Hunter was a Paladin warrior, and that would never change. It wasn't in him to walk away from his duty. But did that mean he couldn't have any joy in his life? Would it make his life better or worse to know that someone was waiting for him with open arms at the end of the day?

Could she convince him to take a chance on their love? Should she even try?

"Ms. Justice!"

She jerked her attention away from the blinking cursor on the screen. Judging by the aggravation on Kincade's face, it wasn't the first time he'd called her name.

"I'm sorry, Mr. Kincade. Do you need more hot water?"

"No, I just wanted to let you know that I'm going for a walk."

He started out the door, then turned back. "I hesitate to ask, but if my friend is delayed and gets in very late tomorrow, would you mind if we stayed a second night? I don't expect that to happen, but I'll need to make alternative plans if that will be too much of an inconvenience."

Since it sounded unlikely that they'd actually be staying, she nodded. "I suppose so, as long as it is just the one extra night for the two of you. I'll fix adjoining rooms for you."

"Thank you. While I'm gone, I would appreciate your asking that employee of yours to carry my bag upstairs for me. You should really teach him some better manners. He wasn't at all friendly." Then he walked out, yanking the door closed behind him.

She managed to hold back her laughter until her crotchety guest was out of sight. What had Hunter done to offend the man?

For now, she'd better leave her heroine to her own devices and get the rooms ready. She'd forgotten that Mr. Kincade often had another man or two with him. And now that she thought about it, those extra guests were unusual in some way. There was something different about them, but what was it?

Oh, well, it would come to her eventually. She picked up the suitcase and headed back upstairs.

Chapter 17

"Damn it, man, get your head in the game!"

Penn deliberately blocked Hunter's view of Tate's house. Normally he would've shoved the jerk out of his way, but the man was right. They had to make plans and needed Hunter's input. It wasn't their fault that his mind was two blocks away in Tate's bed.

"Sorry."

He turned his back on the tea shop and focused instead on the three other men. "Where were we?"

D.J. rolled his eyes. "We know where we are, Hunter. The question is, where were you last night? When we came back up the trail, we almost ran right into Mabel and one of her sisters. They were talking about you taking a walk and debating whether or not to leave the light on for you."

"Where I was is none of their business—or yours, for that matter." He glared at each man in turn, making sure they understood that this particular discussion was over. "Okay, now that that's settled, how did it go last night?"

D.J. acknowledged the change in subjects with a nod. "We posted signs both down on the beach and at the back of Tate's property that the trail is closed for repairs, hoping that will keep the locals and any tourists from stumbling into the middle of our business. To make it look legit, we tore up part of the trail right above that sharp switchback."

"Good thinking."

"Thank Larem. It was his idea."

Larem only shrugged. "While they were doing that, I checked out the cave a few times. No sign of any activity, but the barrier was fluctuating off and on all night."

Now that was interesting. "Was it doing that on its own, or was someone trying to bring it down?"

"Impossible to tell for sure." Penn sipped his coffee before continuing. "But when we checked in with Devlin this morning, he said there were no reports of problems anywhere else in the area. That makes us think someone was screwing with it from the other side."

Hunter struggled to keep his mind on Paladin business. He had a bad feeling about all of this. "So tonight might be the night we finally catch the bastards."

Which also meant these could be the last few hours that he could spend with Tate. Was he a selfish bastard for wanting to prolong their final good-bye? Probably.

"Are you all right?" Larem frowned and pointed at Hunter's hand.

He was crushing the oversized cup of coffee Penn

had brought him with a white-knuckled grip. It took some effort, but he forced himself to relax, at least on the surface.

"I'm fine. Look, why don't the three of you go get some rest. I still have the key to the apartment. Tate won't care if you use it for one afternoon."

Penn peered at him over the brim of his cup of coffee. "Yeah, and what are you going to do while we're snoozing?"

What Hunter wanted to do was drag Tate back upstairs for another bout of brain-rattling sex, but that wasn't going to happen. When D.J. yawned so wide that his jaw cracked, Hunter laughed.

"God, go lay down before you *fall* down. I'll head over to the bluff and keep an eye on things. If someone's trying to break through to our side, there's no telling when he'll succeed." He checked the slide of his sword. "I'll be ready for him."

"Sounds good." Penn pulled a revolver from the back of his waistband. "Take this, too. Shoot off a few rounds if you need help, and we'll come running. Otherwise, we'll catch up with you right before dark."

The two Paladins headed for the car to pick up their gear, but Larem hung back. When D.J. shot him a questioning look, Larem waved him off. "I'll hang out with Hunter for a while."

Hunter didn't need a babysitter. "That's not necessary."

Larem dumped the dregs of his tea out on the ground. "After what happened the last time, I don't think any of us should be alone down there. And before you ask, I'd feel the same way if it was Penn or D.J."

Hunter believed him. "Okay, let's go."

Actually, he appreciated the offer of company because he was in no mood to be alone with his own thoughts right now.

They hadn't gone more than a handful of steps when Larem broke the silence. "I don't meant to pry, but are you really all right, Hunter?"

Okay, so maybe he would've been better off alone, but he couldn't bring himself to tell Larem to kiss off either. After all, the Kalith warrior had shed his own blood to jump-start Hunter's return to the living. He owed the man.

"As all right as can be expected. I don't understand exactly what you did, but all my newest crop of injuries healed up fine." He slapped his bad leg. "Even this has improved a lot, so no complaints here."

He hoped that was enough to satisfy the Kalith warrior, but he wasn't surprised when Larem gave him a disgusted look. "Do I look like your Handler? I thought you'd foresworn spending any more time with Tate. Has that changed?"

"Do I act like I want to talk about this?"

Larem had the balls to laugh. "That doesn't mean you don't need to. Perhaps an outsider's viewpoint would help prevent you from screwing up big time."

Like he hadn't already. He should've kept his pants zipped, and they both knew it. With a derisive snort, Hunter asked, "And what makes you an expert? I don't see a parade of women chasing after you."

For the first time Larem's alien nature showed in his expression. It was as if he'd only been pretending to be human, and his real self briefly peeked out from behind the those pale eyes. That didn't make his pain any easier to witness.

"A man doesn't need a parade, Hunter. One female is enough, as long as she's the right one."

Damn, Hunter hadn't meant to rip open an old wound. "Sorry, Larem. I'm guessing you left someone important back home."

"And you'd guess wrong. She came with me."

Son of a bitch, could it get any worse? "Barak's sister? The one who's living with a Paladin?"

Larem nodded and kept walking. "I never got up my nerve to let her know how I really felt. Funny how you think you have all the time in the world, only to find out that it has slipped away."

"That really sucks."

"Indeed. I would ask you not to say anything. It would only hurt her and make things even more awkward for me."

"You have my word, and I'm sorry."

"Thank you. Maybe she would've accepted my suit, but perhaps not. But either way, I'll never know. However, it is not yet too late for you and Tate, Hunter. Think hard before you walk away from what she can offer you."

"Believe me, I know how much she can offer me." Even now the scent of her skin and the memory of her touch were driving him crazy with the need for more of the same.

They'd reached the edge of the woods. Somehow it was easier to spill his guts in the shadowy sanctuary of the towering firs. "The real problem is how little I can offer her. Hell, after we plug up this leak, I don't know where I'll be sent next. She's already seen me die once. How can I ask her to go through that again?"

"That doesn't seem to have affected her too much. Pardon my frankness, but I'm guessing that if she was totally freaked out by the experience, she wouldn't have invited you back into her bed last night."

Hunter's face flushed hot. "Uh, we were saying good-bye."

His new friend didn't even try to hold back his laughter. "That sure beats a handshake, doesn't it?"

Before Hunter could decide whether he should punch Larem or if perhaps the Kalith might be on to something, he realized they weren't alone. Someone had just disappeared around the bend in the trail just ahead.

Larem looked disgusted. "So much for the signs keeping the locals out."

"Or else he's got pressing business down below and doesn't give a damn what the sign said."

"Do you think—"

Hunter laid his hand on Larem's arm and put his finger across his lips. The sound of voices carried softly on the breezes from the bluff below where they stood. With a slow nod, Larem drew his sword from the harness strapped to his back under his coat. When both of them were armed and ready, they started forward.

With luck, the long-awaited battle was about to begin. Once the enemy was defeated, Hunter would figure out what to do about his future—and what role Tate might be willing to play in it.

• • •

Tate stood at the window in the back of her house, watching Hunter disappear into the woods with Larem.

She said a soft prayer for their safety before making up the bed for Mr. Kincade. Once she brought in some clean towels, she'd get started on the second room in case his friend showed up. Why hadn't she just said no? The last thing she needed right now was the added stress of houseguests.

As she tucked the sheets in, she frowned. What was it about Mr. Kincade's associates that was bothering her? She could only remember him having guests a couple of times when she'd visited her uncle, but there'd been something different about them. It probably wasn't important, but she knew she'd keep thinking about it until she figured it out.

Straightening up, she walked back to the window again. There was no sign of Hunter or his companion. Immediately, her mind pictured Larem and Barak with their accents and Old World mannerisms. Or, according to Hunter, the more accurate description would be alien world mannerisms.

A chill raced through her as the dots began to connect faster than she could follow. When she'd first met Larem and Barak, she'd been too upset by their effect on Hunter to realize why something about them was so familiar. She'd never met them before that day, but she *had* met others of their kind.

Had Mr. Kincade been bringing Kalith into this world, into her home, for years? Uncle Jacob couldn't have known the truth about them or he would've said something. How often had it happened? Maybe she should take a quick peek back through the ledgers and see if she could find something concrete to show to Hunter.

She tossed the towels on the dresser and headed for the small office she kept off the kitchen. Uncle Jacob's old-fashioned ledgers were lined up on a double row of shelves above the desk. She picked a book at random and opened it. The familiar sight of her uncle's nearly illegible scrawl tugged at her heart. How many nights had she played on the floor by his feet while he'd labored over the books?

But now wasn't the time for reminiscing; it was time to hunt for proof. No sooner had she sat down than the shop bell rang. Sighing, she selected two more books and headed out into the shop to see who'd come in. It was with some relief that she saw one of her regulars there to pick up the special blend of green tea that she'd ordered. After a quick transaction, Tate was again alone.

Rather than retreat to the office, she spread the books out on the table that gave her a clear view of the garage apartment and the route Hunter had taken to the woods. With a cup of her favorite chamomile tea to help calm her nerves, she opened the most recent ledger and started scanning the pages for a mention of Mr. Kincade and his mysterious companions.

Sure enough, at least once every few months Mr. Kincade showed up for a two-day stay. Only about half the time did he end up with one of his special guests joining him. She made note of each date and whether or not he'd been alone. There didn't seem to be a regular pattern, although he rarely went longer than three months without a visit.

That had remained true until a few months ago. What if he had already known about Jacob's death? Could that have forced Mr. Kincade to find a new way to operate, like prowling around town at night? What was he really up to?

She sat back and stared at the ledgers scattered across the table. It would be nice to have Hunter come back so she could discuss this with him. Maybe she was jumping to conclusions. After all, she was basing all of this on the vague memories and a personal dislike for an irritating customer.

The lights were on over at the apartment, which probably meant that D.J. or one of the other guys was using it. Maybe she should go talk to them. It wouldn't do to leave the ledgers out, not with Mr. Kincade likely to show up any minute. She also didn't want to risk carrying them over to the apartment in case she ran into him on the way.

She finished marking the pages with slips of paper and stashed the ledgers behind the counter. Then she hurried out the door to see who she could talk to over at the apartment. Failing that, she'd head down the trail herself and see if she could find Hunter and Larem.

There was no sign of her missing guest, which was just as well. This could all be her overactive imagination at work, but she didn't think so. Either way, she had no desire to see him until she knew for sure.

When she reached the top of the garage stairs, she

looked through the window and knocked on the door. Someone was curled up on the couch looking awfully uncomfortable. She knocked again, louder this time. D.J. lifted his head and blinked sleepily.

"D.J., open the door. I need to talk to you."

The urgency in her voice brought him to full alert. He threw back the blanket and sat up. She looked away while he yanked on his jeans and a shirt. A few seconds later, he opened the door.

"Come on in. Let me roust Penn out, too, so you can tell us both at the same time."

Too restless to sit down, she paced the length of the room and back while she waited for the two men to join her. Time seemed to drag, although it couldn't have been more than a minute before they joined her.

Penn stretched his arms over his head, his joints cracking. "What's up, Tate?"

Drawing a deep breath, she did her best to sound calm despite the staccato beating of her heart. "Okay, now this might sound crazy, but I think I know who's behind what's been going on around here."

D.J. looked understandably skeptical as he flopped back down on the couch. "How so?"

"That day Larem and Barak first showed up, my first thought was that there was something familiar about them. But I forgot about it in all the excitement." She still had nightmares about the crazed look on Hunter's face when he'd tried to kill Larem.

"What do you mean 'familiar'? There's no way you'd ever seen them before that day. I know for a fact that neither of them had ever been up this way."

"I know, I know. But early this morning one of my uncle's old customers showed up unexpectedly wanting to rent one of my rooms. Mr. Kincade has been coming here for years. One reason he stuck in my mind was that he's always demanding special privileges." The words poured out, as if the faster she said them, the more likely D.J. and Penn would believe her. She paused to catch her breath.

Penn prompted her to go on. "And the second reason?"

"Sometimes he'd have a guest or two join him. We always wondered what country they were from because of their heavy accents and odd attire." She stared at each man in turn. "They mostly wore all black. Their hair was long and shot through with gray and silver. And I might be wrong about this, but I think they all had those same pale eyes that both Larem and Barak have."

D.J.'s glittered in excitement. "Describe this Kincade. We know a Colonel Kincade, and I'm betting it's the same guy."

Tate pictured him in her head. "Late fifties, just under six feet, carries himself like he owns the place no matter where he is."

"Well, I'll be damned. Who'd have guessed that bastard Kincade was the one behind all of this?" D.J. was already reaching for his cell phone. "How long do you think this had been going on?"

"Before I came over here, I looked back through my uncle's ledgers. I only check out about four years' worth, but I know it went on longer than that because I can remember seeing them pass through here when I was still in my early teens."

"First, I've got to call this in to Devlin. Then we need to—"

He stopped midsentence at the sound of three loud popping noises. Her first thought was that it was an odd time of day for anyone to be shooting off fireworks. But she knew she was mistaken when D.J. and Penn went from relaxed to warrior mode before the last echo died away. Swords and guns seemed to appear out of nowhere.

"Tate, go home and lock yourself in. Then call your neighbors and tell them to stay inside."

D. J. was already on the move and leading the charge down the stairs outside, leaving Tate no choice but to follow along in his wake. "What's going on, D.J.?"

Penn loped on ahead of them as the other Paladin stopped to answer her. "We told Larem and Hunter to fire off a couple of shots if they needed backup. Get inside. It could be nothing, or all hell could be breaking loose. Hunter will have my ass if I let you get caught in the crossfire."

"Okay, but . . ." Her voice cracked.

D.J.'s smile was sympathetic. "Yeah, I know. We'll do our damnedest to keep Hunter from collecting any more interesting scars."

"Not just him. *All* of you be careful. Now go. I'll be fine." She backed away, ready to bolt for home, her stomach churning with fear for Hunter and his friends.

"Here." D.J. tossed her his cell. "Hit two on the speed dial and tell Devlin Bane what you just told me. Let him know what's going on and who's involved. Tell him we'll check in as soon as we can. Now get inside."

She ran for her back door, stopping only when she was inside. She flipped open the phone and hit the button.

A gruff voice answered on the second ring. "Damn it, D.J., where the hell have you been? Do I really need to come up there and kick your collective asses?"

This guy was *so* not going to be happy to hear from Tate instead of his friends. "Uh, I hope not, Mr. Bane. This is Tate Justice."

There was no mistaking the heavy sigh at the other end of the call. "Ms. Justice, I apologize. I assume there's a good reason that you're calling me instead of D.J. or Fitzsimon."

Tate immediately launched into her explanation, starting with the gunshots and ending with her theory about Mr. Kincade and his guests. As she waited for Devlin to respond, she could hear the clicking of a keyboard in the background.

"Okay, good thinking on your part, Ms. Justice. We'll want to take a serious look at your uncle's ledgers at some point. For now, I've got an all-call out for Barak, Lonzo, and a couple of my other men. We'll be on our way inside of ten minutes, but it will be awhile before we can get there, even by helicopter."

The relief of knowing that help was coming went a long way to help her stop shaking. "Thank you, Mr. Bane. See you soon."

"That you will." Then he laughed. "And better make it Devlin, Tate. No use in formality among friends. I have a feeling we'll be seeing a lot of you."

Once she disconnected, she set the cell phone aside and reached for her own phone to begin calling the neighbors. After she hung up from talking to Mabel, she realized she was no longer alone. Slowly she turned to face the doorway, where her unwanted guest stood staring at her.

Before she could react, Mr. Kincade grabbed her by the arm and dragged her out into the shop. He shoved her toward the table in the far corner, and she stumbled backward. By the time she caught her balance, she was looking down the barrel of his gun.

"Tate, my dear, you've obviously been a busy girl since I left. How unfortunate for us both." His smile was cold and nasty. "While we wait for my ride to show up, why don't you tell me exactly what you just said to Devlin Bane on the phone and what he's going to do about it. And maybe, just maybe, you might actually live through this."

Hunter parried and thrust, forcing his opponent to retreat backward toward the barrier at the rear of the cave. Damn, it felt good to be swinging his sword, which was probably twisted and sick. But for the first time since waking up in Doc Crosby's lab, he was doing what he was born to do—protecting the barrier with his sword and his blood.

That he was doing so standing shoulder to shoulder with Larem q'Jones was ironic, but it felt amazingly right despite their different fighting styles. The Kalith warrior was all grace and blinding speed, while Hunter fought with brute strength and determination. But between the two of them, they'd already forced one contingent of Larem's countrymen back across the barrier. Right now, they were trying to block the entrance to the cave to prevent the latest bunch from reaching freedom on the hillside above.

He'd spent his career fighting Others, but this was the first time he'd faced Kalith warriors in full control of their emotions. Sweat poured down his face, and his shoulders ached as he blocked another attempt to separate his head from his body. These bastards knew how to kill and fought with deadly intent.

The barrier flashed bright and failed again. An older Kalith stepped across, his sword up and ready for battle. As soon as Larem spotted him, he screamed in rage and charged forward in reckless intent to breach the male's defenses.

Hunter lunged to the side, blocking Larem's headlong charge. "Damn it, do you want to die?"

Larem gave him a wild-eyed look but fell back into position. "That bastard's why I'm trapped in your world. He's mine to kill."

"Fine, you've called dibs, but another stupid charge like that will get both of us skewered."

Hunter managed to badly wound his most recent opponent as he spoke, but as that one fell back, another took his place. God, if that barrier didn't go back up soon, he and Larem would eventually be overwhelmed. He could only hope that D.J. and Penn had heard the warning shots he'd fired.

Speaking of which, while the barrier was down, it would be safe to use bullets instead of blades. "Larem, hold them for a few seconds."

He moved to the side, giving his partner more room

to maneuver while he drew his revolver. He'd have to pick his targets carefully or risk a ricochet hitting him or Larem. He took aim and dropped two of the Kalith with shots meant to disable rather than kill. With luck, he and Larem would be able to shove the whole bunch back into their own world.

When the barrier flickered to life again, he stuck the gun back into his waistband and rejoined the battle. A shout outside the cave caught his attention.

"Inside, Penn!"

"On your left, Hunter!" D.J. moved up beside him, engaging another of the Kalith. "Penn's outside in case any of them get by."

That was relief. So far, he and Larem had kept the Kalith contained, but even one could do a lot of damage if he got past them. The thought of Tate or any of the residents of Justice Point at the mercy of these cold-eyed bastards made him crazy.

"I had Tate call for reinforcements, but they could be awhile in getting here. If the barrier is down all through the region, they may not be coming at all."

"We'll hold them."

D.J. lunged forward, laughing like a loon when his opponent ran into his comrade and almost went to the ground in a tangle of arms and legs. "Don't suppose you've seen their human buddies down here."

"No." Another worry. He was puffing like a steam engine, and his leg hurt like hell. "We saw somebody on the trail, but he'd disappeared before we caught up with him. Larem and I sensed the barrier weakening. Since then, we've been too busy to hunt him down."

D.J. looked worried even as he reengaged his opponent. Between blows he brought Hunter up to speed. "I was afraid of that . . . you see . . . Tate's customer from this morning has been coming here regularly for years."

He spun and took out a warrior who'd thought to flank them while they were talking. "We're pretty sure our Colonel Kincade is the one who's been working with these bastards."

Which meant the traitorous jerk was still on the loose, and Tate was up there without any of the Paladins or Larem to defend her. Hunter's stomach plummeted.

"Can you two hold these guys?"

Not that it mattered. He wasn't about to stay, not if Tate was in danger.

It was Larem who answered. "Go to your woman." A flash of his sword punctuated his words, and his opponent screamed.

Larem shouted in triumph. "One less of your lackeys between me and you, Guildmaster. Hide back there if you want. I'll get to you soon enough."

Hunter backed away from the battle. "Penn, I'm coming out." He hesitated only for a heartbeat before charging outside.

Penn had his gun trained on him but turned it aside as soon as he recognized him. Hunter sidestepped along the ledge as the other Paladin shifted his position to maintain a clear shot at the cave entrance.

"How goes it in there?"

"D.J. and Larem are holding their own. The Guildmaster crossed over the last time the barrier went down.

It's back up for now. As long as it stays that way, they'll be all right until help comes." He looked up the trail. "If it does. But I'm going up above. Kincade isn't here. If he figures out Tate has identified him . . ."

He couldn't say it, but the threat hung heavily in the air. "I'll be back when I can."

"Do you want backup?"

Hunter appreciated the offer, but Penn was needed here. Hunter charged up the trail, ignoring the shards of pain in his leg. He'd get to Tate even if he had to crawl. At the edge of the woods, he paused long enough to decide which weapon would be best. The gun would be effective at a longer distance, but the sword would give him greater satisfaction. The traitor he was hunting deserved to die piece by piece.

His decision made, he followed the woods around to the edge of the Auntie Ms property. Kincade was familiar with the area and would be watching for any sign of Hunter approaching from the woods. The only chance he had to surprise him was to come from the front.

As Hunter ran past Mabel's house, she stepped out on the back porch. The last thing he needed was to stop and answer a lot of questions, but he couldn't have her hobbling along behind him right into the line of fire either.

"Get back in the house, Mabel. I'll explain later."

"Tate already called and warned us to stay inside, but I saw a man sneaking around the tea shop with a gun in his hand. I tried to call Tate and warn her, but she's not answering. I thought you should know."

Bless the woman. Now he needed a distraction,

something that would keep Kincade's attention focused in the wrong direction long enough for Hunter to make his final approach.

"Mabel, have you ever shot a gun?"

She drew herself up to her full height with pride. "I knew my way around firearms long before you were born, young man. But my eyesight's too poor for accuracy."

He couldn't help but grin. "What I need is a distraction to draw his attention away from Tate. Think you can take this to the edge of the woods and fire off a few rounds?"

She was already coming down the steps. "It will take me a bit to get there, but I won't fail you."

He pressed a quick kiss on her cheek and handed her the gun. "Be careful."

She checked the weapon over with surprising efficiency. "Not a problem."

Then she was off and moving with a stately grace in a direct line for the woods. When he was sure she was going to reach the cover of the trees safely, he waited at the corner of the house for her to start firing. He could only hope it would buy him enough time.

And once he had Tate safely in his arms, damned if he'd ever let her go.

Chapter 18

"I knew it was risky stopping here, but I had to know what was going on," Kincade said. "I suspected that Devlin Bane was up to something, but all of the Seattle Paladins were accounted for. I should've known that he'd import outside help. And I never know where those pet Others of his are."

Tate tried a bluff, hoping to buy some time. "I don't know what you're talking about." She backed up a step but stopped when he immediately brought the gun up to her eye level. Maybe he wouldn't actually shoot her, but he looked too comfortable with the weapon for her to be certain.

"Why don't you have a seat so we can chat?"

He motioned toward the same table he'd sat at earlier, which would block her view of anything going on outside. If he joined her at the table, maybe she could flip the table over and make it out the door. Unfortunately, her captor seemed to be a mind reader.

"Keep your hands were I can see them, and things will stay peaceful. At least for the moment." He walked over toward the window. "I would guess Bane and company are rushing up here by helicopter. That is really very inconvenient. However, if my ride manages to get here in a timely fashion, there will be no need for bloodshed."

His smile sent chills up her spine. "You probably know by now that it's hard to make those freaks out there stay dead. However, that isn't true for the two of us. So as much as I'd hate to pull this trigger, if it comes down to a choice between me and you, well, we both know how that will turn out."

She sneered right back. "Paladins are not freaks. They're heroes. DNA isn't what makes us human; it's things like honor and duty. But then, I guess you don't understand anything but greed."

He wheeled around and slapped her. "I understand a lot of things, like the fact that you've obviously been spreading your legs for one of those bastards . . . or more likely all of them. I'm sure your uncle would be proud to know that you've been whoring for those animals."

She tasted blood and fury. "My uncle was a great judge of character. He never really liked you, but he sure loved beating you at chess."

He moved to slap her again, but this time she was ready and dodged the blow.

"If you need to get out of here, take my car. The keys are on the hook in the kitchen."

"And have your friends be able to track me? I don't think so." He pulled out a cell phone and punched in a number. "Joe, where the hell are you? Fine, but step on it. We'll be leaving as soon as you get here. I'll double your bonus if you make it in less than ten minutes."

Kincade cut off the call and tossed the phone on the table. "Not that he'll live to spend a dime of what he's made."

His cold-blooded words sickened her. If he planned on killing his accomplice, what chance did she have? She wasn't about to wait for him to decide that her time had run out. Right now she had some value as a hostage, but should that change . . .

Maybe if she kept him talking she could figure something out. "How did you end up working with the Kalith?"

"The first time I stayed here at your uncle's place, I happened across the cave down on the bluff. When I saw the barrier at the back, I figured eventually someone would try to escape through it. I left a message. A few weeks later, an enterprising Kalith warrior answered it, offering me a trade. Free passage for some of his buddies in exchange for whatever they had of value to trade. Finally, we settled on the blue garnets. I've been hoarding most of them, but a few have gotten away from me."

His eyes glittered with avarice. "I've got the market cornered, though. Enough to make me a rich man. I've sold enough to finance my plans. Even now, the fools I've been dealing with are trying to analyze them to find out where they can mine the ore themselves. Good luck with *that*."

He walked around to look out front before returning to the side window. "I'll be a rich man when I dump the rest on the open market. Of course, I'll have to disappear for good. My business associates won't appreciate finding out that the stones usually deteriorate on our side of the barrier. Probably something to do with too much light."

No sooner did he reach the side window when a series of gunshots rang out. Tate screamed and dropped to the floor, throwing the table over on its side. Before she could crawl more than a couple of feet, the front door of the shop burst open, kicked off its hinges. Hunter threw himself through the opening, rolling to his feet in a blur of motion.

Her captor spun around, unsure where the attack was coming from. He swung his gun up, taking aim at Hunter, who was armed only with a sword. Facing a blazing gun didn't stop him from charging straight at Kincade, cursing his name at the top of his lungs.

She couldn't bear to see the man she loved die again. Picking up a chair, she ran at Kincade and bashed him over the head as hard as she could. He hit the floor, and the gun went off. The bullet went wide and hit the wall behind her, sending a shower of plaster down on the floor.

Then Hunter was on Kincade, his hands wrapped around the older man's throat. Kincade bucked and jerked as he tried to break free, to no avail. She thought for sure Hunter was going to kill him, but then he eased off enough to allow his captive to breathe.

She hardly recognized Hunter's voice when he spoke. "As much as I'd like to see you die for threatening my woman, I'm going to let you live."

He leaned down close, letting Kincade see the hatred in his eyes. "But don't think I'm doing you any favors. Once Devlin Bane and his buddies get here, they'll come up with some fun plans for what little time remains of your life." He cocked his head to one side, as if listening to something in the distance. "And the helicopter will be landing in about two minutes."

Then his worried eyes studied her from across the room. "Tate, honey, are you all right?"

Other than the fact that she'd lost her voice and was shaking like a leaf, she was fine. He smiled when she managed to nod.

"Good. Do you have some rope handy? I need to truss this turkey up."

Hunter hated the fear in Tate's eyes, not that he could blame her. All she wanted to do was run a quiet tea shop and write the book she didn't think he knew about. Instead, she was once again embroiled in the violence of his world.

After a quick trip to the utility room, she was back with her clothesline. Before he took it, he nodded toward where the gun had landed a few feet away.

"Point that at him while I tie him up. If he so much as breathes wrong, shoot him."

She gingerly picked up the weapon. "But I might hit you."

He gave her what he hoped was a reassuring smile. "As long as the bullet hits him, too, I'm all right with that."

"That's *not* funny." She widened her stance and aimed the gun right at Kincade's head. "But once you're out of the way, I might like a free shot at him."

It didn't take long to hog-tie Kincade.

The whirring clatter of the rotors announced the arrival of reinforcements. Hunter stood up and held out his hand to take the gun from Tate. She surrendered it with obvious relief, and he pulled her in for a quick hug. She buried her face against his chest and wrapped her arms around his waist.

Knowing that she still wanted to touch him made him smile in relief.

A sleek, military-style helicopter was just setting down out in the yard, stirring up a cloud of dust. If they followed the same protocols as the Missouri contingent, the aircraft would take off again to avoid drawing unwanted attention from the local authorities.

Sure enough, the men inside hit the ground and spread out, ducking down to avoid the rotors as the chopper immediately went airborne again. They approached the house cautiously. Devlin reached the porch first, his sword in one hand, a gun in the other. Hunter hollered that it was safe for them to enter the tea shop.

"About time you got here. You almost missed all the fun." He squeezed Tate, letting her know the man was a friend. "Tate Justice, I'd like you to meet Devlin Bane. The tall guy behind him is Blake Trahern."

She turned to face them, keeping her arm firmly around Hunter. He liked her unspoken signal that they were a team, knowing the Paladin leader wouldn't miss the significance of the gesture.

"We spoke earlier, but I'm very glad to meet you in person," Tate said.

"Thanks again for the call," Devlin replied as he sheathed his sword.

"I have the human culprit ready for you." Hunter gestured toward the floor behind him.

Devlin's eyes narrowed, and his smile radiated a dark pleasure when he got his first clear look at the prisoner. "Hey, Trahern, look who we've got here."

Trahern sauntered over to where Kincade lay huddled on the floor. The captive actually whimpered and tried to caterpillar across the room. The Paladin squatted down beside his longtime nemesis and smiled as he yanked Kincade's head up by the hair. "What's the matter, Colonel? Having a bad day?"

"Not now, Trahern," Devlin snapped, glaring at his buddy until he moved away from the prisoner. Kincade's head hit the hard floor with a thunk.

"Fill me in, Fitzsimon."

"We've got to get back down the trail. I left your boys holding off the Guildmaster and his buddies. I'll show you the way."

"What about him?" Trahern nudged Kincade with the toe of his boot. "We wouldn't want to have to track him down again."

Tate spoke up. "And his accomplice is on the way here to pick him up."

"I'll stay here," Trahern offered. "You can trust me to keep them both safe."

Hunter met Trahern's silver gaze head-on and read the man's down-to-the-bone promise to protect Tate, with his life, if necessary.

He pulled Tate back into his arms for one last hug. "I'll be back. Then we'll talk."

Her smile was a bit fragile, but she kissed him and gave him a soft shove. "Go. We'll be fine."

"I know you will. Call Mabel, though, and tell her you're okay. She'll be worried. That was her shooting the gun earlier."

"Who's Mabel?" Trahern asked.

Hunter laughed. "I think I'll let you find out for yourself."

Then he led Devlin and his men back outside and down the hillside to put an end to this mess once and for all.

It didn't take all that long to help D.J. and Larem with the final mop-up, but each minute away from Tate was one too many. Hunter stood at the entrance of the cave, impatient to get back to her.

"So what are we going to do with them?" He glanced at the bedraggled bunch of Kalith sitting along the cave wall. "Personally, I'd just as soon shoot them for trespassing."

Devlin looked like he was considering the suggestion. "As much as I'd love to, I think we'd better turn them over to a friend of Barak's on the other side."

Neither Barak nor Larem had been particularly gentle when they'd administered first aid to their former associates, especially the Guildmaster. They held him in isolation on the other side of the cave.

"These fools are guilty of poor judgment, but the Guildmaster will most assuredly stand trial for crimes against our people." Barak's pale eyes gleamed with satisfaction. "That is one execution I would sell tickets to."

The man in question retorted, "So speaks the traitor! Both of you are outcasts and under death sentences, should you be so foolish as to return to Kalithia. Some might forgive your betrayal, but there are those who will seek *your* death for your crimes."

"That may be so." Larem calmly walked over and stared into the Guildmaster's furious eyes. "But you know nothing of honor and will die begging for mercy."

Hunter understood his friend's anger. Because of this greedy male, Larem would likely never be able to go home. "Uh, guys, I understand why you want to let your people deal with him, but are we really just going to shove him back across the barrier and hope the right people find him?" Hunter asked.

Before anyone could answer, the barrier flared and died. All of those in the cave immediately drew their weapons, ready for yet another battle.

But as soon as their eyes adjusted once again to the dim light, a solitary Kalith stepped forward. He held his empty hands out to show he wasn't there to fight.

Barak smiled and quickly stepped forward to clasp the man's forearm in a gesture that spoke of a long friendship. "Berk, it is good to see you once again, although you missed out on quite the fight."

The newcomer looked at the prisoners in disgust. "I was afraid of that. Word only just arrived that the Guildmaster had slipped his leash. My men and I will be glad to take charge of these vermin for you."

"That would please us to no end." Devlin walked over to stand beside Barak. "I'm Devlin Bane."

The Kalith warrior nodded to the Paladin leader. "I

am honored to meet you in person, Paladin. You are a legend among my people."

Hunter wasn't sure, but he thought Devlin might have actually blushed.

"You're free to take them with you. We have your Guildmaster's human counterpoint in captivity, too. We'll be talking to him to see if there's anyone else we need to be looking for on either side of the barrier. I trust you'll let us know if you find out anything we should beware of."

"Agreed. But how shall I reach you? Crossing safely at the portion of the barrier that you normally protect can be a problem for us."

Hunter decided it was time he got involved in the conversation. "Berk, is it? My name is Hunter Fitzsimon, and I plan on living close by here on a permanent basis. We'll figure out a way for you to contact me."

Larem moved up beside him. "He's a warrior of honor, Berk. I am proud to call him friend and Blademate. I would trust him with my life and yours."

Berk studied Hunter for a second before nodding. "I will return in two of your days to work out the details."

"Larem and I'll both be here. It might be a good idea if I leave some human-style clothing for you here in the cave. Then I can show you where you can find me in an emergency."

"Until then, Hunter Fitzsimon." Berk backed up a step. "Now if you'll help get the prisoners back across the barrier, I'll call in my men to take them back to our headquarters for interrogation."

• • •

Hunter left the others to follow as they would, but he had a driving need to get back to Tate. Other than himself, there was no one better suited to protect both Tate and the prisoner than Trahern, but Hunter didn't care. She was his, and he wanted to be there for her.

As soon as she spotted him, Tate came at a dead run across the yard, shouting, "Trahern caught Mr. Kincade's partner, too. Are you all right?"

"I am now." He squeezed her tightly. "God, Tate, I thought my heart would stop when I realized Kincade had you."

"I was scared, but I knew you'd come." She rested her face against his shoulder. "We make a great team, don't you think?"

His heart filled with something that felt an awful lot like hope. "Care to make this team thing permanent? With vows and rings and the whole shebang?"

"Can Mabel be my matron of honor?"

"Only if Larem can be the best man."

Her smile vanquished the last shadows from his soul. "It's a deal."

Epilogue

Hunter sipped his tea as Larem, Barak, and Penn studied the lists of dates and names he'd given them. Larem was the first to finish.

"There are more?"

"Probably. I've only had time to go through the most recent ledgers, but Kincade has been sneaking Kalith through here for years."

"What are you thinking?" Penn asked.

"That we might want to track some of the Kalith down and see what they're doing. They've most likely built lives here in our world, but I don't like not knowing what they're up to." He set his cup down. "And maybe if they've gathered in one particular area, I thought you, Barak, Lusahn, and her two kids might want to reach out to them."

"What does Devlin think about the idea?" Barak poured himself some more tea. "Do you know what kind of tea is this? I like it."

Hunter sensed Tate's warmth moving closer even before her hands landed on his shoulders. He caught one and brought it to his mouth for a quick kiss as she answered both of Barak's questions.

"It's Scottish breakfast tea. And I believe Devlin was only too happy to turn this project over to Hunter."

Hunter laughed. "More because he thinks I should actually earn my salary, than from any respect for my ability to ferret these guys out. He forgets I'm a historian by training and damned good at research. I'm going to do it anyway, but I thought you guys might want to help."

He braced himself for Penn to explode. To his surprise, he didn't. "I'm in, as long as you guys will continue to work with me on my left-handed sword training."

"Not a problem. I've already converted the garage into a dojo. We'll all have to keep our skills sharp."

Larem smiled, something he did more often. "Sounds good to me. Now, it's late. If you'll excuse me, I'm going back to the apartment."

Penn and Barak stood up as well. "Yeah, and we've got a long drive back to Seattle. When do you want to get started on this?"

"D.J. promised to come back with Cullen to set us up with computers at the end of the week. When he gets that done, I'll let you know."

Hunter followed his friends to the door while Tate gathered up the teacups and plates. Penn and Barak drove off, and Larem disappeared into the apartment over the garage. Lately he'd been dividing his time between there and the place he shared in Seattle with Lonzo. He was working on his ability to heal, using some texts that Berk had left for him in the cave. Until he knew better what he could and couldn't do, he wanted to keep his studies as secret as possible.

Once they were all gone, Hunter remained outside, tempted to go walking in the silver light of the full moon. He rarely needed the walks to find peace of mind, but he still enjoyed the quiet of the Northwest woods.

He headed for the path through the trees at the back of the yard. As soon as he stepped into their shadowy depths, he knew he wasn't alone.

"What took you so long? I've been waiting for you." Tate's voice was laced with laughter and heat. She sidled up to stand in front of him and laid her sweet hands on his chest.

"I'm here now." He wrapped her in his arms, loving the calm her touch brought him. "What do you have in mind?"

"I've never forgotten that first night when you kissed me up against that tree over there, and I want to finish what you started."

"I'm up for it." Literally, but he didn't have to tell her that. She could feel the evidence for herself. "Are you sure that's the same tree?"

"Well, no," she said between kisses, "but I figure we've got time to try them all. Eventually we're bound to get the right one."

"I love the way your mind works."

"And I love *you*, Hunter Fitzsimon. Now, let's get started—time's a wasting."

"Yes, ma'am!"

Turn the page
for a sneak peek
at the next sizzling Talion novel
from
Alexis Morgan

Dark Warrior Untamed

Chapter 1

"Who the bloody hell are you?"

Piper looked up from her computer screen and studied the irate male glaring at her from the doorway. Her stomach flipped at the sight of him. He was, without a doubt, the guy they'd warned her about—Greyhill Danby. She'd been hired while he'd been in England, and she knew for a fact that no one expected him back yet.

"I suppose I could ask you the same question—but I'd like to think I would've been a little more polite." Her smile wasn't meant to be nice; rude was always the best response to rude.

His eyes, an incredible shade of bright blue, narrowed as he walked into the crowded room. That fierce gaze wouldn't miss much. She was willing to bet he'd committed every detail to memory the moment he entered, from the painting on the wall to the number of buttons on her blouse. And he clearly didn't approve of any of it.

When he didn't respond, she continued. "Well, since you've obviously forgotten how to speak, I'll answer for both of us. I'm Piper Ryan, this is my office, and you must be Greyhill Danby."

It took some effort to tear her eyes away from all that masculine intensity, but she managed. Barely.

"Now, since the pleasantries are over, you'll have to excuse me, Mr. Danby. I have work to do."

Her fingers flew across her keyboard to make her point. She'd delete the gibberish she was typing after he left. *If* he left, which right now seemed doubtful. He'd widened his stance and crossed his arms over his chest.

She hit the save button and then looked up, sighing loudly. "Is there something else I can help you with, Mr. Danby? I really am very busy."

His lips tightened. She'd definitely pushed too far.

"I can see that you're busy, ah . . . Miss Ryan, was it?" His eyebrows lowered as he stared at her. "And I'm sure whatever you're doing is important to someone, somewhere. However, since this is actually *my* office, you'll understand why you need to go do your little job somewhere else."

Apparently no one had told him that they'd be sharing the space until the workmen finished remodeling the rooms upstairs into offices for her and Kerry Thorsen.

Thanks a lot, Sandor. You could have warned me.

She turned to face Danby directly. "I'm guessing that you haven't talked to Sandor since your return."

He nodded sharply. "You'd guess right, although I'm not sure what he has to do with you usurping my office."

Piper laughed, fueling the flames. Holding her hand up in apology, she finally managed to speak.

"Sorry, Mr. Danby, but with that British accent of yours, it sounds like this is 1776 all over again, and I'm one of those pesky American rebels. But I assure you, sir, I didn't dump your precious tea in Puget Sound. It's over there on the cabinet, right next to my coffee."

He scrutinized the clutter with a slight sneer before turning back to her. "My advice to you, Miss Ryan, is not to get too comfortable here."

He stalked out, taking most of the oxygen in the room with him. That was the only reason she could come up with for why she was suddenly so breathless. Yes, that had to be it. Slowly, the pressure in her chest eased, leaving her to figure out how she was going to share such a small space with that uptight jerk. Sexy, but a jerk nonetheless.

Turning back to her computer, she deleted the nonsense lines. She'd manage somehow. She always did.

Out in the hall, Grey pinched the bridge of his nose and wished he could rewind and try that whole mess again. Maybe he should take a lap around the rose garden—or half a dozen—before seeking out Sandor Kearn or the Dame herself.

Granted, neither one of them were particularly happy to have Grey around, but to stick a spy—especially that flit of a brunette—in his private office was too much. How was he supposed to work with her in there? She'd already turned his neat and tidy office into complete chaos.

What else had changed in the short time he'd been out of the country? Although Dame Kerry had told him to take his time moving to Seattle, he hadn't wanted to give her the chance to recant her decision to appoint him as her Chief Talion and enforcer.

He'd worked around the clock to close up his flat in London and make arrangements to ship his necessities to the States. He did it in record time, and it was exhausting. It also didn't help that his departure had been delayed for over six hours because of weather, followed by a flight full of crying infants and rough turbulence.

So he was seriously jet-lagged and short-tempered. He'd only intended to stop by the Dame's home long enough to let her know he was back and to drop off a few things in his office. Which, as it turned out, was evidently no longer just his.

Exactly who was this Piper Ryan? And more importantly, how had she managed to worm her way into the Thorsen household so quickly? The last he'd heard, he was supposed to be in charge of security, which included vetting potential employees. Obviously someone had also usurped his job while he was away.

The most likely culprit was Sandor Kearn, Grey's predecessor as Chief Talion. Even though Sandor had happily relinquished the role, he'd probably felt obligated to continue his former duties until Grey returned. That was all well and good, but why hadn't he kept Grey in the loop?

The answer was obvious. Sandor had guessed how Grey would react to finding someone else ensconced in his office. And not just someone, but Piper Ryan. Her image filled his head, another reason to curse his gift of almost perfect recall. Her dark hair looked like it had been cut with grass clippers with no intention other than drawing attention to the streaks of purple and bright pink that clashed with her bright red lipstick and nail polish.

Her dark eyes had a slight tilt to them, hinting at an interesting ancestry. And those full lips with that small mole at the corner of her mouth made him wonder—he cut off the thought immediately. Better not to go there.

He stepped out into the garden, breathing deeply to draw in the damp Seattle morning. It was the one thing his new home had in common with his old one. What London didn't have were the towering peaks of the Cascades and the Olympics that framed the Puget Sound area. Then there was the rather impressive Mt. Rainier, its snow-covered volcanic peak serving as a backdrop to the city itself.

He could come to like it here, provided the Dame and her Consort trusted him enough to do his job. If they couldn't, he'd be banished to serve the Dame at a distance, most likely from London or perhaps even Scandinavia. His skin crawled, remembering the sharp bite of Nordic winters.

Speaking of Europe, Grey needed to check in. Not that he wanted to, as tired as he was, but it was more politic of him to do so. Pulling out his cell phone, he dialed the familiar number. After ringing a handful of times, the call clicked over to voice mail. Considering his mood, it was for the best.

"Listen, you wanted to know when I got back to Seattle. Now you know. So far, no new developments. E-mail me if you have any questions. I might even answer them if the mood strikes me."

He hung up, thankful he didn't have to speak to a man he could barely tolerate. A common interest forced him to be civil, but it wouldn't last past the resolution of the current situation. That was just fine with Grey. Plus, he agreed with that old saying about keeping your friends close and your enemies closer.

"Greyhill, I hadn't heard you were back!"

He automatically snapped to attention as he turned to face the new Grand Dame of the Kyth, Kerry Thorsen. His training demanded he bow to honor his ruler, but he held back. Kerry had made it clear that she preferred a more casual relationship with her Talions than had her predecessor. Besides, courtly behavior seemed out of place when the Dame was wearing a faded T-shirt and jeans that had more than one hole in them.

The radical change in the royal court was only one of many things Grey struggled to come to terms with since the death of their previous ruler. Although Dame Judith had chosen to live out her last years in the Pacific Northwest, she'd held on to many of the customs that had held her in good stead for the thousand-plus years of her reign. Their entire world had been rocked by the combined shock of her death and her choice of successors.

"Grey?"

The puzzled note in Kerry's voice made him realize that he'd been staring at her. He shook his head to clear it.

"I'm sorry, Dame Kerry. After a long, hectic flight, I'm afraid I'm not up to full speed yet. Please let me take those flowers for you." He looked around, searching the garden for some sign of her guards. "Where is everybody? Are you alone out here?"

"For once." Kerry smiled as she handed Grey the basket of roses. She stripped off her gardening gloves and dropped them, along with her pruning shears, on the table beside the door.

"I believe Ranulf is out hunting down some parts for his pet Packard. Sandor took the kids shopping this morning before they head to the airport to meet Lena's flight. I don't expect to see them before dinner tonight."

Grey still studied the garden behind her. "May I ask where you left your guard?" Discreet was one thing; invisible was quite another.

She shrugged, obviously not concerned. "Sandor mentioned something about assigning someone to follow me around. I told him not to bother."

Bloody hell. Sandor shouldn't have allowed her the option of refusing. It was the duty of the Talions to protect the Dame. If Kerry wouldn't let them stay nearby, how were they supposed to keep her safe?

"I will ensure any guards assigned to you will be as unobtrusive as possible."

"But I've never needed one before." Kerry wrinkled her nose and frowned. "Well, unless you count when Ranulf and Sandor get it in their heads to hover."

"We're all concerned for your safety, my lady." He might as well have been speaking to the wall for all the attention she paid to his advice.

"I'll think about it," she said dismissively. But it was all right—he could be stubborn, too.

Kerry started back toward the house. "You must be tired from your trip. Why don't you come in and have a seat while I put those flowers in water?"

As they stepped inside, she added, "I don't know about you, but I'm definitely ready for a break. Care to join me for an early lunch?"

Since it gave him the perfect excuse to stand guard over

her, Grey didn't hesitate. "Gladly. Why don't I let Hughes know?"

"Thanks. I'll wash up and grab a vase."

Kerry disappeared down the hall toward her private quarters while Grey cursed under his breath. Damn it all! What was Sandor thinking? No matter what Kerry thought, the Talions should stand guard 24/7 to protect the Grand Dame of the Kyth. Like it or not, Kerry was the ruler of their people, one of the few to possess a rare combination of powers that qualified her for the job.

That alone dictated that she be carefully watched over. But then there was also the fact that not everyone was thrilled that she'd ascended the throne. Most of the American Kyth simply seemed curious, but some of their Old World kindred were fuming. They'd had their own plans for the succession, and Kerry wasn't what they'd had in mind.

A small but vocal faction claimed that Judith had meant to give Kerry her memories only as a temporary measure to keep them from being lost forever. If Kerry didn't step down soon, they might very well attempt to take matters in their own hands.

Well, he'd certainly be having words with Sandor. Granted, the Dame was married to Ranulf Thorsen, a powerful Talion in his own right. The Viking was perfectly capable of protecting Kerry by himself, but only if he was actually with her. So when Ranulf couldn't be by her side, another Talion should be. After all, Dame Judith had slacked off on security and look where that had gotten her: dead and buried, murdered by one of their own, a Talion warrior who'd gone renegade.

Ranulf and Sandor had obviously let Kerry have her way

a little too often. Yes, she was their ruler, but she was new to the role and to their world. Someone needed to keep her safe. As Chief Talion, it was both Grey's honor and his duty.

Now if she'd just trust him enough to let him do it.

For the time being, he'd use the chance to share a meal as an excuse to remain close by until Ranulf could take over. Grey sought out the butler and requested a pot of Earl Grey tea and something to eat for them both. When he returned to the dining room, Kerry was already busy arranging her flowers.

"Hughes will be in shortly."

"Good. I'm famished." She shoved the last rose into the vase and stood back to admire her handiwork. "Perfect."

To Grey, the arrangement looked a bit haphazard, but his Dame looked pleased with her efforts. She buried her face in the blossoms and drew a deep breath. She carefully set the vase on the sideboard before sitting down in her usual chair at the table.

"So how was your trip, Grey? I had expected you would be gone longer. I hope you didn't rush things on my account."

Was she disappointed that he'd returned so quickly or only surprised? It was hard to know for certain, but he suspected that she'd have been just as happy to have him stay away indefinitely.

"London was London, so it rained much of the time I was there. There wasn't much to do other than shut off the utilities and close up my flat. I've arranged to have my things shipped to Seattle, which means I'll have to start looking for a permanent place to live. Until then, I've extended my reservation at the hotel."

"The hotel?" Kerry frowned. "Are you sure you wouldn't be more comfortable staying here at the house? We have plenty of room."

Kerry's offer seemed sincere, but he couldn't imagine that she'd want another guest imposing on her hospitality. She and Ranulf had recently taken in three Kyth teenagers Sandor found practically living on the streets. Sandor was trying to track down their families, but had no intention of giving the kids back.

"I appreciate the offer, but you already have enough mouths to feed." He hesitated and then asked, "How is that going, by the way?"

"It's definitely been an adjustment for all of us, but especially for the kids. Sean and Tara have been on their own for years, so they're not used to taking orders from anyone. God knows, they've had little enough reason to trust the adults in their lives."

Kerry's smile looked a bit rueful. "Kenny is definitely a handful. He wasn't happy when we told him he had to go back to school, especially since he'll need tutoring to catch up. We're looking into online programs for the older two so they can earn their high school diplomas. After that, who knows."

Hughes appeared in the doorway with a heavily laden tray. "Ma'am, shall I serve?"

Kerry, being Kerry, smiled and shook her head. "No, just leave the tray. We'll take it from there."

The butler looked a bit disappointed but did as Kerry asked. Evidently Grey wasn't the only one who would appreciate a little more formality around the place. He wondered how Hughes felt about the newest additions to the household. The teenagers must present a variety of challenges, and then Piper Ryan was added to the mix.

Did those three kids have any idea how lucky they were? Under the laws of their people, Kerry would've been within her rights to have them executed for the way they'd been stripping life energy from ordinary humans. Instead, Sandor had convinced the new Dame that mercy should also be part of Kyth law.

Grey didn't necessarily disagree but he'd give anything to know if Kerry's decision had been driven by compassion or cowardice. Only time would tell. For now, he could only wait and watch.

Piper froze. She'd been on her way to get the Dame's signature on a stack of papers only to find Kerry was talking to Greyhill Danby. Well, she was in no mood to deal with *him* again. Their earlier encounter had been more than enough.

Especially if he were to start asking a bunch of questions she couldn't afford to answer. She certainly didn't want him to start poking around. Her references and paperwork had stood up well enough to Sandor's inquiries, but she suspected he hadn't looked all that hard. Between the three kids he'd rescued and Lena's whirlwind trip to the East Coast, he'd been distracted.

Piper checked her watch. Another fifteen minutes and she'd be done for the day. If the bus gods were smiling on her, she'd have time to grab lunch somewhere before heading to class. This was one of her long days, putting in hours here at Kerry's followed by the three classes she was taking to finish up her degree.

The thought brightened her mood considerably. It was hard to believe that she was finally going to graduate. It had been a long haul, but the end was in sight.

Deciding the signatures could wait until tomorrow, she hurried back to the office and shoved the papers into a bright red folder labeled with Kerry's name. If something came up after Piper left, Kerry would know where to look for the documents amidst the clutter.

That had her grinning. She bet Greyhill was an "everything in its place" kind of guy and her clutter would drive him crazy. Poor man, it's not like he had any choice about sharing his office. For a instant, she considered straightening up a bit before leaving but rejected the idea.

She'd been raised by a neat freak and had vigorously resisted her mother's efforts to force Piper to conform to her high standards. If Piper hadn't changed her ways for her mom, she wasn't going to for a man she'd only met once. If Greyhill Danby didn't like the mess on her desk, he could just get over it.

She logged off the computer and snagged her backpack off the floor. After flipping off the lights, she charged out into the hall, heading for the front door only to bounce off an obstacle that hadn't been there a few minutes before.

She stumbled backward and was rescued at the last second when Grey latched onto her arms and jerked her back upright. Despite his obvious impatience, his hands were remarkably gentle. She knew she should say something, at the very least apologize for almost knocking the man down. But her brain and her mouth were seriously out of sync when she spoke.

"Are your eyes really that amazing shade of blue or do you wear contacts?"

Her face flushed hot and then cold as his eyebrows shot up in surprise.

"Thank you for noticing and, yes, they're actually that blue. But tell me, Ms. Ryan, do you always say the first thing that pops into your head?"

"I try not to." It was nothing short of the truth. "Look, I'm sorry I ran into you. You see, I've got class."

Okay, that came out wrong. She tried again, hoping to make more sense, but the warmth of his hands had her brain firing on only half its cylinders.

"What I meant to say is that I'm running late for my classes at the university. But that's no excuse for running down an innocent man."

Those blue eyes suddenly warmed up about a hundred degrees, and his stern lips softened as he smiled. At that moment, innocent was hardly the word to describe Greyhill Danby. Good golly, the man was compelling enough when he was angry. She didn't know what she'd do if he turned out to be charming too.

His hands dropped away from her arms, leaving her missing his touch as he stepped back out of her way.

"You mentioned something about leaving."

Piper blinked twice. "What? Oh, yeah, I was. Excuse me, Mr. Danby."

She sidled past him and walked down the hallway, feeling his gaze following her each step of the way. It was hard not to turn around and catch him watching.

Just as she was about to turn the corner, a phone rang. She looked back to see Greyhill flipping his cell open.

His eyes flickered in her direction and just that quickly every vestige of warmth disappeared from his expression. He muttered something into the phone and then stared at her until she gave up and walked away.

What was that all about? It wasn't as if she had a burning desire to eavesdrop on his all-important phone call.

She stalked out into the bright sunshine and stopped to soak up a bit of its heat. She was under enough stress working as Kerry's assistant without adding in a man who ran hot and cold with no predictable pattern. She didn't understand him and wasn't sure she wanted to. Right now she had more important things to do than to waste her time thinking about Greyhill Danby.